Tim Griggs was born in London and studied English and archaeology at Leeds University and University College London. He has lived and worked in four continents as a journalist and science editor, and holds dual British and Australian nationality. Tim Griggs recently returned to England after several years in Sydney, and is now settled in Oxford with his wife Jenny. He is currently working with monk-like devotion on his second novel.

Redemption Blues

Tim Griggs

HEADLINE

First published in hardback in 2000
by HEADLINE BOOK PUBLISHING

First published in paperback in 2000
by HEADLINE BOOK PUBLISHING

10 9 8 7 6 5 4 3 2 1

ISBN 0 7472 6834 7

Typeset by Avon Dataset Ltd, Bidford-on-Avon, Warks

Printed and bound in Great Britain by
Mackays of Chatham plc, Chatham, Kent

HEADLINE BOOK PUBLISHING
A division of the Hodder Headline Group
338 Euston Road
London NW1 3BH

www.headline.co.uk
www.hodderheadline.com

For the whole bloody lot of you who kept the faith –
yes, even Mark Lucas.

1

Before dawn, on the second anniversary of her death, Cobb left the farm and climbed towards daybreak.

Above and around him the rim of the black hills stood against the stars. He breathed hard and, though his breath plumed from him in the bitter air, it was too dark for him to see it. He moved mostly by instinct and memory: he had climbed this path many times before in the cold hours before the light, and he knew it well. First the crunch of frosted turf in the lower paddocks, crisp as spun glass. Then a wedge of sky marked a gap in the hawthorn hedge and the start of the track, muddy ruts frozen into lava, knocking like wood under his heavy boots.

At length he felt for the field's top gate and found its timber, furred with frost. He opened it and stepped through. As the steel latch shut behind him he heard a beast shuffle and stamp nearby. By staring slightly away from the sound Cobb could just make out the bulk of the animal's shoulder, then another beside it, and another, black humps against the starwash. He saw the steam of their bellows breath and of his own, and he turned and stumped the last few yards, feeling with his boots for the low turf ridge which marked the wall of the ancient churchyard. He trod over it and took up his dawn station, seated with his back to the trunk of the oak which stood there.

He liked to think that the oak might have been growing here, a sapling unnoticed against the wall of the graveyard, when the lost village was populated by the living as well as the dead. That was in 1665. Twelve generations ago; not so very long. Recognisable people, speaking a language he would understand, making jokes he would laugh at, loving and cheating and working and sinning, crimes like the crimes he dealt with every day. Believing, all these vanished people, that it would go on for ever, that – God willing – there would be a tomorrow. And then discovering, as Cobb himself had discovered, that God was not willing. That in fact He cared so little one way or the other that He allowed them all, of whatever virtue or beauty, to be swept away by a force whose nature they could not even imagine, for no reason that made any sense, following no discernible scheme of justice or mercy.

Cobb's face was numbed by the keen air which rinsed over the high ground. He could see it now, the first fan of dove grey and pink far away over London. The rising air made the oak above him creak like a ship at sea and he felt the great trunk stir, a living thing, against his spine. To the south he could make out a scatter of diamond lights which must be Oxford: if he stayed here an hour longer he would see the needle spires piercing the roll of mist along the Thames. Somewhere below he was aware of that ancient river, black water slipping eastward in dim channels, cold as death. It was still night in the valley which cradled the farm from which he had set out. A single yellow square marked the light in the kitchen, the light he had left on to guide him back.

He heard Baskerville blundering in the gorse near him, panting harder than he was, ragged and broken-winded. The old dog was searching for him in the dark, stopping at intervals to snuff the air, nearer, nearer, blundering and snuffing again. Then the rough warm head was in his lap, slobber and bristles and hot ripe breath, and Cobb put his own head down and dug his chin into the warm carpet head and felt the dog shudder with delight and swing his big slow tail and turn his purblind eyes up to him and slap at his face with his tongue. Cobb rubbed the mongrel's ears and spoke to him, and the dog lay down on the frosted grass of the gravemound at Cobb's feet and thumped the crisp turf with his tail.

Cobb felt his own heartbeat slow after the effort of the climb. His spirit took joy in the warm presence of the dog and in the salmon wash of light that spread from the east. He took comfort too in the company of the dead beneath his feet. Against such casual extinction his own loss, if not comprehensible, seemed at least part of a shared grief. He stretched back against the oak and it shifted against his spine once more. The net of its roots beneath him cradled the bones of the dead. Clea, for all the vigour she had brought into his life over twelve years, was as completely at rest as these long-dead villagers. Their peace was her peace and in their company he was in hers. He felt less alone.

The dog stirred at his feet and lifted his anvil head. In the gathering light Cobb could see the milky adoring eyes and the swinging tail. The dog knew it was time for food. Cobb's stomach murmured in agreement and he rubbed the dog's head and stood up and stretched in the thin light. Cobb was not bitter. He had been bitter once but not any more. It was less of a life now. He accepted that, and accepting it he was very nearly content.

2

Silver could not see beyond the blast of the lights but he could feel it there, the many-mouthed beast he had to feed. He closed his eyes, his head thrown back, trying to shut it out. But the glare burned red into his brain just the same. The last shrill chord of his treble run hung there, ringing through the vast stadium, and the audience clung to it, invisibly, silently begging him to go on. At the last moment he did so, his left hand flicking up the frets, his head back, his eyes half closed, the patterns in his mind translated with perfect precision to the patterns of his fingertips, tapping, changing, dancing on the fretboard. And then back down – a barré at the eighth, a long glissade, the guitar howling in pain, and at the exact moment the crash of drums and bass smashing the cage of the music, releasing him from the song.

Silver bounded out of the light, the bellowing of the crowd breaking over him like a following surf. The band came after him, waving, as he had not done, at the audience. They blew like horses as they ran, their sweat flying in the lights. Silver stopped and let the musicians stampede past, laughing and cursing at one another, squinting in the darkness after the glare of the lights. He saw the familiar bulk of Tommy Hudson in the wings, clapping the musicians on the back, mouthing ritual congratulations over the din, though they were all too hyped and too deafened to hear.

Silver backed into the shadow behind the scaffolding which framed the stage, his heart bouncing like a triphammer from the adrenalin and sweat cooling on him in the winter night. From here he looked out on to the dazzling cone of centre stage, the abandoned instruments glittering in chrome and mother-of-pearl. He noticed for the first time that a fine rain was falling over the unprotected crowds in the stadium, curtains of drizzle drifting like golden smoke through the laser beams. The huge audience didn't care about the rain. They whooped and whistled and drummed the damp turf with their heels, baying for more. Up in the covered stands they stood and cheered, stamping on the boards and clattering their folding seats. Litter started to drop on the stage – flowers, programmes, hats – falling in the lights like singed moths.

Silver watched the crowd. He remembered the beginning, twenty-five years and more ago, when impatient audiences hurled bottles and chairs, and didn't always wait for him to get off stage first. It had been different back then, in rundown halls in Liverpool and Manchester and North London, crumbling theatres, off-duty cinemas, the back rooms of rough pubs. Back then there were no cordons of smart security guards keeping him safe, with their cellphones and their Mace sprays and their crisp uniforms. Just Tommy Hudson's broad brawler's shoulders. Silver had a vision of one wild night at the Hackney Empire, long before the place was renovated, when a punchy drunk had hurled a bottle which burst clean through the bass drum. Silver remembered Tommy Hudson slipping the steel bracelet of his watch over his fist and sliding from the stage like a polar bear from an ice floe. The smack of knuckle on bone had silenced the whole screaming theatre for a full minute. Silver didn't know why he should remember this incident particularly. It was only one of many, and far from the worst. But there was something in the fierce protective roll of Hudson's massive shoulders that night, something that summed up the big man's faith, his devotion. Hudson, Matt Silver knew, would have waded out there to protect him if every member of the crowd had been a bottle-wielding drunk.

Out in the black gulf of the stadium tonight's crowd was chanting, a hungry, pitiless chant. Silver could not make out the French words but he knew what they wanted. They wanted more. More of him. And more. And then more. They were lighting candles now. In a few seconds the small yellow flames were flickering all over the dark acres, a swarm of bright pinpoints, swaying to the chant, more urgent now, more urgent. Silver could not look away from those undulating lights. He watched, and as he watched it happened again: the black cavern of the stadium swam before him, and the din receded, and something in him retreated from the present.

He was not sure how long it was before the clamour

brought him back, but after a while he sensed Tommy Hudson materialise from the shadows beside him.

'Look at the bastards.' Hudson hissed the words into Silver's ear. 'You know what you are, Mattie? You're the fucking Sun King.'

'Tommy, listen–'

A man with headphones came running up and Hudson said 'Piss off' without turning. Silver opened his mouth again, but Hudson cut him off, his voice knowing and steady. 'We're too old for this, Mattie.' After a moment, the big man added, more gently: 'Give them what they want. You know they only want one.'

Silver pushed past him quickly, snatched the shining Gibson from the stagehand and bounded on to the stage. The audience erupted. But Silver stood motionless in the lights, waiting until the torrent of noise withered away. When the silence was complete, he held it for another twenty seconds, his right hand poised above the strings. Then he struck the first ringing chord and the audience bellowed their approval in a great clap of sound that drowned the first couplet.

> *You people climbing on that Narrow Way,*
> *Can climb from cradle to the Judgement Day*
> *You want to win, but first you gotta lose*
> *That's what they call*
> *That's what they call*
> *Redemption Blues*

Silver sent the aching chords across the stadium. The

sound system picked up the buzz of his fingertips against the binding of the bass strings. Then the last line, hurled high in Silver's diamond-hard voice – and he was finished, flinging his arms wide, the guitar in one fist flashing like an unbuckled breastplate, his black hair swinging. And then he was running, racing the damburst of the crowd's frenzied adulation, hurling himself out of the dazzle of lights and into the wings.

Suddenly spent, Silver hung against Hudson's rough coat until his breathing steadied and the din engulfed them once more. The stage structure rocked as the crowd surged against it. Hudson felt it move and in an instant took charge, standing Silver upright, tossing the guitar to an aide, slinging a jacket across Silver's back. 'OK, my son. We're gone.'

He gripped Silver's upper arm, steering him quickly away. Shouted orders, a hard, straight-armed, shoulder-barging rush down crowded corridors of grey cement and staircases smelling of piss and thronged with shouting people, then out into the sweet cold night behind the stand, where a stretch limousine stood with its back doors open.

Silver straightened, pulled his arm free. 'You go ahead, Tommy. I'll meet you later.'

Hudson glanced up at him. 'Don't be a prick. Get in.'

But Silver's strength had returned. He swung the jacket around his shoulders like a hussar's tunic, cocked his head mockingly at Hudson's tone.

'Get in, for Chrissake.' Hudson was growing testy.

Silver backed away, his hands raised, palms up. 'Need some space, Tommy. No big deal.'

'Mattie, we've got a meeting –'

'Catchya, Tommy.'

Silver backed out of Hudson's range and into the darkness, smiling. It was a smile out of another era, the smirk of a kid scrumping in the parson's orchard, and, seeing it, Hudson knew it was pointless to argue. He got in the limousine himself, banging the door behind him. He lowered the window with a whirr and shouted: 'It's Berlin tomorrow, you tosser. Don't you forget it. You hear me?'

3

Silver did hear but gave no sign of it. He was already lost in the chaos of trucks and generators and trailers behind the stadium, breathing the stink of diesel and fried food. The drizzle was heavier now, turning to rain, glistening on the sides of the vehicles and gathering in pools on the tarmac. The shouting men and cranes and arc lights made him think of a depot behind the front line of some forgotten war. Staring up at a reversing truck, he tripped on cabling and fell against a toiling man who swore at him in French. The man was wearing a tour T-shirt with Silver's face on it but gave no sign of recognition.

He found himself coming down. The anonymity helped. It was a while since he had kicked over the traces and it felt good – irresponsible, unprofessional, and good. Unprofessional because he would miss one of Tommy's late-night business gatherings in some exclusive Paris restaurant. There was a time, and not long ago, when Silver had enjoyed this sort of thing. He would listen to Tommy talking big money with the dealmakers while he sat back, pulsing with that after-show energy that was better than sex.

He caught the smell of fried onions on the night air and found a hamburger stand and bought a paper thimble of coffee as thick as tar. The French girl who served it looked at him narrowly and he moved quickly away and leaned against a trailer in the shadows to drink it. The cold rain slanted through the lights. Something, perhaps the foreign accents around him, flung him back thirty years to Dr Gottschalk's tiny basement studio at the Conservatorium, a place of yellowing sheet music, and hot water pipes, and the smell of stale cigars. He saw himself again, a truculent boy of sixteen, hunched over his guitar, staring rudely out of the window at the garbage cans in the lightwell.

'You are a very bad classical student, young Mr Matthew Silver,' Dr Gottschalk told him in his clockwork English. Then the old man folded his sere fingers over the neck of his own instrument. 'But you haff something very big to say. Get out from my sight and say it.'

Something to say. But what story was so important that this vast weight of manpower and equipment and transport and technology was needed to tell it? There had been a time when Silver had said whatever he had to say with an old acoustic guitar and no more gear than would fit into the pockets of a donkey jacket. He finished his coffee and screwed up the paper cup and tossed it away among the big wheels. He was not a romantic. He did not believe in the good old days. They had been hard days, hard and squalid, and he had no faith in the improving power of poverty. But he also knew he had lost touch in some way, somewhere between there and here. At some point his own voice had been drowned out by the grinding of this great machine designed to project it.

Twenty thousand in the crowd tonight, many of them unborn when Dr Gottschalk had confronted him with his destiny all those years ago. He should have been incandescent with the power they sent him, these unknown young people. Two years ago – less – he would have been airborne with it. But now it seemed the circuits had somehow been switched. It left him drained, confused. What did these young French people see? What could *Redemption Blues* mean to them?

The song had come to him as he huddled in a bus shelter on the outskirts of Hull on a bleak November evening a hundred years ago. Their Dormobile had finally packed up on the ring road and Tommy was off scaring up new transport, though how he would do it without money was beyond Silver's power to imagine. Exhausted and near defeat, Silver was not even sure that the big man would ever return, and he could not have blamed him if he had not. From the grim council estate across the road came the jagged sound of a kitchen shouting match, people yelling above the chatter of a television show. Lauren, feverish and ill, slept curled in a sleeping bag on the spit-stained concrete of the shelter. A solitary bus prowled past, a patchwork of yellow light. It did not trouble to stop and Silver remembered the desolate whine of its gears as it pulled away. He did not know why it depressed him so. They had no destination in any case.

At his feet Lauren moaned softly in her sleep. He

knelt down and stroked her hair, murmuring to her, to himself. She nuzzled against his hand. Then, unbidden, the refrain was in his mind. He let it play, finding its form, until it was clear enough for him to hum it aloud. When the girl was sleeping again, he moved quietly away and found the cardboard lid of a takeaway container in the gutter and scribbled on it in fitful blue biro, scribbled and scribbled, until the cold locked his fingers, and then scribbled more with the biro pushed through the barrel of his fist. It took him perhaps twenty minutes to get the verses down. No longer than that. When he had finished he looked up to find Lauren watching him, propped up against the seats, the sleeping bag pulled tight around her. She looked like death under the yellow streetlight, sick and shivering. But she smiled at him, a smile of such confidence and courage that he felt his heart lift and he knew it would be all right. It had been her song from that moment.

Silver pushed himself upright. As he did so the children's Christmas letter crinkled in his breast pocket. He dragged out his mobile and clacked it open and punched the keys. Engaged. He swore, tried again. And again. And again. Hunched in the wet night while this toiling army of strangers deconstructed the world around him, he dialled and redialled endlessly. His knuckles shone white where he gripped the phone.

4

Lauren Silver paused by the door of the rumpus room and watched her daughter reading. Serious little Freya, after nine years on the planet, was as grave as a medieval bishop behind her big glasses. Was she even more quiet than usual tonight? Gudrun, naturally, was not quiet at all. She was already setting out the red-and-yellow cartons of food on the table, chattering to herself, singing snatches from the school musical in which she had starred just the week before. It gave Lauren a pang. There would be no more musicals for Gudrun. Not in that school, anyway. She wondered if her bright, talented, irrepressible daughter would ever forgive her. But she knew, even as the thought formed in her mind, that of course she would. Gudrun did not hold grudges. She didn't have the time. She was too busy living – living with a spirit which Lauren recognised only too well because it had once been her own. Yes, Gudrun would forgive her.

Freya, though, would be a different story. You could never tell with Freya. Well, Lauren thought a little unkindly, the child could brood and sulk in one house as easily as another. Gudrun was so much easier to decode than her sister that it was sometimes hard to believe the two girls were twins. As she stood watching, both her daughters glanced up and saw her. Gudrun smiled her careless smile, as open as a sunflower. Freya gazed solemnly at her, her eyes owlish behind her glasses. Lauren wondered if they suspected anything. Perhaps they just thought tonight was special because Christmas was only a few days away. She waggled her fingers at them, made a funny face, closed the door gently and crossed to the room she called her study.

It was a pleasantly dim room, all dark wood and bookcases and brass lamps. But it was foolish to call it her study. In reality it was the room she came to when she wanted to drink and smoke in peace. To call it a study was pretentious, like so much else in her life. Lauren had to admit she had never truly studied anything. She had barely started her first year at Leeds University before she heard Matt Silver play at the Union, and that had been it, more or less. Within a few hours she found her way into his tobacco-smelling sleeping bag in a chill tenement overlooking the University. She remembered standing at the window the next morning, pulling on a Rugby Club jersey, her breath pluming in the raw air, with the brutish concrete campus spread out at her feet. That was the last time she ever saw the place. Later that day she climbed aboard Matt Silver's rusting camper van, wedged herself in the back between the battered guitar cases and the drum kit, and smoked dope with the keyboard player all the way to their next gig in Newcastle. She had not even gone back to her digs to collect her books and her clothes.

At the time, and for many of the years afterwards,

she thought that dropping out of university in this dramatic way had been her big break, her bid for freedom. Freedom from the awful suburban primness of her mother, with her pastel lambswool cardigans and her Women's Institute domesticity. Certainly Lauren had never been happier in her entire life than for those three hours in the back of that booming panel van, her head swimming with dope and lust, watching Matt Silver's Aztec profile against the light. He was beautiful that day, and the more beautiful for not knowing he was observed. Or perhaps he did know. You could never tell with Matthew.

Looking back she could see that her flight with the young Matt Silver had been the opposite of escape. He had snapped his fingers – perhaps he hadn't even done that much – and she had followed. Naturally she had never finished her studies. Her course was English and drama, but she could not now remember ever attending a single lecture. Of course not. She hadn't gone to university to study English and drama. For all her talk of independence she had gone there for the same reasons her mother had gone to secretarial college in the 1950s: to find someone who would snap his fingers at her and tell her to jump in the back and do as she was told. And it had been like that for most of the years since.

Lauren stopped herself there. There had been good times – many of them in the early days. She could not bring herself to pretend it had all been bad from day one, even though that might make tonight easier to bear. For tonight marked their final failure, hers as well as his. God knows, she had fought hard enough, year after year, to avoid it. If he had only fought with a tenth of the same tenacity, maybe she wouldn't have to do this – maybe none of them would have to go through it. Lauren felt suddenly weary and tearful. She supposed in a way Matthew could not help it. It was in the nature of the beast, and it was a beast she had loved well enough for long enough. But she could not carry their relationship alone. It was so dreadfully heavy. If she did not put it down now, it would crush her.

It was odd to be thinking this way now. She knew what people thought of glamorous Lauren Silver when they read her celebrity interviews in the women's magazines. They thought of her as an actor. She insisted on the word 'actor'. She had won a rich-bitch reputation for publicly bawling out interviewers who questioned her right to it. It was a little hard even for Lauren to see how she had sustained this fiction for so long on the strength of bit parts in soap operas. But Matthew had been rising like a comet then – indeed, he had never stopped – and nothing stood in the way of what he wanted. Well, she thought now, maybe she had been an actor after all. The truth was, when it came right down to it, that she was merely Matt Silver's wife. And lately that had become the hardest role of all to play. He had seen to that.

All that ended tonight.

The thought of him made her glance at the phone on the desk. She had thought that perhaps this

Christmas he might at least call. She was far from sure that she wanted him to, but even so. She glanced at her watch. It was exactly eleven. Midnight in Paris. He had been off-stage for an hour or so. Lauren felt a spurt of anger, not with him but with herself. Why should she care? It was demeaning that she should. And yet she did care and this made her angry. She crossed to the desk and flicked the handset off its rest, so that it lay rocking on the leather.

She walked to the sideboard, poured herself a vodka, bigger than she intended, and, ashamed of herself, tried to tip some back in the bottle. The dismounted phone, sounding some automatic warning tone, squawked like a nestling at her and she jumped, spilling most of the drink on the desktop. She swore, reached behind her for a cushion and smothered the phone under it. She turned away, rescued her drink, noticed she was trembling, lit a cigarette and pulled hard at it. She caught a glimpse of her reflection in the ebony square of the window and saw a strained woman of forty with dry blonde hair, screwing up her eyes against the smoke. The expression gave her a shrewish look. She hadn't always looked that way. There had been times when she had almost liked herself and the way she looked. When she was pregnant, for example. She had thought then that she and Matthew might make it work out despite everything. And earlier, too, in the first flush of his success, when she could still convince herself that she had something to do with it. God, what a ride it had been! And earlier still, when she had been – or so her mother told her – just the way little Gudrun was now: a blithe, sunny child who loved to dance and dress up. She had liked herself then, and other people had liked her too. They didn't like her now. The vodka was making her maudlin and she felt her eyes fill. She glimpsed her reflection again and knew that she was past the age when she could weep appealingly. She pushed the heels of her hands into her eyes and stubbed the cigarette out ferociously. Dammit, she would put all this right when she was free. Really free. Not make-believe adolescent free like twenty-two years ago in beautiful Matthew Silver's beaten-up minibus.

She checked her watch again and looked out into the dark garden, leaning her forehead against the glass. Through the pool of her own shadow she could see the black cypresses along the drive standing like spears against a sky of Arabian Nights indigo. There was a scatter of flinty stars high up in the blue above the glow of London. It was very cold out there. The frost was already crisping the grass under the bare trees and glinting on the rockery. She could see it sparkle in the light from her window. If it stayed clear like this the children would have another year without a white Christmas. That was a pity. They had never yet seen snow at Christmas . . . she caught herself. Maybe this year they *would* get a white Christmas. Did it snow at Christmas in North Yorkshire? Probably. She took another drink.

'Mummy, are we going out?'

Lauren spun on her heel so quickly that vodka slopped from her glass. 'God, Freya! You scared me to death! Creeping in like that.'

The girl watched her gravely through her big round glasses. She said nothing. She had asked her question and now she was waiting for her answer. Lauren found the child's composure unsettling and even a little contemptuous. But tonight she knew it was important to be calm. She took a deep breath. 'Going out, sweetheart? What gave you that idea?'

'You left the car out. You always leave the car out if we're going somewhere.'

'We'll start calling you Sherlock Holmes, huh?' Lauren pinched Freya's nose gently, but the child was not to be charmed so easily.

'Where are we going?'

'Never you mind.'

'When's Daddy coming home?'

Lauren stiffened. 'Daddy's touring. In France. You know that.'

'When's he coming home?'

'I'm not sure, sweetheart.'

'When—'

'Freya, for Chrissake, don't interrogate me!' She saw the girl flinch and in a second was across the room and on her knees and sweeping her daughter into her arms and hugging her hard. 'Frey, Frey. I'm sorry. I don't mean to shout. But you mustn't question me like this. I'm doing my best. For all of us.'

She felt the child's arms creep hesitantly round her

---

neck. 'Why are you crying, Mummy?'

'I'm not really crying. I'm just having a hard time tonight, that's all.' Lauren rocked back on her heels and again pushed her palms across her face. 'Hey – and why aren't you having dinner with Goodie?'

'Not hungry.'

'Go and eat something, sweetheart. For Mummy.'

The child's eyes were full of suspicion. She turned away from her mother's arms and walked towards the door. With her back still to Lauren she said: 'I don't want to go anywhere. It's nearly Christmas.'

Lauren watched the child go and felt the weight settle like a yoke across her shoulders. She splashed another inch of vodka into her glass. She was drinking too much, she knew, not just tonight but for months past. A couple of years, perhaps. But – what the hell? If she couldn't make it a little easier on herself tonight, when could she? She ran through the preparations again. Her single case standing in the corner. A bundle of money – her escape fund – in the drawer. She opened the drawer and put the money on the desktop. A couple of big stretch bags for the twins' toys and clothes. And a box of sandwiches and drinks in the fridge. Today was the fourth day in a row she had packed that box. Each morning when she found herself still here she threw all the food out and made a fresh batch. But this had to be the last time. Matthew's tour finished in Berlin tomorrow. That was her deadline. She wanted to know exactly where he was when she made her move, and that meant she had to go tonight.

5

Sergeant Dennis McBean stood by the wooden barrier and beat his gloved hands together against the cold of the London night. The workmen would not catch his eye, labouring with ostentatious vigour under the arc lights. It was as if they sensed his mood and feared to share in the dressing down the site engineer was about to get. Or maybe they just wanted to keep quiet so they didn't miss any of it.

Good, McBean thought, bouncing up and down on his toes. That was the way he liked it. A bit of trepidation always helped. And besides, he *was* bloody annoyed. It was eleven-thirty at night and the after-theatre traffic was grinding south across Lambeth Bridge towards him, the glittering batteries of lights creeping, bunching as they edged past the roadworks. Beside him he heard a paper wrapper rustle in the probationer's pocket.

'Hayward, do you ever plan to stop filling your face?'

'Sorry, Sarge.' Hayward's voice was muffled with food.

'That's "Sergeant".' McBean glanced around at the boy. Hayward reminded him of a camel. He was enormously tall with a prominent Adam's apple and joints that seemed to bend the wrong way. 'You get any bigger, you won't fit in the bleeding car.'

The boy blushed, swallowed, then brightened again. 'You wouldn't fancy a bite, would you, Sergeant?'

'No.'

Hayward stiffened into something close to attention. 'Right, Sergeant. Silly question.'

McBean looked away quickly. It was difficult not to laugh at Hayward. He was putting on his tough Cockney voice again, though McBean knew he was from a good middle-class home in the Cotswolds. The young man tried hard but everything about London confused him, not least the fact that McBean, his senior by ten years and by several light years of experience, was black. Hayward had never had a black man in authority over him. He wouldn't for a moment have considered himself racist but he was stuck for a proper form of address all the same and retreated into this pseudo-Cockney all-mates-together argot as a defence. McBean could not resist teasing him.

'You were looking for me, Constable?' A small tweedy man in anorak and hardhat stood behind the barrier. A generator clattered suddenly into life and the man had to shout the rest of his introduction. 'Brian Dawson. I'm the site engineer.' McBean noticed without surprise that Dawson spoke not to him but to Hayward. When there was a choice, white people always spoke to white cops, even if, like Hayward, they were the most unlikely authority figures.

'This is a mess, isn't it, Mr Dawson?' McBean said, so that the engineer had to turn awkwardly to face him. McBean flicked his gauntleted hand at the shovelling men, the tarmac truck, the stalled traffic. 'Your blokes were supposed to be out of here before the traffic tonight.'

'And it's Sergeant, not Constable,' Hayward put in boldly, before Dawson could recover. Then added, less confidently: 'Him, that is. Not me.'

Dawson shifted his gaze uncertainly from one to the other and when he spoke again his tone was more careful. 'We did inform your people we were going to overrun a little, Sergeant.'

'Oh, yes? Nobody told us.'

'Never said a word,' said Hayward.

'It's all arranged with the Council.'

'The Council isn't us. You should have let us know direct and maybe we could have done something about it.' McBean stared around the floodlit site and pointed out Dawson's sins in sequence. 'Look at it. You've dug up half the nearside lane. No one said anything about that. And taken out the streetlight. Now we've got traffic snarled up as far as the Elephant. For three days running this has been going on. Rush hour was diabolical. Maybe you've forgotten it's Christmas this week?'

'Yes, well, I appreciate–'

'I don't know why the job takes three days anyway.' McBean beat his hands together again and looked out through the gap in the railings to the black water of the Thames. 'You're only fixing the fence.'

'Yeah,' said Hayward, moving his shoulders belligerently, 'a bit of fence.'

'It's not quite as easy as that,' Dawson protested, stung. 'These are custom-made cast-iron sections. You have to treat them like glass. And we've had bloody awful weather all week. And we've got English Heritage on our backs–'

'OK, OK. How much longer?'

'We're just clearing up now, Sergeant. We should be finished just after midnight.'

'That's midnight tonight, is it?'

'Of course.'

'And I mean all cleared away? The streetlamp working? No barriers, no holes in the road, no flashing lights for the Hooray Henries to toss in the river when they come out of their Christmas piss-ups?'

Dawson relaxed as he realised there would probably be no complaint made. 'No more than the odd "Wet Paint" sign, Sergeant. Cross my heart and hope to die.'

McBean did not smile back. 'Yeah, well. Just make sure that's done, won't you, sir?' McBean stopped just short of prodding the little man in the chest. 'Because I have enough to do on this patch without Christmas piss-artists falling into the river through gaps in your railings. OK?'

'That's right,' Hayward said.

'Be quiet.'

'Sergeant.'

26

6

Silver abandoned the cab near the Gare du Nord and walked the rest of the way, cursing the Christmas traffic and the revellers and the rain. He was angry with himself for refusing the ride back with Hudson when he had the chance.

He stopped in a doorway near the Pont Neuf and tried her number again, water running down the inside of his shirt as he dialled. When that didn't work he checked the street, crumbled a little of the white powder on to the back of his hand and snorted it clumsily, licking away the residue. He hoped it would calm him but the chemistry was wrong. His skin was mottled blue in the streetlight and it felt as cold as a corpse's under his tongue.

Silver reached the hotel wild-eyed, stoked with synthetic energy, trembling on a hair-trigger. The doorman eyed his wet clothes haughtily for a moment without recognising him, and, when he did, ushered him quickly out of the foyer into a glaring bathroom where a uniformed attendant waited. They brought in fresh towels and fussed over him until he shook them off and escaped back into the foyer. He rode the VIP elevator up to the executive level, rubbing rain out of his hair. The doors whispered open. In the lush lift lobby an elderly French security guard sat at a marble coffee table, leafing through a magazine.

The guard stood smartly, pulled a notepad from his tunic pocket and held it out, smiling. His English was carefully rehearsed. 'Mr Silver, sir. My fifteen years grand-daughter likes very much your music—'

Silver slung the damp towel in the guard's face and pushed past him to hammer on the door of Hudson's suite. When it opened, he strode into the room, his shoulder banging the door back against its hinges.

Hudson glanced across at the elderly Frenchman, who stood like a hatstand with the towel draped over his shoulder. 'Bad timing,' he said. The man jerked up his chin in disgust. Hudson closed the door behind him. 'That's one Christmas CD you won't sell.'

'I've sold enough for one night.' Silver threw himself down on to the grey leather sofa, pushing his hands through his long wet hair.

'You're soaked, you silly bastard. Where you been?'

Silver did not reply and Hudson went into the bedroom and found a fresh shirt and a towel and tossed them on to the sofa. Silver stripped off and scoured himself with the towel and stood to pull on the dry shirt. As he did so he glanced through the half-open door into the next room. Three young women sat at the glass-topped table, chatting and sipping drinks. They were elegantly dressed and reminded him of confident young executives at a seminar. Catching Silver's eye, one of them smiled. Then the three of them went back to their conversation. He said: 'Who the hell are they?'

'At least they don't want your autograph.' Hudson crossed to his desk, sat down and settled a pair of surprisingly dainty half-moon glasses on to his nose. They made him look headmasterly. He moved documents about then regarded Silver over the top of the lenses. 'You been so bloody miserable lately. Think of it as a Christmas bonus.'

'Get them out of here, for Chrissake.'

'It's not like you to be particular, Matt.' Hudson took up a gold fountain pen and began to initial papers.

Silver crossed to the dresser, opened a drawer and banged it shut again, returned to his seat. 'I'll find my own whores, Tommy, if it's all the same to you.'

He drew two neat lines of powder on the glass coffee table, patting them into exactly parallel tracks with the edge of a platinum American Express card. The girls' conversation continued in the next room with the too-steady rhythm of people who are determined not to notice an argument.

Hudson put down his pen, watched Silver for a moment. 'Loosen up, Matt. You're getting to be a real pain in the arse. Relax, why don't you?' He nodded towards the half-open door and the women beyond it. 'Take a couple of them and have a lie down.'

Silver snuffed up the first line. 'I need to talk, Tommy,' he said, his head tilted back. 'So get them out. Please.'

'Mattie—'

29

Silver swept the crystal bowl from the table and exploded it against the wall. Fruit thudded and rolled and one of the women squealed. Silver quietly resumed his ritual while Hudson ushered them out. There were whispered and indignant negotiations and a rustle of money and the door closed.

Hudson crossed to the bar and took a couple of miniature brandies and broke some ice out of the freezer. He brought glasses and bottles over to the table. He slid one drink across but Silver was already working on his second line. It was a little act for Hudson's benefit, both men knew, and Silver frowned with concentration until he had completed it. Hudson had a puritanical streak and the cocaine ritual irritated him. At length Silver sat back against the cushions and closed his eyes and sighed. This time it seemed to be working.

Hudson put his big fists on the table. 'Mattie, I'm too old and it's too late at night and the tortured artist bit is beginning to make me want to spew. Is there any danger of you telling me what the fuck's going on with you?'

Silver opened his eyes. 'I'm going home, Tommy.'

Hudson straightened up slowly, all his senses straining to see where this was leading. 'It's the end of a bloody hard tour, Matt. We're all knackered.'

'It's not the tour.' Silver swept his hand in a gesture which took in the tiny casket of cocaine, the sterile opulence of the hotel room, the very hour of the night. 'It's all this.'

'You should get some better grade angel dust,' Hudson said. 'Go sleep it off. We'll talk tomorrow.' He flipped his hand at Silver in dismissal.

Silver didn't move. After a while he said: 'I've been having some trouble with Lauren.' He frowned at the sound of this and rephrased it. 'I mean, we've been having trouble with one another.'

'Oh?' Hudson moved his head cautiously. 'And that's news?'

Silver looked directly at him. 'I'm going back, Tommy. Now. Tonight. Fix it for me, will you?'

Hudson sipped his drink, watching him. 'You'll be home in time for Boxing Day. Kiss and make up then. Laurie'll forgive you. She always does.'

'That's not good enough.' When Hudson didn't speak, Silver tapped on the table with his forefinger. 'By tomorrow.'

'Don't be fucking silly, Matt. It's just a spat, like every other time.'

'I'm serious, Tommy.'

'You're not serious. This is serious, what we're doing here.'

'I haven't had a Christmas at home with my kids for five years, Tommy. They're nearly ten. And I'm forty-five.' Silver cocked his head in a characteristic gesture. '*That's* serious.'

Hudson opened his mouth to reply then let his breath out slowly. He patted the leather back of the sofa. Finally he walked around the chair and sat down opposite Silver. He twisted the cap off the other miniature and poured it over the remains of the ice, swilling it thoughtfully. He set it on the table in front of him. 'OK, Mattie,' he said. 'Let's think this through, before we get all aerated about it. First off, we're going to call Laurie up, right now.'

'It's off the hook.'

'You've tried ringing her?' Hudson was astonished that Silver had made the attempt. He reassessed rapidly. 'Well, OK. I'll send one of the lads round to check she's all right—'

'Tommy, listen.' Silver leaned forward urgently. 'Get this straight. I'm going. Tonight. Are you going to fix it or am I?'

Hudson straightened in his seat and his face hardened. 'Matt, get real. We've got Berlin tomorrow night. You know that.'

'Cancel it.'

Hudson closed his eyes for a moment, as if to shut this out. He said: 'After Berlin you can go back.'

'Cancel it, Tommy. I mean it.'

'Don't talk like that.' Hudson's voice dropped a tone and Silver could see him begin to smoulder. 'We don't do things that way. Laurie wouldn't want you to do things that way. You're not thinking straight.' He moved forward and grabbed Silver's arm. 'Look, Mattie, you know what I feel about Laurie and the girls. Nearest thing to family I'll ever have. Goodie's my god-daughter, for Chrissake. Now, I promise you we're going to find a way—'

'It was those bloody candles.'

Hudson blinked. 'Candles?'

'Christmas. And twenty thousand French kids light candles for me.' Silver looked up at the big man frankly. 'I do something for those kids, Tommy. It's time I did something for my own.'

Hudson sat back and looked at him. 'This is a joke, right, Mattie? You treat them like shit for years on end, and now you want to put things right in five minutes flat?'

Silver held his eyes. 'Tommy, they're still my kids. And I'm still their father.'

'You, Matt?' Hudson gave a bark of contempt. 'You're not their father. You just fucked their mother.'

Silver stood up slowly. Already anguish and guilt were spreading across Hudson's heavy face. Silver picked up his wet jacket, swung it around himself.

'Mattie . . .' Hudson was on his feet too. 'That came out all wrong. You know I didn't mean—'

'It's all right, Tommy.' Silver walked quietly to the door, leaving Hudson standing in the middle of the room, his big hands opening and closing helplessly at his sides. Silver took pity and said again more softly: 'It's all right.'

But it was not, and never would be again, and they both knew it.

7

One of Tommy Hudson's lads had brought the Jaguar on to the Stansted tarmac to meet the jet. It was just after three in the morning. Silver's clothes were still damp and the cold had crept into his bones and even the two Scotches he had swallowed on the flight had not helped. He came stiffly down the steps and let Hudson's man usher him into the passenger seat. He was never quite sure where Tommy found these people: at his gym, possibly. They came in all ages and all sizes, and Silver hardly ever saw the same man twice. This one was tall and good-looking and about twenty, smartly turned out in a blue blazer with gold buttons. He had even dug up a chauffeur's cap from somewhere and wore it at a rakish angle. If he found it a strain to be summoned by Hudson in the middle of an icy winter night, and told to drive halfway across the country at a moment's notice, he did not show it.

'Good flight, Mr Silver, sir?' the boy said, unnecessarily checking Silver's seatbelt.

Silver grunted. He didn't want to talk; he needed time to think. He said: 'Drive round to the cab rank.'

'You won't need a cab tonight, Mr Silver.'

'The cab's for you. I'm taking the car.'

The driver pushed the heels of his hands against the

wheel and splayed his fingers. 'Mr Hudson wouldn't like that, sir.'

'Which bit don't you understand?'

The young man chewed his lip for a second then drove unhappily round to the taxi rank in front of the neon-lit terminal. He started to protest again but Silver climbed out and walked round to the driver's side and stood over him until he got out too. When he did, Silver slid into the warm seat. Before the boy could speak again, Silver shut the door and drove off. When he rounded the end of the taxi rank and turned towards the airport exit, the young man was still standing in the bitter night, the peak of his jaunty cap shining in the lights. He didn't look cocky any more. He looked anxious and deflated, and his eyes followed the Jaguar all the way down the sliproad until Silver swung the car on to the motorway and headed south.

Silver felt his spirits lift as soon as he saw the curve of the motorway before him. He was a little drunk and a little high but he drove fluidly and well, gliding down the empty lanes, the car as soundless as a great owl. It would take less than two hours at this time of night. By 5.00 or a little earlier he would be there. That was early in the day, but even so – for just an instant – he wondered if it might not be too late. His stomach muscles tensed. He breathed hard and mastered the feeling, and smiled to himself in the dim cavern of the car: stage fright. Matt Silver had stage fright. Wouldn't the papers love that! And with that thought all the old confidence flooded back to him and his soul soared, doubts falling away. He could hack it. He could always find it in him somewhere. Finally here was a performance that mattered: he would not blow this one. He put his foot down and the Jaguar surged forward. He was in control. He was calling the shots. It was the way he liked it.

8

Lauren jolted awake to the thud and bounce of the empty glass on the carpet. She felt sick and confused. Her tongue was glued to the roof of her mouth and her neck hurt. She peered at her watch but couldn't read it in the gloom. The furred green numerals of the digital desk clock told her it was 4.37 in the morning.

'Oh, Christ.' She fumbled for the empty vodka bottle. It was empty. 'Oh, Christ. Oh, Christ.'

Maybe she could leave it until daylight. She craved her warm bed, the security of knowing where she would wake up tomorrow morning, hangover or no hangover. She knew people thought of her as tough and feisty but right now she could not seem to remember why. She desperately did not want to go out into that empty darkness beyond the glass and enter a cold world of strangers and their strange houses. Perhaps she really could leave it till tomorrow, until after Christmas, until the New Year. But a voice in her head told her: Go now. Walk through to the rumpus room, bundle the twins into their bedclothes, dump them in the car. Don't stay to pick up their toys or food or your jewellery or your clothes. One trip out to the car, one child under each arm. Go *now*. She turned, the bottle still in her hand, and headed for the door.

'Hello, Silvergirl,' he said, 'am I too late to join the party?' He lounged against the doorframe, unshaven, unkempt, smiling that smile, car keys dangling from his hand. She stood in silence, her reactions locked. He tilted his head quizzically at her, and even in that he had a tiger's grace. 'I've come back, Laurie.'

'Back?'

'Back for Christmas. Back home.' He pushed himself upright. 'You probably won't believe it. I don't blame you.'

'Home?' she repeated stupidly. She squeezed her eyes shut and pushed one hand through her tangled hair.

He seemed to hesitate for a moment, and then took two strides across the room towards her. As he touched her she felt herself flinch, and she knew with absolute clarity that this was going to go horribly wrong.

'No,' she said. She reached behind her to unlace his fingers, found she was still holding the empty vodka bottle in one hand, and tossed it on to a chair. 'No, Matthew.' She pushed him away and straightened her spine, brushed down her clothes. 'You can't just bounce back in here like a pantomime genie. Flash-bang and a puff of smoke. Change everything.'

'Sure I can, Laurie.' He smiled that smile at her again. 'I just did.'

For the first time she noticed his eyes. 'You're flying, Matthew. Did you drive in that state?'

'I got nervous before my big entrance.' He laughed.

'Me! So I did half a line in the street outside. It's no big deal.'

She shook her head to clear it. 'I don't understand. How did you get here?'

'I cancelled the tour.'

'You did *what*?'

He bowed from the waist, a magician completing a trick. 'Cancelled it. *Finito*.' He brushed his hands together, grinning, delighted with himself. 'All over.' Then in a different voice he said: 'It's all going to change, Laurie, I promise you that.' She didn't speak and after a moment he added: 'Do we have to stand here like strangers?'

She groped behind her for a chair and sat on the vodka bottle. She hooked it out from under her, dropped it, and watched it roll on the carpet. He sat in the leather swivel chair by the desk. She felt hollow and sick. Even now a part of her wanted to forget it all, to give up. But his confidence goaded her. Her life was in ruins and his very optimism was an insult.

'You've rehearsed all this, haven't you?' she said. 'You've gone through this scene so many times that you really think it ends the way you want.'

'Laurie, it doesn't matter. All that stuff that went before. Believe me. All that matters is that it's all over.'

'Just like that?'

'That's right. That's how I do things, Laurie. Just like that.'

'And what about the way I do things?'

'Laurie. Let's not argue. Not now.'

'Why not now? We can't argue any other time. You're never bloody here.'

'Laurie, you don't understand. That's all over. Gone. Behind us.'

'No, Matthew. This is what's all over and gone and behind us. This. Us.'

He suddenly looked tired. 'Don't say anything you'll regret, Laurie. I don't expect this to be easy. But don't let's be hasty.'

'Hasty?' she heard herself laugh, a short ugly sound. 'This isn't hasty, Matthew. This has taken a fucking lifetime.'

He watched her, his silence breaking her rhythm. He nudged the bottle with the toe of his boot. 'How much of that have you had?'

'Cheap shot,' she hit back. 'You're in no position to pull that one.'

He sighed. Put his hands behind his head. 'You think this is a time for posturing, Laurie? This is the real bit, the bit that matters. Here and now.'

'And the rest doesn't? All that went before.'

He looked puzzled. 'No. No, it doesn't matter.'

'It matters to me.'

'OK, OK.' He began to lose patience. 'Look, Laurie, I've given up a lot for this. All I want—'

'You?' she cried. 'You haven't given up a damn thing, Matthew! In six months you'll be bigger than ever. There's nothing you could do that won't make you bigger. The only thing you've given up is me.' She found she was shouting, leaning forward out of her chair. She caught herself, surprised at her loss of control. Silver looked at her and shook his head with weary disappointment, as if, somewhere inside him, he had expected this all along. He shifted in his seat and the back of his hand brushed against the bundle of money she had left on the desktop. He picked it up, frowning.

'I'm leaving, Matthew,' she said quite calmly. 'I've had enough. I'm leaving and I'm taking the girls. I put everything I had into making this work, and it isn't enough. I should have realised it a long time ago, but I realise it now.'

She stood up, collected her bag, smoothed down her skirt. When finally she looked at him, she saw that a small tic was working in the corner of his mouth.

'No, Laurie, listen.' He seemed confused, and there was a new note of alarm in his voice. 'This is crazy. This isn't what either of us wants. Not any of us.' He moved his arm to include the girls sleeping in the other room.

'It's what I want, Matthew.' She edged past him. She saw he was still holding the bundle of money but she did not quite have the courage to ask him for it. 'It'll be best for all of us in the end.'

She was through and into the hallway, and in the wider space she felt more of her spirit return. She turned back and he was standing where she had left him, staring at the wad of money in his hand, as if wondering how it had got there. As if wondering how the scene had unfolded this way. It was the first time she had seen him look pathetic, but instead of stirring her pity it fuelled her anger and contempt. Contempt for herself, she realised, for allowing this man to dominate her so long by trickery and charm. She drew herself up, fully awake now, fully in control at last.

'I'm taking them, Matthew. Give me my money.'

He looked vaguely at her outstretched hand. He seemed unable to believe that this was happening to him. He said: 'Laurie – wait. We can work it out.'

'Good line,' she said, showing her teeth. 'Why don't you write a song about it?'

Perhaps this was what triggered it. His head came up quickly and he looked directly into her and then through her, and to Lauren it was as if something slipped out of place behind his eyes. He dropped the heavy bundle of money into the pocket of his leather jacket and took one step towards her so rapidly that her boldness collapsed in an instant and she heard herself cry out. She waited for the blow with her eyes screwed shut. When it didn't come she opened them and saw that he was standing awkwardly in the middle of the room. He seemed disorientated, as if he had just come to and was puzzled to find himself here. It frightened her.

Across a gulf she called to him: 'Matthew!'

He looked distant. 'Do you know, Laurie, I chartered a jet to get back? So keen to get home.' His voice trailed away. He frowned at her: 'Did I do something wrong?'

'Matthew, you must know I'm not doing this just for me.'

'I would honestly have tried, Laurie,' he said. 'Just for once, I really meant it. Ironic, huh?' He smiled at her, a rueful *kismet* smile. Then he turned and walked away from her and into the room where his daughters lay sleeping.

She flailed at him with her fists but her blows had the weakness of blows in a dream: they seemed to float off him. When she tried to scream her voice was hollow. He brushed past her, swept up the sleeping Gudrun and marched straight down the hall and through the open front door. She followed him out on to the gravel, trying to shriek, trying to beg. His car was slewed across the drive, engine running. Hers was a white mound of frost, its windows opaque. She was over-whelmed by the realisation that he would win, as he had always won, and the last of her strength trickled out of her. She sat down on the frosted stones and sobbed.

Silver laid the sleeping child in the front seat of the car and strode back into the house. In a second he returned with Freya. Lauren, weeping on the gravel, could see the silent girl's white and wakeful face against the black of her father's jacket. Lauren reached out her arms as Silver placed the child in the back of the car. He closed the passenger door and walked over to where Lauren lay crumpled on the driveway.

'Matthew . . .' She fought for breath. He hunkered down in front of her, balancing easily on the balls of his feet. She swallowed hard and won some control.

'For God's sake, Matthew. You don't need to do this. You've got everything you ever wanted. The whole world thinks you're fucking God almighty.'

'But they're my kids, you see, Laurie.' He spoke softly but there was a strange wild light in his eyes.

She hooked his sleeve with her hand. 'I'm their mother, Matthew,' she moaned. 'I'm their mother.'

He turned away from her and she lunged at him and gripped the cloth of his jeans and he slapped back at her as if swatting a wasp. The edge of his hand caught her across the mouth and she felt a tooth crack and fell back on to the stones tasting blood. A second later the car roared past her, flinging gravel into her face. She caught a glimpse of Freya's grave and ancient eyes searching for her through the passenger window. Then the tail lights were ruby streaks in the darkness and the rumble of the car's engine shrank away to nothing.

9

He would soar away, far away from the accusations
and the reproaches, and he would find peace. And
when he had found that peace he would consider what
was right. It wasn't easy to know what was right, but if
they would just leave him alone he would be able to
work it out. The car swept down the black tunnel of
the highway that would take him to the city – his city –
and to freedom. He guided it as expertly as a charioteer,
his hands light on the wheel. Cat's-eyes in the road
flashed like tracer across the edge of his vision. He
drew the charged air into his lungs and felt new power
rush in his blood.

'Daddy?' Freya's voice quavered from the back seat.
'Why was Mummy crying?'

He shut his mind to it. He must shut his mind to it.
The lights of the suburbs rushed towards them and he
swung the car on to a two-lane highway sharply enough
to make the back wheels tramp. The road was lit by
sickly yellow streetlamps, the houses dark behind tall
hedges. He accelerated and the wan lights stretched
into golden rails.

'She fell over. I saw – Mummy fell over on the drive
and you didn't stop.'

Somehow, everything had gone wrong. But he could

make it all right again. If only he could find enough peace to think it through. Life would be different. His life would change. All their lives would change. He would make amends. If they would just all leave him alone long enough to get it straight in his head.

'Where are we going, Daddy?' There was a rising note of fear in Freya's voice but he closed his mind to her, closed his mind and desperately held it shut. It would be all right now.

Dennis McBean stopped the patrol car in a pool of shadow a few yards short of Clapham High Street. That was merely habit. With its Day-Glo markings the car was obvious to anyone who looked, shadow or no shadow. Not that anyone would be looking now. It was too late – or too early, whichever way you looked at it – and the night was polar. He and Hayward might get the odd call to a break-in or a fire, or just possibly a domestic, but otherwise McBean expected the shift to end quietly. That was why he had taken a probationer out with him in the first place.

'Time for a bite, you reckon?' Hayward asked him, opening the remains of his fish-and-chips. McBean had told him fish was a bad choice. The garage manager would give them a royal bollocking for stinking the car out. 'Want some?' Hayward persisted. McBean waved the food away. The boy shrugged and made a big thing of digging into the cold slab of cod. He spoke with his mouth full. 'Sergeant, you from round here?'

'Why?' McBean asked, too sharply. 'You think all us

jungle bunnies come from Clapham?' He was touchy about this one. He had been born in a tough estate not half-a-mile from where they were now parked.

Hayward's mouth dropped open. 'I didn't mean that.' His accent fell back into southwest educated. 'I just meant, you seem to know the area.'

'Of course I know it. I'm a police officer. It's my job to know it.'

'Look, no offence. Sergeant.'

'Forget it.'

Hayward hesitated for an agonised moment. Finally he thrust out the greasy bundle. 'Go on,' he said pathetically. 'Have a chip.' The congealed mess was such a grotesque peace offering that both men burst out laughing.

The Jaguar rocketed through the junction a few yards ahead of them in a blur of light and noise. It left a small whirlwind of litter in its wake and seemed to rock the police car with the power of its passing.

'Fuck me,' said Hayward simply. He tossed the food over the back of the seat and grabbed for the radio. McBean was already gunning the engine. They swerved away from the kerb, lights and siren springing on together, and fishtailed into a turn that took them in hopeless pursuit.

Silver saw the blue lights flashing in his wake. There were lights everywhere now, streaking past in bands of blurred neon, riding in voluptuous waves up the bossed bonnet. Why would they not leave him alone? The yellow beacon of a rubbish truck loomed up and he swept by so fast that the noise of its brushes merely hissed in his ear for an instant like a spitting cat. A bus pulled out and Silver swerved past it on the wrong side of the bollards and a black cab bounced up the kerb to avoid him and through the plate-glass window of a store. He heard the curtain of glass come down like water on tin and saw the glitter of it flood across the road in his rearview. He swung right and the great river was spread out beside him, polished ebony daubed with colour from the high crystals of the city, spires he recognised from a fairyland of memory, pinnacles and battlements and castellated towers and glass ziggurats and festoons of lights strung from wrought-iron posts which ticked past with tiny thuds of air. There were more blue beacons now, one ahead which he closed upon and left spinning in his wake, another jumping out of a street just abreast of him, two, three, more behind. There was a wailing too which he associated with the blue lights and yet which was plaited together in some way with a child's terrified screaming, very close to him.

It came to him all at once. Aim for the dark. Fly into the dark where they would never find him. There was a gap to his left up ahead and he trod on the throttle so that the car sank down on its haunches then leapt as he spun the wheel. There was a splintering impact and debris spun past him like the disintegrating heatshield of a spacecraft. And then the thin shriek of the child: 'Daddy!'

And at last her terror broke through to him. In the fraction of a second left to him he saw the gap in the railings ahead and saw the black water smirking below and he wrenched the wheel to save them all and felt it spin loose under his hands and knew that it was too late.

A moment of sweet silence. And in that silence for the first time that night he spoke to her. 'It's all right, Freya. Daddy's with you.'

A monstrous concussion and something like a great white flower bloomed in his face and he was stunned and in terror and the world was turning over and turning black and a pistol-shot bang near his ear and something ripping at his face and a torrent of icy cold was crashing against him, hosing his body, stinking like a tomb, utterly black, and he knew he was not a god after all.

McBean pulled up just short of the bridge and he and Hayward left the car with its lights still flashing and ran past the shattered barriers of the roadworks to the parapet. The Thames was sliding westwards, pushed by the incoming tide, bunching like coils of tar against the piers of the bridge beneath them. McBean saw the Jaguar at once, wheels up but afloat in the current. Its lights were still on and they lanced across the river just under the surface and steam rose in clouds from the ruptured engine.

'Jesus!' Hayward said, his voice breaking. 'What a fucking *jump*! He must be forty feet out.'

McBean watched, peering at the sinking wreck for

any sign of life. There were other noises behind him now, shouts, running feet on the road, more patrol cars pulling up, more sirens, the squawk of someone's radio. The current nudged the Jaguar around and pushed it towards them, towards the piers of the bridge. Hayward, nearly weeping with frustration, was fighting his way out of his anorak.

McBean put a hand on his arm. 'What d'you think you're going to do? Nick the hubcaps?'

'They might still be in there!'

'Don't be a prick.' McBean brushed his gloved palm along the parapet. His hand came away white with frost. 'Water like that? You'd last about a minute.'

'But we've got to—'

'See if you can make out the plates. Do something useful.'

'Right.' Hayward pulled himself together. 'Right, Sergeant.'

A small crowd was at the parapet now, shouting questions, gabbling to one another. McBean and Hayward ignored them as the Jaguar, now directly beneath them, dipped sharply by the nose, lifting the back wheels out of the water for a moment, and then began a slow dive down the wavering ramp of light thrown by its own headlamps.

'Did you see the plates?' McBean asked. 'I couldn't make them out.'

'MKS or maybe MBS 001,' Hayward said, drawing the numbers with his fingertip in the frost. 'Personalised plate.'

'Call it in.'

The Thames closed over the Jaguar, and now all they could see was the pinprick rubies of its rear lights and the eerie white spokes of its headlamps. The beams lurched and circled, still falling, and abruptly died. The crowd fell silent. McBean made to turn away but Hayward hung back, craning over the wall.

'Wait.' He gripped McBean's arm and pointed. There was a small flurry of movement in the depths and a second later a trickle of bubbles boiled up through the water, then a fat belch of air which rocked the river's surface.

'Hayward!'

But he was already across the road, shedding jacket and cap as he ran, and in a moment he was clattering down the steps and McBean heard him crash into the black water.

10

It was before 7.00 in the morning and still dark, but London was vibrantly awake by the time Cobb drove off the overpass and on to Cromwell Road.

He glanced at his watch. It had taken him an hour and ten from the farm, which wasn't bad in this old heap. The call had come through at five-thirty while he was failing to milk his father's one cow, a Guernsey called Mrs Buckets. Sometime during every visit to the farm Cobb failed to milk Mrs Buckets. The cow never lived up to her name whenever he was involved. Doris, who came in to clean for the old man during the week, told Cobb it was all in the subtle squeeze of finger and thumb, and she should know since she'd been a real live milkmaid over the border in Gloucestershire about sixty years ago. Cobb's own view was that Mrs Buckets was about as likely to produce milk as Doris was, no matter who was subtly squeezing. He didn't care. He was a city man and was expected to fail at such tasks. Cobb didn't want milk as his reward for getting up at five. He wanted the clean cold dawn and the animal's warm hide against his skin and the medieval stamp and shuffle of beasts in stall.

Cobb had been in the act of resting his forehead against Mrs Buckets's flank when the mobile had buzzed. He had meant to leave the phone turned off, back at the house, but must have zippered it up in his anorak pocket the night before and by some miracle the battery had lasted. It was an irritation but Cobb didn't mind much. The truth was that he liked to be summoned, and he was especially glad of it today. He wondered how he would handle it in a few weeks when the phone would stop buzzing altogether. No, the main problem with being called back into the city at this hour was that he had not had time to change from his farm clothes. Kapok was hanging out of the sleeve of his jacket and his boots were balled with mud from Mrs Buckets's stall. The boots worried him. He could change in the office – he kept a spare suit there – but he had a nagging suspicion he had forgotten to throw a decent pair of shoes in the back of the Land Rover. Well, there was nothing he could do about it now.

The city had that special brand of Christmas excitement he remembered from his childhood. Every Christmas Eve Cobb's father had driven him and his brother in the family's old Rover 90 to see the great tree in Trafalgar Square with its lights and decorations. It had been one of their few family rituals. Cobb always felt that London took Christmas more seriously than any other festival. Perhaps it was because Christmas had more or less been invented by a Londoner, complete with stagecoaches and mulled wine and snowy cobblestones. Cobb thought that even the visionary Dickens would be pretty startled by the capital's evolution in the last one hundred and fifty years, but on the other hand just beneath the surface he would find plenty that was familiar, plenty of squalor and hopelessness and pain. And he would certainly recognise this old river. Cobb crossed the Thames southwards at Vauxhall Bridge, slowing the Landrover long enough to get a good look northeast towards the city as he crossed. The sky was just beginning to pale and a dawn wind was pushing down the river from the estuary thirty miles away, driving a thin sleet before it. The tide had turned and was flowing out, so that a tug and three barges thumping upstream towards him had to labour against it. Cobb turned left and followed the southern bank.

Ahead of him at the end of Lambeth Bridge he saw a knot of ambulances and police cars, lights splintering the darkness. There were barriers of striped tape across the road and men in luminous jackets were setting up signs and directing traffic. A heavy crane, up on its jacks, squatted on the crown of the bridge with its jib jutting into space. Cobb parked and climbed out, hunched himself into his coat against the sleet and ducked under the tape. A dozen police and paramedics on the bridge were leaning over the parapet and nobody seemed to notice him. A tall black Sergeant was standing back a little from the others. Cobb walked across to him.

'McBean?'

Cobb could feel the man checking him out, taking in his rough outdoor clothes, the mud on his boots and jeans.

'Yeah. And you?'

'I'm Detective Inspector Sam Cobb.' He flipped open his warrant card wallet and noticed with approval that McBean took the trouble to check it.

'Sorry, sir. It's just that we're nervous about the media. It'll be a circus when they get hold of this.'

Cobb tucked his wallet away and glanced out over the river. It was a bleak enough stage for the great Matt Silver's last performance, he thought. 'Who else was in the car?'

'His two little girls, sir. Twins, they were.'

'Out with Daddy at that time of night?'

McBean hesitated. 'Sir, Mr Liston is in charge here now. He's down there on the pontoon. I'm just hanging around to see the end of it. I'm off duty, by rights.'

'I'll speak to Liston later. I'm asking you.'

McBean stiffened. 'Sir.'

'So where was he taking the kids?'

'They've got this massive place in Virginia Water. Silver turns up in the middle of the night and just bundles the kiddies into his Jag and away he goes. Mr Liston got the local station to send a couple of their people over to break the news to the mother.'

Cobb grunted. He tried to guess what kind of a job two young constables would make of telling Lauren Silver that her husband and her daughter were dead. Nobody ever made a good job of that. He did not envy them. It crossed his mind that, judging by her celebrity bitch reputation, Lauren Silver would not make it any easier for them. At once he felt guilty for thinking so.

'Silver's not in the car, sir,' McBean said after a moment. 'One of the divers went down. The driver's door's busted open, but no body.'

'It'll turn up. The tide running like this, it'll be at Battersea Bridge by now. A nice surprise for the Christmas shoppers, if they're looking.'

Cobb, not a tall man, pushed himself up on his hands to see over the parapet. The cable from the crane was taut and straining. It passed directly down into the water on the outside of one of the bridge piers. Two blue and grey Thames Division launches hung in the current and the cable lanced down between them. Men on both boats were peering into the water as the cable jerked upwards, the tension flicking droplets off it like dew from a bowstring. Three divers in drysuits floated mask-down in the water, the rods of their torch beams probing beneath them, following the angle of the cable. Cobb pitied the divers. He had done a little amateur diving himself years ago, and had even dived in the Thames once or twice. Despite his fascination with the river he had found diving in it a joyless experience. It was filthy in summer and hideously cold in winter. But for the police divers that wouldn't be the problem. The problem was that diving, unlike most police work, hardly ever brought a positive outcome. You generally knew what you were looking for and you knew it wouldn't be good, and it was never pretty when you found it. These days, Cobb knew himself better: he was not truly a man of action after all. For some reason that pill of self-knowledge had been a hard one to swallow, but it was getting easier to digest now he had reached middle life. With Clea gone there seemed less to compete for. It wasn't all bad. In a way it was more comfortable like this. Cobb jerked his thumb back towards the road.

'He went through there, did he?'

Where the main road turned on to the bridge the granite parapet gave way to wrought-iron railings. Several sections of railing were missing. Inside the police tapes lay a scatter of lamps and traffic cones and broken chunks of timber.

'They were fixing the railings last night, sir. They told me they'd be finished by midnight. I'll have something to say about that at the inquest.'

'Did you see him go over?'

'We were well behind, so we couldn't see much. But he must've just sailed through the gap. It was like he thought the road carried on through.'

'Speed?'

'Hayward and me, we both guessed at about a hundred and twenty. He just flew off into space. He missed the ferry pier by a mile.'

Cobb thought about more questions but McBean seemed strained, which surprised him in so experienced a man, and he decided against saying more. Instead he pushed himself up on the parapet again and took another look over. The rear bumper of the Jaguar was just breaking surface. There were some shouted commands from the police boats and another cable was slung over the bridge and hooked on to the car before winching began again. Black water spouted from a shattered rear window. Someone raised a hand to the crane operator and winching stopped again and the divers swam in close and wrenched at the passenger door and poked inside as if the beams of their torches were swordblades.

'You always hope, I s'pose,' McBean said. 'For the kiddie, I mean.'

Cobb glanced at the man's face and McBean saw his look. In answer to the unspoken question he said: 'We've only got one, sir. A daughter.'

'Of course. You would have.'

The arc-lit scene below them fell silent and a diver emerged from half inside the hanging car with a broken doll in his arms. Several of the men on the police launches looked away, and one of the divers crossed himself in a quick and furtive motion out of sight of the others.

Cobb and McBean turned away from the parapet and leaned against it. After a while Cobb said: 'The mother can be thankful for your partner, at least.'

'Hayward? He did well, sir,' McBean said hotly. 'Really well.'

'I'll remember it.'

'Did you hear how she was, sir? The kiddie he pulled out?'

'They say she'll be all right. Physically, I suppose they mean.'

'Christ.' McBean's voice was awe-struck. He knew how close he and Hayward had come to missing the tiny figure face down in the water. 'And they were twins, too.' He said it as though somehow he had expected them to share the same luck.

They stood together for a minute longer. McBean seemed reluctant to go, but when he finally did Cobb moved quietly along the bridge through the gathering crowd, checking the scene from different angles. It was no more than a habit of inquiry on his part, for it was obvious what had happened. Contractors replacing the railings on the southern end of the bridge had left the work half done, with wooden crash barriers across the gap in the railings. Probably they intended to get back at first light and finish the job before the fearsome Sergeant McBean came to check up. Cobb ducked under the tape, flashing his warrant card when a Constable challenged him.

Splinters of striped wood and nuggets of glass lay scattered over the tarmac. Down at the water's edge below him Cobb could see a couple of automatic warning beacons, one of them still stabbing a yellow shaft of light across the river. He wondered if some pre-Christmas revellers had thought it funny to throw them over the edge. Cobb checked the road behind him. The police were waving the early traffic past and the near half of the roadway was clear. Even in the wan light of the winter morning he could see no skidmarks on the tarmac. The Accident Investigation people would check that but it looked clear to him. Silver had not braked, which meant that he had not seen the hazard. Or that was presumably what it meant.

Cobb moved down among the uniformed men and the paramedics. A few recognised him but for most he was a shabby presence in the background, which, for the moment, was the way he liked it. It gave him time to think. The arc-lit Jaguar, hanging like a great steel shark from its cable over the water, had attracted a sizeable crowd now and Cobb could tell that the officers were distracted by their audience. They would all know by now whose car this was. Within moments someone would tip off the press and then there would be chaos. Cobb thought he probably had a few minutes more of calm before that happened.

They were winching the wrecked car towards the road now, clearing a space for it, backing up a hired transporter to receive it. Cobb caught sight of the uniformed Inspector Liston trotting up the stone steps from the water's edge. He knew the man slightly, a dull but solid officer nearing retirement. He looked more energetic than usual this morning, striding around and bawling commands as the car swung closer overhead. He seemed in his element. Perhaps he was enjoying his audience, building up to his last chance at a few minutes of fame. He would get that, too, when the cameras arrived, and as far as Cobb was concerned he was welcome to it. He moved away and positioned himself to one side so that the car would swing past within a few feet of him.

At first sight the vehicle looked only slightly damaged. The windscreen, driver's window and sunroof were gone and the driver's door hung open. The bonnet

and the driver's side were scratched and dented.
Perhaps that was from the crash barrier. Perhaps the
door had been damaged by that impact and that was
why it had burst open under water. Perhaps anything.
Through the open door Cobb could see the white
collapsed balloons of airbags, upholstery smeared with
filth, and nothing much else. He shrugged himself
deeper into his coat. He could smell the sour river
mud which dribbled out of the car, a smell which
reminded him of gravedirt, and he could not help
wondering what it must have been like inside. The idea
of being trapped underwater, trapped and sinking and
in the dark, was one of his private horrors. He had
never been able to understand why people thought
drowning was an easy death. To see it coming, to sense
the growing weight of the black water leaning on the
windows, to see it spurt in through chinks in the
bodywork, to hear that frail cocoon creak and buckle
as it slid into the pit . . . Cobb shuddered.

He decided he could leave Inspector Liston to it,
and turned away and stooped under the tape again and
walked towards his Land Rover a hundred yards away.
A solitary ambulance was parked at the roadside, with
a knot of paramedics clustered around it clapping
themselves against the cold, their luminous jackets
blazing in reflected light. They looked an unusually
grim lot. As he walked past, the back doors of the
ambulance opened and threw a splash of hard light on
to the pavement at his feet. A man in white police
coveralls stepped out and almost collided with him.

'Sam?'

Cobb looked up in surprise.

'It's me. Phil Latimer.'

Cobb took the doctor's hand and shook it. 'Sorry, Phil. Miles away.' He had met Latimer a dozen times at crime scenes and knew that the doctor – like other players in these dramas – felt that this bonded them in some way. Cobb supposed this should have been true but he had never felt able to respond to battlefield comradeship of this kind. He didn't dislike Latimer but he didn't want to talk. There was an awkward pause.

'Have they put you back on accidents these days, Sam?'

Cobb laughed, but it suddenly struck him that this was literally true and for a moment he found himself stuck for an answer. Finally he said: 'Someone at Area's leaned on Horrie Nelson. He just wanted me to take a look.'

He knew this sounded apologetic, but it was the best he could do. Perhaps tactfully, Latimer didn't pursue it. Instead, to change the subject, he nudged Cobb conspiratorially and stepped back into the rear of the ambulance, beckoning.

'Get in here out of the cold. I've got something to put some fire in your belly.'

Cobb, unable to escape now without rudeness, followed him. 'I'm pretty filthy.' He hoped Latimer wouldn't notice his clotted boots. 'I just came in from the farm.'

'Won't make any difference in here now,' Latimer said, his back turned. Latimer's bag was at the end of the aisle between the bunks, and he rummaged in it and found a leather-clad flask and handed it behind him to Cobb, who hovered half-crouched in the low space. 'Sit down, Sam. Wherever you can find room.'

Cobb took the flask and perched himself on the red-blanketed bunk.

'Not on that one,' Latimer said. 'That one's occupied.' He flicked down the red blanket and the dead child stared into Cobb's eyes. Black hair lay daubed in shocking streaks across her blue-white face. Cobb stood up slowly until his head touched the roof. Her eyes followed him. Her mouth was slightly open, as if she was about to speak to him.

Latimer was talking, his attention elsewhere. 'Get that down you, pal, that'll fuel you up.' Cobb wanted him to shut up so that he could hear what the child had to say. Then Latimer looked up and saw him and stopped. He quickly folded the red blanket over her, suddenly embarrassed. 'Sorry. I should've thought. Not the pleasantest way to start the day.'

Cobb pulled himself together. He sat on the opposite bunk, looked as casual as he could manage. 'It's OK. She just reminded me of someone for a second.' He took a nip of the flask. It was more brandy than coffee and he was grateful.

'We get a bit blasé,' Latimer said awkwardly.

Cobb noticed that the 'we' excluded him. He had reacted. He was no longer one of the boys. He felt an odd sense of relief as if he had finally managed to get a point across.

'Don't worry about it,' he said.

Cobb drank again from the flask. It was really very strong and he wondered how much of Latimer's nonchalance came out of it.

'It gets to people, when it's children,' Latimer said. Some of his bounce seemed to have gone out of him. 'The paramedics always get screwed up about it. But you haven't got . . .?'

'No kids,' Cobb said. 'It wasn't that. Forget it.' He felt a little sorry for Latimer, as if he had let him down, broken the rules. He lifted the flask again, took a final nip and handed it back. 'This is great stuff.'

'She didn't feel much,' Latimer said, ignoring the flask. 'Her neck's broken. She'd been in the water for an hour, but we tried everything anyway.'

'Of course you did, Phil.'

To Cobb's surprise Latimer uncovered the dead face again and stood staring at it. 'Poor little bitch.'

After a moment's hesitation Cobb looked too, and when he did her eyes were still fixed on him, as of course they always would be, always had been.

11

Cobb drove to the office and edged the Land Rover under the roof of the underground car park. He bundled the torn anorak under the driver's seat and took the fire stairs up to the front office. He was unsettled by the events at the bridge, and uncomfortable with the scruffiness of his appearance. He wanted to get changed, to have a coffee, to find a couple of minutes to get his thinking straight again.

He pushed through the swing doors into the front office. The room carried the exhausted taint of the small hours, stale weariness and the wet-dog smell of winter coats. Striplighting buzzed above half-a-dozen pale people waiting on plastic chairs. A suited businessman type preparing to be outraged, a woman who sobbed while her embarrassed husband murmured to her, a youth with a Canadian maple leaf sewn on to the backpack which lay on the floor between his feet. To Cobb they looked an average mix: stolen car, teenage runaway, lost passport.

'Morning Mr Cobb,' the Desk Sergeant greeted him and added quickly, 'why don't you pop back down for your messages later, sir? I would.' He made urgent signals with his eyes, but Cobb was too slow.

'Cobb!' boomed the mad Brigadier from behind

him, and the parade-ground heels knocked briskly towards him. 'There you are, man.'

The Sergeant pulled a sympathetic face. 'Full moon, sir,' he muttered.

'That man!' the Brigadier roared. 'Take his name, Cobb. Talking in the ranks.'

Cobb turned and straightened to attention. 'Yes, Brigadier. Right away, sir.'

'Good man, good man.' The Brigadier stood slapping his trouser leg with his swagger stick. He was an impressive figure for a man in his seventies, with sandy hair, clipped moustache and a long, brown face. The Brigadier tugged down his yellow waistcoat and barked: 'Now pay attention, Cobb.'

'Sir.'

Over the Brigadier's tweed shoulder Cobb saw the red-eyed mother look up and forget to sob for a moment.

The Brigadier noticed Cobb's clothes. 'Good God, Cobb! State you're in, man.'

'Sorry, sir. Just come in off ops.' Cobb heard the Canadian student snort with laughter.

The Brigadier swung on the boy. 'Sergeant! Take that man's name!'

'Right away, sir.'

The Canadian boy clutched his face in both hands and rocked silently in his chair.

'Ops, eh, young Cobb?' The Brigadier slapped his trouser leg again, twitched up one eyebrow. 'Bit sticky, was it?'

'A bit, sir.'

'Sorry to hear it, Cobb. Did your best, no doubt.'

'Thank you, sir,' Cobb said, and found himself thinking that, yes, it had been a bit sticky, and that in some odd way he valued the crazy old man's concern.

'Still, must keep up standards, Cobb.' The Brigadier stiffened his spine. 'No excuses, what? Got to set an example.'

'Yes, sir. For the chaps, sir.'

'Correct! That's the spirit. Smarten your ideas up a bit, that's my advice to you, young Cobb. And you'll go far.' He jammed his swagger stick under his arm, and spun on his heel. 'Carry on!' He marched out on his conker bright shoes.

When he had gone the Sergeant handed Cobb his messages. 'The old boy's getting cunning. Hiding round the corner like that.'

'That guy,' the Canadian boy's voice was pitched between awe and delight, 'is he for *real*?'

'Depends what you mean by real,' Cobb said, pushing open the door on to the fire stairs. He waved his hand over his shoulder. 'Carry on.'

On the third floor he dodged quickly past the CID office. It was after eight now, and the place was thoroughly awake, and he was anxious to avoid meeting any of his team before he had a chance to clean up. Nevertheless, he was glad to be in off the chill streets. The shrilling of the phones and the shouted questions and the noisy bustle of the place were reassuring. That surprised him: he had not realised that he had need of reassurance. Cobb tapped on Horrie Nelson's door, walked in as soon as Nelson answered, and closed the door behind him. Nelson surveyed him from behind his desk.

'Well, if it isn't the gentleman bloody farmer.'

'Morning, Horrie.' Cobb pointed at the wardrobe, already shrugging out of his sweater and shirt. 'Is it OK?'

'You carry on, lad.' Nelson affected his martyred voice. 'Don't mind me.'

Horrie Nelson looked more like a great tragedian than a Superintendent. His magnificent head of silver hair was legendary and he had the kind of patrician profile associated with leading men in black-and-white movies. He was well aware of his dignified presence and paid a good deal of attention to maintaining it as his grasp of high-technology policing slipped away. His care for appearances was the reason he was the only one of Cobb's colleagues who had a wardrobe in his office with a full-length mirror inside the door. Nelson had grown accustomed to Cobb using his office as a changing room whenever he was called in at short notice from the farm. Since Cobb had first talked about resignation these visits to Nelson's office normally attracted a lecture, but Cobb liked the big Yorkshire-man, who had been good to him when it mattered, and he thought that access to the mirror was just worth the lecture.

Nevertheless Cobb hoped Nelson wouldn't start in today. The sight of the dead girl had left him feeling jumpy and ill-at-ease. What worried him most was that it worried him at all. He had seen all manner of death before. He did not want to ask himself too closely why this one had got to him. He glanced into the mirror to see how badly he needed a shave, caught sight of his own dark-shadowed eyes, and popped a button off the collar of his shirt. He cursed unreasonably and slung the loose button hard against the door.

'This wasn't your idea, was it, Horrie?'

'My idea?'

'Turning me into some sort of an accident investigator.'

Nelson regarded him with innocent blue eyes. 'Well, now, Sam. I suppose you'll have to be like the rest of us and take the assignments you're given.'

'This isn't an assignment. It's a car crash. Liston could do it all right. He'd enjoy it.'

Nelson laid his silver pencil down on the blotter and steepled his blunt fingers. 'What's brought this on?'

Cobb hesitated but he found it impossible to lie to Nelson. 'I went to the scene just now, like you said. There was a dead child. Threw me a bit.' There was no one else in the office to whom he would have admitted this, but Nelson knew other things about him that no one else did, and Cobb felt instantly better for confiding in him.

'Oh.' Nelson sighed, stretched back and put his hands behind his head. 'You never get over it, Sam, you know that. Not when it's the little ones. Ugly, was it?'

'No.'

'Ah, well.' Nelson paused, as if he understood how

this made it worse. 'And for the record, no, it wasn't my idea. Mr Sykes called me as soon as he heard, and told me he wanted you to handle it. He thinks it'll be another Princess Di. This chap Silver was so big, apparently.'

'It's a car smash. A routine RTA.' Cobb savagely buckled his belt. Stopped. 'What does he mean, "handle it"?'

'Well, go to the scene. Take a look.'

'I took a look. It's a car smash.'

'Mr Sykes also tells me the wife is saying this banjo-player isn't really dead.'

'He's dead all right.'

'Well, you have it your own way, Sam. You usually do. But you'll still have to handle it.' They were silent for a minute, and Nelson said: 'I suppose you'll be going over to the hospital now?'

'I suppose.' Cobb straightened his tie: dark blue for authority. Fortunately the suit was dark too, not funereal, but sombre enough to show respect. Not that he supposed the poor woman would give a damn. He checked himself in the mirror. After a shave he'd look pretty good. Down to the ankles, anyway. Nelson seemed to decide something, got up, walked round his desk and leaned against it.

'Sam, you can call me a superannuated old fart if you like . . .'

'You're a superannuated old fart.'

'. . . but I think you're a bloody fool.'

'I know you do, Horrie. But I'm leaving, and that's it.'

'It's not as if you haven't got plenty of time. What are you? Forty? Forty-two?'

Cobb shot him a glance and straightened his lapels. 'You know I'm forty-six, Horrie.'

'Well, when I was—'

'Yes, I know. You were still on the beat. And here you are a Super. But things have changed.'

'Not that much.' Nelson straightened, resplendent in his midnight blue uniform, his buttons as polished as a guardsman's. 'Not that bloody much they haven't, my lad.'

Cobb turned to face him. 'Horrie, we both know why Stan Sykes leaned on you to give me a shit job like this.'

Nelson stiffened. Despite his affection for Cobb, Nelson was a formal man who believed in discipline, and this was very plain speaking. He and Cobb had a gentlemen's agreement to leave personalities out of these discussions and he was unhappy that Cobb had violated it. 'The Detective Chief Superintendent is an excellent police officer,' he said stiffly.

'I didn't say he wasn't, Horrie. But he doesn't like me. I'm not . . . dedicated enough for him. I'm not into "total policing".'

'I don't think you've got that quite right, Sam.'

'I've got it right,' Cobb said. 'Dead rock stars are real heavyweight stuff for a DI, wouldn't you say?'

'You want everything at once, Sam. And on your terms.'

'Stan Sykes is an old-fashioned thieftaker. He hasn't got any time for failed fast-trackers who spend half their lives in the country when they're not telling him how to run the police force.'

Nelson took a deep breath. 'I can't imagine why that is,' he said.

'And while he's there I'll never go any further.'

Cobb turned back to the mirror and brushed down the suit with his hands. Not bad.

Nelson tried again. 'Mr Sykes won't be at Area for ever.'

'They said something like that about income tax.'

Nelson pursed his lips. 'Sam, are you sure that Stan Sykes is the problem?' He waited for a long moment, but Cobb did not answer. 'It's been two years, you know.'

'So it has. Two years yesterday, in fact.'

Nelson sighed. 'Sam, no matter how hard it is, it might be better if you'd just get your head down and get stuck in.'

'I don't need the hassle, Horrie.'

'I'd have thought . . .' Nelson's voice grew harder for an instant. It was unusual enough to make Cobb stop and look at him.

'You'd have thought what, Horrie?'

'I'd have thought it was more a case of whether the hassle needed you.' Nelson tossed his silver pencil on to the blotter for emphasis.

'Horrie, can I ask you something personal?'

'Of course, lad.'

'What size shoes do you take?'

'Ten.'

'Bugger it.'

12

The Staff Nurse led Cobb along a bright corridor hung with Christmas decorations of tinsel and coloured paper. The nurses had made a big effort with the children's wing, but to Cobb it remained a hospital just the same, with the familiar thrill of fear vibrating just below the surface. A hollow-eyed man blundered out of a ward on their right and walked blindly past them, clutching a handful of child's drawings, stick figures and fluffy clouds. Cobb was glad he had never had children.

'I don't know how much you'll get out of any of them,' the Staff Nurse was saying. 'The doctor's in with the little girl right now and the mother's not really with us, if you take my meaning.'

Cobb liked the Staff Nurse at once, liked her practical busyness and her Midlands accent. The sense of competence she exuded reminded him of his own authority and he felt himself hit his stride for the first time since Lambeth Bridge.

'How is the child?'

'She's a bit knocked about, poor lamb. Cuts and bruises. I think she'll turn out to have a greenstick tib and fib.'

'That's leg, isn't it? I can never remember.'

'Yes. Right leg.' She glanced at him. 'We won't get you to run any first-aid courses.'

'Good move.'

'She must have been thrown around in the crash.' They stood back while a team of green-clad medics wheeled a trolley past at speed, then set off again. 'But you know, Mr Cobb, people get worse taking a tumble down the stairs. I don't think she'll even need stitches. It's a miracle, really, considering.'

Cobb thought again of the crushed car and the cold black river. 'Yes, it is.'

'But of course she's in shock. She hasn't said a word since they brought her in. Not a word.'

'Is that usual?'

'It's not unusual.'

'Do they get over it?'

The Staff Nurse shrugged without breaking her busy stride. 'In the old days they did. Kids will bounce back from most things. Of course now they have to deal with therapists and counsellors all telling them how bad they should feel. That's her, by the way, poor little pet.'

She pointed to a double door and through the porthole window Cobb had a glimpse of a doctor and a nurse, forcing smiles and bending over a figure so small it seemed to be lost in the bed. Cobb paused, seized with a sudden curiosity, but he could not see the girl's face behind the doctor's shoulder. The Staff Nurse had marched on and he had to hurry to catch up.

'And the mother?'

'Can't get much of a fix on her. But that great hunk of a minder is a pain in the backside. Keeps shouting for a private ward, and for this and that.' She sighed. 'But, you know, it takes people different ways.' They stopped outside a set of double doors. The nurse said, 'Here,' and made to open them. She paused, her nose wrinkling. 'Can you smell something? Like cowpats maybe?'

'Not a thing.' Cobb quickly pushed open the door and walked in.

A big man in a loud check jacket was standing by the window. He turned with an expression of irritation as they entered. A woman sat perched on the edge of a green plastic sofa, smoking in defiance of hospital regulations.

The Staff Nurse ignored that, walked across the room and bent over the woman solicitously, touching her arm. Her voice was tender. 'Mrs Silver, Mr Cobb's here from the police. It's just one of those routine things.'

Lauren Silver looked up vaguely, frowned, and gave a small couldn't-care-less shrug. Cobb did not recognise her, though he must have seen her a dozen times on TV. She looked crushed and exhausted, with a translucent duck-egg pallor that told him she had been vomiting. Her clothes were crumpled and ill-matched and her hand quivered as it held the cigarette. As she parted her lips to smoke, Cobb saw that one of her front teeth was broken off at an angle, and he noticed too that her lip was cut.

'The doctor will be finished in there soon and you can go back in,' the nurse was saying. 'But your little girl seems to be fine, thank the Lord. Do you need anything? No?'

As the nurse clucked over her, Cobb found himself feeling sorry for the way the Silver woman looked. He had no special interest in celebrities – they were usually a nuisance – but Lauren Silver had fallen such a very long way from glamour that it moved him to see it. As he watched her she glanced up at him with a flicker of interest, but before he could speak the big man stepped across from the window and bulked between them.

'Why the plain-clothes? What do we want the p'lice here for anyway?' The voice was East End, addressed to the room at large. 'No one's done a crime, have they?'

He was six inches taller than Cobb and he stood too close, close enough for Cobb to smell stale adrenalin and body odour. Cobb ignored him and turned to thank the Staff Nurse, who lifted an eyebrow in sympathy as she marched away through the swing doors. Then he turned back. 'And you are?'

'Matt Silver's manager.' The man stared rudely over Cobb's head.

'Have you got a name?' Cobb said. 'Sir?'

The big man faltered. 'Hudson. Tommy Hudson.' Recovered a little. 'And I'm a friend of the family. And–'

'Well, Mr Hudson, in answer to your question, two

people are dead. That's why the police are involved.'

Distress sat almost comically on Hudson's battered face. Cobb tagged him as an instinctive protector – there was often one involved when there was a widow. Protectors, in Cobb's book, were usually a pain in the arse, but nevertheless he was glad the woman had a friend. He dreaded to think what the media would do to her in her current state. And there would be media. This was Lauren Silver. So he was glad that Hudson looked effective, even if he didn't look subtle.

The big man rubbed his face, took a deep breath and started again, his tone conciliatory this time. 'I'm sorry – Mr Cobb, was it? We're all really upset, see.'

Hudson's pain was so obviously real that Cobb relented. 'I understand that, of course, Mr Hudson.'

'But what I meant was, it's not like someone's done a crime, exactly.'

'There was a crime.' Her voice was very clear and much stronger than Cobb had expected. He wondered what gave it such force.

Hudson said: 'I don't think you ought to say anything just now, Laurie–'

'Matthew stole my two babies–'

'–Laurie–'

'He stole them from me and he murdered my Gudrun.' She looked up suddenly at Cobb. 'He murdered Gudrun, Mr Cobb. That's a crime, isn't it? Murder is still a crime in this country?'

'It certainly is, Mrs Silver. Tell me what happened.'

'She's not up to this.' Hudson's voice was anguished.

'Can't we do this later, Mr Cobb?'

'Let me just get a few basic facts while they're still fresh in everyone's mind,' he said, 'then I'll leave you in peace.'

The woman tossed back her dry hair and reached for cigarettes and lighter again. 'You haven't found him yet, have you?'

Cobb waited while she groped in the bag. Something in the way she phrased her question suggested to him that she wasn't talking about her husband's dead body. If she thought he was still alive, Cobb didn't want either to buy in, or to contradict her. He had a feeling that to do so too brutally might unhinge her entirely, so he said nothing and sat watching her instead. She fumbled with the gold lighter, holding it the wrong way up at first and taking too long to discover her mistake. Then she dropped it on the sofa, and recovered it clumsily. He was sure now. The woman was drunk. He didn't blame her. But it was nine in the morning. He filed the fact away. She was not about to let him get away with silence.

'I said, you haven't found him yet. Right?' Her voice was slurred and belligerent.

'Mrs Silver, it's true we haven't found your husband's body yet–'

'Not his *body*, Mr Cobb,' she said with heavy emphasis. '*Him*.' She found her mouth with the cigarette and snapped at the lighter with such force that Cobb could see her biceps bulge. Finally the gas caught and she made a number of passes before getting the flame to the tip and inhaling the smoke and holding it in her lungs with her eyes shut and her head thrown back.

Cobb thought briefly about it then took a decision. He swung a chair around and sat on it so that he faced Lauren Silver directly. 'Mrs Silver, I'd like you to listen to me a moment.'

'This won't do any good,' Hudson protested. 'Can't you see the state she's in?'

Cobb ignored him. Lauren Silver said nothing but, her eyes still shut, blew the smoke out of her lips in a long plume towards the ceiling. 'This is probably hard for you, Mrs Silver, and maybe you won't believe it. But I think you should start to accept that your husband is almost certainly dead.'

'You don't know him.' She parted her lips over her broken tooth as she said this, opened her eyes and looked at him directly for the first time.

Cobb went on: 'Let me just say these things, Mrs Silver, and then you can work on them in your own time, OK? Your husband's car is badly damaged. I've seen the damage myself and in my opinion the driver could not have survived.'

'You don't know him,' she repeated in a flat voice.

'The Thames at Lambeth Bridge, Mrs Silver, is thirty-odd feet deep at high tide. There is a current of three knots running, and at this time of year the water temperature is about five degrees. Very few people survive in those conditions for more than a few minutes, especially if they're injured or shocked.'

'She doesn't need to know this now!' Hudson cried.

'Yes, she does.' Cobb kept his eyes on the woman's and thought he saw a glimmer of deeper understanding there, through the shock and the alcohol. He said very quietly, 'She does need to know it.'

Then the moment was past. She broke his gaze and tossed her head defiantly. 'Freya got out. So did he.'

'All right, Mrs Silver.' Cobb got to his feet. 'Just as you wish. We'll talk later.'

As he turned to the door it opened and a white-coated doctor leaned in. 'Mrs Silver, we're about done in there for now. Would you like to come through?'

She tossed her unfinished cigarette away for Hudson to stamp out and marched quickly past Cobb and through the door and down the corridor with the doctor following. Cobb watched her until she found the door of her daughter's room and pushed through it. He wondered how long it would take her to accept the truth. He wondered whether she would ever learn to be grateful she had one child left, and whether she could survive the loss of the other. He wondered whether anyone could. He pitied her, but he didn't fancy her chances. In particular he didn't like the drinking. Most people didn't drink during tragedies like this: after them, maybe, but not while the drama was unfolding. No, he didn't give much for her chances. He followed her out of the door and began to walk away down the corridor.

'Mr Cobb? Hang on a minute.' Hudson caught up with him outside the door of the ward. He looked somehow less jagged without Lauren Silver present, less like a gorilla and more like a large distressed bear. Cobb felt sorry for him too. Hudson spoke in a low voice: 'I just wanted a word, Mr Cobb, without Laurie – Mrs Silver – around.'

'Sure.'

'You're not just preparing her for the worst, like? You really don't think there's any hope?'

'None at all, Mr Hudson. That's my opinion.'

'I guess it will be easier when you find him. His body.'

'They turn up sooner or later. It's usually better when they do. I'm not trying to play psychiatrists here, Mr Hudson, but I've got a feeling she won't come to terms with one death until she's accepted the other.'

'Right.' Hudson looked away. 'You're right, I expect.'

'Were you close friends with Matt Silver, Mr Hudson?'

'Brothers. We was brothers.' Cobb saw the big man's eyes fill with tears. 'He wasn't always the way Laurie says. And that little kiddie was my god-daughter. Might as well've been my real daughter, I loved her that much.'

'I'm very sorry.'

Hudson pulled out a vast handkerchief and snuffled into it. Cobb looked away while he recovered himself. After a moment Hudson cleared his throat. 'This is all my fault, you know.' His voice was overloud, falsely matter-of-fact.

'Mr Hudson, in my experience nothing of this kind is ever all anyone's fault.'

'I said some things . . . in Paris last night. Just last night.'

'Oh?'

'He wanted to come home, Matt did. He wanted to put things right with Laurie.' He looked at Cobb. 'I tried to stop him.'

'Well, you failed to stop him, evidently.'

'But I tried, Mr Cobb. That's the point.'

Cobb knew this territory. He said with deliberate cruelty: 'Don't flatter yourself, Mr Hudson. He was a big boy, and even you weren't big enough to be your brother's keeper.'

He might have left then but Hudson burst out: 'It's this business, y'know? This fucking business does it to people. I should've fixed it for him to get back when he asked. I should've seen to it he wasn't going to drive in that condition.'

Cobb waited a moment. 'In what condition?'

Hudson was alert at once. 'What d'you mean?'

'Was he using last night, Mr Hudson?'

'I wouldn't know, would I? Using what?'

Cobb smiled inwardly at the speed with which the drawbridge came up. 'Don't worry about it, Mr Hudson. Even if he was, we can't prosecute a dead man. I was just asking.'

But Hudson seemed to feel a need to say more, perhaps to expiate. 'You don't know what it was like,' he went on in a rush. 'He could be a bad boy, Mattie could. But he was a good man. The trick was to tell which was which. The one time it mattered, I got it wrong.' He turned away and stared out of the tall Victorian windows at the opposite wing of the hospital. 'I loved that man, I don't mind saying. Loved 'em all. Loved Laurie. And that poor child lying dead in a fridge down the hall there. If you'd known her, Mr Cobb. So full of life . . .' Hudson's voice caught and he shook his big head in disbelief.

'At least her sister's alive,' Cobb said. He was unreasonably nettled. Perhaps because a young policeman had risked his life to save this girl, he felt somehow that Hudson was being ungrateful.

Hudson glanced at him. 'Frey? You're right, of course. Absolutely right.' But then his voice faded away. 'Still, you should've seen Goodie, Mr Cobb. You should've seen Goodie.'

The exchange troubled Cobb, but there seemed no point in pursuing it. Then Hudson was holding out his hand, thanking him for sparing the time to talk, and Cobb took the warm paw and shook it. Hudson turned and pushed open the swing door into the child's room. It was Cobb's cue to leave but at that moment curiosity seized him again, more strongly this time. On impulse he stepped forward and blocked the door with his shoulder before it closed. For a moment Hudson's back obscured the child from him, but he could see Lauren Silver seated on a straight chair on the far side of the bed. Her face was carved in marble and the child's small hand lay limp and untouched in her lap. Cobb tried not to be judgemental but it saddened him that the woman had not taken her daughter's hand in her own, that she was not sprawled sobbing over the bed with her child in her arms, for God's sake, with nurses trying to drag her off.

After a moment Hudson moved around the bed and put his big hand on Lauren's shoulder and Cobb could see the child's face clearly for the first time. A plain little girl with mousy hair, eyes downcast and staring at the coverlet. He felt strangely relieved; she might be Gudrun's twin but she looked nothing like her dead sister. And then something else. As he stood propping the door open with his shoulder she lifted her head and stared directly at him. Her eyes focused and he knew that she had seen him, in a way that she had seen no one since she had come here and perhaps for a long time before that. He felt his spine stiffen and his chin lift at the silent interrogation and he looked straight back at her and smiled and said clearly: 'Hello, Freya.'

Her mouth opened a little and for an instant he thought she might actually answer him. But then Hudson, sensing the atmosphere and glancing up with surprise, broke the spell. 'You've got a way with kids, Mr Cobb.'

'No,' Cobb answered. 'No. Not at all. Excuse me.' As he turned to leave he glimpsed her face again, eyes vacant once more.

Outside on the hospital steps a scrum of TV crews and reporters had already gathered in the thin light. Their vans blocked the street and knots of them were gathered, testing their equipment, rehearsing reports to camera, calling questions to hospital staff coming off duty. Police were already moving them back, clearing the steps, marshalling them behind metal barriers. None of them noticed Cobb and he passed quietly into the throng. On the whole, he did not dislike journalists in the visceral way that some policemen did. They were professionals, just as he was. And this was a typical selection, hard, competent men and women, most of them young. They cursed the cold and the waiting, shouted ribald greetings to new arrivals, warmed their hands around paper coffee cups, blew steam into the keen air. A cameraman in a sheepskin jacket was talking, more or less to himself, as Cobb pushed past.

'Why d'you think it is,' the man hefted his camcorder and squinted experimentally through the viewfinder, 'that celebrities always have to top themselves at dawn?'

Beside him a woman in a wide scarf and carrying a clipboard answered without looking up. 'Look on the bright side. They don't usually take their kids with them.'

'Still, you have to admit, it's bloody inconsiderate.'

Bloody inconsiderate. They'd said that about Clea, that she was always a law unto herself. Dying at Christmas. Bloody inconsiderate. He had heard someone actually say that at the funeral, innocently no doubt, trying to take the sting out of things, not knowing Cobb could hear. Bloody inconsiderate. He walked on through the crowd of journalists, angry and unsettled. Then he found that today he resented these media people after all and that truly alarmed him. That was something he could not allow to take hold. For they were real life, just as he was real life. The lost child and that ugly bear Hudson and the shattered mother in the ward just a few yards away, they were not real life. They were characters in a drama. The drama might be real enough to them but it was their drama and not his. That was the way it worked, and the only way it could work.

Cobb pushed through to the far side of the crowd and found a granite kerb and savagely knocked the last of the dried cowshit from his boots. The activity bought him a measure of composure. He breathed deeply. He knew the way this worked. He was an old hand at it by now. Grief was like malaria. Just when you thought you were clear of it, something would happen to lower your resistance and off you'd go again. A breakthrough, the medics called it. But there was a bright side. Each time the bouts of fever were less debilitating and they knocked you down for a shorter time. Even if you never quite got rid of the disease, after a while it ceased to matter.

He repeated this mantra until he believed it, and then walked away to work.

13

It was strange how calm she felt. Lauren did not fool herself that this was healthy, nor that it would last for ever. But it was useful. In a cold and practical sense it allowed her to function. At least, she supposed that was what she was doing. Functioning.

The calmness had settled on her hours ago when the two police officers – a boy child and a girl child, really, dressed like police officers – had come pounding at the door. She had been in the bathroom throwing up at the time, spinning in a vortex of terror and nausea so deep that for minutes on end she had not heard them. Finally something had got through to her: not their incessant thundering on the door but the sawing voice from their radio, braying through the house, like one of those bullhorns cops used in old movies to order the villains to come out with their hands up. It was this that told her that what she so dreaded had come to pass, with the finality of a biblical prophecy.

When she opened the door to these child-police she was already calm. She saw them staring at her stone face and at her broken mouth, scared by it like the children they were. Even so the girl had proved competent enough: taking charge, ordering her about, quickly checking for drugs, pills, signs of a suicide attempt, Lauren supposed. The police-girl pushed her to a seat, called an ambulance, made tea – *tea!* – found her fresh clothes. Lauren didn't want tea. She didn't want an ambulance. She didn't want fresh clothes. But it had all happened, and she had let it happen around her. Other things happened after that, urgent things involving men and women in important uniforms, lights, sirens, and people softly speaking to her in language she seemed unable to understand. She was the centre of attention and yet was required to do nothing. It was strangely comfortable.

She could see everything very clearly now. Far too clearly. She could see, for example, how much she resented this dumb little figure in the bed in front of her. Resented the love she was supposed to lavish on this child when she had none to give, had nothing at all to give. It wasn't Freya's fault. It was just the way it was. Lauren looked down at the girl's soft hand in her lap, like a little white starfish. She wasn't sure how it had got there. Maybe the nurse had placed it there. She knew she should take it in her own hands, chafe it, murmur to her baby. But she simply did not have the energy. Freya would live, whether her mother cared or not. Lauren registered that as good in an abstract way. She just could not see, as she sat there, quite what it had to do with her.

Lauren glanced at the child and saw that she was sleeping, curled into her big pillows. She remembered they had said something about a sedative and was glad. It meant she no longer had to sit here. There was a nurse in the room, she noticed for the first time, a pretty Asian girl, and for a moment Lauren watched her work.

'Give me a drink, Tommy,' she said abruptly, and held out her hand. The nurse looked up quickly and then away again, and Hudson was speaking, protesting. She ignored his voice – it was like a rumble in the background – and clicked her fingers impatiently until she felt the weight of the flask in her palm. She drank from it. She wasn't sure whether she needed the alcohol or not, but it felt natural to drink and there seemed no reason to resist. 'I want to see my daughter,' she said.

'Your daughter's right here, Mrs Silver,' the Asian nurse said gently, thinking perhaps that she did not know what she was saying.

'I want to see my daughter,' Lauren repeated without any change of emphasis, for she knew quite well what she was saying, and she stood up.

'You shouldn't be doing this, Laurie.' Hudson had to hurry to keep up with her brisk stride. 'There'll be time for this tomorrow. When you're rested.'

'Tomorrow?' she said scornfully. 'And what's she supposed to do until tomorrow?'

Hudson, unhappy and afraid, said no more. She couldn't see what was wrong with him but she didn't much care and strode on, gathering a retinue as she moved quickly down the corridors. There were whispered consultations around her, snatched conversations on the run. A Staff Nurse whom she vaguely recognised tried urgently to get in her face and speak to her. A doctor walked backwards in front of her complaining in a plummy voice. A security man barged into her path and tried to sound authoritative, as if he were directing traffic. All brushed aside.

Rubber doors, a chill bright cavern, metal tables glimpsed through a porthole window, a reek of chemicals. She waited, tapping her feet on the brilliant tiles, as green-clad attendants hurried to make unscheduled preparations around her. Someone drew curtains around a cubicle and she was ushered in by an indignant fat man in glasses and coveralls. He smelt of antiseptic and authority and had a green surgical mask tied under his chin, and it was obvious he had been pulled away from some more pressing task. He was still drying his hands and there were slick marks on his rubber apron. The fat man was plainly furious at the interruption and the effort of repressing his outrage made his voice wobble. It wobbled more every time Hudson, in despair, tried to explain or to apologise. Lauren did not know why Hudson should do any of that, but the fat man's impotent rage was so funny to watch that it was only the whisper of a steel drawer opening somewhere close by that stopped her from giggling aloud.

A trolley trundling on rubber wheels. The curtains moving aside. The green-clad figures stepping back. Hudson's arm clutching around her waist, locking there.

The blanket was folded back over the china white face with its bell of black hair, washed and combed now. Hudson gasped audibly beside her and Lauren felt his shock. But she was not shocked. That was no longer possible. She turned the blanket down further, revealing the birdbones of the child's shoulders.

'For God's sake, Laurie,' Hudson begged. 'Leave her be.'

So small. So very small. Too small, in fact. Gudrun took up so much more space in the world than this cold doll. Lauren touched the silken hair, let it trickle between her fingers, ran her knuckle down the white cheek. It was chill and alien, like a joint of meat. This was nothing like the child she had thrust into the world, hot and bloody and squalling, one hundred months ago. Nothing of the girl Lauren had seen springing up sapling-fast to mirror herself at the same age – pretty, talented, open. Nothing of the girl who was destined to carry those things for her into adult life, as she had been unable to carry them. Lauren stared hard at the pinched little face. She felt nothing. Disappointed, perhaps. Irritated at this pointless deception (did they think she would fall for *this?*). She felt nothing for this snow carving, this facsimile. She flipped the blanket back into place.

'Laurie, this isn't doing you any good. Let's go now.'

'Don't be silly, Tommy,' she said in a clear voice. 'I can't *go*. Not until I find her.'

She felt eyes glance at her questioningly, eyes which had been averted. She could not imagine why they looked at her.

'She's gone, Laurie.' His voice cracked a little. 'We've seen. Now let's go home.'

'But where is she?' She was unable to comprehend his stupidity when the matter was so clear to her. 'You don't imagine *this* is Goodie, do you?'

'Come on now, love.' He steered her away a couple of steps and in a flash the gurney was rolled out of sight.

'You're not going to let them get away with this, Tommy?' They were back in the glaring anteroom now, Hudson's powerful arm locked around her, half carrying her. Others came to help him. Someone opened the door for them. Twisting her head around in sudden panic, she caught sight of the fat man with glasses standing near the far wall. 'You!' she screamed at him. 'What have you done with my daughter, you bastard?'

The fat man, all his outrage gone, looked sadly at the floor as they dragged her away along the echoing corridors, shrieking like an animal in a trap.

14

Cobb was not called to give evidence until midday, but after that the case moved rapidly and by two in the afternoon he was walking out of the court and into the rain.

He enjoyed court, watching the miniature drama unfold, the small thrill of knowing he had to perform in it. Most police officers loathed it, and the fact that he did not feel that way made him wonder from time to time whether he might have missed a turning some way back in his life. It amused him to think so but he did not take the thought very seriously. He enjoyed watching the gladiatorial courtroom contests, and he understood the need for them within the system, but he could never have taken part. Cobb privately felt that the real victims of the legal system were the lawyers themselves. Forced to set aside personal values, they often came to forget where they had left them. That was why so many of them became cynical and corrupt. If you fought purely as a mercenary, Cobb believed, it soon ceased to matter for whom or for what you fought. He had too much self-knowledge to think that he could do that. He was involved, every time. It was a constant struggle for him to maintain distance. Unlike lawyers, who believed in the law, Cobb believed in justice, and sometimes in an Old Testament version of it. He liked to see criminals locked up. Cobb knew that virtually every defendant is guilty, and though he understood the need for a competent defence, he was almost always glad when it failed. Which was why he emerged from the court into the gloomy London afternoon in a better mood than he had gone in.

It was raining hard now and he dodged into an Italian coffee shop near the court and took a stool near the rain-streaked window and ordered bruschetta and espresso. He could smile at himself when he became righteous. Clea always had. His food appeared and he began to eat. Well, she would be on his mind, of course, this week of all weeks. That was OK. He forgave himself for that. It was only that the dead child had looked just a little like her. It didn't mean anything. He had all that in perspective now that the day, with all its action and pressure, was throwing him forward. File and forget, as Horrie Nelson always said. Cobb never knew whether Nelson realised this was quite a good military pun – probably not – but it was apt anyway. A man is dead. A child is dead. Her sister is struck dumb with horror and her mother broken beyond hope of recovery. That's tragic. That's life. File it away. Forget it. His pager buzzed.

A few minutes later, Cobb took the lift to the third floor and at the end of the corridor used his security pass to open the double doors. The CID room was the usual wasps' nest of activity, a clatter and buzz of keyboards, phones, raised voices. It struck Cobb that for a late afternoon it was even more frenetic than usual. He moved through the mêlée towards his own desk, where his workstation stood plastered with yellow post-it messages. Before he got there Nelson appeared in the doorway of his office, gesturing to him.

'Sam?' Nelson had to shout over the noise. 'A minute, lad.'

'I'll be right there.'

'Right now, Sam.'

This was unusually authoritative for Nelson and Cobb followed him into the office and pulled the door half-closed behind him, shutting out some of the machine-room jangle.

'What's up, Horrie?'

'We can't have this, Sam.' Nelson waved him to a seat and paced in front of his desk. He seemed restless.

'Can't have what, Horrie?'

'Well, look at it!' Nelson cried, as if this had been his cue. 'The whole place is in pandemonium over this *bloody* Matt Silver business. It's going just like Mr Sykes said it would.' He sat down with a thump and pounced on his silver pencil, sliding it through his fingers to tap on the blotter, first one end, then the other.

'Spit it out, Horrie,' Cobb said, lacing his fingers behind his neck and pushing his head back into the cradle they made. 'I know I'm not going to like it, but let's hear it.'

'Mr Sykes wants us to set up a task force, Sam.'

'A task force? For a car smash?' Cobb was

incredulous. He just stopped himself from laughing. 'What are we looking for? Bald tyres?'

Cobb failed to register Nelson's warning glance or the sudden drop in the din from the CID room so that Sykes was through the door and standing behind him before he knew it.

'We're looking for another corpse, Cobby,' Sykes said, with his usual mix of aggression and jocularity. 'We've only got one of those so far.'

Cobb stood up. 'Sir.'

Sykes gestured for him to sit down again and himself took the chair opposite. 'Did you meet the grieving widow?' He was a hard man in his mid-fifties who grinned a lot, baring small teeth. He was of middle height but there was something shrunken about him, something wizened and cunning. Cobb supposed there had to be, for him to reach Detective Chief Super on the strength of old-fashioned policing.

'Yes, sir. I talked to her at the hospital.'

'She doesn't think hubby's dead. She keeps calling to remind us about that. Keeps asking for you, as a matter of fact.'

Cobb wondered where this was going, but he already had a fair idea. 'The woman's in shock, sir. She doesn't know what she's saying.'

Sykes grinned.

'Silver's body will turn up in a few days,' Cobb said. 'Maybe sooner. Sir.'

'Well, that's fine. Because I've just told Horrie to put you in charge of looking for it.' Cobb stared at him and Sykes continued: 'There you go, Cobby. The Matt Silver Task Force. What you always wanted. Your very own team.'

Cobb swallowed. 'Sir, I've been working with DI Peters on the Beulah Road break-ins. And I'm on the West London Car Crime programme—'

'Put them on hold. Hand over your notes.'

Cobb said, 'Sir.'

'I'll get them to keep you in the loop, Cobby. You won't miss anything.' Sykes turned to Nelson with a look of mock surprise. 'I don't think he likes it much, Horrie.'

Nelson frowned at his desk blotter. Cobb said: 'With respect, Mr Sykes—'

'Listen, Cobby,' Sykes cut across him, 'I know it's a pisser, and you probably think I've done it to shaft you, but I need it done. There's a feeding frenzy out there and I don't want anyone saying we haven't done every last fucking thing to find this bloke. Because that's what they will say. And it'll be us at Area HQ they'll point the finger at. And I'm sensitive about that, see, Cobby?'

'Silver's dead, sir,' Cobb said. 'It was an accident.'

'Of course it was, Cobby. This isn't about reality. This is about public bloody relations.' Sykes stood up. 'You look all right, Cobby. You can give an interview without saying "fuck" too often, unlike me. And you're not doing anything important. So you deal with it.' He rose to go. 'Get in touch with those jokers at public affairs and fix it. Horrie'll give you an

incident room and assign some people.' He saw
Cobb's expression and stopped. 'Just look busy until
they stop asking questions, Cobby. And we can all go
back to work.'

Sykes grinned at both of them and left. Nelson and
Cobb looked at one another.

'Well, don't blame me, Sam,' Nelson protested, eyes
wide. 'Maybe the Commissioner's a Matt Silver fan.
Every other booger is. Speaking for myself I'd never
heard of the bastard before this morning.'

Cobb, who had grown up with Silver's music,
wondered who or what Nelson had thought Matt Silver
was: some sort of photographic process, perhaps. He
felt strangely lightheaded, as if a decision which had
worried him had suddenly been taken out of his hands.
'You know what this means, Horrie?'

'Now don't get on your high horse, Sam. You just
drew the short straw, that's all.'

'A Detective Inspector? I'll be on points duty next
week.'

'I believe Mr Sykes wants someone with sufficient
authority,' Nelson said loyally. 'That's his thinking, I
understand.'

'Right,' Cobb smiled at him with his mouth. 'Right,
Horrie.'

'Look at it this way, Sam. It is a task force. It's quite
a coup to get it, really.'

'A coup?'

'I'll find you some lads. You can have 4D for an
incident room.'

'No one's got two hours to waste on this, Horrie, and 4D's a broom cupboard.'

Nelson tossed his silver pencil down with a clatter. 'If you're going to jump ship, Sam, why don't you stop talking about it and bloody well do it? Put us all out of our misery.'

Cobb stood up. 'I'll give it some thought.'

15

It was Hudson's voice that woke her. He was giving an instruction to the driver, telling him to pull up. Lauren opened her eyes, careful not to move, unwilling for the moment to attract his exhausting compassion. The windows of the car were plates of ebony. So it was night again. But then, between the backs of the seats, she saw the green numerals of the digital dashboard clock and it told her that it was only six in the evening.

Lauren moved her fingers and toes, flexed her muscles gently. She was wrapped in a coat or a blanket, warm and comfortable, curled in the back seat of the car. She didn't remember getting there. She was sleepy and dull and knew that she must have been sedated. She didn't blame them. She knew how she had been. She could see it replayed in her mind, as if she had been floating outside her own thrashing body, and had watched Tommy Hudson fight to pin her down – and fight damned hard too, despite his weight and strength – long enough for someone to slip a thread of steel into her arm and squirt oblivion into her. She tensed her muscles again, experimentally, but no, she was not restrained. It would hardly have surprised her if she had been. But this new movement must have alerted him. She saw the angle of his profile shift and he whispered: 'Laurie? Are you awake?'

'Yes, Tommy.' The concern in his voice was so palpable that she stretched out her hand and squeezed his arm. 'It's OK now.'

'Jesus, Laurie.' His rough slab of a hand came down on hers and rubbed it so hard that it hurt her. 'Jesus, I been so worried.'

'I'm all right, Tommy.' She shuffled herself into a sitting position, discovering that her body was raw and bruised. He heard her catch her breath.

'What they done to you . . . I had to help them, Laurie. I hope I never . . .' He shook his head. 'How are you now?'

'OK. I'm OK.'

She glanced out of the window. From this new angle she could see big handsome houses set back in ordered grounds. The area looked familiar but she could not summon up the energy to decide whether or not she knew where she was. Many of the homes had Christmas lights strung over the eaves or in the branches of the fir trees in the gardens. The merry blinking of the lights wearied her. It struck her as important that she ask Tommy to see that the lights festooned around her own house were taken down. As she formulated that thought it came to her that that was where she was. Home, or very nearly home. She could not decide whether this was good or bad.

Hudson had punched numbers into a mobile and was murmuring into it. The voice that squawked back was clearly audible to Lauren.

'It's pretty crazy here, Tommy. We'll have all the overseas media here by midnight, too, and the local law aren't much help.' The voice paused. 'You might think about giving this a miss. Stay away for a day or two.'

Lauren curled into the corner of the back seat and pulled the coat more tightly around her. Hudson covered the phone. 'Laurie, we ought to go somewhere else. We can come back here in a couple of days maybe.'

'I'm going home, Tommy.' Her voice surprised her with its firmness but once spoken the decision seemed obvious. She stretched across in the darkness and patted his arm again. 'You'll take care of everything.'

'You there, Tommy?' the phone bleated again.

'Yes.' Hudson's voice took on a new edge. 'We're coming through. Right now. OK?'

'Just as you say, Tommy.'

Hudson slipped the phone into his pocket and leaned forward to slide open the driver's partition. 'Give it a bit of welly as you go through, Col, but try not to kill anyone.'

'Right.'

'Tommy –' Lauren stirred beside him.

'You stay down for the next minute and it will all be OK.'

She moved her hand down his sleeve and gripped his thick wrist briefly. 'Couldn't have got through today without you, Tommy. Thanks.'

She uncovered her face and gave him a pallid smile. The broken tooth made her look strangely like a teenager again, a half-grown gamine. Then they were sweeping towards the lights and lenses. He told her to duck down, but she was too dazed to care and as they drove through the popping flashguns her lost white face against the glass was an offering to the cameras.

The car bounced to a stop on the drive and the security men ran up and Hudson helped them bundle her towards the house. The dark garden leapt into stark negative behind them as TV lights sprang on in the slanting rain and a riot of scuffling and shouting broke out beyond the security cordon. Then the front door was open and Hudson pushed her through and slammed the door behind them and locked it and leaned against it. She could feel him watching her as she moved away from him down the hall, shedding her jacket in a heap on the floor. It was reassuring to have him watching her and she was grateful for it. Yet she found she could walk well enough without help. She felt hollow, nearly weightless. It was no huge effort to move when you were weightless. At the top of the steps leading down into the lounge she leaned for a moment. She could feel her strength returning, and some involuntary process in her – some opening out – told her she had been right to insist on coming back here tonight. Maybe this was where she should be, after all.

'I'll call someone for you,' he said. 'A friend or someone.'

'A friend?' She executed a little tottering pirouette and made a sad face at him. 'Not many of those any more. All Matthew's. Everything was Matthew's.'

'That's not true, Laurie. You'll see.'

She turned away and glimpsed herself in the hall mirror. She pushed up her tangled hair and ran her finger around the dark circles under her eyes, slid her tongue down the broken angle of her tooth.

'We'll call someone tomorrow about that,' Hudson said. She could tell the broken tooth worried him. 'Get that fixed. Good as new.'

'Good as new,' she repeated absently. And then something seemed to slip into place in her mind and she stood up straight and tugged down her clothes. 'I'm going to take a shower, Tommy. Freshen up. You're a sweetheart for bringing me back here but you don't need to wait.'

'You *are* joking?'

'Truly.'

'I'll wait, Laurie.' He stood at the end of the hallway, his back to the door. 'I'll wait.'

She looked at him. 'OK, Tommy. You have a drink and wait for me, and when I come down I'll call someone to come over and stay. Will that make you feel better?'

'It will.'

She walked back up the hall to him with unfaltering steps and kissed him quickly on the cheek. 'Dear Tommy. Always there.'

When she had gone upstairs, Hudson poured himself a Scotch at Silver's dining-room bar. He would have been happy with any old cooking Scotch, but all he could find was a vintage Glen Morangie. That was typical. The bar was of Indonesian teak. The glass was Waterford crystal. That was typical too. He sipped the Scotch, set it down and then moved around the room ripping down the Christmas decorations. Lauren hadn't asked him to do this but he felt sure that was what she would want. It was certainly what he wanted. If it had been left to him he would not have come back here for a long, long time.

Hudson fetched a rubbish sack from the kitchen and bundled up the bright tinsel, the smiling Santas and reindeer, and crushed them all into the sack. Only when he had finished did Freya cross his mind. He hesitated for a second with his hands full of bright paper. Should he have left something for her? He wrestled with this for a moment but could not work out the best thing to do. The truth was, he acknowledged to himself, that he didn't much care, and he could not even find the energy to feel guilty about it. He had tried to be good to both children at the beginning but Freya had always held back. It was her nature, he supposed, but the result was that now he really had no room for her. It was a pity but there was.

Hudson stuffed the bag of ruined decorations out of sight behind the sofa and then stood and nursed his Scotch, gazing mournfully around the room. The house had been home to Silver's family – and a second home to Hudson himself – for twelve years. Matt could have had something far more spectacular, anywhere in the world, but he had chosen to keep this place. Hudson suspected that he wanted to hang on to the house where his kids had been born. Perhaps he saw it as an anchor in his own turbulent life. Whatever his reason, Hudson was glad. He couldn't count the number of hours he had spent here in this room. It was, perhaps, the only place he had ever truly felt at home and over the years he had come here as often as he could, bringing presents, staying over. He was Matt Silver's friend, sometimes his confidant, sometimes Lauren's, Goodie's godfather. Yes, Lauren and Matt might have troubles, but who didn't? Personally, he thought Matt was mad to risk losing her – a woman like Lauren – especially when she worked so hard to make a go of things. Maybe it was different when you had women throwing themselves at you day and night, like Mattie did. But whatever their problems the Silvers were family, and to Hudson this was home. He thought of his own apartment, a costly modern warehouse conversion south of the river, smelling of pine-scented cleaner and emptiness.

He stared moodily around at the handcarved furniture and polished mahogany floors and the drapes with their gold fleur-de-lys motif. Tommy Hudson knew quite well that his own appreciation of style was strictly limited. But even making allowances for that he could never quite warm to this decor. It was a bit showy for him. If he was honest Hudson had never much liked the stuff Silver packed the house with. Hudson's attachment ran much deeper.

All over now. All over for Silver, and for little

Gudrun. The image of the child's face appeared to him again and Hudson sat down on the brocade sofa with a bump. He had never expected grief to be like this; every time he thought of Goodie it caught him by surprise. Once, years ago, Hudson had sparred a demo bout with Henry Cooper. The champion was long retired by then while Hudson was a magnificent gladiator of twenty-five. The whole thing was set up as a bit of fun for a TV variety show, with Cooper – well over fifty – keeping everyone laughing with a running commentary on his age and infirmities. At the very end, when everyone was laughing too hard to notice, Cooper tapped Tommy Hudson hard between the eyes, hard enough to make his legs wobble, and Hudson caught a look in the old prizefighter's eyes which warned him not to forget who was boss. Hudson felt that way now. Every time he thought about Goodie the memory knocked him sideways. The impact never seemed to get any less brutal and he was never prepared for it. His vision blurred and he squeezed the bridge of his nose hard. Laurie didn't need any of that nonsense right now.

Lauren walked through the littered bedroom to the en suite bathroom, turned the shower on full and left it that way. With the rush of water masking all other sounds, she returned to the bedroom door and locked it from the inside and then walked across to the dressing table and sat down. It surprised her to find that her reflection looked much the same as it had twenty-four hours before. The woman in the mirror was strained and pale, but if she didn't look too closely at the swollen mouth, if she didn't part her lips over the snapped tooth, she could almost be the same person as before: not a happy woman, certainly, but a woman with two fine children, a woman with choices, a woman with a life.

The change since then was absolute and yet, so far, invisible. Lauren parted her lips and examined the broken tooth. She could see the nerve exposed and she prodded it with her fingertip, hard. She was aware of a current, like a jolt of electricity, which leaped up into her jaw. She supposed this was pain. She supposed everything she had felt since four this morning had been pain, perhaps since long before. Yet she no longer felt confused or angry or hysterical. She did not feel anything. There was a photograph on the dressing table beside her. It showed her and Matthew with the two girls at the Eiffel Tower. She remembered that it had been taken two years before on the last of their reconciliation trips. She wasn't sure why she had kept that photo particularly. His recommitment to her had not outlasted the Paris trip by more than a week. Yet now it was his image that she gazed at, this unreasonably beautiful man, his head tossed back, laughing as if to challenge the whole world.

'Matthew,' she told the picture quietly, 'you've killed us all.'

Lauren went through the drawers of folded clothing until she found what she wanted and when she did she drank from the bottle. She drank again, rose to her feet and walked into the bathroom. She found surgical scissors and half-a-dozen bottles of pills. She emptied some of the pills on to the coverlet and sat on the bed and tossed the scissors on to the blanket beside her. How good it would be if they did find him, against all her instincts, bloating like a cat in a weir. Perhaps then, the threat removed, she could let go. How she longed for that. And it would be so simple. Extinction, the end of all her failures. She found a loose coin on the bedside table and played at tossing for it: heads the bottle, tails the blade. After a while she stopped and tossed the coin on to the blanket. For of course she could not be that easy on herself. She reached across to the dressing table and lifted down the photograph. She opened her blouse and cradled the picture there, the glass cold against her bare breast, and rocked it against her like a baby.

Tommy Hudson realised he had finished his drink and that made him aware that time had passed. He set down his glass and walked quickly through into the hallway. He peered upstairs and could see the line of light under her bedroom door and could hear the hiss of the water.

'Laurie? You OK up there?' Probably she couldn't hear him, but the silence worried him anyway. He trotted up the stairs and knocked hard on her door. 'Laurie?'

He tried the handle. The door was locked. He put

his big shoulder against it and popped the oak inwards like plywood. The shower was rushing in the bathroom and steam billowed through into the disordered bedroom. Lauren sat cross-legged on the bed, nursing the picture, watching him. There was an odd, resigned calm about her that he could not quite decipher. An empty vodka bottle stood on the bedside table next to an ashtray overflowing with butts. The coverlet was scattered with small bottles and plastic pill containers and loose multicoloured tablets. He saw the glint of the scissors against the blanket. He tore his eyes away from her and marched through to the bathroom. He turned the water off and came back and stood over her. He gripped her shoulders and shook her so that her head snapped back.

'Did you take any?'

'Tommy—'

'Did you?'

'No. I didn't take any.' He let her go.

He turned away, breath coming fast, then he swung back on the ball of his foot. 'You got a little girl to take care of!' he shouted suddenly.

She stared at him, motionless. 'I know that, Tommy.'

'A little girl!' His fists were opening and closing, his head swaying like a bull's with a lance in him. When he spoke again his voice was tight. 'Laurie, you know I always . . .'

'Tommy,' she said, 'none of that matters now.'

He seemed about to say more but stopped himself and straightened slowly to his full height, so that he towered above her, and stood there silent for a long while. Drops of water from the shower head fell heavily into the bath, like the ticking of a grandfather clock.

'She was you,' he said at last. 'Goodie was. When you asked me to be her godfather, it felt like you was giving me a bit of you.'

She said nothing.

'I remember that first time when you climbed in that van, all them years back,' he went on. 'Matt and me, we both knew you was the one. You was what – eighteen then? I'd've given anything to see Goodie at eighteen. Anything.'

'I know.'

He nodded quietly to himself for a while, then seemed to notice the disordered state of the room for the first time. Bending as if with great weariness, he scooped up a wastebin and moved slowly around the bedroom gathering up her litter, the empty bottle, a handful of pill boxes, an ashtray foul with butts, the discarded scissors, clattering them into the metal bin. He stopped distractedly and shook the bin at her as if she were a naughty schoolgirl. 'I won't stand for all this, you know,' he said. 'I won't stand for it.'

She rocked the framed photograph in her arms, watching him. 'Just take care of everything for us, Tommy.'

16

'The cops again? Why don't you let a chap get some peace?'

'Open up right now, old man,' Cobb commanded. 'It's bloody cold out here.'

When the low front door opened a crack, Cobb shouldered through it into the hall. He noticed that Fred was wearing purple pyjamas with a smiling pig motif on them.

'Are you ever going to leave me alone?' the old man muttered, stumping away down the long hallway. 'Damned police around here at all hours of the day and night. What am I supposed to have done to deserve this?'

Cobb closed the front door and followed him. The house was dark and Fred snapped on a light and, with a tetchy jerk of his arm, waved Cobb through into a pleasant firelit lounge. 'What are the neighbours going to think, eh? Answer me that.'

'Give it a rest, Dad,' Cobb told him. 'Long day.'

'It's not natural, hanging around your father day and night. Man of your age.'

Cobb smiled to himself as the old man grumbled on. They both knew, but neither could admit, that Fred lived for his visits. Cobb followed him into the kitchen, fetched a beer from the fridge and then went back into the lounge and turned on a soft light and put the TV on low volume. He sat in the leather armchair next to the banked fire and poured the beer so that it trickled luxuriously in the glass. Baskerville lay slumped across the rug in front of the fire, his chops fallen open in black pleats. In the low room the old mongrel looked the size of a small pit pony.

'Please don't get up,' Cobb told the dog, nudging him with his boot. Baskerville thumped the floor a couple of times with his tail but stayed where he was. The old man, still in full flight, came back into the room and stood in front of Cobb's chair.

'Why didn't you stay in town? Drive all the way back here at this time of a Monday night . . . kill your stupid self.'

'Dad, I had to bring the truck back and pick up my car.'

'What's wrong with my Land Rover? You could have kept it till the weekend.'

'Call me old-fashioned, but for my job I need a car with doors in it. And some shoes without shit up to the ankles.' Cobb sipped his beer. 'Anyway, what would I do in town? Sit in the flat and watch TV. Just like this.'

'You could go out to one of those nightclubs all you policemen are supposed to go to. That's the sort of thing any red-blooded young chap ought to be doing. Find yourself a . . .' he groped for the words '. . . a bit of crumpet.'

'You silly old sod.' Cobb shied the empty beer can at his father, who caught it with surprising dexterity.

'Fine way to treat your ageing parent. I suppose you want a sandwich now?'

'Right. And make it snappy.'

The old man bustled out, grumbling. After a moment, Cobb could hear him humming in the kitchen. He would be as happy as one of the pigs on his pyjamas, Cobb knew, now that his ritual protest was over. All the old bastard wanted was to have a purpose in life. All any bastard wanted, Cobb supposed. And yet he knew that Fred was right. Maybe it wasn't altogether healthy that he should start coming down here midweek as well as most of his weekends. He sipped his beer. To hell with it, he thought. He'd had enough of making hard choices.

Silver's disappearance was top of the late news. A girl with copper hair and a low, urgent voice traced Matt Silver's career for twenty-five years, backed by a full-length photo of him in song. Cobb thought she had probably not been born when *Redemption Blues* hit the charts. There was old footage of Silver on stage, his long black hair flying as he sang, his trademark gold earring flashing in the lights. The camera cut every few moments to wildly applauding fans. There was no doubt the man had charisma, Cobb had to admit. Unlike most rock stars Silver was genuinely handsome and evidently knew it. He was tall and narrow-hipped, and it struck Cobb, as he watched him strut the stage, that there was a buccaneering air about him. He would not have looked amiss with a rapier at his hip and a pair of flintlock pistols in his belt. The later shots showed a man who'd aged well, with a square jaw, a full head of hair and a lean body. Footage from interviews projected an image of an articulate, intelligent, sardonic personality, one who handled fame easily, who always looked in control.

The report cut to the steps of St Thomas's Hospital where the camera caught Lauren Silver through a cordon of security men, hurrying across a rainswept pavement to a black BMW. As the group reached the car Tommy Hudson materialised in front of the camera and spoke to the journalists, distracting them as the car pulled away behind him.

'What's happened is a tragedy,' he was saying, his broad homely face stricken with grief, 'a terrible tragedy. We haven't given up hope, and we know the police are doing everything they can. But we're trying to come to terms here with the loss of a great man. A great man and a truly great talent.'

They jostled him, threw questions, thrust microphones, but Hudson handled it all with dignity and aplomb, the rain running down his battered face. Yes, they were all devastated, but none so devastated as Lauren. She'd lost her husband of nearly twenty years and her darling daughter. No, there was no truth in rumours that their tumultuous marriage had been on the rocks. In fact, Silver had been coming home for Christmas. No, he did not know why the accident had happened at Lambeth Bridge, but he thought Silver might have been taking his daughters to see the Christmas lights.

Cobb smiled at that one. A quick spin around the West End at five in the morning with two nine-year-olds? Yet it was well done, Cobb thought. Well enough done to deflect the obvious questions, at least for the moment. Hudson had covered Lauren Silver's escape, and managed to say a few of the right words at the same time. Cobb did not doubt Tommy Hudson's sincerity, but he acknowledged at the same time that the big man was smarter than he made out. Cobb wondered again what the reporters would have made of Lauren herself, with her broken tooth and slurred speech. She was lucky to have Hudson batting for her.

Cobb wondered what had really happened last night between Silver and his wife. It didn't surprise him that the marriage had been in trouble. Cobb didn't see how the strained, bitter, drunken woman he had met that morning could have held her own in a relationship with this charismatic man. Yet this line of thought troubled him. There must have been better times, even for people like Matthew Silver and his wife. Ordinary times. Times when they left one another funny notes on the fridge, when they laughed together like other people did, when they held hands. Cobb glimpsed for an instant something of the cavernous loneliness of fame, and felt sorry for the woman. Before this morning he – like millions of others, presumably – had only ever seen her as Silver's wife, and if she was not that, she was nothing. And yet that could not be true. It could not be true.

At that moment the TV flashed up a picture of two little girls. Gudrun, at once radiant and coquettish, beamed like a searchlight. Beside her, Freya might have been sketched in sepia.

'Little Gudrun Silver,' the voiceover intoned. 'Dead tonight at the age of just nine. Meanwhile, as hope fades, the search goes on for her famous father.'

Sipping his beer, Cobb found himself hoping that they soon found Silver dead, for his own sake. It was impossible that anyone could live with himself after bringing about the death of his child and the destruction of what was left of his family.

He shook himself and realised he was hungry. 'Hey, old man,' he called into the kitchen. 'Are you ever coming out of there?'

'Come in and get me, copper.'

But Cobb did not need to go in and get him, for Fred emerged almost at once with sandwiches on a tray. Cobb always let him do this: cooking for his son had been one of Fred's great joys for as long as either of them could remember, even while Cobb's mother had still lived with them. In his own eyes Fred would have lost authority over his home – over his world – if anyone had sought to take the job from him. Clea had learned that on the first occasion (almost the only one) that she had been well enough to offer to cook. Cobb flicked channels while he ate, running into the Silver story again almost at once.

'Pity about this chap,' Fred remarked, nodding at the screen. 'I rather like his stuff.'

'You do?'

'And what's so surprising about that?'

'Dad, you're seventy-eight. He's a rock star.'

'I'm sorry? I fail to see the connection.'

Cobb knew better than to rise to that. He gestured at the screen with a half-eaten sandwich: 'Then you'll be pleased to hear that Matt Silver's my new case.'

'Really?' Fred sounded impressed.

'You're looking at the head of the Matt Silver Task Force.'

Fred watched his son carefully. 'That's rather good, isn't it?'

Cobb sighed and set the plate of sandwiches aside and snapped the TV off with the remote. 'I'm resigning from the Met.'

Fred blinked. 'I see.'

'I decided a while ago, as a matter of fact. I was going to tell you.'

'Well, now you have.'

'Dad, I knew you'd be disappointed.'

'You're not a child, Samuel. You must know your own mind.' Fred stood up, ramrod straight. 'And am I allowed to know what your plans are?'

'I don't really have any. I'm all right for money, more or less. I just thought I'd–'

Fred swung to face him square on. 'Don't think for one moment, Samuel, that you're going to hang around here.'

'Well–'

'Because I too have plans for the rest of my life, however long or short that may be. And watching my own son mooning around in some sort of endless mourning is not included in them.'

'That's not fair.'

But Fred was not to be stopped now. 'There's life, you know, Samuel. There's life out there. It goes on despite you. You can't turn your back on it for ever.' Then he swung on his heel and marched to the door. Cobb heard him stamp away down the polished boards of the corridor and slam his bedroom door hard enough to make the crockery rattle in the dresser. Baskerville raised his broad head an inch at the sound.

'And you can shut up,' Cobb told him. The dog dropped back on to the rug with a thud.

Gloomily, Cobb munched the rest of his sandwich in silence. When he had finished he banked up the fire for the night, turned off most of the lights and took his plate to the kitchen. He roused Baskerville and ordered him out into the yard, waiting while he shambled around on the cold cobbles and found somewhere to pee in a cloud of white steam. Then he let the dog back in and walked past his father's door to his own room. But the cold night air had awakened him. At the last moment he changed his mind and walked back through the lounge and the kitchen and across to the short passage that led into the garden room.

He had not planned to come in here tonight but it seemed like a pointless piece of self-punishment to stay away, when to be here always brought him a measure of comfort. He turned on the desklight and closed the door behind him and patted the bed in which Clea had died. It was a small ritual which said hello to her. Cobb was not superstitious. He did not feel presences or hear things go bump in the night. Or not any more. He simply felt better in here. Calmer. And the ritual was part of that.

He sat at the desk and swung round in the swivel chair. He had left a few of her books on the shelves, ones that seemed too personal to throw out. They were not very personal even so: books about fighting back, about managing life crises, about positive thinking. It was typical of Clea to approach death as if it were a hostile takeover. There were also three framed photographs of her on the dressing table and a few of her tennis trophies. The room was reminiscent of her but Cobb was satisfied it hardly qualified as mawkish indulgence. He would have been sensitive to that. He had sent her few intimate possessions back to her family in the States, and for himself had kept only a handful of letters and photographs which were now packed away. Here in the garden room there were none of her clothes hanging moth-eaten in the wardrobe, no mouldering pieces of wedding cake in boxes at the backs of drawers, no locks of her hair under glass. That was neither his style nor hers. The room was pretty businesslike which, he reflected, was appropriate for both of them. Clea was not the vapid type. She was always too busy for that sort of thing. She was almost too busy to die, when it came to it, which was perhaps why it had taken her so long.

The only truly personal memento of her was a pink stuffed toy which now sat grinning on the mantelpiece.

It had cost him nearly £20 to win it for her at the St Giles Fair in Oxford the October before she died. He went over, picked the thing up and dusted its nylon fur. He was a little embarrassed about keeping it but Clea had taken such an uncharacteristically sentimental liking to it that after she had gone it seemed a betrayal to throw it out. He turned it over in his hand. It beamed at him with idiot glee. What was it supposed to be? A dragon? The Loch Ness Monster? He had never really thought about it before.

Fred's tapping on the door did not startle him: he had been half expecting it, hoping for it. He opened the door.

'Room for an old 'un?' his father said. He carried a small wooden tray with the Laphroaig and two shot glasses.

'That'd get you in anywhere,' Cobb said, taking the tray and setting it on the end of the bed and turning a chair for his father. He poured the smoky spirit and handed one to Fred.

The old man lifted his glass towards the light, squinted at the Scotch, sucked in his cheeks. 'You know, Samuel . . .'

'I know, Dad.' Cobb lifted his own glass and touched his father's with it. 'Cheers.'

'Flew off the handle a bit . . .'

'I know.'

'Will you stop telling me you know?' Fred said testily. 'I want to tell you that if you really must go ahead with this resignation nonsense, of course you can spend as long here as you need. It's your home. Always has been.'

He looked away awkwardly, sipped his drink. 'Cheers.'

'I won't say I know. But I do.'

They were silent for a while, drinking. Then Fred lifted his head and looked around the room as if he had never seen it before. He nodded appreciatively. 'Nice room, this,' he remarked. 'Always liked it.'

Cobb smiled into his Scotch, wondered if he should say it, and did anyway. 'Too nice for a shrine, eh, Dad?'

'Good Lord, Samuel. You tread heavily.'

'Perhaps I do. It comes of being a flatfoot.'

'I just meant –'

'You're right, Dad. I'll clear it out after Christmas. Redecorate it maybe. Put in that extension for the en suite. I'll have the time then, I suppose.'

'Samuel, you must know that all I want . . .' Fred's voice trailed off, helplessly.

'Yes, I think I do.'

'Well, then.' Fred put his glass back on the tray and slapped his knees in their pig pyjamas and stood up, as if something important had been resolved. He crossed to the dresser and picked up one of the photographs of Clea. He burnished the glass with his sleeve and looked at it. 'Handsome woman,' he said. 'Tragedy, no disguising it. Thorough tragedy.'

'Yes.'

'Have you noticed how people try to avoid facing that nowadays?' Fred replaced the photograph. ' "Celebrate the life" they say. Make out that somehow there's some compensation to be had.'

'Yes, I had noticed that.' Cobb drank, topped up

their glasses, waited curiously. His father was rarely this loquacious. Fred picked up the second photograph: it showed Clea with her eyes squeezed shut with laughter, her bell of black hair shining in sunlight. She was inexpertly holding a child, a neighbour's newborn, and laughing at her own clumsiness.

Fred said suddenly: 'One might have wished for grandchildren.'

'But you've got grandchildren,' Cobb said in surprise. Geoffrey, his elder brother in Johannesburg, had two superbrat boys in their early teens.

'I said grandchildren,' Fred said scornfully, 'not the Hitler Youth.'

'Oh. I'm sorry we didn't oblige.'

Fred set the photograph down rather too smartly on the dresser. 'Damn it all, Samuel. You know what I want to say.'

'I do, Dad. It's OK.'

'You can't . . . close down. Not at your age.'

'I understand.'

'I mean, leave the force if you must. It's not treated you especially well in my view.' Fred was sniffy about his son's lack of promotion. 'But start something new. Build something. Don't . . .' He thought hard about it, and bunched his fist and thumped it softly on the dresser top. 'Don't retreat. Don't ever retreat.'

'Dad, I hear you.'

'My boy, if you heard me, I wouldn't have to say it.' Fred straightened, sighed. 'And maybe you wouldn't be standing there cuddling a stuffed dinosaur.'

17

Six hours later Cobb stood at the kitchen window, sipping coffee, and stared out at the night which people called morning at this time of year. It was raining gently – he could hear it trickling in the gutters. Another degree or so colder and there would be sleet.

He had vaguely planned to climb to the abandoned village this morning. It seemed to be a significant enough day. Resignation day. But the rain made it unappealing. He noticed that Baskerville, who loathed the rain, was still determinedly asleep in front of the collapsed embers of the fire. Besides, Cobb had only got to bed at midnight, and with a little too much Laphroaig inside him too. He could feel the whisky now, like dry heat in his blood. In another hour or so his headache would begin to tap the inside of his skull, just above the right eye, like a chick trying to break out of its shell. He decided upon pre-emptive strike and took a couple of painkillers with his second cup.

Despite his hangover, the black rain and the hour, Cobb felt good. He had told Fred: that meant he had crossed the Rubicon. The old man might not like it but he had come up with no argument Cobb himself had not already considered. It was time for a big step. Resignation was no retreat. Or not as the old man understood it. Fred was from an era when a career was a lifelong commitment and you stuck at it. His own career with the Diplomatic Service had been just like that. Things were different now. Cobb would spend a couple of months at the farm, get some peace and quiet, think things through calmly. Then he would work out what else to do with his life. He closed his eyes and listened to the wind fling the rain against the windows. He could feel the weight of the thick ragstone walls; hear the heave and grunt of the hard men who had built the place, five hundred years ago or more. Six months, maybe. Perhaps he could stretch it to six months here. Maybe even more. There was no hurry.

He locked the back door and crossed the yard to the barn. He threw his parcel into the back seat with his briefcase, slid in a Bach CD and then backed the Saab out and drove up the rutted track to the main road. The very contrast with the rattling ride of his father's beloved Land Rover reminded him that he had made the same trip just yesterday with his boots clogged with mud and the feel of Mrs Buckets's leathery teat still on his fingers. It was not until he called this to mind that he saw how yesterday's events had crystallised his decision. That sobered him a little, for he had to confess to himself that there was after all an element of escape to it. The sight of the dead girl had jolted him. It still jolted him when he thought about her jet hair slashed across her blue face. He could not afford to feel like that. He could not afford to see his dead wife in a dead child's eyes.

He turned the car on to the M40 and joined the twin tracks of light heading east. There was no sign yet of dawn and it struck him that this was the shortest day of the year. Or the longest night, depending on which way you looked at it. On impulse he decided to go to the hospital first.

It was still only 7.30 when he stepped out of the lift at St Thomas's. There was a sense of offstage bustle, jingling trays, a rattle of crockery and the smell of food. A uniformed policeman dozed in a hardback chair against the wall. He recognised Cobb and made to stand but Cobb waved him back down again. A nurse with auburn hair was leaning against the desk in the reception area, chatting to an orderly behind the counter. Both wore red felt Christmas hats. She looked up as he approached. 'Why, Inspector Cobley. Don't you ever sleep?'

Cobb saw that she was the Staff Nurse from the day before. He recognised in particular her no-nonsense North Midlands accent. Derby, was it? He liked it. It was warm and mocking. He realised that she was a pretty plump woman in her mid-thirties, and that she was looking at him archly from under her silly red hat. He began to feel heavy and formal in his expensive blue suit, the way he used to feel in uniform.

'Sleep?' he said, a little gruffly. 'What's that?'

'Well, don't ask me, love. If any of us got any sleep around here our eyelids would heal up.' She straightened. 'So what brings you here so early, Inspector, keeping you away from Mrs Cobley?' She hesitated just a heartbeat. 'Or whoever?'

'It's Cobb,' he said. 'Sam Cobb.'

He realised she had been teasing him. It came as a shock, a pleasant one but a shock. It flustered him. He wondered what this healthy, attractive woman could suddenly see in him. He met her eyes. They were brown and sleepy. She put her head on one side and spread her arms out along the top of the desk behind her. Her breast put him in mind of a dove's, soft and full.

'I'm Annie Lockwood,' she said, with mischief in her voice. 'And my face is up here.'

'I've come to leave something for the child,' he said, more brusquely than he intended.

'Oh, I see.' She crossed her arms again. 'I'll find out if she's awake.'

'That's not necessary. I just wanted to leave her something.' He patted his parcel. But she sensed his hesitancy and her playfulness returned at once. He saw the corners of her mouth twitch.

'Oh, no, Inspector Sam,' she said firmly. 'That won't do at all. Little Freya would love a visit. Just you come along with me.'

'I can't visit her at this time in the morning . . .'

'Breakfast's in half an hour. She'll be awake anyway by now. You won't get a word out of her, of course, but never mind.' She set off at the brisk pace he remembered from yesterday and he hurried to catch up.

'I really can't visit her. There should be people present–'

'Why? What are you going to do? Use thumbscrews?'

'It's a regulation–'

She strode on. 'I won't tell if you won't.'

They stopped outside the door.

'Look, Staff . . .' he made an effort to use her name '. . . Annie, I don't really want to get into this. I shouldn't be hanging around here before the kid's mother even arrives. It doesn't look right.'

'The mother threw a fit yesterday.'

'She did?' Cobb told himself he didn't want to know. He began to wish he had not come.

'Insisted on seeing the body, then wouldn't believe it. You know the sort of thing. They won't be told, poor people.'

'Where is she now?'

'She wouldn't let us admit her. That big ape took charge. I must say, he was useful when it came to it. But she threw a real wobbly. Restraint, sedatives, the lot.' She checked her watch. 'Not that I blame her. I don't know how you'd ever get over losing your own child. Not like that, anyway.'

'Are you keeping the girl in? Who's taking charge here?'

She made a face. 'Taking charge? Love, things are just lurching from crisis to crisis, like they always do in the real world. Didn't you know that?' She paused, adjusted her red hat and looked straight at him, and despite her briskness he could see behind her eyes how tired and sick at heart she was; how, giving comfort herself all day, she was so badly in need of some herself. He wished for a moment that he had some to give. He might have spoken then but at that moment she said:

'The point is it's Christmas Eve tomorrow and she's not going to see her mum any time soon. So just you pop in and say hello, all right?'

She swept him into the room. The child was sitting up, lost in the bed. There were dark rings under her eyes and she did not look as if she had slept, which did not surprise him. There was a graze on her jawline and a patch of her hair had been shaved above her right ear. A square of sticking plaster was taped there. They had found her some glasses. They were evidently not her own, for they had severe black frames and were too big for her. Through them she stared owlishly at Cobb over the Staff Nurse's shoulder as she fussed around her, plumping the pillows, smoothing the sheets.

'This is Mr Cobb come to see you again, sweetheart. Do you remember him from yesterday?' She ruffled the child's mousy hair. 'But of course you don't. Never mind. Mr Cobb's just come to see how you are, that's all. Breakfast soon, pet.' She kissed the girl lightly on the forehead and bustled out of the room. As she passed Cobb she whispered: 'They don't bite, you know, Inspector Sam. Not the little ones.' And winked at him.

The door swung to behind her. Cobb felt oafish in the bright room under the child's solemn gaze and began to wonder how soon he could decently escape. He braced himself.

'Hello, Freya,' he said, with what he took to be the right level of heartiness. 'I just wanted –' Then he stopped. She was not looking at him but at his shoes, craning over the side of the bed to see them. 'You do remember,' he said quietly, and could hear the wonder in his own voice. He had a ridiculous urge to call Annie Lockwood back and tell her, to show off the big impression he had made. 'You really do remember.' He laughed aloud, and she lifted grave eyes to look at him then dropped them again to his shoes. 'They were pretty filthy, Princess, weren't they? Do you think anyone else noticed? But look – they're clean this time.' He lifted one polished black shoe and then the other, hopping around, clowning for her. She gazed steadily at him. 'Hey, I nearly forgot. I've got a little present for you. It's a bit early for Christmas and it's not much.' He put the parcel on the bed. 'But open it anyway. Go on – rip it. It's always more fun if you rip it.'

Rather to his surprise she did. Within a few seconds the neat bed was littered with Christmas paper and the pink dinosaur was bestowing its beatific grin on her. She looked at it thoughtfully for a long moment then gathered the dinosaur up in her arms and rocked it hard against her.

'There you go, Princess,' he said. 'From one lovely lady to another.'

Abruptly he felt his throat tighten and turned quickly away to stare out of the window. It was growing light now. There was a Christmas tree in the courtyard below, its lights still bright in the gloom. Beyond there were decorative lights in office windows, illuminations strung down the streets, a glittering cone that might have been the huge tree in Trafalgar Square. That was the tree his father had taken him to see every Christmas Eve in the old Rover 90, so many years ago. He could still remember the way the car had smelled of leather and mould and pipesmoke. He was suddenly flooded with loneliness and loss. He started talking quickly, without thinking, to distract himself.

'She's called Bronty, Princess,' he said, turning back to face the child. 'We have lots of them on the farm. Great big ones. Much bigger than Bronty. She's only a baby. Cows and chickens and horses and things too, of course, but our specialty is pink dinosaurs. You don't believe me?' The girl stared at him, rocking the toy against her face. 'Well, I'll tell you what. If you don't believe me, you can come down and see them for yourself, as soon as you're out of here. How's that? And that's a promise.'

The door swung open sharply and the Staff Nurse bounced back into the room.

'Mr Cobb—' She stopped, glanced at the pink toy and at the child clutching it. 'Well, sweetheart,' she said, eyes twinkling, 'is that what the big tough Inspector brought you? That's lovely, that is. Who'd've thought he was a softy?'

Cobb looked away.

'But I have to take the nice Inspector outside for a minute, love. So say goodbye now.'

'Goodbye, Freya.' Cobb leaned forward to pat the child's hand and she instinctively held the toy out to him, as if returning it. 'No, Princess. She's yours now. You take care of her. And yourself.'

He followed Annie Lockwood out into the corridor.

'Sorry to drag you away just when you're playing Santa,' she said, 'but Mrs Silver is about to make a liar of me.' She gestured to the reception desk at the end of the corridor. It was bustling with people. Among them he saw the tall, square figure of Hudson, arguing with the uniformed Police Constable. There were others, too, men with mobile phones, nurses and orderlies.

The Staff Nurse clicked her tongue. 'I'd better sort this out.' She half turned to him, giving him one last chance. 'Another time, maybe?' And when he didn't respond, gave a wry no-hard-feelings flick of her Christmas hat and strode away towards the mêlée.

Cobb threw on his coat and moved off in the opposite direction. He had barely rounded the corner when he almost collided with Lauren Silver, pushing through the doors from the fire stairs. She was alone. They both stopped. She looked, Cobb thought, as fragile as cut glass, as if she might be held together by some crystalline lattice of forces and would shatter at the smallest impact. Her face was sharp and white, and her ash-blonde hair plated her skull like bright steel.

'Mrs Silver, I'm Sam Cobb. Perhaps you remember?'

'I know who you are. Have you found him?'

'No. I just came by to drop in a present for Freya.'

'A present?'

'It's nothing. Just a toy. I hope you don't mind?'

She looked through him without interest. 'She doesn't need presents.'

'No, I don't suppose she does, Mrs Silver. I just felt like giving her one.'

She made to walk on. Then she hesitated and her eyes focused on him for the first time. 'I know how to look after my own child, Mr Cobb.'

'Of course you do. I only meant–'

'I know my duty as well as you know yours.'

'Your duty?'

'Perhaps you had better get on with your job, which is finding my child's killer, Mr Cobb. And I'll get on with mine.'

'Your *duty*, Mrs Silver?' He stared at her in disbelief as she brushed past him and he continued to stare at the door after she had walked through it. It stunned him that she could say such a thing, and stunned him still more to discover how it outraged him. He got a grip on himself and for reassurance crinkled the resignation letter in his pocket. This was definitely the right decision. Definitely.

18

There were four male and two female officers in the incident room and the moment he walked in Cobb could sense their resentment. It did not surprise him. They were hardly the pick of the bunch. They knew it, and obscurely they blamed him for it. Only a young DC named Rossiter could be considered a real catch but Cobb suspected his inclusion was purely nominal. Rossiter's time was already split between two other teams investigating separate murders, and his DCI would never release him for more than a couple of hours at a time. Cobb was a little surprised he had got to the briefing at all. All the others were from uniformed, and what little Cobb knew of them was uninspiring. Two of them he recognised at once – a solid Welshman called Owens who was under investigation for assault and might soon be suspended, and a coarsely pretty female Constable called Carlow who was sleeping with a Drugs Squad DI. Cobb looked around the crowded room and thought sourly that both he and Matt Silver had got the task force they deserved.

'Settle down, people,' he said, and shuffled his notes while they arranged themselves in world-weary attitudes.

There was more than resentment in the air. More than cynicism. He could see it in their eyes. They didn't like him. He'd been going places at one time, fast-tracking. Now, it was as if they blamed him for making promises he could not keep. Well, he thought, he didn't like them either, and he didn't like this bullshit job one bit. But to spite the whole bloody lot of them, he'd do it meticulously, right up to the very last moment.

He stood up. When they fell quiet he leaned over to the noticeboard and flicked the glossy enlarged print with his nail. 'Matthew Kelso Silver. He is a missing person and we are going to find him.' He looked belligerently around. 'You have a problem with that, Constable Owens?'

'No, sir. Not exactly, like.' The Welshman pulled a face. 'Well, what I mean to say is, we know where he is, sir, don't we, reely? He's in the river. He'll float up in a day or two.'

'Where?'

Owens spread his hands. 'Well, how would I know that, sir?' He looked around for support.

'Get on to the Thames Division as soon as we finish here and find out. And I want to know by tomorrow. The ten most likely places, given the tide.' Cobb looked around. 'Any more comments before we get on with this?'

He dismissed the briefing half-an-hour later. He felt better as he watched them file out. Took some pride in refusing to court their sympathy. They didn't have to like him, and they didn't have to like the job. But they'd bloody well do what they were told, just as he had to. When they had gone he moved back to his desk and shuffled through the messages. One from the public affairs directorate warned him there would be a press conference on the Matt Silver affair at 12 noon. Another note told him that someone had taken a call on his line from Dennis McBean. McBean's mobile number was scrawled on the message pad. Cobb glanced his watch, decided he just had time, and keyed in the number.

'McBean? It's Cobb.'

'Right, sir. Let me just pull over.'

Down the line Cobb heard an engine die away and the creak of the handbrake coming on.

'Sorry to call you direct, sir.'

'What's on your mind, Sergeant?'

'It's the kiddie, sir. Me and Hayward, we just wondered how she was?'

'Someone should have called you about that, I'm sorry. The girl's in shock but I think she'll be OK.' Cobb guessed Hayward was in the car too and raised his voice. 'Tell your pal Hayward he did a fine job. It's been noted.'

'Thank you, sir. That's all we wanted to know.'

'Right.' Cobb went to hang up, hesitated. 'Wait . . .'

'Sir?'

'There's been a task force set up to find Matt Silver. I'm heading it.'

'Oh, yes?' McBean's tone was wary.

'Listen, Sergeant, I can't officially co-opt you but I'd

like you and Hayward to keep your eyes open, just until Silver's body turns up.' McBean did not reply at once and with a jab of irritation Cobb added: 'Unless, of course, you think it'll be a waste of your precious time.'

'Like you do, sir?'

'What did you say?'

'Sorry, Mr Cobb, out of line. We'll keep our eyes and ears open.'

'Thank you, Sergeant.'

Once again Cobb moved to hang up but this time it was McBean who spoke. 'Did you ever hear of a bloke called Billy Bananas, Mr Cobb?'

'Billy who?'

'I didn't think so. Billy Bananas was a sweet old guy, soft in the head. Used to dance with the buskers down at Embankment Tube. Every night for years.'

'So?'

'So one night last year, Mr Cobb, a bunch of yahoos chucked him into the river. Just for a laugh. Course, he couldn't swim, poor old bastard, and that was that. We never caught them.'

'There's a point to this story, is there, Sergeant? Only I'm in a hurry.'

'It's just that I never heard of a Billy Bananas Task Force. But then he was poor, crazy, old and black. Have a nice day, sir.'

Cobb took some of his bloodymindedness to the media relations briefing and then into the press conference.

The event had been hastily convened to introduce him to the media, and Cobb dealt with it all calmly enough. He enjoyed the challenge of public performance, as he enjoyed court appearances. He did not think of himself as a natural but he was a steady performer and in this case it was simple enough. No, they had not found Matt Silver. No, he had very little hope of the great man's survival. No, there were no indications yet as to how the accident had happened. But, he gravely told the cameras, he would conduct the inquiry with the utmost thoroughness until they had a result.

Cobb was grimly amused by the whole charade. It should have been clear to everyone that the Matt Silver Task Force was a fiction for the media's benefit, designed to show that the police were doing something. But apparently it wasn't clear to everyone. The crowding journalists seemed prepared to take it all seriously enough. Another time the whole thing would have infuriated him, but today Cobb felt relieved. It would make it easier to walk away, would give him leverage if anyone tried to argue him out of it.

But once the conference was over, and throughout the day, a pressure began to build in him, a pressure that demanded release. He felt like a terrorist with dynamite strapped around him. He longed to place himself in front of Detective Chief Superintendent Sykes and then detonate.

But it was not so easy to find Sykes. By 5.30 his moment still had not presented itself. Cobb logged off his workstation and stretched back in his chair as the screen shrank to a point of light. He swept a couple of loose paper clips off the desktop and returned them to their packet in the top drawer, straightened the phone, arranged a scatter of photos into a neat stack.

'There's a name for that condition, my lad,' said Horrie Nelson from behind him. 'That's a syndrome, that is.'

'I'll bring my crochet in next week.' Cobb packed his battered black legal case and snicked the lock closed. 'If there is a next week.' When he looked up, Nelson was still there.

'This the Jag?' Nelson took the pictures and dealt through them like a deck of cards, clicking his tongue at each new image of twisted metal. Something about the way he did this made Cobb think he was not really looking at them. Nelson said, too casually: 'Still no sign?'

Cobb took the photos back and put them away in the top drawer. 'Horrie, you know and I know that Matt Silver is either stuck under a barge, in which case he'll bloat and float in a week or so, or he's past the Thames Barrier by now. Some Dutch holidaymaker will find what's left of him on a beach come summer.' Cobb hefted his case as a signal that he was about to leave. 'Not that anyone will convince his poor bloody wife of that.'

Nelson nodded, but showed no sign of moving away. 'She needs help,' he observed.

'Yes.'

'Good psychiatric care is what she needs.'

'You're right.'

'Got to come to terms with it sooner or later.'

'Horrie, is there any danger at all of you letting me go home?'

Nelson looked guiltily at him and blurted: 'Come to the club for a drink.' He saw Cobb's expression and added, a little plaintively: 'It's Christmas, Sam.'

'You know I never go to the club. *You* never go to the club.'

'Mr Sykes would like you to go to the club, Sam.' Nelson looked away. 'And don't argue for once. Just bloody do it.'

It reminded him of all the things he had hated about the Union Bar at university twenty-five years ago: a cavern full of smoke, loud heartiness, shouted laughter and the click of snooker balls. At this time of night its clientele was split between young policemen anxious to show off their macho credentials, young police-women equally anxious to check them out, and a handful of oldtimers with nothing better to do after eight or ten hours at work than to spend another three drinking. Police work was notoriously hard on marriages. That, Cobb supposed, was one reason he loathed coming here – the fear that they would take him for one of them and enfold him in their beery embrace.

'Cobby! We got you here at last.' Sykes was leaning against the bar in the centre of a knot of junior detectives. He had interrupted himself mid-story. Sykes was famous for his stories, mainly about the old knock-

'em-down-drag-'em-out days of the Flying Squad. Cobb believed that the ability to listen to these tales and laugh in the right places, even after six or eight pints, was a key criterion for promotion. He had never mastered it. 'What'll you have, Cobby? Wine? Scotch?'

'Prefer bitter, sir.'

'Bitter, is it?' Sykes made big eyes as if this were a daring request. His football bladder face creased and his band of acolytes laughed on cue. Cobb noticed that every one of them was drinking bitter. 'Well, we'd better get you the real thing, then.' Sykes called the barman, ordered the drink and turned back to his audience. 'Now this bloke, DI Cobb here, he's a smart character. One of the smartest. I've seen his file.' Cobb felt the team inspecting him as if they had never seen him before. 'He's so bloody smart, you'll never find him in this shithole. In fact, he's only here now because I put it about that I wanted a quiet word with him – so the fact that he's showed up *proves* he's smart.' Sykes nodded and winked until they all nodded and winked back, then he let his face go stony. 'And if you lot were half as smart, you'd've all buggered off by now and left me and the DI in peace.'

Sykes turned to the bar to pick up Cobb's beer and by the time he had swung back with it the entire group had fled.

He handed the pint to Cobb. 'You think I'm taking the piss out of you, don't you, Cobby? With this task force and all. Prostituting your professionalism. Right?'

'Sir.'

Sykes sipped at his pint, replaced it on the counter and grinned. 'Don't be a bolshie cunt with me, Cobb.'

Cobb should have said 'sir' again but didn't. He didn't need to be polite now: this was the moment he had waited for.

Sykes said: 'Horrie Nelson tells me you're thinking of leaving.'

Cobb opened his mouth and closed it again. He moved his hand towards his breast pocket.

Sykes grinned. 'Don't give it to me now, Cobby,' he said. 'Swear to God, if you do, I'll burn it in that ashtray without so much as opening it.'

Cobb put his hands on the bar, collected himself. 'With respect to Mr Nelson, sir, he shouldn't have told you any such thing. I could then have told you myself.'

'Yes. But I wanted to deny you that pleasure, see, Cobby. So I wheedled it out of the old bugger. You must realise that my entire mission in life is to thwart your every move.'

'I'd begun to think so, sir.'

'Because you want to go to Regional Crime and I won't let you? Because I give you bullshit assignments like this one?' Cobb said nothing and Sykes pulled at his beer and set it down again. 'Look, I know what you think. You think I've got it in for you and that's why you don't get moved up. Well, it's true I don't much like you, Cobb. You're some kind of smartarse on the surface and something else underneath. I haven't figured out what yet. But the reason you haven't moved on is because you're no more than an all right copper.

It's as simple as that. You'd be better, but you spend too much time inside your own head.'

'It's more interesting in there, sir.'

Sykes watched him steadily and drank a little more. 'Tell me, Cobb, why are you with the Met at all? You think most of us are pricks. You got a social conscience or something?' Sykes curled his mouth around the words as if they tasted bad. 'Because I did have another look at your file. You've done some interesting stuff. I never knew you were in the Army . . .'

'Just a short service commission. I wasn't much good at it.'

'You were in Northern Ireland. I was there too for a while.'

Cobb wondered what kind of a contribution to Anglo-Irish rapprochement Sykes would have made. But then, he thought, he hadn't done much better himself. Nobody had.

Sykes said suddenly: 'You know, I've got a theory – you can tell everything about a man by his sports. Maybe some bloody shrink will jump up and tell me that went out with the Romans, but I believe it. Now me, I'm a soccer man on the weekends, and I still get around a squash court one night a week, believe it or not. What does that make me? I'll tell you. It makes me a team player when I want to be, but with lots of aggression and a big will to win, that's what. Now what about you, Cobb?'

He couldn't help himself. 'Ballet and baroque music, sir.'

'Kayaking, it says on your sheet. And fell-running, whatever the hell that is.'

Cobb did not recall having ever given these details, and was surprised at his effrontery in doing so. Their revelation now made him feel defensive, as if he had been caught at something illicit.

'I haven't done either for years, sir. Not seriously.' He had a momentary fear that Sykes might be about to order him to compete in the Metropolitan Police kayak slalom, if there was such a thing. He wondered if he could still remember how to get the spray deck off during a wet exit. He'd never been very expert at it.

Sykes was speaking again: 'Solitary sports, ain't they, canoeing and running? Don't have to compete, do you? You don't have to . . . mix it.'

The beer boiled in Cobb's belly. He hoped Sykes would drop the subject, but he knew he would not.

'What's your problem with mixing it, Cobby? People tell me you used to be different in the old days. Used to be a better officer too. Could have stayed on the fast track.'

Cobb set his glass down on the bar. 'What's this about, sir?'

Sykes watched him, glanced down and then up again. 'I heard about your wife, Cobb. I didn't know. Me being a newcomer.'

'It's no secret, sir.'

'I might have thought twice about this Silver business if I'd known.'

Cobb realised with surprise that this was as close to

an apology as he was ever likely to get. It disarmed him a little. 'I'm just not the sociable type, Mr Sykes. I never was, really. I used to play up a bit to compensate, but these days I don't bother. I'm sorry if that makes me unpopular.'

Sykes shrugged. 'Have it your own way, Cobby. I'm still not going to recommend you for Regional. Or take you off the task force.' He pushed himself away from the bar. 'I don't suppose we'll ever be mates, Cobb, but even I know you need all types in a job like this. Not just beer swilling old warhorses like me.'

'Sir.'

Sykes paused. 'No man is an island, Cobb, or whatever the bloody quote is. Who the fuck said that, anyway?'

'Maybe you're thinking of Simon and Garfunkel, sir.'

'I always thought it was John Donne. But then, you'd know.' Sykes made to move away across the room, then turned back. 'Think about it over Christmas, Cobby. Maybe this is a bad time for you to make decisions. If you still want to resign after the break, I'll accept it.'

Cobb took the fire stairs back up to the office, three at a time, and barged back into the CID room. He marched across to his desk, ignoring the half-dozen men and women still at work, grabbed his briefcase and turned to go. He would have to return to the Baron's Court flat, of course. It was too late for the farm. He considered going out and getting drunk. He felt humiliated, betrayed by Horrie Nelson, outsmarted by Sykes. Most of all he was furious with himself. He had decided to resign. Why had he not done so when he had the chance? Let Sykes burn the letter if he wanted to go in for theatricals.

'Sam?'

He swung round, astonished to hear Nelson's voice. He had imagined the mild Yorkshireman would have made himself scarce, not risk a confrontation after what he had done. But there he was, at the door of his office, resplendent in blue and silver.

'You've got a bone to pick with me, I think.'

'Bloody right.'

'Well, do it in here.'

Cobb slammed down his case and strode across the room into Nelson's office.

'What do you think you're doing, Horrie? Passing that on to Sykes?'

'Spoil your scene, did I, Sam? So sorry. And if you're going to have a tantrum, close the door behind you.'

Cobb closed the door, just managed to avoid slamming it. 'You betrayed my confidence, Horrie.'

'Oh? I didn't realise this were the boy scouts. I thought this were the Metropolitan Police.' Nelson was unrepentant, even defiant. It put Cobb off balance.

'How could you do that, Horrie? I was going to resign today. If I could've caught Sykes earlier I'd have done it already.'

Nelson moved behind his desk, sat down and found his silver pencil. He tapped his front teeth with it. 'Sit down,' he said.

'I don't want to sit down.'

'Sit down!' Nelson shouted suddenly. Cobb sat. 'You listen to me. Now you can take it or leave it, but I did it with your best interests in mind.'

'My best interests?'

'It may come as a shock to you, Sam, but I am a police officer first and your personal counsellor second.'

'What does that mean?'

'It means I've got more things to worry about than your finer feelings.'

Cobb began to feel himself losing steam. 'I told you in confidence–'

'There's a chain of command round here,' Nelson said, his face colouring. 'Mr Sykes is my superior officer. I am required to be open with him about anything which may be germane to the efficient running of the department–'

'Germane to the efficient running . . . You sound like a bloody manual.'

'– and in case you'd forgotten,' Nelson went on more loudly, 'I am *your* superior officer. Perhaps you'd better see if you can remember that occasionally. Detective Inspector Cobb.'

Cobb sat back, speechless. Nelson had never spoken to him like this before and he found himself lost for an answer.

'Sam, Sam,' the older man's voice lost some of its edge, 'what did you expect to happen? That you'd hand in your letter and then go swanning off, just like that? You've got an inquiry to run.'

'The inquiry's bullshit.'

'What on earth's that got to do with anything? They throw shit at us, we do our best with it. Sometimes we know the reason and sometimes we don't. Sometimes there isn't one. Don't you know yet that's how the system works?'

'I've had it, Horrie.' Cobb looked away. 'I don't want any more to do with the Silver family. They're screwing me up.'

'Aye, I thought that might be it at bottom. But you see, Sam, when it comes down to it, you'll do what you're told and a little shellshock won't be a good enough excuse.' Nelson sighed. 'Look, I'll cover for you for a couple of days over Christmas. But you can't just turn your back on this stuff, Sam. It won't go away.'

'I should've shoved the bloody letter down his throat,' Cobb said bitterly, aware of how childish he sounded.

'Well,' Nelson shrugged, 'perhaps you'd better ask yourself why you didn't.'

Cobb stumped down the fire stairs and barged through the double doors into the front office, heading for the street and freedom. He desperately wanted time to think.

'Ah, Cobb,' barked the mad Brigadier, turning from an inspection of the Sergeant and Constable on duty. The two officers stood to ramrod attention by the front desk, their faces twitching with suppressed laughter. The Brigadier saw Cobb's expression and his sandy eyebrows shot up. 'Palaver with the top brass? Red tabs? Staff wallahs?'

'You might say that, Brigadier,' Cobb said, thrown by the accuracy of the old man's guess.

'Word to the wise, young Cobb.' The Brigadier tapped the side of his own nose with his swagger stick. 'Chaps upstairs know a thing or two. Fine job of work, most of them. Damned difficult, disposing the lives of men. Should remember that, you young fellers wet behind the ears.'

He spun on his heel and marched out.

The Constable slumped against the counter, shaking with laughter. 'Christ, sir! He thinks you're the dog's bollocks, don't he? Crazy old bastard.' The man wiped his eyes, stopped. 'Oh. Didn't mean it like that, sir.'

'Sergeant!' Cobb said. 'Take that man's name.'

19

They had settled Freya on the lounge in a nest of cushions. If her injured leg pained her she gave no sign of it. It lay stretched out in front of her, strapped with flesh-coloured tape.

Lauren rolled her glass between her palms while she watched her daughter. She had been rolling the glass in this way for a long time and all that was left in it was a warm slurry of gin and flat tonic water and shreds of lemon pulp. Noticing this at last, she tossed down the tepid liquor, made a face, set the drink down on the side table. She deliberately knocked the base of the tumbler sharply on the wood. The child did not react. She lay in her soft nest, brushing her toy's pink fur against the nap then smoothing it down again, turning it so that it grinned its imbecile grin at her from a dozen different angles. But she did not smile and she did not speak. Lauren knew that if she had fired a gun in the room the child would not have looked up at her.

Merilda, the Portuguese maid, bustled in with a tray, filling the room with noisy sympathy, fussing around the child, pushing her tear-stained face close to Freya's, talking too loudly at her. Lauren watched for a while longer, but something about the scene set her teeth on edge. The poor woman was inconsolable, partly because Lauren's own brittle calm horrified her. Back in Merilda's home in Oporto, Lauren knew, the house would have been filled with shrieking relatives and the surviving child would have been showered with all the care that could nevermore be lavished upon her dead sister. Merilda did not understand how things could be otherwise, and though she tried not to show it, her every glance at Lauren carried an accusation.

Lauren knew the woman was right to despise her. She would have liked to deny it but she was stripped bare, with nowhere to hide within herself. It was as if she had lost the will or the energy for self-deception, even as if this might be part of the punishment. She had been told that trauma could lock the mind solid, like a seized engine. It did no such thing for her. Her mind worked with a dreadful efficiency, banging like a steamhammer, unstoppable, punching out truths like new minted coins, hard and bright and unanswerable.

The bloody woman was sobbing, Lauren registered with distaste, and looked across at Freya again, bundled up against the maid's heaving breast, her face blank. She concentrated hard on her daughter, noted the curl of hair behind her ear, the cleft in her chin, the tight button of her mouth. She barely recognised the features of her face. Gudrun's hair did not fall that way. There was no cleft in Gudrun's chin. Gudrun's mouth was always wide open with laughter or chatter.

The steamhammer in her mind banged once more and minted another coin. There was no question of denying its currency. It was the currency of resentment. If she could have thrown a switch to make it so, Lauren knew with complete clarity that Gudrun would be cradled there in that nest of cushions, not this strange child in a stranger's arms, nursing a stranger's toy.

When this realisation frightened her enough, Lauren got up and walked out of the room, down the hallway and into her study. She snapped on the light. Tommy Hudson was sitting in the leather chair by the desk, his elbows on it, staring out of the black square of the window. He looked up as she came in.

'Sorry,' he said. 'Did I startle you?'

'I don't think anything will ever startle me ever again, Tommy.'

'No. I s'pose not.' He gazed miserably out into the night. The lights put up by the security people and the TV crews threw the scene into stark black-and-white, like a Cold War stand-off at some Berlin checkpoint. He said: 'I just had to sit somewhere quiet for a bit.'

'Shall I leave you in peace?'

'You, Laurie? Are you kidding?' He turned to look at her and his big face crumpled. He swung his head away again and she put her hand between his shoulderblades and rubbed his broad back, perhaps murmured to him, she wasn't sure. It was no more than she would have done for an animal in pain, yet she could not do even this much for her own daughter. 'I know it wasn't always easy,' he was saying, his voice thick. 'I know he was a bastard when it suited him,

Laurie. I do know that. But I sort of thought it would go on. Just go on.'

'I know, Tommy.'

'Like we was sailors or some damn silly thing, and we'd go off around the world, Matt and me, and then we'd come back home. Maybe we'd play silly buggers when we was away, but it's like we always knew where home was.'

'Matthew didn't,' she said with certainty. 'You maybe, Tommy. But Matt never discovered where home was. He's still out there looking for it.'

She stepped away from him and her foot struck an empty vodka bottle on the carpet. It was strange to think it had lain there for two full days. She nudged it again with her toe and it rolled. The smallest touch shifted it yet here it was, just where she had let it fall forty-eight hours before, motionless while the whole of the rest of the universe had lurched so far off course. She bent to pick it up. There was a trickle of oily spirit still rocking in the curve of the glass. She found that she was tempted to tip the last few drops into the back of her throat, and it shocked her to be so tempted. She set the bottle down on the desk.

'You don't really think he's alive, do you, Laurie?' Hudson was looking at her with the eyes of a wounded spaniel, pleading to be convinced of something, but she couldn't tell what. Perhaps he didn't know himself. 'He couldn't be, could he?'

'Get me a drink, Tommy,' she said abruptly.

He sat up straight. 'Laurie, you ought to take a

couple of those pills and get some rest. We all need some rest.'

'It's Christmas Eve and I want a drink,' she said, and when she could see how the harshness of her tone hurt him, added: 'Be a sweetheart. Please.'

Hudson made no further protest. He got up and walked through to the kitchen. Lauren waited, rocking herself in her chair. Alive? She would never be able to explain it to him. To anyone. Matthew had always been beyond normal rules. Now, perhaps, he was beyond even this. Had he escaped? Of course he had. He had escaped into his own mythology. The papers had sensed that at once. They used words like 'mystery' and 'legend' and 'vanishing' in their headlines. Within days, she knew, they would be reporting sightings of him from Brazil and Australia. Mad-eyed German boys would pay homage at his shrine, as they did at Jim Morrison's grave in Père Lachaise. They would exchange fables about the way the CIA had killed him. Or had kept him alive. Or both at the same time.

But to Lauren he was another order of being altogether. She knew he was the Elf King, luring the loveliest of children to annihilation, possessed of a lambent spirit which burned with beauty and evil in equal measure. To talk of him dying was simply absurd. She would never see him, as she had seen Gudrun, cold and shrunken on a steel trolley. He would have found a way out.

The line of her thinking led her to Cobb, who thought he was merely looking for a corpse in the river.

A remarkably clear vision of the detective flashed into her mind, as he had looked when she walked into him outside Freya's room at the hospital: a square, compact man, serious in his dark suit. She knew she needed his quickness and intelligence, but it wasn't that alone. It wasn't even his flash of kindness to Freya, though she registered that in the abstract way she appreciated all kindnesses to her stranger daughter. It was something else about him, something unrelenting. He did not even believe his quarry was there to be found. But despite that, once he was set on the hunt he would track the spoor to the very end. He was that type. She wondered how she would feel when the hunt was over. Might there be a flicker of hope for her to escape from Matthew then? She did not know. She only knew instinctively that Cobb was the kind of man for such a task, the kind of man to whom duty was a religion and a curse. Duty. Her vision of him darkened. He had used that word to her, and she could still see the contempt in his face as he had used it: 'Your *duty*?'

She got up quickly and walked out of the room, brushing past Hudson in the hallway as if she had not seen him.

'Laurie –' He followed her, concerned, setting the spilled drink down on a window ledge.

In the lounge Merilda was still sitting over the child, cooing to her, tempting her with sweets. Freya caressed the fur of her toy, her face closed. The maid looked up as Lauren walked in.

'Get out,' Lauren told her.

The woman got to her feet, her eyes full of pain and hostility. She seemed on the point of speaking out, but after a moment she took her tray and with massive dignity left the room. Lauren crossed to the couch and sat on the edge of it. After a moment she began, hesitantly, to stroke Freya's hair. She did not recognise the feel of it. The child did not interrupt her silent play to look at her. 'Frey – Frey,' Lauren said softly. 'I know that you know. It's not your fault. But perhaps it's not mine either.'

And finally the child lifted her face and looked at her. She nursed the toy against her, her eyes huge and dark and filled with an unreadable sadness.

20

Probably nothing would have called him back if it had not been for the thrashing of the dredger's propellor. It did not belong in the comfortable womb in which he rocked. It demanded attention, a distant chirping noise, inhuman, metallic. And it was stronger now, stirring something buried inside him, so deeply buried that he did not at first recognise it as fear. Then suddenly the water was foul again and stank of diesel and shit. Pain erupted in his hands and feet and burned inwards to his chest and brain, and all at once the thing was on top of him, a black fortress of gantries lurching past so close he could hear the steel groaning. The big prop was churning a few feet away, wildly rocking the black water, and once again he was plunging down, down, and his lungs knotted for lack of air and then drew in the liquid cold.

The knocking on his door was irregular but insistent. Tap-tap. Tap-tap-tap. He came awake reluctantly, keeping his eyes closed. He had the troubling conviction that he had overslept, that he was missing something important, but equally that however late he might be, this was a wholly unreasonable hour for anyone to summon him.

His confusion did not strike him as particularly

strange. He thought perhaps he was drunk. That had happened before, waking up in a strange hotel, disorientated and uncomfortable. He opened his eyes. But when he did it all made even less sense. There was a solid wall of black above him, and beyond that a high indigo sky with streamers of brick red cloud racing across it. Running up the side of the wall from his eyelevel was a flight of steps. He could make out strips of moonlight gleaming along each one. It occurred to him that maybe he had fallen down these steps and stunned himself, and now he was just coming round. He could see his legs, black against the glittering water. They did not seem to belong to him.

Silver moved his head experimentally and two things happened at once: he was filled with a ballooning fireball of pain, and the knocking stopped abruptly. As it did he realised it was made not by knuckles on wood but by his skull, knocking against the bottom step as the water moved him. Then he saw there was a figure at the top of the steps, apelike against the wild sky. As the creature moved forwards and down it was clear that it had not seen him. Silver could hear big boots, clumping down; could hear something else too, a harsh crooning sound. This was a man, of sorts, singing to himself. Silver even recognised the song. It was *Blue Moon*.

The man stopped halfway down, grunted and fumbled a little, and the scalding stream of his urine fell across Silver's hands and face. He lay listening to the stream ringing into the water around him, the hot reek of piss in his nostrils. He wondered if he could push himself away from these steps back out into the chill river and finish it, but he could find not an ounce of strength in his body to do so. Perhaps at that moment the man's eyes became accustomed to the gloom, for Silver clearly heard his intake of breath and a questioning resentful grunt, as though Silver had somehow violated his space, instead of the other way around.

The man stood quite still, his unfastened coat flapping like a sail in a gust of wind. Silver knew he was watching him, watching the bundle of shadows at the foot of the steps, wondering, perhaps, whether he was alive or dead. Silver lay half on the stones, wishing desperately that he might be left in peace, but knowing with certainty that peace was something he was not to be granted. The man called something – a question, a demand. Silver heard the words, gruff, full of bluster, but his mind did not trouble to translate the individual sounds into meaning. There was no point. The man moved a couple of paces. The steps were narrow and the stones were slick underfoot as the Thames slid past a few inches away. He stopped, shouted again. The boots were close to Silver's face now in a bar of moonlight, scuffed Army surplus boots with the laces tangled. The wind gusted again and Silver caught a whiff of bonemeal body odour.

He closed his eyes, weary to the point of death, hoping that perhaps it might come and release him even now, and in that moment the man reached down and gripped the collar of his leather jacket and hauled on it convulsively. Silver felt his body bump up a couple of steps, felt it grow heavier as the river released it, felt the pain flare up again, but less keenly this time, and realised that his mind was drifting. Sounds and images came to him without connection. From his new position a few inches above the water he could see to the lights of the far bank, perhaps a quarter of a mile away, the moonlight a silver track across the surface. He could hear the filthy water drain out of his clothes and run in torrents down the steps. His rescuer was wheezing from his effort and sat back on his haunches, sucking his teeth, muttering to himself.

'Can't leave you in the drink, son. Against the rules.' The tramp's voice was a rasp, thick with drink and smoke. 'We don't leave the floaters in for the little fishes. Dead or alive, my son, we pull 'em out. Dead. Or. Bleeding. Alive.' He spoke, and as he spoke his hand stole down inside Silver's jacket. 'No good to you now, you poor bastard, is it?' the man protested to himself. 'Not when there's them as needs it, eh?' Silver felt the hard warm hand against the skin of his chest. The pigskin wallet slid out of his breast pocket. The man did not open it at once. He tapped it thoughtfully on his other fist for a while, as if he needed an excuse, and after a moment he thought of one. 'Feller can't die without a name, now can he?' The wallet flipped open and the moonlight glinted on a dozen gold and silver credit cards. The man stared at them, transfixed. 'It's not natural, without a name. Like you never been born.'

Something stirred painfully in Silver's mind, some revulsion at this creature and the world they both inhabited. With a huge effort he lifted his hand and gripped the derelict's wrist. The man shouted and stumbled back and tore his wrist free so violently that he fell back up the steps. Silver heard the wallet slap against stone and then the splash of it and he knew it was lost and was glad. The man scrabbled with his heels, pushing himself up, panting with fear, and at that moment a woman's voice shrilled: 'What the fuck are you up to now, Stevens?'

Another slighter silhouette stood at the top of the steps, arms akimbo. Silver saw a flag of hair flap in the wind, bone white in the moon.

'Christ on His cross, Maggie! It's alive down there!'

'You've been on the piss again, Stevie, ain't you?'

The man called Stevens pushed himself up past her and she snorted at him in contempt. Silver saw her crane over the edge, a shrivelled old woman. She looked directly at him. In a different voice she said: 'You stupid bastard. What have you got me into now?'

Stevens got to his feet on the dock beside her and Silver saw him rub his big hands nervously down the serge of his coat, over and over again. 'I just pulled him out, Maggie. That's all. Out of respect, like.'

'He's a jumper, you stupid bastard. It's where he wanted to be.'

'Can't leave 'em in, Maggie.' The man stiffened with a certain sullen defiance. 'Can't leave a man in the 'oggin.'

161

'You and your bloody Navy. Nobody'd think you was thrown out.'

'Honest to God, Mags, I thought he was dead. I just wanted to pull him out.'

'You wanted his wallet too, while you were about it.'

Stevens rubbed his hands on his coat some more and sulked. 'Thinking he was dead, mind. We need it. He don't.' The woman looked at him until he answered the unspoken question. 'He chucked it in the river.'

She snorted again. 'Move aside and let me take a look.'

Silver watched the woman hitch up her skirt and tuck it into her belt then step cautiously down the steps towards him. Water slapped against stone in the darkness.

She bent over him and touched him on the neck. 'Jesus. You're more dead than alive, you are.'

He did not recognise the noise from his own throat, a barely audible gargle, but the woman heard it and craned forward, pushing her shadowed face close to his.

'What's that? What you saying there?'

He could smell her bad breath and supermarket scent. He tried again. The muscles of his throat were clamped: they ached with the effort of speech.

'Leave me.'

The woman sat back on her haunches on the wet stone steps. 'Leave you?'

'Please.' Silver fought to stay conscious. Somehow he knew that she was an ally, that she might understand, that she might even do as he asked. He moved his hand far enough to reach his jacket pocket and tapped it with his forefinger, again and again. 'Please.'

She spoke gently to him, as if to a child. 'What you got here, then, sunshine? What's this here?' She felt inside his pocket and pulled out the wet wad of notes, fat as an airport novel. 'Show old Mags.'

The water ran glittering off the wad. Silver saw her freeze at the sight of the money. He heard her suck in her lips, weighing it. Then she sighed, and he knew she had made up her mind. She stuffed the notes somewhere in her clothing.

'Sorry, my luv,' she said, with what sounded like real regret. 'But it don't work that way.' Then she stood up and screamed in her harridan's voice. 'Stevie? You get down here and give me a hand with him, you useless article.'

He was vaguely aware of being dragged, bumping, up the steps with the man grunting in his ear. He would have resisted if he could have found an ounce of energy or will. He felt himself dropped, dumped, on the dockside above while the man struggled for breath. Falling half on one side he could see he was on the apron of a warehouse washed in acid light by a three-quarter moon. Dead weeds spiked up between the concrete blocks of the forecourt. A row of cranes stood like dinosaurs jutting their necks out over the black and silver acres of the river. Way off to the left he could see the pinnacles of Tower Bridge and beyond that the stacked lights of the City climbing into the sky. He recognised it all, of course, automatically, and yet it seemed bizarre to him that he could still do so, that anything could still look familiar to him. The world had changed so profoundly, and yet it still looked the same. It was not right that it should be so. He drew in the chill breath of the river, a dank breath with a hint of fuel oil and – perhaps just perceptibly – a tang of the salt marshes far to the east.

The grinding rumble of a roller door. A bell-peal of kicked bottles which echoed in a great hollow space. Growled curses. A crackling and a popping near him, a sound he could not place but which seemed strangely comforting. Finally it was another noise which brought him round again, a strange clattering which sounded very close. It took him a moment to realise that it was the chattering of his own teeth. He tried to control it, but the very core of his body seemed to be shuddering. He struggled to open his eyes. Only one of them would obey but it was enough to show him wild flame shadows flickering among iron pillars, and he understood that the crackle and hiss was a fire. Now he could feel the warmth of it pulsing against his back. There was a rough blanket against his skin and he registered that he was naked under it and that the blanket stank. It was impossible not to yield to the animal comfort of the flames and the dry touch of the wool, but beyond that he had neither thought nor recollection. Something primeval in his mind told him not to seek either. There were voices.

'If he's going to die,' the woman was shouting, 'he'll bloody die in the warm. Fair exchange, that is.'

'But Jesus, Maggie,' the man whined. 'What're we going to do with him? When he goes?'

'You should've thought of that before you pulled him out.' Silver heard her stand and then the pad of bare feet moving towards him across the concrete floor. 'It's thanks to you, Stevie, that I got to make decisions now.'

The feet – dirty bare feet – came into view. The ankles had varicose veins and the toenails were yellowish and horny. He registered all this, but he could not lift his head to see the rest of her. Then she squatted down and he saw an ugly woman in her late fifties, with grey hair in rats' tails over a haggard face as strong as an axeblade. She was dressed only in an old coat and it fell open as she squatted. She did not trouble to pull it closed and her exposed breasts hung like dugs. She shook her head as she looked at him.

'My Christ but you're a sight,' she said. She dropped the coat over him and as he drifted away again he was aware of her bare body against him, as bristled and warm as an old hound's.

She was digging about in the ashes of the fire and it was grey daylight. From where he lay he could see out through the gap in the roller doors. Fragile winter light lay across the yard and a wedge of it fell through the open steel door. He realised he had pissed in the blankets during the night and he lay in a cold pool of it. He could hear gulls.

'Jesus and Mary, you fair sucked the heat out of me,' she told him conversationally.

She was groping in the soft ashes with one hand and holding her coat closed across her with the other. The veins stood out blue and knotted in her ankles and wrists. He could see she was shivering, and realised that, for the moment, he was not. Finally she found a live ember and, grunting with satisfaction, placed a curl of paper next to it and blew asthmatically on it. In the half light, Silver could see the glow of it. A worm of fire hurried along the edge of the paper and then with a small pop it blossomed into yellow flame. She blew on it again and then hawked and spat in the fire. The gobbet of spittle sizzled like an egg in the ashes. She placed splinters and shreds of wood and a cigarette carton over the nest of flame, and in a second it was crackling. For a few moments more she fed it carefully with pieces of a broken wooden pallet heaped on the floor beside her.

'Reg'lar girl guide, me.' She looked up and leered at him, showing discoloured teeth. 'Not what we're used to, Stevie and me. But we was turned out last week. Again.' He thought she was probably the ugliest woman he had ever seen. She moved nearer to him and pulled up a milk crate and sat on it, warming herself at the fire, peering at him. 'Hear me, can you? You with us for five minutes this time, or you going off again?'

'Why did you have to interfere? Why?' It was not the

voice he remembered but it was his voice.

'Well, that's nice, I must say.' The woman moved her shoulders and chin in a pantomime of offended dignity. Even in his state Silver could tell she was utterly unconcerned by his ingratitude, would be untouched by any insult he could find to hurl at her. 'I sent Stevie out for some tea and stuff from the takeaway, the useless bugger. Should be open by now.' Incredibly to him, she spoke as if he might be interested. He lay in silence, watching her with one dull eye. 'I give him some of your money.' By her tone, he knew she expected him to protest. When he didn't she went a step further. 'You give it to me, y'know. Last night. Remember? A great fat wad. Never seen so many shekels in me life.'

'Take it. Just take it and go.' He closed his eyes, desperate to shut out the sight of her, the daylight, the warmth of the fire.

'But that'd be stealing,' she said. He opened his eyes again and looked at her in exhausted disbelief, and she read the look correctly. 'You can say a lot of things about me, sunshine, but I never been lightfingered. Not never.' She straightened the shabby coat around her scrawny body and stuck out her chin. 'So there.'

Silver lay, barely breathing, and stared at her in pain and misery. At last he said: 'Who are you?'

'Me? I'm Maggie Turpin. Everyone knows me.'

But that wasn't what he had meant. He didn't care what her name was, and he closed her out of his mind. He tried to move but he was as weak as a kitten. He could flex his right arm a little, though his shoulder hurt him fiercely when he did so. He still seemed to be able to use only one eye. Nothing else answered at all. His legs were as dead as if they were carved out of wood.

'I shouldn't struggle, dearie, if I was you. You got things broke inside, I think.'

He ignored her and strained against his weakness but within seconds he was spent. He dragged down half a breath and shouted feebly at her: 'For God's sake – why couldn't you let me die?'

'It wasn't your time,' she said easily. She got up and fed the fire, raking the embers towards the middle. She sat down again. 'That old river don't give folks up easily, and when it does, there's a reason.'

'Jesus,' he whispered in despair. 'Jesus Christ.' For a second he wondered if he might be dreaming it all.

'But now you're a bit of a problem. Seeing as you're still in the land of the living.' She looked down at him with a strange, detached benignity. 'I give you till this morning, see? I reckoned if you'd passed on in the night, well, that was meant to be. But now – well, this is a poser.'

'Just leave me here, for God's sake. Just fuck off.'

'Can't do that, luvvie.' She fingered a crucifix around her neck, perhaps unconsciously, perhaps as part of her explanation. 'Stevie's got his old Navy rules. I got mine. Now, what I *should* do is call the law, and be gone when they get here.'

Silver had not thought himself capable of alarm,

and for the first time it brought the woman into sharp focus. He said, in a clearer voice: 'Don't do that.'

'Oooh,' she said. 'That got your attention, eh? Well, don't you worry. That'd be breaking another rule.' She paused. 'Because you've done something, luv, ain't you?' Silver was silent and she went on, more gently: 'Well, I'm not going to be calling any policemen. But – see the problem? Can't call the coppers. Can't leave you.'

Silver heaved his head up an inch or two. 'You crazy old witch – why can't you just forget you ever saw me? You know I'm going to finish this just as soon as I'm strong enough.'

'Oh, yes,' she said, quite unruffled. 'You have to do what you have to do, dearie. Just like I do.'

21

Cobb struck the rhythm, sinking the spade and turning the greasy slabs of soil, again and again, moving slowly up the length of the hedgerow.

He liked to dig. He liked to feel his body warm and loose with labour, muscle sliding over bone, keen air flooding his lungs. It was Boxing Day and it was better now, the anniversary past. He sank the spade with extra force and stopped, leaning on it. He was sweating and could feel his heart thumping comfortably. The afternoon was unusually crisp and fine, the sky a distant duck-egg blue. Through the glassy air he could see Arthur Riordan's blue Ford tractor, crawling over the neighbouring hillside, and above it a plume of gulls following the harrow, shrieking like harpies.

'You're not impressing anyone, you know,' Fred grumbled beside him. 'Any fool can dig a ditch. Why don't you do something useful?'

'Like what, for example?'

'Like shoot a couple of damned foxes. Why do you think I bought the gun?'

'I don't like guns. Guns go bang and nasty things come out of them.'

'Fine cop you are. What'll you do when you meet a hoodlum with a forty-five, eh? Tell me that.'

'A hoodlum? Christ, I'll run a mile.'

'All the more reason to practise on foxes, then.'

Cobb suppressed a smile. Fred's hatred of foxes was legendary, but they both knew that foxes were not the problem. Cobb looked at his father with affection. The old man was lost inside a bulky padded anorak. He wore a woollen hat with bobbles on it and carried a tray with two mugs. The mugs gave off great roiling clouds of white steam, aromatic with coffee and brandy. Cobb took his mug and saw that the bare skin of his own forearm steamed slightly too. This evidence of his own animal heat made him feel vividly alive. 'It'll be all right, Dad. Relax.'

'You'll be a bloody agricultural labourer,' the old man snorted, squinting at Riordan's tractor. 'You'll go mad here. Look what's happened to me.'

Cobb drank, smiled to himself, said nothing. He knew his father loved the farm and understood perfectly why he loved it too. Cobb let the scented steam bathe his face for a while, and then said: 'I cleared out the garden room.' He indicated a clutter of cardboard cartons on the cobbles by the French doors.

'You did?' The old man looked momentarily pleased, and then troubled. 'You didn't need to, you know. I mean, not at this precise moment. It could have waited.'

'No. It's already been too long coming. I'll take the books down to Oxford next week and give them to one of the charity shops.'

'Well. If you're sure.'

'I'm sure.' He was. It was one of the reasons he felt

good today. It was strange, but giving away the foolish toy dinosaur had broken some dam in him, and the rest had been easier than he had imagined. He straightened his back, stretching the muscles. 'You know, I've been a bit selfish about all this.'

'Nonsense. There's no need.' Fred looked away into the middle distance, shifted his feet. He was uncomfortable with intimate revelations and he felt one coming. 'I mean to say–'

'You used to tell me that for more than four centuries Christmas had been celebrated in this house every single year. I think I've broken that tradition in the last two.'

Fred stared at him. 'I didn't mean the word "celebrated" literally, Samuel. Not with crackers and paper hats. I meant it was *observed*. And so it has been. Quietly and decorously for the last two years. But observed nevertheless.'

'I know. All the same.'

'There's no all the same about it.' The exchange seemed to have nettled the old man. After a pause he said: 'When are you going back to work?'

'Horrie Nelson says he'll hold for another couple of days. His wife's away. I'll go in Thursday.' Cobb waited a second and added: 'And then I'll go and see Sykes, and I'll resign.' Fred grunted his exasperation. Cobb said: 'Dad – I love it here, OK? Is that so bad?'

'And what do you love so much about it, Samuel? The endless Pantheon of Nature, is it? Rebirth? Regeneration? Great Cycles of Being?'

Cobb tried not to laugh. 'Something like that, I suppose.'

'Well, let me tell you, Samuel,' Fred lectured him, 'that sort of psychobabble is for old farts like me. I am the one who needs rebirth and regeneration. I'm falling to bits by the bloody day!' In an uncharacteristically extrovert display he waved his free arm in a windmilling motion. 'I'm the one who needs to be reminded of Great Cycles of Cosmic Being. Not you. You're just a stripling. You've got it all to do yet.'

Cobb bit his lip to keep from smiling. In a moment he asked: 'Are you finished?'

'Probably.' Fred thumped his empty mug back on the tray, held it out for Cobb's. More quietly he said: 'Don't you be in such a hurry to get old, Samuel. It's not for the fainthearted.'

As he turned to stump away the phone rang shrilly in the farmhouse.

'It was wrong of me, Mr Cobb,' she said. 'The way I spoke to you at the hospital.'

Cobb stood just inside the conservatory door with the phone to his ear. He was simultaneously surprised, angry and resentful at being called at home: it shattered his peaceful mood in an instant, darkened the thin sunlight over the fields. But Lauren's apology disarmed him, that and his understanding of her trouble. He found himself locked in silence.

'Mr Cobb?'

'Yes. Yes, I'm here.' He juggled the phone to his

other hand. He noticed that his earthy hands left brown prints on the white plastic and he composed himself with an effort. 'Mrs Silver, you have nothing to feel sorry about. Especially not at a time like this. In fact, I should probably apologise to you.'

'Oh?'

'Going to Freya like that without asking you. I can see–'

'As a matter of fact, that's another reason for my ringing.'

'Why? Is she talking yet?'

'No, that's partly my point. Tommy and I both feel she has taken to you in some way.'

Cobb just resisted a brutal urge to dismiss this out of hand. He found that he passionately did not want it to be true. 'I only gave her a toy, Mrs Silver. Nothing more.'

'Yes, there was something more.'

He closed his eyes and took a deep breath. 'Mrs Silver, I ought to make it clear to you that I can't get involved . . .'

'You are involved.'

'Not for very much longer, Mrs Silver.'

'Come to the funeral,' she said abruptly.

'I'm sorry?'

'Goodie's funeral is tomorrow. It's at a very quiet little church–'

'Mrs Silver, it wouldn't be appropriate–'

'– at a place called Leighford, down in Surrey. I'll give you the address. A very brief service. It's been kept quite secret. Tommy has seen to that.'

'But, Mrs Silver, I'm a police officer–'

'Don't policemen usually attend funerals?' she said, with some of her old acidity. 'To see if the murderer comes back to gloat?'

This wrongfooted him for a fatal couple of seconds. In the gap he left her she read him the address of the church and the time of the service, and before he had regathered his wits she rang off.

22

Cobb left the car in the car park of the Cross Keys pub, where Hudson's security people had directed him, and walked across the field to the church. The churchyard was unkempt, with last summer's uncut weeds drifting in grey-brown tangles against mossy gravestones. The weather had broken and a light drizzle fell like muslin over the countryside. The far ridge of the South Downs swam in and out of focus behind it. The greystone church was small and squat, with a blockish Norman tower. It seemed half swallowed by the land, as though it had sunk into the soft sward over the years under its own weight. The church looked deserted and Cobb paused for a moment in the shelter of the roofed lychgate. Above him a gang of crows flapped like black flags in bare poplars, cackling raucously, stumbling through the treetops and snapping twigs in their clumsiness. The broken wood clattered on to the lychgate's slate roof.

As if at a signal the crows were gone, beating away over the sloping land, their jeering cries fading as they flew. A convoy of black limousines swept up the lane and came to a halt and the doors opened and useful-looking men got out and moved away, and after them a knot of people in black emerged and hurried against the rain into the church. From his distance Cobb recognised Hudson, shepherding, directing, and saw a hospital-style wheelchair with a slight figure huddled in it. He waited until they were inside and then he followed and sat at the back and watched the raindrops sparkle on the sleeve of his coat while the service began. It was the first funeral he had attended since Clea's.

After a while he looked up. The casket was absurdly small – so small that it reminded him of a violin case as it lay in front of the altar. He ran his eyes along the line of mourners. There were very few of them, no more than fifteen including the main players, not even enough to fill the first two rows of pews. An elderly couple, two middle-aged women, a very fat bald man, a boy in an ill-fitting jacket . . . he stopped paying attention. They were nondescript – relatives, he supposed. Even the children of superstars had relatives. Whoever they were they were not glamorous show business types, and he was glad about that. He relaxed a little. The chrome winter light fell aslant through the high windows. He watched it.

When the service was over he stood back and let the small procession shuffle past him, careful to keep his eyes on the worn flagstones. He looked up just a fraction too soon. Freya was being wheeled past him in her chair, pushed by a distraught Latin woman Cobb had never seen before. Against the child's sombre clothes the pink toy made a flamingo splash of colour. He caught Freya's eye and smiled. She did not smile back, but her eyes stayed locked on to his as the weeping woman pushed her away.

The grave seemed cavernous, a chasm swallowing up the tiny coffin. Cobb moved from behind the mourners to the far side of the pit while the vicar read the closing phrases and the coffin was gently lowered down. The rain was heavier now and the fat drops starred the polished wood, scattering like quicksilver. At length the shadow of the grave engulfed it. Cobb looked up. The elderly woman was sobbing, and the old man put his arm around her. It looked as if he had not done this for years. The boy in the ill-fitting jacket stared awkwardly at his feet. Hudson stood like a soldier on parade, rigid in every muscle. But his lower lip wobbled uncontrollably, twisting his mouth into a grimace. Lauren, her veil lifted, stood with her cold face sightless in the rain, utterly remote, beyond the touch of sympathy. Cobb could sense the grief within her like a black hole, sucking the very light out of the world in which she moved. He looked at her with useless pity: there was nothing to be done for her.

And then the priest had finished. He turned back through the rain towards the church, and the little group moved to follow. At the last moment Lauren seemed to rouse herself. She shook off Hudson's proffered hand. As Cobb watched, she drew a white rose from inside her jacket, kissed it, and tossed it down into the grave. The gesture surprised Cobb. For some reason it gave him a flash of hope for her, and that pleased him. Then she flicked down her veil, turned, and walked steadily and alone towards the church. Cobb watched her straight back until her figure blurred into the rain.

On the far side of the grave from Cobb the Portuguese maid, half-blinded by tears, was trying to turn Freya's wheelchair on the soft ground. She slipped and caught one rear wheel in the mud. She strained to shift it, failed, and in a second her fragile control was gone and her legs buckled and she was on her knees on the muddy ground, wailing aloud, clutching at the canted wheelchair, close to hysteria. Cobb moved quickly around the grave but Hudson was there first, catching the woman under his arm and lifting her easily against him.

'I'll bring the girl,' Cobb told him, and Hudson nodded and moved away towards the church, half-carrying his helpless burden between the wet gravestones.

Cobb freed the wheelchair easily. Then something made him look down at the silent child with Clea's toy nestled against her, and quickly he swept her up into his arms. 'Come on, Princess,' he told her. 'You've been pushed around enough, I think.'

'Wait,' she commanded.

Cobb froze, aware that something extraordinary had happened but for a fraction of a second unable to recognise what it was. When he did, he said softly: 'Princess.'

Her arm moved in a jerk and the pink toy flew from her and fell with a small thud on to her sister's coffin far below where it lay grinning at the sky, the rain cloying its lurid fur.

'I thought Goodie might like to take him,' Freya said.

'I expect she would, Princess,' Cobb said. 'I'm sure she would.'

'Frey!' It was Hudson, hurrying back from the church. 'Did I hear you . . .?' He turned to Cobb, his battered face shining. 'Did she . . .?'

'You'll have to ask her,' Cobb said. He hefted the child in his arms and handed her to Hudson, then walked quickly away down the field path.

Lauren stood beside the car. She lifted her veil and let the rain drive into her face. Looking down, she could see the silver runnels of water snake down the black wool of her coat from her shoulders and along her sleeves, dropping in a small cascade into a clay red puddle at her feet. Behind her, in the back of the limousine, Merilda sat moaning in a half-swoon, crushed by grief. A driver in a chauffeur's cap, his face averted as if he wanted to avoid looking into her eyes, tried to usher Lauren in through the car's back door to shelter from the rain beside the other woman. She ignored him and after a while he turned away. He hovered unhappily for a while then left her and slid into the driver's seat, closing his door softly behind him.

Hudson shouted from beside the grave. Lauren lifted her eyes with an effort. She did not particularly want to look, but it was that kind of shout, like a hook in the mind, impossible to ignore. She noticed that Merilda had heard it too and had stopped sobbing. Hudson shouted again. It was too far for her to hear his voice over the drumming of the rain on the car roof but she saw the delight in his face. She saw him smile in wonder at her, mouthing words across the wet churchyard, holding Freya up like a trophy for her to see. She knew instinctively what had happened. Merilda sensed it too and in a second the woman was stumbling through the mud past Lauren, dropping her shawl, then her bag, shouting hope and entreaty to the grey tent of the sky. At the graveside Hudson pulled up the collar of his coat to cover the child and carried her at a half run to meet them so that they collided with the maid in an untidy tangle, Merilda hopping in the mud and clutching for the child's hand, Hudson trying to push past her, trying to carry the girl to where Lauren stood silently watching.

' 'Swonderful, Laurie, ain't it?' His big face was glowing as he came up to her. 'Bloody miracle, eh?' He pulled Freya to him and hugged her hard. 'Eh, ya little darlin'! Talking again! Eh?'

Lauren watched her daughter's dark eyes as they gazed at her from under the shelter of Hudson's coat. Those eyes tracked her as Hudson swivelled and shouted the news to the others, as Merilda shrieked prayers of gratitude and grabbed for the child. Those eyes reminded Lauren of the eyes of some small fierce animal in a cave. They unnerved her. She was surprised to find that she was still capable of being unnerved.

'Take her, Laurie,' Hudson was saying, moving the child on his hip so that Lauren could reach for her. 'Go on. You take her.'

The group around them fell quiet, waiting. Lauren frowned. Hudson seemed to be speaking to her from behind glass. It did not seem possible that, simply by reaching out, she could touch this surviving cub of hers, feel her weight. She felt herself take a sharp breath and realised she could not do it, that in some strange way it was forbidden her.

'Put me down,' Freya commanded.

'You got a bad leg, Frey,' Hudson said. 'You can't–'

'Put me down *now*!' the child spat, and this time he obeyed at once, sliding her down so that she rested her good leg on the ground and balanced for a moment on it, stork-like. When Hudson put his hand out to her, she slapped it away, her eyes fixed on her mother's with that same fierce gaze. It seemed to Lauren that the others had shrunk away to nothing, leaving just the two of them alone in the universe.

Slowly Lauren reached out her hand. Freya took it and steadied herself. Freya's hand was cool and dry in hers. The touch of it sent her a message, she realised – not a message of warmth and comfort, but a challenge. It frightened her. She found that she was breathing fast and felt the fear trickling cold inside her. To break the spell she guided the child into the car and got in after her, closing the door behind them in the faces of the others. She locked the doors. She found the switch which controlled the glass partition and pressed it. Mother and daughter sat in silence for a space, the rain streaking the windows. Lauren was vaguely conscious of muttered discussions outside, the slamming of the doors in the other cars. Finally the engine murmured into life and they pulled away between the high wet banks of hawthorn. Lauren glanced at the child beside her, but Freya's eyes stared directly ahead. The car emerged on to the main road and headed north through the sodden country, its tyres hissing on the wet surface. For a long time there was no other sound.

'Why did he go?' Freya said suddenly. 'Why did he leave us?'

'He didn't leave you, Frey. He took you. It was me he left.'

'Why?'

'I don't know, Frey. I don't know much of anything any more. I did everything I knew how to keep us all together.'

'Well, he's left both of us now, hasn't he?'

'Yes, Freya. I suppose he has.'

'Was it my fault?'

'You mustn't think that,' Lauren said quickly. Her mouth seemed to be full of ash. She knew she must speak but it was difficult to form the words. 'Don't ever think that.'

'There must be a reason,' Freya said. Her voice was full of a grim certainty.

Lauren licked parchment lips. She leaned forward and clicked open the walnut cocktail cabinet.

'Don't,' Freya said sharply.

Lauren swallowed hard and squeezed her eyes closed. Very deliberately she shut the cabinet again and sat back in her seat.

'I don't think I can do this, Freya,' she said.

'You have to,' her daughter told her. There was no pity in her voice. 'You just have to, that's all.'

23

Silver became aware of a low angled ceiling and a luminous rhomboid of window. The window was dark blue, and he knew it was night.

He had no clear idea how he had got here. He remembered being roughly bundled up and pushed into the back of an old station wagon. He remembered noticing, in moments of lucidity, that the car was shabby, full of litter, and smelled of takeaway food and vomit. He'd noticed too that the woman had driven it lovingly even though it misfired and jumped out of gear every few hundred yards. After that the images had slipped and blurred. There may have been some sort of altercation in a car park: from where he lay in the back of the car he recalled a pub sign, and the black zig-zag of a fire escape across red Victorian brick. He distinctly remembered the man called Stevens smacking the upholstery so that the springs twanged, and shouting in fright: 'You stupid cow! He's going to die on us.'

And Maggie Turpin replying, imperturbably: 'Gently Bentley. Mind me motor.'

That seemed long ago now. He was drifting comfortably again and, though his skin burned and his throat and lungs were raw, he floated above all this in a strange euphoria. He knew, as if he were experiencing these sensations on someone else's behalf, that he was running a fever. There was a splash of yellow light through a curtain and the reassuring sound of voices in a room downstairs. More than voices. Music. A girl was singing plaintively to a guitar. She had a singularly beautiful voice, untrained but wonderfully pure. It reminded him of his childhood, when he would be sent to his attic bedroom while his older sister and her boyfriends played their records downstairs. Records like this one. The singing was muffled, perhaps two floors below, but he identified it effortlessly. *Virgil Caine is my name* . . . Joan Baez. It was as familiar to him as the voice of a friend and he allowed himself to be lulled by it, sensing it would be his last moment of comfort. And sure enough, the memories surfaced like a broaching whale, black and monstrous, and with them the pain and fever became his own and not someone else's.

Silver explored the inside of his mouth with his tongue. Even that landscape felt foreign to him now. On the right side of his jaw he found a mound of what might have been splintered china, and when his tongue touched it a white light exploded in his brain. It was the first pain in this life and he felt strangely glad of it. He touched the place again and another starshell exploded, harsher this time. The pain sent saliva squirting into his mouth and he rolled it around and swallowed some. A door slammed below and there were heavy footsteps on the stairs, and voices, a man's and a woman's. The door was pushed wide and garish light flooded the room and blinded him. The woman came in first, the same shrivelled grey-haired Maggie Turpin woman he had seen before. After her came a smiling thickset man of fifty in a hairy tweed jacket.

The woman cawed at him. 'Back with us at last, eh? Thought you'd either be awake or stiff. And it looks like you got two eyes after all.'

The smiling man shouldered her aside. 'Move your wrinkled ass now, Maggie, will ye?' It was an Irish accent, so strong that to Silver it seemed the man must be hamming it up. The bluff and merry face came closer to his, and Silver saw that the eyes were cold. 'Jaysus – where did you find this one? He's as hot as a feckin' furnace. And he stinks. Couldn't ye have hosed him down, y'auld bitch?'

Silver swallowed again and found his voice. 'You're a doctor?'

'I'm Kilpatrick. Where I come from, mine is not a lucky name for a man of my profession. Though it proved prophetic enough.'

'I don't want a doctor.'

'Well, ye're safe then, for they tell me I am one no longer.' Kilpatrick's smile broadened and his eyes became chips of flint. 'Still and all, I'm the best you'll get.'

Kilpatrick's big hands were strong, competent, and utterly uncaring. He stripped the coverings off and felt the bones of Silver's legs under the bruises, forced open his mouth and dug around with his broad forefinger among the broken teeth, flexed each rib so

187

hard that Silver felt the fractured ends of bone grate together before he passed out. In interludes of semi-consciousness he felt something cold injected into his face, more than once, and then the prick and drag and tug of stitching. When he came round again he was on his side with his head hanging over the edge of the cot. He had puked, though he had nothing much to bring up. Someone had slid a newspaper under his head, presumably to make it easier to clear the mess up later. Silver drifted in and out of this strange new world, tasting bile, feeling his body throb with pain with every heartbeat. He could see the blur of the newspaper's front page under his eyes, swimming in and out of focus, and just beyond the edge of it he could see Kilpatrick's brown brogues. He realised the man was talking.

'Well, your golden goose has got about a 50/50, Maggie. I've stoked him up with antibiotics and sewn him back together, but that's about all I can do. The ribs will heal on their own, most likely. He has a constitution like an ox, whoever he is. If this doesn't turn into pneumonia he'll probably see the New Year.'

The brown shoes moved away and Silver heard Kilpatrick gathering his things together and cleaning up, the clink of metal instruments and the slop of water in a basin. The door was opened and Kilpatrick's footsteps moved out on to the landing and clumped down the stairs. He heard the cheery voice one last time: 'Oh, Maggie! I near forgot! D'ye want it for a keepsake, now?'

'What?'

' 'Tis his finger. Had to snip it off, ye know.'

Whatever reply she gave was drowned by Kilpatrick's guffaw, and Silver could hear him laughing as he clumped all the way down the stairs in his shiny brogues.

She returned after a few moments and stood silently in the doorway. He rolled his head and looked at her, a hardbitten old woman in a dirty sweater.

'Which one was it?' he said.

'Does it matter?'

'It would have, once. It would have mattered a lot.'

He tried feeling his hands but both seemed to have been bound up stiffly, like paddles. Maggie Turpin held up her left hand and wiggled her ring finger.

'This one.'

Left hand, fret hand. How would all those chords sound now, without that one? He was surprised how little he cared. She was right. It didn't matter now.

He let his head loll back and the movement brought the stained newspaper before his face again. He watched it idly as it swam in and out of focus, a fuzzy patchwork of print and a single big photograph. It looked oddly familiar and with a sudden surge of energy he forced himself to concentrate. He felt his heart begin to bump. The headline read simply MIRACLE GIRL and the photograph was of Freya, sitting up in a hospital bed, glowering at the camera.

'And now there's another thing,' Maggie said, and

her voice was heavy with meaning as she watched him. 'What do we call you?'

He breathed hard, fighting for control, feeling his damaged ribs spike him with pain. Freya was alive. He had killed Goodie, but Freya was alive. Where did that leave him? How could the debt be cancelled now? He could hear himself panting.

'I said, what do we call you?'

Downstairs in the bar the woman had started singing Joan Baez again, her muffled voice carrying up the stairs. While his conscious mind spun, his subconscious unerringly – uselessly – identified the song, filled in the words.

> *I dreamed I saw Joe Hill last night*
> *Alive as you or me.*
> *Says I, 'But Joe, you're ten years dead.'*
> *'I never died,' said he.*

'Joe,' he said. 'Joe Hill.'

'Right,' Maggie said. She reached down and crumpled the soiled newspaper into a ball. 'Joe Hill. Right.'

24

It was gone eight by the time Cobb reached the Baron's Court flat. He had bought it as little more than a bedroom in town, but he had grown fond of it over the years and was rarely lonely here. He could never convince his father of that. The old man was forever pressuring Cobb to buy a bigger place, perhaps something more like the handsome Primrose Hill house where Cobb had lived with Clea. Old Fred's thinking on these matters was convoluted. Secretly, Cobb knew, Fred suspected that his son might be visiting him at the farm only out of duty. He reasoned that if Cobb moved into a place he could call home, then he would have less need to head into the country every weekend. That way Fred would not have to live with the dread thought that he was becoming a millstone about his son's neck. On the other hand, of course, it would have broken the old man's heart.

Cobb climbed the stairs. He let himself in and brought the flat to life, snapping on lights and igniting the old-fashioned gas fire. It caught with a soft plop and burned magenta. The truth was that Cobb visited the farm for peace and pleasure and out of love for his father. On the other side of the ledger, he also enjoyed the solitude of the flat. There were times when he felt it had kept him sane – not so much the flat itself as the knowledge that it was here, a refuge which was entirely his own space.

Cobb poured some red wine and positioned himself by the window. The flat was on the second floor and he could not see much of London from here, only the patchwork of lighted windows in his own street, a jumble of dark rooftops, and a section of the tube line running into Baron's Court a hundred yards away. Nevertheless he felt and heard some of the rhythm of the city here: the clatter of a taxi's diesel in the street, music from a pub, the rumble of a train. He could see the lit caterpillar of carriages rocking away towards the suburbs. The room was almost bare. He liked its Japanese starkness; a desk and a work chair, a single large armchair on one side of the gasfire with a television and music centre facing it, two rows of bookshelves along one wall. It pleased him to stand at his eyrie by the window and look out on the other windows, and to imagine all those innumerable cubes of light and warmth in the winter night, floating above the layered history of the city, each cube bearing its own freight of love, hate, fear, hope. It reminded him of how unknowable were the lives of others to him, as his life was unknown to them, and the thought gave him a sense of peace in his own insignificance.

Cobb sipped the wine. It had been open two days and was almost dead, but that didn't matter. It was merely a ritual. And he needed some ritual, some stability. He could make no sense at all of the events at the funeral, nor of his feelings about them. He was glad for the child, liked the child, hoped he would never see her again. Never see any of them. He wished he had forced his resignation on to Sykes and simply walked. It was a lousy way to behave, and it would have cost him dear. But he did not think it would have cost him as much as this entanglement was costing him. At least here he didn't have to think about it.

The tapping on the door was as swift and light as a woodpecker. The sound was so unfamiliar that it took Cobb a moment or two to recognise it. He turned on his heel and listened, disbelieving, for it to be repeated. No one had knocked on his door here for two years. He set down his drink, walked quickly across the room and pulled the door open.

'I know you'll be angry, but I had to come.'

'Mrs Silver, how did you get this address?'

'That doesn't matter.'

'Yes, it does.'

'Can I come in?'

'No.'

Her eyes met his in irritation. 'Look, I'm rich, OK?' she said as if it might be answer enough. 'I can get that kind of information. Even from the police.'

'Someone at work told you?'

She shrugged. 'I might have lied a bit. Look, can we pull the plug on the outrage, Inspector Cobb? I really need to talk to you.'

She walked straight into him, so that he had to choose between stepping aside or pushing her childishly back on to the landing. He let her pass and closed the door behind her.

'I'm sorry for your trouble, Mrs Silver. Terribly sorry. But I want you to know this is totally out of line.'

'Inspector,' she swung on her heel to face him, 'I buried my little girl today. You watched me do it. You should know I don't give much of a shit about anything.'

She walked across to his own favourite spot by the window, her heels clicking on the polished boards. Her face was so white against the black of her suit that the contrast was painful. She leaned on the back of his work chair and looked around the room with frank incredulity. 'And this is your place? There isn't room to swing a cat.'

'I don't have a cat. Mrs Silver, this is not the way these things are handled. About your husband–'

'This isn't about Matthew.' She turned the hard-backed chair round, banged it down on the bare boards and sat without invitation, facing him. Cobb noticed, irrelevantly, that she had had her broken tooth fixed. He had not seen this at the funeral. Perhaps she had not parted her lips. She took out a gold cigarette case, flipped it open, looked at it and put it away again. 'Have you got a drink?'

She said this with a certain defiance and it struck Cobb that she expected him to comment, to absolve her perhaps, or else dissuade her. He said nothing and went to the tiny kitchen and poured the last of the red wine and handed it to her.

'Mrs Silver, I think you need to talk to somebody about all this.'

'About all what?'

'You're not behaving rationally. Coming here. Asking me to the funeral, even. In a way I appreciate it, of course, but it's not appropriate.'

'You didn't have to come.'

'I did have to, Mrs Silver. You gave me no choice.'

'There's always a choice.' She waved her glass scornfully. 'Look, fuck appropriate, Mr Cobb. It worked. My daughter's speaking again.'

'Yes, I'm glad about that.'

'So stop quoting the regulations at me.'

'It's not that I blame you, of course–'

'Oh, well, that's all right then.'

He started again. 'Nobody expects you to be super-human, Mrs Silver. Human beings weren't supposed to get through this kind of thing alone.'

'I'm not alone. I've got Tommy.'

'Good. That's good, Mrs Silver. Tommy Hudson seems like a strong person to me. Would you like me to call him for you right now?'

She sipped her wine and looked at him thoughtfully, half-smiling. 'You think I'm totally out of my tree, don't you?'

'If I were in your place, I think I might be.'

'Mr Cobb – can I call you Sam?'

'I'd much rather you didn't.'

'Mr Cobb, then,' she said, as if weary at such game playing. 'This isn't about me. You should know that it wouldn't matter to me right now if I didn't wake up tomorrow.'

'I can't imagine what you're going through, Mrs Silver. I haven't a clue what the right thing to say to you is.'

'And I thought all you policemen did counselling courses along with your MBAs?' She looked out of the window. After a while she said: 'For me, I wouldn't care. But I've got a daughter to go on living for.'

'You're right. She's a beautiful little girl.'

'Beautiful?' She repeated the word vaguely and her voice began to drift. 'I never thought of Frey like that. Not beautiful. Not like Gudrun.'

'Well, I never knew Gudrun,' Cobb said, harshly enough to make her look at him, 'but your little girl is bright and brave and intelligent, and in my opinion, if you want a good reason to live, you couldn't ask for a better one.'

She straightened and her mouth hardened. 'All right, Mr Cobb. You can cut the sermon. As I was trying to tell you, Freya is why I'm here.'

'Oh?'

'It was right, what I said on the phone. You have a way with her.'

'Mrs Silver, Freya started to talk when she was ready. It happens like that sometimes. You don't want to read too much into it.'

'She blames herself in some way.'

'That's ridiculous.'

'Of course it's ridiculous. What difference does that

make? I need to get her mind off it. I need to get her interested in life again.' Cobb said nothing, and she correctly interpreted his silence. 'You promised her, Mr Cobb.'

'I was trying to cheer her up, that's all.'

'You promised. Cows and pigs and sheep and pink dinosaurs the whole bloody lot. She told me. In her own voice.'

'Mrs Silver, I'm a police officer. You're involved in a case I'm working on. I cannot–'

'Just a day, that's all. We'll drive up any day you say. We'll be no trouble.'

'Mrs Silver–'

'Tommy told me you'd say no.'

For some reason that gave him pause. 'Let me think about it.'

'No.' She saw him waver. 'It's for my daughter.' She took a deep breath. 'Please.'

Cobb stared at her unhappily, not quite sure why he found it so hard to give way. He passionately didn't want them on the farm, a half-crazy Lauren Silver and new friend Tommy Hudson, with his big knuckles and his Hawaiian shirts. The farm was his home. He did not want them invading it. The thought had no sooner formed in his mind than he saw how colossally selfish it was. Of course she was right. It was nothing to do with any of them. It was for the child, and it was for one day. It was little enough. He felt ashamed of himself.

'Mrs Silver, of course, if that's what Freya wants.'

She screwed her eyes closed and turned her face away from him.

'Thank you.' Her head dropped forward an inch as she said it.

'But I'll do a deal with you on this,' he went on. 'I don't want you to ever come here again, or to the farm, without my invitation. I'm sorry if that sounds harsh, but my privacy is important to me and that's the way I want it.'

'Anything you say.' Her shoulders sagged.

'Are you all right, Mrs Silver?'

'Can I have another drink?'

'It's late. I'll call you a cab.'

She nodded, resigned. He glanced at her while he called the cab: he did not believe he had ever seen anyone look so pale without passing out. Her face was a sculpture in ivory.

'Shall I call you a doctor, Mrs Silver? I can get one here in a moment. Pull a bit of rank.'

She lifted her head and focused on him with an effort. 'Why won't you let me call you Sam? We both know it's your name.'

'I see a good many tragedies in my job, Mrs Silver. I have a walk-on part in lots of them. I don't want a bigger role than that.'

She stood up, steadied herself. 'You're not a kind man, are you? For all your correctness, you haven't got much heart.' She walked past him. 'I'll wait for the cab outside.'

25

'Not so fast, Commie swine!' Fred hunched in the cockpit, his shoulders working like a dancer's as he jockeyed the F-16 into position. 'Let's see how you like this!' He thumbed the gun button and released converging streams of tracer at the fleeing shape of the Ilyushin. The Soviet fighter bloomed into lurid flame. Debris spun past Fred's windshield and the farmhouse filled with the simulated din of explosion. 'Got him!' The old man slapped the desk. 'Right up the tailpipe!'

Sensing excitement, the dog lifted his anvil head an inch from the hearthrug.

'Take it easy,' Cobb said. 'Baskerville's having hysterics.'

Fred flung his F-16 into an expert victory roll and crowed in triumph across the room. 'That's one for the good guys!'

'I'm beginning to wish I'd never bought you that machine.'

Fred spun his chair so that his white hair floated out briefly like a wizard's. 'You know, Samuel, I'd never have guessed computers could be so therapeutic. When the Cold War was actually going on I had to be polite to the Russians. Now I can just – blow them away! Years of frustration swept aside at the wiggle of a joystick. Wonderful.' Fred rubbed his hands with glee.

'Who was this particular evil Commie bastard?'

'An actuary from Bath.'

'Serves him right, then.'

'Quite so.' Still chortling to himself, Fred shut the computer down. Then he slapped his knees hard and said: 'Right.'

Cobb folded his paper and set it aside, knowing what was coming next. His father had used brisk, mock military movements of this kind ever since Cobb was in short pants to signal that he wanted to discuss something delicate. Cobb said: 'I should have taken the bloody dog out.'

'Too late. Fetch the bottle.'

Resigned, Cobb rose and brought the Laphroaig from the black oak dresser under the stairs. He didn't particularly want to drink or to talk. It was close to midnight. He had very nearly escaped to take Baskerville shambling round the frozen yard, and after that could decently have gone to bed. But once initiated, the ritual could not be derailed. It stretched back to Cobb's teens, when to be offered a drink by his father was a rare privilege indeed and always meant that some key issue was about to be raised. Cobb remembered every one of these occasions, always with a shadow of the awe he had felt on the first time that bottle and the two shot glasses had appeared.

It was on the veranda of a palm-shaded bungalow in the suburbs of Jakarta, where his father had just started a two-year stint as assistant trade secretary. A luminous blue dusk was settling over a garden loud with insects, and a gecko hunted gauzy flies around the porch light. Cobb, just fourteen, was finishing his homework at the rattan table. He loved the glamour of his father's overseas postings. He was thrilled by the colour and mystery of foreign places. Experience made him feel exotic and powerful. He straightened from his school-books as a file of farm workers drove a water buffalo past the garden gate. The men were laughing and joking. They and their beast were silhouetted against the pearl sky like characters in the *wayang* shadow play. The clove scent of *kretek* cigarettes drifted through the night. In that instant, with the scent of *kreteks* and the clump of hooves and the chuckle of men's voices, fourteen-year-old Sam Cobb decided that he was happy.

'Your mother has left us, Samuel,' his father announced from behind him, setting the bottle and glasses on top of his son's history homework. 'My fault entirely, of course.' And then an astonishing thing happened. His father began to cry.

'Were you rubbing that bottle in the hope of attracting a genie?' Fred asked him.

'Sorry.' Cobb poured the smoky spirit, took his own and sat down again next to the dying fire. He poked moodily at the embers. He said: 'I'm not happy about them coming here, that's all. I shouldn't have agreed to it.' He could hear the snap of resentment in his own voice.

'I see.'

'The woman's a rich-bitch TV starlet. She's not your kind of animal.'

'She's a mother, too, I think? Possibly even a human being?'

'Yes, yes. I'm very sorry for her. I wouldn't wish this on anyone. But you don't know what these people are like.'

'I see,' Fred said again, stiffly. 'And what are they like?'

'Why don't you just take it from me for once, Dad? I don't want Lauren Silver here with her booze and her grief. I don't want the poor traumatised kid here. I don't know how to deal with her. And I don't want their wide boy ex-pug minder here either. I don't think you should have to put up with any of them.'

'Me? I'd be glad of the company. All I have is this comatose hound, and rather too much of you every week.' Fred sipped his Scotch. 'And what is a "wide boy ex-pug", anyway? Is it something I might see at Crufts, perhaps?'

Cobb tossed the poker down in the hearth with a clatter, and was suddenly angry with himself. 'Oh, Tommy Hudson's all right. At least he cares about her and the girl, which is more than Silver ever did.'

'Well, then.'

'I just don't want to get mixed up with them. I'm a policeman, not a social worker. They're not my problem. Besides, the file isn't closed yet. The man only drowned a week ago. I shouldn't have any social contact with his family at all.'

'Why not?'

'It's unethical, it's unprofessional and it's bloody awkward.'

'Unprofessional, unethical and bloody awkward?' Fred smirked. 'These are a few of my favourite things.'

'You silly old sod. You've never had so much as a parking ticket in your entire life. That's why you spend half the night annihilating actuaries from Bath.'

'Don't change the subject,' his father said primly. 'And incidentally, don't try to make out that all this concern is on account of your dear old father.'

Cobb could see where this was leading. 'Dad, we're only talking about this woman at all because she gatecrashed my flat and invited herself down.'

'Good Lord,' Fred said. 'Stormed the inner sanctum. Goodness me.' There was an edge to the old man's voice that made Cobb pause.

'You don't understand,' he said lamely.

'I understand quite well.' Fred set his glass down. 'I understand a distraught woman comes to you the very day her child is buried in the cold earth and begs a favour of you – a small thing – on behalf of her surviving daughter.'

'It wasn't like that.'

'And I understand that you *hesitated*.'

'Dad, listen–'

'You *hesitated*, and, having reluctantly agreed, you are now trying to weasel your way out of it.'

Cobb knew when to shut up. He sucked morosely on his whisky and stared at the fire.

'Good Lord, Samuel!' Fred's voice rose. 'You've been offered a privilege. The child trusts you, speaks to you. She asks if she can spend a few hours with some ducks and chickens in the countryside. And you refuse her this?'

'I *didn't* bloody refuse her.'

'But now you wish you had!' Fred boomed. 'My God, Samuel, are you so locked in your own bleak little world—'

'Jesus, Dad, all right!' Cobb raised his hands in submission. 'Look, you win. I give up. It's selfish of me. I'm a prick.'

'And?' Fred's voice quivered magnificently.

'And of course they can come here, and I'll be just as nice as pie to all of them. I'll be so nice it'll make you vomit.'

Fred sat back in his chair, his prickles settling back like an old hedgehog's. 'Splendid,' he said sweetly. He lifted the bottle. 'A nightcap?'

Cobb looked across at his father and gave a snort of laughter.

'I think we should.' Fred tilted the Laphroaig.

'Mad if we don't,' Cobb agreed, closing the circuit with the response they had rehearsed for thirty years.

26

Cobb drove into London and worked methodically until midday. It was Monday, the first of the New Year, and he found himself grateful for the day's routine dullness after the dislocation of the last couple of weeks. Already he could feel the machine start to turn again with the same familiar rhythm, tedious and reliable. Cobb knew it would go on with him or without him, and that knowledge took some of the pressure off him. He was glad to be back behind his desk, however temporarily. He decided that he hated Christmas and would always hate it, and he wondered why he tried to convince himself otherwise.

Horrie Nelson was catching up on the leave he had failed to take over the holiday, and Sykes was away until the end of the week at a conference in Scotland. Cobb was glad about that. He did not want another confrontation just yet. He wanted a day or two to recharge, and the absence of his superiors gave him a measure of peace for the rest of the week. Barring extraordinary circumstances he would be left to himself. He returned half-a-dozen e-mails, chased up the pathology report for Gudrun Silver, dealt with five media calls and ignored a handful more. He set up a 'Matt Silver Task Force' folder under his own password

on the system, and amused himself for an hour or
more creating subfiles within it: Witness Reports, Biog,
Notes, Statements. Warming to the task, he called every
member of the task force team as if they might really
have fresh information, and contrived to sound surprised when they did not. Three new witnesses to the
crash had turned up, but they had nothing to add. The
Jaguar was brand new and the Accident Investigation
people at Barnes could find nothing obviously wrong
with brakes or steering. There had been no reports
over Christmas or the New Year of bodies floating
downriver.

Cobb found that the activity helped to refocus his
mind. It had been nine days now, and still Silver's body
had not turned up. That was curious, he had to admit.
At least it was a little unusual. When the *Marchioness*
pleasure steamer had gone down in the Thames they
had found all fifty-one victims within hours. Cobb
would have expected Silver to be washed up somewhere by now. He took another look at the report
Owens had prepared with the River Police. The ten
most likely sites had not proved likely enough, evidently.
He made a note to call Owens back and get him to go
through the exercise again. The parameters would have
changed completely by now. After nine days and
eighteen tides the body could have drifted clear out
into the Channel. Or it might still be stuck under a
jetty within yards of Lambeth Bridge. Cobb sat back in
his chair. So they did at least have a little mystery to
clear up, after all. He supposed that was something.

Which reminded him. Cobb took the letter of resignation out of his breast pocket and turned it over in his hands. The envelope was beginning to get a little dog-eared. He tore it open, tossed it on the desk, and made out a crisp new envelope. As he did so the heavy paper of the letter unfolded itself before him and he found it impossible to resist the urge to re-read it.

It was strange how different it looked now, in the grey workaday light of a Monday morning. When he had roughed it out at midnight in Clea's room, a couple of days before Christmas, its tone had seemed stately and high-minded: now it looked pompous and belligerent. Cobb was a little ashamed of it, and relieved that he now had the chance to rework it before he needed to deliver it. He resolved to do so that night, back at the Baron's Court flat.

'Mr Cobb?' The female Constable, Carlow, appeared beside his desk. 'It's the path. report you wanted.'

'Right.' Cobb stuffed his resignation letter into the top drawer of his desk. 'Thanks.' If she noticed his hurry she did not show it. Cobb thought that she looked too bored to notice much at all. He took the plastic-bound folder from her and waited while she slouched away across the half-empty room. He flipped open the pathology report.

There was nothing in it which surprised him, and a little which relieved him. The girl had not drowned. Her neck had been broken, as Latimer had guessed, possibly by the impact of the passenger side airbag, which seemed to have caught her across the left ear, judging by heavy bruising there. With no seatbelt attached she would have had very little chance and the bag, inflating in a fraction of a second as the car smacked into the river, must have hit her like a heavyweight's knock-out blow. She was dead, or as good as dead, by the time the car had settled in the water. She had been spared the horror of seeing the black water climb the windows, shutting out the light. Unlike her sister, Cobb reminded himself. Unlike her sister.

He flicked through the remaining pages and then through the sheaf of glossy enlarged photos. The sight of her no longer touched him. He had always found it difficult to be moved by photographs, no matter how graphic. The camera could snapfreeze a sliver of the past, but it could not recreate that past in the present. The glossies looked exactly what they were: clinical, two-dimensional, impersonal. Looking at them now Cobb found it hard even to see the resemblance which had struck him so forcefully at the time. Gudrun had short dark hair like Clea's, and a certain reminiscent squareness to the jaw. It was the most passing similarity. He recognised, with a sense that one more thing was falling back into its proper place, that Gudrun Silver had nothing in common with Clea Cobb except that she had died too young, and on the same day of the year. The phone buzzed and Cobb answered it.

'Mr Cobb? It's Lauren Silver.'

Cobb sat up straight and quickly closed the file to shut out the image of the woman's dead child. He felt as if he had been reading her private letters and that somehow she would know.

'Mrs Silver, I was about to call you.'

'You were?' A note of urgency entered her voice. 'Have you found him?'

'I'm sorry, no, we haven't.'

'Oh.' He could hear the hope drain from her.

'I was going to call you about Freya and the farm.'

'You promised, Mr Cobb. You promised me.'

'Mrs Silver, if you'll let me finish – I've had a word with my father, and I was going to suggest you bring Freya down on Saturday week. It can't be any earlier, I'm afraid. I'm working through next weekend–'

'That will be fine,' she cut in, as if trying to seal the bargain before he could change his mind. 'Saturday week will be fine. Perfect.' Her relief was palpable and it took her a moment to recover her composure. Down the line he heard a glass clink. The pause was so long that he wondered if she had anything else to say. Then she spoke again: 'You need to interview me, don't you?'

'Well, yes–'

'You said at the hospital you'd need to interview me. About that night.'

'When you're up to it, Mrs Silver–'

'I'm up to it. Freya's out of the house. Come down today.'

'Today?'

'Yes. You want me to send a car for you?'

'Of course not. But–'

'You know where it is. Security will let you through.'

She rang off. Cobb replaced the receiver and looked at it for a while. He was tempted to ring her back and explain to her gently but forcefully that minor celebrities did not summon police officers just when they felt like it, even if they were prepared to send cars for them. But he decided he would be doing no one any favours if he let his personal distaste get in the way. He locked away the file, signed himself out, and took the lift down to the basement car park.

The roads were still holiday empty and Cobb reached Virginia Water in a little over forty minutes. He enjoyed the drive. The weather was fine and clear, and a weak sun struck gold bars horizontally through the car as he turned south off the M25 and put the London sprawl behind him. But his mood did not last long. He had not been to Virginia Water for years and had forgotten how much he disliked these fat complacent stockbroker suburbs, their mock-Tudor houses with sweeps of gravel drive unscrolled before them, cluttered with shiny cars. At the age of eleven Cobb had spent a three-month stint at an uncle's house in just such a ghetto while his father attended a Foreign Office course in London, and he remembered it as one of the loneliest periods of his life. He had hated the regimented gardens with their sterile ornamental shrubs and untouchably neat lawns, hated the silence, hated above all the dull suet people under their dull wet skies. They didn't really have a chance, he reflected now, with more charity than he had been able to muster at the time. He had been fresh from his father's posting in

Mombasa then. Portfolio managers from the City could not compete with Masai tribesmen, leaning one-legged on their spears, or with smugglers who fished the reefs off Zanzibar with handgrenades.

Now that he was here, Cobb was surprised that Silver should have had a home in such a place. He had not thought much about it before but he might have expected the man to have an opulent apartment in Mayfair, all blond wood and chrome. Or something at the other extreme – a private island off the wild coast of Ireland, perhaps, inhabited by goats and men with Armalites. Either way he would have expected something exotic. This area was hugely expensive, but exotic it was not. It was in fact eminently respectable. Cobb wondered if this should tell him something about the sort of man Silver had been. And whether it mattered.

He spotted the first security men half a mile away, and soon saw the knot of TV vans clustered outside the tall cypress hedge which screened the house. The media presence had dwindled as the story faded from the front pages. It was one that needed to be fed. Without Silver's dead flesh to sustain it, without any new morsels at all, it was starving away to nothing. Cobb assumed that this must be some sort of relief for Lauren Silver, still besieged here as she was. On the other hand he wondered if she had the capacity to care one way or the other. There were three or four vehicles outside the house and a huddle of weary photographers, stamping in the cold. Security men waved him through on to the drive and a couple of the photographers were bored enough to flash off shots at him and to shout the usual hopeless questions as he drove past.

The house itself was a hundred yards away down a drive of tawny gravel and it repelled him at once, a big, gloomy redbrick place under dark stands of larch. It reminded Cobb of an Edwardian rectory, which perhaps it had been. The whole building had a severe and disapproving air about it, its steep gables lifted in distaste like circumflexed eyebrows. A man was unnecessarily raking twigs from the gravel path at one side of the house and another was polishing a white Citroën nearby. From the mirror brightness of its finish the car looked as if it had been polished several times in the last week. These patently bogus activities and a pattern of inexpertly repaired skidmarks in the gravel were the only traces of drama about the place.

Cobb parked and was met at the door by the Portuguese maid he had seen at the funeral. Even now her face still seemed puffy with weeping. The woman showed him down a long panelled hallway and into a huge sunken room cluttered with oriental teak furniture. One entire wall was clad in leatherbound books behind glass. The red and gold carpets were deep underfoot. The last of the day's delicate sunlight streamed in through glass doors, firing the room's rich colours.

'Mr Cobb.'

He had not seen Lauren, her small figure lost in the scale and complexity of the room. She was smoking.

An ashtray full of butts stood on a sidetable next to a bottle of Stolichnaya vodka which was only a quarter full. She was dressed carelessly in trousers and a sweater of ribbed cream wool which showed up the strain and pallor of her face. Cobb noticed she was wearing no makeup. He wondered how she could stand to wear the heavy wool. He found the room airless. The raw smoke caught at his throat and he would have liked to throw the French windows open to the cool winter parkland outside. It wasn't just the smoke. Tension had somehow seeped into the stale air and hung there like firedamp, waiting to be ignited. She did not rise but waved him to a seat on a blue and gold brocade sofa opposite her.

'Coffee, Mr Cobb? You don't look the drinking type.'

'Coffee's fine.'

'Good choice. Merilda is very good at making coffee.' The implication unmistakably was that Merilda wasn't good for much else.

The woman slid Lauren a stiletto of a look and marched out of the room. Cobb had the feeling that the whole scene was for his benefit – ostentatious drinking and smoking, insults to the servant. It made him uncomfortable and impatient. He felt a fresh rush of misgivings about allowing this woman on to the farm, his haven: he could not imagine how Fred would handle her, and did not think he should have to. But if it was too late to do anything about that now, at least he did not have to put up with this. He resolved to get away as soon as possible. He had better things to do than watch this failed starlet put on her sad little *Sunset Boulevard* performance. Perhaps she read his expression.

'You think this is self-destructive, Inspector?' She held up her glass so that it caught the light. She looked amused by his disapproval. 'That's what Tommy thinks too. But in fact it's the opposite, Mr Cobb. It's self-preservation.'

'There might be better ways of achieving that.'

'Oh, such healthy counsel. But at least I poison myself with care. Not in front of the children, you know.'

Cobb wondered if this was really an accidental slip of the tongue, or a grotesque attempt to seek his attention and perhaps his pity. He said: 'How is your little girl now?'

'You mean, the one that isn't dead?'

So it was grotesque after all. Cobb tried to make allowances for the woman but it angered him all the same. It was a cheap attempt to sting a reaction out of him, all the more infuriating because it had worked. It was an insult to both living and dead and it made him brutal. 'I don't normally ask after the health of dead people, Mrs Silver.'

Her eyes faltered for a second, and he felt mean, but she recovered almost at once, lifting her chin to him. 'Freya may be talking again but that doesn't change the fact that she is depressed and withdrawn and uncommunicative. I cannot reach her, Mr Cobb. I thought she blamed herself for all this. Now I realise that she blames me.'

'I'm sorry about that, Mrs Silver. Very sorry.'

She made a dismissive movement with her cigarette, brushing aside his sympathy, and drank some more vodka. 'She's with her therapist right now. But I doubt they'll get any more out of her than I have.' She shifted in her seat into a pose which was almost a parody of the theatre, cigarette hand flipped back at the wrist beside her face. 'What I can't get them to understand is just how depressed and withdrawn and uncommunicative she was to start with.'

Cobb realised she was very drunk. He waited but she said nothing more, seemed almost to have forgotten his presence.

'Mrs Silver, I really only need to establish exactly what happened on the night of the accident.'

'And that's all you're interested in. Right?'

'It's as far as my job goes, Mrs Silver.' He wondered if he would save time by leaving now. He pulled his legal case up on to the sofa beside him and snicked open the catches.

'He is out there, you know.' She blew smoke in a cloud and peered at him through it. She looked as if she were testing him, challenging him to contradict her, enjoying his discomfort. It was a technique which he imagined she had used in media interviews, projecting an image that was tough, streetwise, a little brassy, in control. It was obvious and it irritated him.

'Yes, well. We'll keep looking.' He might have managed to rise at this point but all at once she was speaking again.

'You know, Mr Cobb, when I met Matthew I thought he was the most magnificent creature who ever walked the earth.'

Oh, Christ, he thought. The poor bloody woman wants to talk. There was a time when Cobb had a reputation as a good listener. Bereaved relatives would ask for him to visit them. It had used up a lot of his time but on the whole he hadn't begrudged it. He wondered what had happened to all that. He just managed to avoid looking at his watch.

'He was an extraordinary talent,' she went on. 'A genius. It put him beyond the normal rules.' She sipped her drink and regarded him over her glass without blinking. 'Do you imagine that genius of that order could just be snuffed out, Mr Cobb? Just like that?'

'Yes.' He stood up, patted his pockets for his car keys. 'Yes, Mrs Silver, I do. I think Matt Silver played some great guitar and wrote some great songs. But when all's said and done he was just an ordinary joe like the rest of us.'

'Well,' she blew a plume of smoke, 'a philosopher *and* a policeman. That's refreshing.'

'And I'm sorry, Mrs Silver, but I believe he's just as dead as the next joe would be, and the sooner you accept it, the more comfort you'll be able to find.'

He dug out his keys, jingled them once, turned on his heel. At that moment Merilda reappeared with the coffee. The maid stared at him in surprise and disappointment as he stood preparing to leave, and the coffee things jingled on the tray she held before her. It seemed she might burst into tears. He found it impossible to walk rudely past her and reject her offering, and as he hesitated Lauren Silver said quietly: 'Please don't leave, Mr Cobb.'

He sat down again and let the woman pour the coffee. The small ceremony took place in a bell jar of strained silence. He lifted his cup and sipped, still avoiding Lauren's eyes. 'You're right,' he said, mainly for Merilda's benefit. 'This is wonderful coffee.' The woman managed a half smile and left the room. Lauren watched her go.

'I can handle this, you know, Mr Cobb,' she said, tilting her glass towards him. 'This stuff, I mean. It's not a problem.'

Cobb nodded and tried not to show his doubt.

'It may look like a problem to you,' she went on, enunciating too clearly, 'but it isn't. It's just because Freya's out.'

'I'm not judging you, Mrs Silver.'

She looked away. After a while she spoke again, in a smaller voice. 'What did you mean when you said "not for long"? On the phone?'

'I'm sorry?'

'I said you were involved, and you said "not for long". What did you mean?'

He put his cup down precisely in the centre of the saucer, so precisely that it made no sound. 'I'm leaving the police, Mrs Silver. I'm resigning.'

'No. You can't do that.' She said it with finality, as if she were a parent refusing him permission to spend a holiday somewhere just a little too adventurous. He could have smiled at the tone, it seemed so inappropriate.

'I'm afraid I've just about done it.'

'But you haven't found Matthew yet. You can't leave.'

He looked at her carefully. Her manner had changed altogether. The pose was gone and she was breathing a little faster. 'You have to find him first.'

'Mrs Silver, I'm part of a team. I don't work alone on this investigation.' As he said this he realised that both statements were essentially false, and stopped talking.

At that moment a door banged. Footsteps clattered in the hallway and someone shouted a greeting. Tommy Hudson came barrelling into the room, shedding coat and scarf as he came. 'Mr Cobb, sorry I'm late. I planned to be here but – well, you know how it is. Something came up.'

Cobb rose and shook hands and Hudson strode over to Lauren and bent to kiss her on the cheek. The caress was brotherly but Cobb detected something different about Hudson, a new assurance, a sense almost of possession. It was not the kiss which alerted him to this so much as the cast-off coat and scarf, slung untidily over a chair as a man might dump his own clothes in his own house. He reminded himself that he had only ever seen Hudson once before in the flesh, and that was at the hospital when the man was grief-stricken and exhausted. It was hardly surprising he seemed more in control now.

'Tommy,' Lauren said, reaching up and urgently gripping Hudson's elbow. 'He says he's resigning.'

'Oh?' Hudson looked up in surprise. 'Laurie wouldn't want you to do that, Mr Cobb. No, we wouldn't want that. Neither of us.'

Cobb could not quite work out how he was supposed to take this. Their concern was so genuine that he was obscurely flattered, and for a moment he was stuck for an answer. He said, feebly: 'I haven't actually resigned yet.'

'Oh, well, that's OK, then,' Hudson ploughed through him. 'Still time to talk you out of it!' He laughed rather too jovially and before Cobb could speak again, turned back to Lauren. 'I'm just taking Mr Cobb into Matt's studio for a minute, Laurie. Something I want to show him. OK?'

Whether it was OK or not, Hudson took Cobb's arm with an irresistible pressure and steered him quickly out of the room. As soon as they were in the hallway, Hudson released his pressure and brushed down Cobb's jacket sleeve where he had gripped his arm, as if he might brush away his uninvited touch.

'Sorry about the manhandling, Mr Cobb. Let's go and have a bit of a chat.'

Cobb allowed himself to be led through the house – a polished dining room, a kitchen suite which would have served a small hotel, a children's playroom bigger than Cobb's flat – and finally through a locked door into a seating area which smelled as if it had been shut up for some time. Leading off this area was a door with

a dark porthole in it and a red light above the lintel.
The heating was off in this part of the house and Cobb
found the chill air a relief after the stifling tension of
the last half hour.

'Mattie's studio,' Hudson said. He pushed open the
portholed door and ushered Cobb through it.

The room was stacked with guitars and keyboards
and computer and recording equipment. There were
no windows and the walls were dull black, so that
when Hudson snapped on the lights the instruments
and electronic gear shone like treasure. A series of
framed photographs hung on the back wall behind the
door and Hudson pointed to each in turn, talking half
to himself.

'That's Matt with McCartney and me at the Trianon
in Park Lane. Night that was! And Mattie and the
Queen at some charity do last year – big royalist he
was, you know. Mightn't think it. Then Matt and
Clapton and Jagger at a gig a couple of years back.
Don't know where I was: taking the picture most
probably . . .' he trailed off.

He turned and waved Cobb to one of the chrome
and leather stools which stood before a control desk as
impossibly intricate as the flight deck of an airliner.

'I spent days in here with Mattie, Mr Cobb. I can
see him now, sitting just where you're sitting, scratching
out riffs on that old Gibson he always used for practice,
playing back old stuff, cursing and swearing.' Hudson
pulled up a second stool and sat down. Cobb wondered
where all this was leading but knew better than to

interrupt. Hudson continued: 'Oh, he was a real perfectionist, Mattie was. Listen to his own stuff over and over – on those headphones right there – till he got it just right. Me, I couldn't hardly tell the difference after the first couple of takes. It all sounded pretty good to me. But not Mattie. Oh, no. Had to be just right for Mattie.' Hudson toyed for a moment with the discarded headphones, turning them in his hand. 'Hey, how about that?' he exclaimed. A single bright black hair was caught in the left earpiece and Hudson touched it, gently, lifting it for Cobb to see. 'Little message from the grave, eh?'

Cobb smiled neutrally. He instinctively distrusted sentimentality, especially Hudson's lachrymose East End variety, but these days he did not feel he had the right to sit in judgement. To him the discovery of the dead man's hair was faintly disgusting, while Hudson would probably make a locket out of it. Cobb supposed one way of handling grief was as valid as another.

'You know, Mr Cobb, Christmas Day I come in here, sat down where you are now in front of that phone and – d'you know what I did?' Cobb looked dutifully interrogative. 'I called him up on his mobile. Mattie, I mean. Crazy, huh? Don't know why I done it.'

The small confession gave Cobb a stab of unease. He had a disturbing vision of Silver's phone warbling hopelessly somewhere far below, rolled among nameless dead things, nudged by a sightless tide. It lifted the hairs on the backs of his arms.

'Talked for about ten minutes, I did.' Hudson smiled at the memory. 'Told him I was sorry for what I done. For stuff I said. Told him I'd take care of things. I'd've looked a proper idiot if he'd answered, eh? Funny thing, though. Felt better afterwards. Could accept it, like.' He stopped, then looked up, blinking quickly. 'Could you do me a big favour, Mr Cobb? Could you put off resigning – just until you find poor Mattie's body?'

'I don't quite–'

'It'd have to turn up in a few days anyway, wouldn't it? Just a few days, Mr Cobb. It'd mean a lot to Laurie.'

'She doesn't even believe he's dead.'

'No, but you do. And when you find him, she'll be able to accept it. Just like I did. She trusts you, Mr Cobb. After what you done for Frey and all. So long as she knows you're looking, she can hold it together. See?'

'Listen, Mr Hudson,' Cobb stood up, 'I'm not making you any promises. We might never find him.'

'She's trying hard with the drink,' Hudson said, as if he had not spoken. 'It mightn't look like it, but she is. I feel like we all owe her a bit of support, know what I mean? Couple of weeks, Mr Cobb. That's all.'

Cobb stared at the ceiling. He did not like being backed into a corner in this way, but on the other hand he could hardly leave the office within two weeks even if he redrafted his resignation that night and put it in the next day.

'Two weeks,' he said.

'Good enough, Mr Cobb. Now let's go back in there and get you a proper statement.'

The thin sun had set by the time Cobb left. He drove back through the dark afternoon oddly liberated by his commitment to Hudson. He tried for the first few miles to convince himself that he resented it, that he had been foolish to allow himself to be thus manoeuvred. But it would not stick. He had to admit he was glad to have a two-week breathing space, a calm period when he could at least go through the motions of doing his job, let things settle. At the end of that time he would be able to go to Sykes with his decision, and hand in a dignified and intelligent resignation – one that didn't read as if it had been written by an undergraduate. And by then the Silver investigation would have resolved itself. The likeliest scenario was that Silver's body was simply snagged somewhere and very soon would bloat with its own gases, pull itself free and bob up to the surface like some monstrous balloon. Cobb could not guess how Lauren Silver would react when it did. He was certain, though, that closure would be better than uncertainty for her and the child, and for their sake he hoped it happened quickly. He only half admitted to himself a less generous hope: that Silver would make his final entrance before Saturday week. Perhaps that would generate enough confusion to make them all forget about visiting the farm.

Cobb joined the ribbon of tail lights on the

motorway, a chain of rubies, snaking ahead into the deepening night at a steady 50 m.p.h. He found a Corelli CD and slipped it into the player. It began to rain a little and the music and the sighing of the wipers and the assured rhythm of his driving relaxed him. Quite unexpectedly Cobb felt a layer of self-deception peel away, like a scab sloughed from a wound. He might have put on a convincing show for the task force but he had not been doing his job. He had let personal problems cloud his judgement. There was more he could do if he was serious about his assignment. And he should be serious. If not, he would be buying into a cynical agenda set by other men. This suddenly made sense to him and he felt his spirits lift at once. It might be a lousy job but it was the job he had been given. If it were to be his last one as a police officer, he would at least allow himself the satisfaction of doing it meticulously well.

Cobb turned the volume of the music down and used the carphone to call Accident Investigation at Barnes.

27

Sergeant Maxey, who met Cobb at 8.30 the next morning at the Barnes garage, was a small, neat man with the precise manner of a lecturer in engineering. He had receding hair and a beard without the matching moustache, which left his mouth looking exposed like a soft polyp in a nest of trimmed hair. The affectation amused Cobb. It made him think of mill workers from the days of the Industrial Revolution. He decided that Sergeant Maxey was a connoisseur of real ale and that he restored old steam engines as a pastime – restored them immaculately, by hand, and with a watchmaker's precision. He followed the other man's straight back out of the station and across a car park into a steel hangar crowded with vehicles, some twisted almost beyond recognition, some apparently unmarked.

The Jaguar lay halfway along one row, leaning slightly to one side on a flat offside front tyre, the driver's door open a little but taped to prevent it swinging wide.

'It's hard to know what to show you, Mr Cobb, without a clear idea of what you're looking for.' Maxey's small mouth was pursed with disapproval. Cobb's visit was irregular and inconvenient and had interrupted his careful routine.

Cobb, who had very little idea himself of what he was looking for, moved around the car slowly. Now that he was here, it disappointed him. It seemed sad and diminished, its dark blue paintwork smeared and dirty. A film of rust was already blooming on exposed patches of metal where the impact had stripped away the paint. One headlight assembly hung half out of its fitting, like an eyeball from its socket. The Jaguar's sunroof, windscreen and driver's window had all been shattered, and this was more obvious under the striplighting of the garage than when he had first seen the car at Lambeth Bridge. The Jaguar looked smaller than he remembered, and was entirely shorn of the fatal glamour it had possessed when he had watched it swinging in on a crane jib above his head, the Thames sluicing out of every opening.

Cobb mooched around the wreck, feeling Maxey's gaze follow him. The Sergeant's air was quietly proprietorial, as though he owned the car and Cobb was a prospective buyer, and an unlikely one at that.

'Just trying to get a feel for what happened,' Cobb said, resisting the urge to kick the tyres.

'It'll all be in the report, of course.' Maxey sniffed. 'You could always wait for that. Sir.'

Cobb stared at him. To his satisfaction, Maxey stiffened and looked away into the middle distance. Cobb let him stew for a few moments. Finally he said: 'You're the expert, Sergeant. How do you think this happened?'

Such an appeal was calculated to unbend Maxey at

once. He would have a theory, Cobb knew. He was the sort of man who always had a theory. 'After she hit the water, you mean, sir?'

'That's right. That's exactly what I mean.'

'Well, not wanting to pre-empt the report in any way . . .'

'This is informal. I'm just interested in your opinion, that's all.'

'Well, sir, I see it this way.' Maxey positioned himself in front of Cobb, his humourless face suddenly alive. His hands began a small ballet in the air. 'He clipped the railings with the driver's side. That popped the headlight and accounts for these gouges. You see? That might have been what burst the driver's door open too. But also the impact flipped the car over so that it hit the water more or less on its roof. By then it's travelling at – oh – sixty or seventy. Out goes the side window. Bang. Out goes the screen. Bang. Maybe the sunroof too. Bang. She fills up with water, and down she goes.'

'Not quite immediately. It was still afloat when our lads arrived.'

'Yes.' Maxey raised one finger. He had this covered. 'Quite right. There's a good deal of air trapped in the back of the car, do you see? The boot stayed closed. That kept it afloat for a minute or two. Long enough for the two officers to get to the bridge and watch it sink.'

'The divers say the car was the right way up on the bottom.'

'That's quite correct, Mr Cobb.' Maxey was

animated now. He was the type of man who could forgive anyone for ignorance provided they showed interest in his subject and thus allowed him to shine. 'That's quite so. But –' he held up a finger '– think about it. Most of the car's weight is concentrated in the wheels and the subframe, and of course the engine. As it fills up with water and sinks it will gradually right itself and go down by the nose, faster and faster.' Maxey demonstrated this with a twisting, descending movement of his flattened hand. 'See what I mean?'

'I'm with you. Can we look inside?'

'Of course, sir. The forensic people have already been over her.'

Maxey produced a Swiss Army knife and folded out a pair of scissors from it. Cobb knew Swiss Army knives had scissors but had never seen anyone take the trouble to use them. The Sergeant snipped the tape and tugged on the door to open it. It was stiff and twisted on its hinges and it groaned a little as it opened. Cobb stuck his head inside. It still stank of the river, a tomb smell, and the tan hide upholstery was streaked with filth. The deflated airbags lay draped across the dashboard.

'What do you think happened in here, Sergeant?'

'Oh.' Maxey sucked his teeth; this was a little too far into the realms of speculation. 'I wouldn't like to hazard a guess, sir.'

'Me neither.'

Cobb leaned in, poked between the seats. Nothing. He felt inside the glove box: a plastic-covered manual, some sort of insurance folder. He wanted the car to speak to him but there was nothing here. Despite the filth, the Jaguar had the sterility of the showroom. He was not surprised that the Accident Investigation people had not found so much as a loose coin under the seat.

'Me neither. But hazard one anyway.'

'Well, Mr Cobb,' Maxey looked doubtful, 'I don't think they'd have known a lot about it. They weren't strapped in, you know. Not that that would have helped, probably.'

'So.' Cobb pulled himself out of the car and wiped dirt off his fingers. 'We've got one little girl in the front. She was dead virtually on impact. We've got the driver – dead or unconscious, his body thrown out through the open door, presumably, when it hit the water.'

'Not right away, sir. There's water rushing in through the window and the screen, remember. Tons of it. It would tend to pin the deceased in there till the car sank far enough and the pressure equalised. Then it might float him out through the open door.'

'Fair enough. But meanwhile we've got the other kid in the back, protected by the front seats, injured but perhaps conscious.'

'She must have had a very nasty time of it, sir,' Maxey said. 'Very nasty indeed. Completely black. The car filling up. The noise. The pocket of air squeezing down to nothing. She wouldn't have known which way was up. Literally, I mean.'

'But she got out. How?'

'The sunroof, sir. At least, that's the theory.' Maxey coughed delicately.

'Oh, yes?'

'Well, sir, the idea is that once the pressure equalises – that is, the water has more or less filled the car and stopped rushing in – then it would be technically possible for her to get out of the broken sunroof. Or be washed out. Maybe as the car settled on the riverbed the last of the air escaped that way, and sort of belched her out. Could happen.'

Cobb felt his interest quicken. It was an instinctive prickling of his senses. There was nothing logical about it.

'You don't sound very confident, Sergeant.'

'I wouldn't say that exactly, Mr Cobb.' But Maxey clearly could not wait to take a shot at the authorised version, and Cobb only had to wait politely for him to do so. 'The other lads say I've got a bee in my bonnet, but – well, you have a look at this, Mr Cobb.' He stepped over to the car and leaned across the roof. 'You feel the edge of that, sir. Mind the glass.'

Cobb ran his hand along the lip of the broken sunroof. A few crumbs of shatterproof glass dislodged and fell pattering inside the car.

'What about it?'

'Just there. Excuse me, sir.' Maxey took Cobb's hand and guided it to the forward edge of the fitting. 'There. Feel that? The sunroof assembly sits inside these channels. That's what it slides in to open and close.

Just here the edges of the channels are bent upwards. Outwards.'

'You think it was forced out from the inside? Not pushed in when the car hit the water?'

'Maybe the air pressure inside the car blew it out,' Maxey said carefully. 'That's what the lads think. Myself, I wouldn't have thought the pressure would be nearly great enough. But I'm in the minority.'

'So in your mind you've got a picture of this Jaguar settling on the bottom of the Thames with the sunroof still in place.'

'Correct.'

'If you don't think the air pressure popped it out – what did?'

'Oh, any number of things,' Maxey said, closing down. 'Maybe the sunroof stayed in place all along and the child got out some other way. In that case our lads might have broken the roof when they fished the car out.'

'Is that likely?'

'It's perfectly possible.' The Sergeant shrugged. 'When you've seen as many crashes as I have, Mr Cobb, you know that almost anything can happen.'

'Does that include miracles?'

Maxey smiled knowingly, as if he had expected this. 'There's always an explanation,' he said, stroking his polyp of a mouth complacently, 'and usually a boring one.'

Cobb drove thoughtfully back to the office and

immediately put in a call to John Piggott. He had not expected to reach Piggott straight away but in fact contacted him at the first try in his office at the Institute for Naval Medicine near Gosport. He had known Piggott, a large, pink man with a sly sense of humour, for over twenty years. They had met on a diving course during Cobb's short service commission. Piggott had stayed in the Navy and was now a Surgeon Commander, carving out a niche for himself in survival medicine.

'So your man's in pretty good physical shape?' he was saying, checking the notes he had taken while Cobb was talking.

'By all accounts, yes.'

'But stuffed full of laughing powder and grog?'

'Right.'

'And injured. Though you don't know how badly.'

'Personally I think he's dead by this time, but—'

'Oh, now if he was dead, I doubt his chances of survival would be very high at all. You can't quote me on that, of course, but I believe most medical opinion would concur. Not all of it, I grant you.'

'John, are you planning to be any help at all?'

'Well, there's not much I can tell you, Sam, if you don't know whether the poor bastard twisted his ankle or ruptured his jugular. Such details affect his chances just a bit.'

'The car hits the water at speed. He isn't wearing a seatbelt but there are airbags and they do operate. The car has a collapsible steering column and all the other safety gadgets. The front end isn't too badly damaged. I think he might have survived the crash.'

'And you want to know if he might have survived the river too?'

'Right.'

'In December? The Thames? Yes, he might have. In theory. People survive all sorts of things, even when they're impossible.'

'What does that mean?'

'An example, for your edification. If you fall into the Arctic Ocean at this time of year – and it's a bit nippy up there, with ice floes and such – you should live about two minutes. That's literally one hundred and twenty seconds I'm talking about. But we know of cases where people have survived for hours. Days, sometimes. It's very rare, but it happens. There's not always a logical reason we can find. And let me tell you, the Thames is a warm bath compared to that. All the same, about twenty-five per cent of people who fall in will be dead in two or three minutes. Another twenty-five per cent could last up to two hours. The rest somewhere in between. There's no telling.'

Cobb was silent for a moment.

Piggott said: 'What's up, Sam? Blown another pet theory to buggery, have I? Don't despair. If it makes you any happier, the entire scenario is pretty unlikely. Your man might be in good nick, but he's still an ageing drug-crazed rock star.'

'He's only our age.'

'That's what I mean. The people we look at are

normally young, trained, and at least familiar with the sea. Mental preparedness is a big factor. Your chap isn't planning to end his evening on the bottom of the Thames in a bent Jag. It comes as a surprise to him. Quite a shock, in fact. And even if he hasn't been too badly chewed up, he's just been belted in the face by an airbag, which – let me tell you – packs a punch like Mike Tyson. Hard enough to break your nose. A thing like that affects your thinking, especially if you're underwater, in the dark, it's bloody cold and you're scared shitless. For him to gather his wits and get out of that, he'd need to be Harry bloody Houdini, if you want my opinion.'

'Right.'

'And on top of that, you'd have to ask what he'd have done if he did manage to get free. I know what I'd do. If I couldn't reach the bank, I'd be thrashing around and hollering until you chaps pulled me out. But he didn't do that.'

'He had just killed his own daughter.'

'Too clever. This is survival, Sam. Morality doesn't come into it.'

'What if he was unconscious?'

'Then you're right on one score. He'd be doing a lot less thrashing about and hollering. But on the other hand he'd probably be dead anyway. Unconscious men float on their faces. Women float on their backs. It's the tits.'

'Always?'

'Not always, but usually, unless there's a good deal

of air trapped in the clothing. You know, a nylon anorak or a flying suit can act like a lifejacket.'

Cobb held the phone and said nothing for a moment. He thought again of the mud-smeared upholstery, and of Maxey's hand guiding his own fingertips along the buckled runner of the sunroof.

'John, it'd all be adrenalin, right? Pure blind instinct?' He was not sure exactly what he wanted to say and let his voice trail off.

'I think he's trying to tell us something,' Piggott said in a stage whisper, as if to a third party.

'What I mean is, there'd be no chance of . . . thinking straight, of acting logically?'

'You want to know what it was like in there?' Piggott said, interpreting Cobb's line of thinking only half correctly. 'You still dive, don't you, Sam?'

'Not much.'

'But still, you know the answer to that one better than I do. It's cold. It's dark. He's in shock and he's hurt and he's trapped. If he sees a way out of that and can get his head together enough to take it, he'd be out of there and heading for the moonlight like a fucking Trident missile. He wouldn't stay to look for his car keys.'

'No,' Cobb agreed. 'Not for his car keys.'

28

He sank to a bitter black place. A nameless roaring filled this place and a dank and rotting taste. Strange flashes spiked the blackness, spokes of blurred light. The monster had him now, the swamp monster, plunging down, down into the pit while he clung to it, beating at it, his body streaming upwards in the night. The creature's eyes threw poles of yellow light into the dark, poles which wobbled and canted as it dived. The eyes illuminated nothing. The blackness roared ever louder and crushed in on him until the anvil weight of it was unendurable. He locked his lungs against his lust for breath, for here he could breathe only the death he knew he had earned. There was agony but at a remove, as if the pain were twisting some other body. He was damaged, he could feel torn flesh, broken bone, but he clawed at the monster as it plunged, flailing at it with helpless, futile blows. He knew he must rip through its carapace and open its steel belly to where his very soul lay suffocating. And yet, as he struggled, he knew he had already failed, failed past all hope of absolution. The monster plunged on, faster, belching out silver orbs which roiled up past the man and wrenched his grip away as they passed. When he looked again it was gone, its insane eyes spinning into the void below him. He breathed death.

Being dead, he awoke at that precise moment every time. How many times he did not know: such matters had lost all meaning. It was more in the nature of a continuous loop of horror that brought him back to the same awful place, again and again. He was trapped in the ever-repeating loop, and trapped in this place, forever sucked down into the same vortex, clutched by the same monster. Over and over again he would hear a voice shrieking in panic and know it to be his own. And then the screaming would twist into the wailing of a siren and the frightened cry of a child and he would feel himself vaulted out into blackness again and there would be a vast explosion and then a nameless roaring would fill the world and he would be diving once again into the same black and bitter place, clinging to the carapace, watching the wobbling lances of the eyes.

And then one day it stopped.

On that day he awoke and knew that he was back in the world. That much he did know, though it was hard to be sure of anything else. He recognised the familiarity of things without being able to identify what they meant, or even what they were. The harshness of wool on his skin, the cool flow of an indrawn breath, a girl's voice singing somewhere close. He could not place these things at first, but he knew clearly, and with the freshness of rediscovery, that they did have a place and that on some level they were familiar to him. Perhaps he had been drifting in and out of sleep during a long drowsy afternoon and had slipped gently back into wakefulness on some grassy bank, comfortable, rested, but unsure of exactly where he was. Who he was. He was aware that his mind had been dislocated in some way and that now, somehow, it had booted up again and the dormant aisles of his memory were beginning to flicker alight once more. Something animal in him took comfort in this. Something more human told him to dread it.

Perhaps the girl's voice had touched him awake. She was still singing sweetly, a little off-key, a song in which his name was intertwined. The childishness of her voice soothed him. He did not need to ask questions about the song or the singer – their origin, their meaning. For the moment the song was enough. Indeed it seemed to him as he lay there that the girl's song had always been with him; that it was all he needed. That – if he had only known it – there had never been need for more than this.

> *I dreamed I saw Joe Hill last night*
> *Alive as you or me.*

He remembered patterns and sensations from a time before the song, as a baby might. A lattice of light which shifted in a slow and stately rhythm around the space in which he lay. The light was warm when it brushed over him. A clattering and roaring which came with the swelling light. And later, when the light had gone and his space had grown blue and chill, laughter and shouting and the clinking of glasses from somewhere below. He did not know what any of this meant, but he knew he was not alone in this universe. Sometimes, he had no idea how often, the body he now knew to be his was gripped, moved, lifted. This handling did not hurt him, although it was often clumsy. He was aware only of the sudden sting of cold water, sometimes on his skin and sometimes in his throat. He was aware of voices. He could not understand the words these voices used, but sometimes he recognised aggression in them, as he would recognise it in the snarling of a dog, and sometimes a certain rough kindness.

Sounds and images of remarkable clarity began to float in to him. The vision of a woman, seated in a chair in a slant of moonlight, smoking, watching him. Her face was ugly and should have been frightening, but it was not. The jingle of bottles on a milk float somewhere close and the whine of its electric motor. The rough honest texture of bare roof timber just above his head. It was as if his mind were beginning to string these vignettes together, as if he were beginning to glimpse some cohesion in them.

> *Says I, 'But, Joe, you're ten years dead.'*
> *'I never died,' said he.*

'I never died,' Silver said, and suddenly he was entirely conscious.

'Didn'tcha, now?' Maggie Turpin's voice answered him from the gloom under the attic roof. 'If you didn't, you was pretty bleeding close.'

'I never died,' said he.

Silver rolled his head with an effort and saw her lumpy silhouette in the cool evening light. The singing came to an end and there was a distant popping of applause, a few bawdy shouts, the chime of a till and a ringing of glass.

'Playing your song, was she?' Maggie Turpin said, rising, taking up a plastic drinks bottle. 'Is that what done it?'

'I know it,' he said. 'The song.'

'You should. She's played it every Saturday night for the last three weeks.'

'Three weeks?'

She lifted his head up an inch and tilted the plastic bottle against his lips. The taste was unbearably exotic. It was orange juice.

'Three weeks,' he repeated.

'Oh, you been here and not here. Don't remember much, eh?'

'But three weeks.'

'Since we come to the Nile.'

The Nile? It seemed no crazier than anything else. Silver lay back and closed his eyes, his mind beginning to churn and mesh. He meant to ask her questions but when he looked again the woman had moved quietly away, thinking perhaps that he had drifted off. He was in a cot of some kind – perhaps a folding bed – in a low, angled space under the roof of some quite large building. He remembered the clinking glasses and the beery laughter and knew that he was in some kind of space above a bar, and in his mind's eye he saw a pub sign: a ship-of-the-line, spewing smoke. The Battle of the Nile. He could not see the street but the dull boom of the traffic was almost constant some way below him, the whining gears of trucks and buses, occasional whooping sirens from police cars or fire engines.

The attic had been planked and roughly partitioned with chipboard and sacking tacked to the upright timbers. A bare bulb hung from the centre of the space, roped to the battens of the roof with cobwebs. It gave a miserable yellow light. A chimney breast of red brick rose through the floor, fluffy with soot and dust. It was as if someone had begun to convert the loft of the place into a flat and had given up well short of halfway. In one recess there was a toilet bowl and an old enamel bath and a sink growing out of the wall, like a clumsily made china flower on the stem of its waste pipe. Silver rolled his head to see more. A section of the roof space near the head of the stairs was partly screened off with sacking and loose plywood. Through a gap in this screen Silver could see a stained mattress and a ruck of blankets, a crucifix hanging crooked from a beam, a scatter of McEwan's Export cans on the bare boards. There was a collapsed armchair in there too, and as he looked he noticed for the first time that the man Stevens was slumped in this chair, watching him from the shadows, one of the tall cans cradled between his hands. Silver read hostility and contempt in the man's look, a slow-burning aggression which made him feel weak and vulnerable. He turned his eyes away to avoid it, and as he did so he heard Stevens crush the beer can in his fist and toss it clattering against the wall.

After a while the woman came back into his field of vision. He saw her move across to the sullen Stevens and hiss commands at him, half-dragging him to his feet. Then she took up an old shopping bag and pushed Stevens in front of her down the wooden stairs and out through a street door, and all at once Silver was alone in the mean shambles of an attic. He heard the door close and her footsteps tapping across the car park, the busy steps of someone with a mission, with Stevens clumping beside her. Silver felt strangely hollow to be left here, helpless and alone. The remaining light faded as he watched. Perhaps he had been alone before during the three weeks she spoke of – probably he had – but he could not remember it. He felt a twinge of panic and fought to control it, forcing himself to think.

Three weeks. That would make it mid-January. He could see a slice of window from his cot: a parallelogram of grey sky with a bare treetop etched across it, like cracks in the glass. Three weeks. Gudrun, the child of his flesh, the child he had killed, dead three weeks. And yet the world ground on somehow. He thought there had to be a message in this but he could not work out what it was. He tried to move and found he had the strength now to lift his knees a few inches to tent the blanket. He could flex the muscles of his shoulders too. He could not see his hands, what was left of them, but he could make weak fists of them. He did so, again and again, under the urging of some primitive impulse. He could not guess at the reason but his body was healing around him in the dimness. He thought of the web of arteries and veins, the skeins of muscle, the long snake of gut, feeding it all, the constant, relentless repair. It made no sense. It seemed that he healed just as quickly as a man who had not murdered his own daughter.

He lay in the dark and forced his mind to focus, but he could not call her face up before him. He was not to be granted that. He could remember a Gudrun, but only as an abstraction, as someone else's laughing, pretty, warm-skinned, milk-scented child. He could not see her beyond that. Instead his brain conjured up a jumble of disconnected images, gravid with a meaning he could not clearly interpret. He had a vision of a man on a stage before a vast audience, of an airport at night, the grumble of an engine, the creak of leather, the smell of power. He remembered Lauren's white and frightened face, begging him. After that, something snapped like the released string of a crossbow and he felt himself bolted out along some long ramp of light, meteors flicking past, a shining Camelot spread below. And then . . . After that he knew the dream began again, and, terrified, his mind closed to it. Of Gudrun herself he saw nothing, or only at a remove, as if he looked at a photograph of her. These were the climactic moments of her short life, but he, her father, her killer, had no memory of them. It seemed like the final betrayal. He breathed alone in the dark room.

Three weeks. Why had they not found him? Presumably because they were not looking. Whatever the reason, he was glad not to be found, though he could not decide why it was important to him. If he could have finished it on that first night he would have done so. Had been desperate to do so. Yet here he still was, his body knitting back together, growing stronger, undetected, unsought. In some sense free. Three whole weeks later.

There was an elderly upright paraffin heater in the corner and the heady smell of it filled the space under the angled roof. It was a comfortable, old-fashioned smell and it gave him some comfort to listen to the tune the metal sang as the stove heated. He remembered an old aunt of his in Whitby had owned a stove like this, years ago, when he was a child. The aunt also owned an ancient piano of lacquered wood, a Steinway, which even then he could play well – better, probably, than anyone had ever played it. He stared up at the dim timbers. Between the exposed tiles he could see cracks of light and they faded as the winter evening fell. The steely light reminded him of the north, and for the first time he thought of Freya. He still lived, after a fashion, and she still lived, when both should have died. But what was this grotesque half-life for? He could not decide. He felt as if he had been given a coded message, but without the cipher. Perhaps he slept then, though he was not aware of either sleeping or waking. He heard the street door bang and the woman's footsteps on the stair again, and was glad not to be alone any longer.

Later he sat naked on the edge of the stained bath. The cold enamel branded his buttocks but he was unwilling to stand up again for the moment. The effort of standing was enormous. Without the old woman's help he would never have got this far – had never got this far, apparently, in all those three weeks. It didn't surprise him. He looked down and surveyed his ruined body. He was perhaps seven stone. He had always been a big man. Now he was a camel, a spider, with stick limbs and big knobbled joints. His hands and feet seemed huge to him. The stump of his missing finger itched as his body gradually came alive. His muscles were milk weak. Every action exhausted him, and even now he could feel his heart banging. When he looked down he could see it fluttering the skin between his ribs, among the untidy knots of bone where the broken cage had half-healed.

Silver steadied himself against the enamel bath, drew in a breath, and stood as quickly as he dared, hooking his good hand through a hole in the fibreboard of the wall. Now he could almost look into it, the triangle of light which hung on the joist above the cistern. Another shuffling step and he was there, his panting breath steaming the glass. For just a second as the mist cleared he thought he had been mistaken and that this was a window into some other desperate soul's hideaway up among the roof timbers. He felt his strength ebb. He took another breath. Another. His right knee began to give and he locked it against the edge of the toilet bowl or he would have fallen. It was not a window. It was a mirror, or a shard of mirror, and he was the broken derelict who looked out from it. Another breath. Another. He felt a cold sweat began to distil on his skin and leaned his forehead against the timber of the joist. He was desperate not to let go. Standing upright, like a man again, was a precious agony. At length his pulse steadied. He lifted his head and looked again.

The face was gaunt and yellow, the jawline grizzled with stubble. Most of the hair was gone, inexpertly hacked off close to the scalp. Where it was growing back it was iron grey. The eyes were huge and luminous like a starved animal's. Three puckered scars ran diagonally across the face, as deep and coarse as the stitching on a leather ball. The deepest of them ran from the right eye socket to the mouth like a sabre slash. It tugged down the edge of both eyelid and lip, leaving them out-turned, red and dry.

'You won't be pretty no more, Joe,' the woman observed. She sounded strangely indifferent. She had pulled the sacking aside and was watching him. He touched his face with his fingers, felt the length of the scars. 'I'm not much at nursemaiding but I done me best for you. All the same, you won't be pretty no more.' He leaned into the reflection, fingering the contours of his new, ravaged face. Something in the way he did it made her cock her head like an old rook and look at him narrowly. 'All the king's horses, Joe, and all the king's men . . .' He fingered his ruined face again, tugged at the shiny scarred skin. It was impossible to believe that this grotesque mask belonged to him. She went on cheerfully: 'I even tried praying! You ask Stevie. He thinks I'm proper cracked, he does.'

Silver leaned on the edge of the bath, fighting for breath and for control. She did not seem to notice his distress. After a while he forced himself to stare into the shard of mirror again.

'Look at me,' he whispered. 'Just look at me.'

She focused her ancient eyes on him for the first time and her voice changed. 'No one wants to look at you no more, Joe.'

He said: 'I killed my little girl.'

'That's right.' Maggie Turpin glanced at her cheap wristwatch as if she might be late for the hairdresser's. 'But then, you got another one.'

29

'So people used to live up here, is that right, Mr Cobb? I mean, it was like a regular town in the old days?'

Tommy Hudson was trying so hard that Cobb found it embarrassing to watch. It was impossible not to take pity on him. 'We'll have to stop this Mr Cobb business. Call me Sam.'

'It's force of habit with policemen. But Sam it is, then.' Hudson smiled ferociously and stuck out his paw from the folds of his anorak. Cobb took the big scarred hand uncomfortably. 'So, Sam, this was a town, eh? What d'you think of that, girls?' he shouted over his shoulder and swept his arm out towards the low green hummocks which spread across the paddock and into the commonland beyond the hedge.

Within the field boundary the mounds had been ploughed almost flat over the centuries but on the common they still stood out sharply, two or three feet proud of the turf, overgrown with ash and hawthorn. Cobb turned and saw Lauren, still hunched in the Land Rover twenty yards away, staring through the streaked windscreen. Cobb could see the smear of her cigarette smoke as the wind whipped it away through the passenger window. For a moment he couldn't see the child but then spotted her, half hidden behind the oak in the corner of the field, a small figure in a red parka, watching them through the rain. As his eyes met hers, the girl left the cover of the tree trunk and trudged towards them through the wet grass. She stood three feet away from Hudson's leg, her head reaching the level of his thigh. The big man moved to rest his broad hand on her shoulder but she took a step away. Cobb pretended not to notice.

'What d'you think of that, Frey?' Hudson cried. 'A whole town. Right here.'

'A village, anyway,' Cobb said, speaking to include the child. 'It even had a name. Funny name, too.'

Freya frowned at him suspiciously. 'What name?'

'It was called Piddle in the Sludge.'

'Piddle in the Sludge!' Hudson shouted. 'You hear that, Frey? You're a card, you are, Sammy boy.'

Cobb winced but Hudson didn't register it. He was too busy slapping his thigh and bellowing with laughter.

'You're tricking me,' the girl told Cobb coolly. 'Like you did about the dinosaurs.'

'The dinosaurs? Oh, they don't hatch out till spring. Like ducklings. Couple of months and the fields will be pink with them.'

'That's a fib.'

'Would I lie to you? I'm a policeman.'

'You're tricking me,' she repeated, glowering at him. If this was a game, she wasn't playing.

'Yes. Guilty as charged, ma'am. It was really called Upper Durning. That's why the farm is called Lower Durning. Only now, Upper Durning's lower than Lower

Durning, if you see what I mean. So maybe we should call it Lower Upper Durning. Or maybe Lower Lower–'

'Don't make fun,' she told him. 'If it was called that, why did you say it was called Piddle in the . .' She tripped over the foolish, nursery-naughty word and for a moment Cobb saw the mask of her gravity slip and his heart went out to her in a swoop that caught him off guard. He crouched down to meet her eyes.

'To make you laugh, Princess,' he said. Freya gazed up at him unblinking through her rain-speckled glasses, holding his eyes, and he repeated, 'I said it to make you laugh.'

'Well, he made *me* laugh,' Hudson shouted, proving it by guffawing like a maniac in the rain. 'Oh, he made me laugh all right!'

'That's because you're stupid!' the girl spat at him with sudden malice and flung away from the two men, stumping off towards the tumuli of the ghost village. Hudson pulled a face, inviting commiseration, but Cobb could see he was hurt and felt sorry for him.

'Let's go grab a beer, Tommy. We're all getting soaked out here. You go back to the car and I'll fetch her.'

Hudson hesitated for a moment, then nodded and plodded off to the Land Rover.

The rain was rolling in grey waves across the hills now and Cobb could hear the water chuckling in the ditch under the hawthorn hedge. She was standing on the highest of the mounds, under the oak where he habitually sat. Bare winter saplings whipped around her in the wind. Cobb climbed up beside her.

'Let's go, Freya. We'll all grow gills if we stay out in this, like little fishes.'

'Did people really live here?'

'Yes, they did. They had houses and streets and shops too. In the spring, when the new wheat is just coming up, you can see where the main street went – right across that field. There's a sort of depression there. The road went all the way to Oxford. There's still a footpath along the route of it.'

'When did people live here?'

'More than three hundred years ago. Up to the 1660s.'

'Why did they leave?'

Cobb had this one covered. The people left because the river silted up and they couldn't get the boats up any more, so they all moved to Burford. It wasn't true but he had rehearsed it and knew it would work. But as he paused, Freya looked up at him from under the hood of her parka.

'The Plague,' he said, meeting her eyes. 'There was a dreadful disease which swept the whole country and so many of the people here died that the others couldn't carry on working the fields. The few who survived just moved away.'

She nodded. 'But you tricked me about the dinosaurs,' she said.

30

'You mean, I can talk to anyone in the world with this thing?' Fred sounded incredulous.

'I told you,' the girl said crossly. 'It's e-mail. We use it at school all the time.'

'Well, blow me down and shiver me timbers, and all that sort of thing. You mean, I could do that and I never knew it? I must be a silly old duffer.'

Freya gave him a look through her glasses which suggested he might be just that. 'Everyone knows about e-mail,' she told him, and then added in an undertone: 'Except Uncle Tommy.'

'Frey.' Lauren spoke sharply from the fireside, but without looking up. It was the first word Cobb had heard her speak since lunch.

'Well, it's true,' the girl said sullenly. 'He's stupid.'

This time Lauren turned to face her daughter across the room. 'Freya! I've told you.'

'I think Uncle Tommy and I must be in the same boat, then,' Fred put in, defusing the exchange. 'Because I've never heard of this she-mail thing either.'

'E-mail,' she insisted. 'It's called e-mail.'

'He-mail. Right. Maybe you'd better show me how to use it, young Miss Freya, since you know so much about it.'

Freya hesitated. For a moment Cobb thought she would not be able to turn her back on the challenge. But then she slipped down from the chair, walked across the room and silently pulled herself up on to the monk's seat beside Cobb.

He let his hand rest across the child's shoulder. It struck him that it was an occasion indeed when anyone found him more charming than his father. Fred was a natural diplomat. Cobb had seen him, with his snowy hair and his old tweed jacket, enter a room full of aggressive student activists and within ten minutes have them roaring with laughter at his dreadful jokes. The old man could still quieten a noisy council meeting just by walking into the chamber, using some mystical alchemy of authority and good manners. Cobb well knew he had inherited little of this. He told much better jokes than his father, but people always detected an edge in them. Though they found him smart, they knew his father to be wise.

But even Fred's diplomatic skills had been stretched today. Cobb knew the dull afternoon could have been a disaster without him. He found that he loathed having these people here every bit as much as he had feared he would, but had done his best to plan a busy and entertaining day for them, nevertheless. He had in mind a visit to the abandoned village, a walk along the river and a pub lunch at the Feathers, then an hour or two annoying Mrs Buckets and the other animals back at the farm. He would be nice to everyone. He would talk to Freya if the poor girl wanted to talk. He would treat

Lauren gently. He would be friendly to Tommy Hudson. He would be the perfect host and countryside guide. And at the end of the day he would get rid of the lot of them.

But it hadn't worked out like that. The January weather had turned so foul that they had been imprisoned in the farmhouse since mid-morning. Fred had been equal to it. Cobb suspected that his father enjoyed the challenge of making this odd crew of visitors feel at home. He had certainly succeeded as far as anyone could. He filled the dim farmhouse with light and music, made great theatre out of cooking an enormous roast and co-opting Freya to help, allocated an endless stream of jobs to Cobb and Hudson as if they were small boys: build up the fire, open the wine, set the table.

Only the woman had been left alone. She sat close to the fire, staring at the flames, while activity broke around her like surf. If Hudson had not helped her, Cobb doubted she would have stirred even to take off her coat. Cobb watched her during the meal. She wore no makeup and her fair hair was scraped back so severely that it looked painful. He could see blue veins under the tight skin of her forehead. She ate little, and said just enough to register her presence. She reminded Cobb of a nun, sitting silent and obedient with her eyes cast down. She responded meekly to Hudson's clumsy attentions, allowing him to seat her at the table, to pass dishes to her. In response she gave him an occasional distracted smile or a quiet word. There was a profound servility about her that seemed out of character. Cobb noticed that she did not touch the wine and wondered if the effort of self-denial was taking all her strength. He was ashamed of himself but could not suppress his resentment. She was a cold presence, like a corpse laid out in a room: it was impossible not to look at her, and having looked, impossible not to feel his own life stilled a little. He did not want her in his home.

Cobb noticed Hudson stealing a glance at his watch and guiltily he felt his heart lift. Perhaps they were about to leave. Then abruptly Hudson sat up and looked towards the kitchen. 'Was that my phone?'

Cobb said: 'I didn't hear anything.'

'I bet it was. It's in my coat out back. Be right back.' He made for the kitchen like a halfback, and as he left Cobb distinctly heard the burr of a mobile phone from near the back door. He glanced up at the sound and saw Lauren Silver watching Hudson's retreating back, for the first time with a light in her eyes that might almost have been cunning. In a few moments Hudson was back. He held out his mobile phone for the group of them to see and tapped it accusingly. 'Bit of a problem, folks.'

'Is it Paris, Tommy?' Lauren prompted.

'Yes, that's it. Paris. They're trying to sort out Matt's contract. He was going to do three concerts, and then he goes and . . .' He floundered. 'I'm really sorry, but I'll just have to go over and fix it.'

'To Paris?' Fred raised his white eyebrows. 'You mean, right now?'

''Fraid so.'

Cobb watched the exchange carefully. It was so amateur that he found it amusing. It did not take a detective of his experience to see that this was a rehearsed performance. He was tempted to call Tommy Hudson's bluff, but for the moment he could not puzzle out the point of it all, and was intrigued enough to let the little scene run its course.

'Will you be able to drop us in town first, Tommy?' Lauren asked, and this time Cobb had no doubt she was feeding Hudson lines.

'I don't see how I can, Laurie.' The big man was theatrically doleful. 'I'm booked on the six-thirty from Heathrow.'

'Already?' Fred said, mystified at all this sudden urgency. 'Good Lord, you do move fast.'

'I got the last seat, Mr Cobb. I was lucky. I booked it just then. But if I don't leave now I'll miss it.'

'Don't worry, Tommy. We'll get the train back,' Lauren said. She looked up at Cobb, her expression unreadable. 'I suppose it's easy enough to get a train at this time on a Saturday afternoon?'

'Sure,' he said quickly.

'Nonsense,' Fred protested. 'You can't–'

'It's no problem,' Cobb said. 'I'll drive you and Freya to Oxford later.'

'Don't be ridiculous!' Fred was outraged. 'Stay the night. Stay the weekend. Pleasure to have you.'

Cobb thought: So that's it.

'You're very kind,' Lauren said sweetly, but did not take her blank eyes from Cobb's. 'It's such a drag getting through town and down to Virginia Water on the train.'

'Settled, then.' Fred smacked the desk, jumped to his feet and took Freya's hand as she came back into the room. 'Come along, young lady. Here's an adventure. We'll put your mummy in the garden room and you in the box room over there. It's the nicest room in the house, and she won't be able to see if you keep the light on late. How about that?'

Cobb was caught off guard.

'The garden room?' he said. 'There'd be more space in the coach-house.'

Fred led the girl across the room and stopped in front of his son.

'We'll put Mrs Silver in the garden room, Samuel,' he said evenly. He was smiling but he spoke directly into Cobb's face. 'We wouldn't want anyone to have to go traipsing across the yard in this weather, would we?'

Cobb swallowed and looked away.

'Look, I'm sorry to cause all this trouble.' Hudson looked crestfallen. 'It's just one of those things.'

'No trouble, Mr Hudson,' Fred cried, leading Freya down the corridor towards the bedrooms. 'Our pleasure. You dash off and catch your plane.'

'This is really good of you, Mr Cobb.' Hudson stepped across the room and put his arms around

Lauren. 'Take care. I'll ring you when I get there. You sure you'll be all right?'

'Don't worry, Tommy.' She patted his broad back. 'We've got both Mr Cobbs to look after us.'

Cobb looked up sharply and caught her watching him over Hudson's shoulder.

31

The night was velvet black and Cobb could see only a faint track of sky between the over-arching trees. He strode out along the sunken lane while the old dog shambled beside him, grunting in protest. They both knew the way from long habit, but Baskerville was not used to this pace. By the time they reached the top and crossed into the upper paddock they were panting, their breath steaming in the cold.

The couple of beers he had drunk during the long, tense evening sat heavily in him. Cobb wanted to burn them off, to feel light again and unburdened. He wanted the keen night wind to rinse him clean of resentment. They followed the black wall of the hedgerow with the farmland falling away towards the house a mile below. He could see the porch light now, trembling in the darkness, and began to feel better. He always felt calmer up here, especially in winter, with the black air flowing over him from the ancient hills, across the dead village, rattling gibbet branches. It should have been hostile, this sightless landscape, but he did not find it so. He paused to catch his breath, and drank in the chill air. It had a sense of eternity which touched him, showed him the pettiness of his own pain. He moved on and felt the turf crunch with frost beneath his boots.

There was a flicker of movement at his feet and something, probably a rabbit, jinked away downhill. Cobb could see nothing but Baskerville was after it at once, blundering in pursuit, and Cobb felt his heart lift. There was no hope at all of the dog catching anything – he was twelve years old and could probably see less than Cobb could – but he never ceased trying. Cobb admired dogs. They never gave up. They always thought life was worth a try. You could amputate one of their legs and they would never waste a moment in self-pity. Cobb had heard it said that self-awareness was the one distinguishing factor between man and animals. He thought that was probably true: he just doubted it was much of an advantage.

He clicked his tongue and Baskerville gave his asthmatic bark in answer from the far side of the field. Cobb followed the sound and almost tripped over the exhausted dog in the darkness as he lay panting and slavering in the joy of his fruitless chase. Cobb felt for the warm head, rough as carpet, and rubbed it.

'Come on, you old fool. We won't get any more miles out of you tonight.'

He turned to walk back down the field towards the farmhouse, and as he did so the kitchen light sprang on, and he knew what it meant, and he felt the bitterness rise up in him again.

'Well, well. If it isn't the long legs of the law.'

She sat at the end of the scrubbed pine table. She was wearing a man's grey sweater and it hung on her thin body. Cobb realised that the sweater was his, from the wardrobe in the garden room, and felt a pang of unreasonable indignation. Her hair was loose now and she had lost the tight, locked-down air of earlier in the day, but something slightly sluttish and brassy had replaced it. He could see why. A square green bottle of Gordon's gin and a half-full tumbler stood on the bare wood in front of her. Cobb noticed she had not troubled to replace the cap on the bottle. Despite everything he could not hold back some pity for her. Not simply for her trouble but for the desecration of herself. Back in the office he had early file photos of her with Silver. He called to mind one shot which showed her dancing with her laughing mouth wide open, blonde hair swinging across her face. Her blue eyes, catching the light, shone directly into the lens. She had been a fine-looking woman then, Cobb thought, with her high cheekbones and clear eyes and that strong clean line to her jaw. And packed with the vibrant energy that attracts the camera. There wasn't much of that vibrant woman left now. The alcohol was desiccating her. There were hard creases at the corners of her eyes and the skin of her face was growing sere and pouchy.

Cobb closed the door behind him quietly and knelt to unlace his boots. Baskerville shambled over to the table and nuzzled Lauren's bare knee, thumping the table leg with his tail. She ignored the dog and tapped the bottle with her nail. 'It's yours. I'll pay you.'

'You're a guest here. Have anything you want.'

'What I want, Sam the man, is vodka. But you haven't got any.'

'No.' He hung up his coat, snapped his fingers to call the dog away, opened the door of the potbelly stove. 'It's almost dead. Aren't you cold?'

She shrugged, indifferent. He rattled the grate and threw on a couple of logs and the flames sprang up at once. She tapped the bottle again and cocked her head at him inquiringly.

'No thanks.'

'There's enough for two. There's another bottle, I checked.'

'Yes, there's enough. But I don't want one.'

'And neither should I?'

'You can do what you want.'

'Aren't you going to lecture me? I was hoping you would.'

'You're a grown woman, Mrs Silver. You know what you're doing and why you're doing it.'

'Mrs Silver, for Chrissake!' she snorted. 'Don't be such a hardass, Sam. It's boring. Get a fucking drink and call me by my name at least. I'm not Mrs anybody any more. Not until you find him.'

Cobb hesitated then relented, fetched himself a Scotch from the hall cabinet and sat at the opposite end of the table nursing it.

'That's better,' she said. She leaned on her elbows and took a drink, then rolled the glass between her palms. She seemed amused. 'You don't want me here, do you, Sam?'

'The great flight for Paris drama . . . what was all that, an alarm call that came in late?'

'British Telecom and poor old Tommy. What a team.'

'So what was the idea?'

'Freya needs to be here. Not just for a couple of hours. For a couple of days. Maybe more.'

'Why?'

'She needs to be near you. I'm damned if I know why.'

'You could have asked.'

'You might have said no. I couldn't risk that. She'll probably need to come back too, and when she does, I'll fix that as well.'

He sat back. 'Lauren, I think maybe you need–'

'Understand this, Sam,' she said with sudden fierceness. 'I will do anything – anything at all – to give my little girl what I failed to give her sister.'

'I think you're going the hard way about it.'

'I can't afford to be in your power on this, Sam. You don't like me. You don't trust me. You'd refuse me if you could.'

'So you get my old man to ask you? Because he's too gentle and compassionate not to?'

'You got that right,' she said. 'And I'd do it even if he was some mean old bastard instead of being twice the man you are, which he is.'

Cobb felt trapped and exposed at the same time, like an animal caught in headlights. He could feel his anger rising, but could think of no way of voicing it that would not be merely destructive. In the end, she was just a woman who had been forced to face too much. She needed treatment. She deserved his pity, his help if he could give it. Yet her pain gave her such power over him. She was wrongfooting him, manipulating him at every turn. Surely at some point he was entitled to call a halt to it? His very helplessness maddened him. His heart banged so hard in his chest that it sent ripples through the whisky as he gripped the glass.

'Who's the woman?' she asked suddenly.

'What woman?'

'The picture. In my room. It was in a drawer.'

He cleared his throat, feeling the conversation spinning out of control again, but in a new direction. 'Clea. My wife. Dead now.'

'That was her room?'

'In a way, yes. She died in it.' It slipped out. 'In the bed you're sleeping in.'

Lauren pursed her lips, considering him. 'Why did you tell me that?'

Cobb shook his head, confused. 'I'm not sure.'

'To give me a jolt? Win a bit of sympathy? Freak me out?' She refilled her glass. 'Won't work, pal. My leads have been pulled.'

'I shouldn't have said anything. I'm sorry.'

'No, I'm supposed to say *I'm* sorry. "Your wife's dead? How tragic. I'm sorry." That's how it goes. Only I don't feel sorry. Nothing personal – I don't feel anything. That's what I'm trying to get across to you. That's why I can do or say anything I want.'

Cobb tossed back the Scotch and gripped the edges of the table with his fists so hard that he could feel the muscles quivering in his forearms. He lifted his face to look into hers.

'People die, Lauren. I don't know what happens, but I know they go away and they don't come back. And I know something else. We can't start again until we let them go. My wife. Your husband. Your little girl.'

'Oh, please!' she laughed, tossing her hair and rocking her chair back. 'Spare me the sermon on healing!'

Cobb felt his lip twitch but he kept going, speaking fast, determined to get it all out. 'I'm being strictly practical here, Lauren. Life starts now. And now. And now. You'll never make sense of the past by trying to pull the present into line. You just stuff up the future.' He realised she had stopped laughing and was watching him. He let go of the table edges and spoke more slowly. 'It gets better, somehow. You don't know how but it happens. Something goes on putting you back together time after time. Even if you don't want it to. Some day you wake up and you start noticing the sun on your back, or laughter, or the sound of the sea.'

She watched him for a moment longer.

'Nice try, Sam,' she said at last. 'But I'm not interested in getting better. The only reason I'm interested in staying alive is because Freya needs me to.' She lifted her glass to him in a mock toast. 'Cheers, Inspector Cobb,' she said, and drained the gin.

Cobb stared at the table for a while and then slowly

lifted his head. 'I don't think that's true, Lauren,' he said. 'I don't think you can help wanting to stay alive. You're too strong.'

He got up and turned his back on her and had almost reached the kitchen door when he heard her forehead hit the table like a mallet and the glass clatter and roll. He got back to her in time to stop her sliding off the chair, but her lolling arm caught the bottle and it toppled and shattered on the stone flags.

'Pity. Good gin, that,' Fred observed from the door. He was in orange floral pyjamas this time. He crossed to the sink, stepping over the broken glass in his tartan slippers, and poured himself a glass of water. He took a sip. 'Well, you'd better do something with her, Samuel, my boy. You'll look mildly foolish standing there like that all night.'

Cobb got one arm under her shoulders and the other in the crook of her knees and lifted her. He was surprised by how light she was.

'You're a great help,' he told his father.

'Sciatica,' Fred said. 'Lumbago. Weak heart. Asthma.'

'You haven't got bloody asthma, you old fraud.'

Cobb hefted the unconscious woman against his shoulder.

'Dizzy spells. Blackwater fever.' Fred turned and shuffled off down the corridor and Cobb could hear his voice fading away. 'Neuralgia. Alzheimer's. Bubonic plague. Flat feet.' His bedroom door closed emphatically.

Cobb carried her through into the garden room and

laid her with reasonable care on the bed, Clea's bed, and pulled a blanket around her and stood back. She seemed frail and vulnerable and he could not help staring at her, searching her slack face for the hard and cynical woman of a few minutes ago. It would have reassured him if he could have found that woman, but it was no good. All he could find was exhaustion and grief.

He killed the light and made to leave the room. But then he glanced back and saw the moonlight falling through the French doors, and heard the woman's breathing from the bed, and the scene lanced him with a sudden aching familiarity. Without knowing why, he did what he had always done and sat in the winged chair by the window, watching her quietly for a long time until he was sure she was asleep. After that he rose and went back to his own room.

32

Cobb was up before first light, following his normal Sunday morning routine. He rescued the fire in the potbelly stove, so that by the time he had finished cleaning up in the kitchen the small window was glowing cherry red and warmth was beginning to leak back into the air. He laid the fire in the living room. Then he took the dog out into the dim chill morning and set off up the sunken lane and across the fields towards his lookout in the abandoned village.

He shut his mind to everything except the turning world on which he walked, noticing the first spears of bulbs in the hedgerows, the gathering knots in the hazels that would soon be buds, the grey-gold light which broke a little earlier now over the Chilterns. It would be spring before so very long. For a man who trod this path every week the changes were there to be seen. He saw them and believed that these were the changes he felt.

By the time he got back, Fred was already at work in the warm kitchen in a clatter of bright pans and a blare of talk from Radio Four. He was singing very loudly over the radio, wearing a full-length apron with a lewd picture of a rooster on it, over the caption 'Morning, Old Cock'.

Cobb took off his coat and sat at the deal table. 'You are a noisy old bastard,' he told his father, by way of greeting.

'Two out of three,' Fred conceded, waving a spatula over his shoulder. 'Try harder.'

Cobb noticed a speck of light on the flagstones and bent to pick up a sliver of green glass. He said: 'The place still stinks of gin. I'll give it another scrub later.' Fred waved a couldn't-care-less arm without troubling to turn. Cobb said: 'I'll get another bottle in town today.'

Fred straightened from his work, moved the sizzling pan off the heat, turned the volume of the radio down and faced his son. 'Are you attempting to apologise for the lady, Samuel?'

'I warned you what it would be like.'

'I didn't need warning, thank you.'

'I don't think you know the half of it, Dad,' Cobb said at last.

'Oh, really?' The old man gave a knowing laugh. 'You mean, I don't know that Mrs Silver would drink the horse liniment if I didn't make sure there was enough gin for her to steal? That's what I don't know, is it? Good Lord, Samuel. Sometimes you act as if the seventy-eight years of experience I have amassed on this earth count for nothing at all.'

Cobb looked at his father. 'When are you going to stop outguessing me?'

'When you learn to give your ageing parent a little more credit. Which means probably never.'

'You're making a lot of noise,' Freya said from the door. 'You woke me up.'

'And high time too.' Fred cracked an egg one-handed into hot fat. 'Breakfast is almost ready, young lady.'

'Hello, Princess.' Cobb moved a chair round for her and she climbed up on to it, opposite him, knuckling her eyes. 'Is your mum coming to eat?'

'She's asleep,' the child said, looking down. 'She never has breakfast.'

'All the more for us, then.' Fred gleefully set a plate of bacon and eggs in front of her. She blinked at it.

'Is that all mine?'

'If you think that's a lot,' Cobb told her, 'just you wait till the dinosaur eggs start coming in. One of them lasts us a whole week. And then we sell the shells for swimming pools.'

'That's very funny, that is,' she said. 'Ha, ha, ha.' Cobb grinned at her and fetched himself a coffee. Fred brought his own plate over and sat next to the girl. She jabbed a loaded fork towards Cobb. 'He's always telling me silly stories about dinosaurs.'

'I know,' Fred said mournfully. 'I've tried to train him, but what can you do? Pink, were they, the dinosaurs?'

'That's right.'

'Well . . .' Fred held his fork up to his temple and made a circular motion with it to indicate insanity. He whispered: 'Little bit loopy, you know. We have to be nice to him.'

She frowned from one to the other. 'Are you his daddy?' she said.

'That's right. It's incredible, isn't it?' Fred dangled a bacon rind. 'I don't know where he gets it from. Certainly not from me.' He nonchalantly stretched the bacon rind like an elastic band and shot it across the room at Baskerville. The dog lurched to his feet and devoured the rind while the child watched in wide-eyed astonishment. The dog, deciding his luck was in, shambled across the kitchen and stuck his nose against Freya's knee.

'He licked me!' she cried, outraged and delighted at the same time, and struggling to maintain her dignity.

'He's OK,' Cobb said. 'Just don't make a noise like bacon.'

'You're tricking me again,' she told him, her eyes narrowing. He winked at her and sipped his coffee.

After a while Cobb walked through to the living room and lit the fire he had laid earlier, deliberately busying himself for ten minutes at the job. Finally, when he heard the back door open and close, he returned to the kitchen. The two figures were moving across the yard: Fred stooped and white-haired, and Freya bright in her red parka, limping a little on her healing leg, looking up solemnly at him.

'He's a wonderful man,' Lauren said.

Cobb had not seen her sitting at the table. He had the impression she had been waiting for Fred and the child to go off together, just as he had waited.

'Yes, he is. Coffee?'

She nodded. 'Please.'

Her face was sharp and tight, and there was a

greenish pallor to the column of her neck and a dull bruise above her right eye. But she was no longer wearing his old sweater, and her hair was now gathered back severely, and she had about her none of the brassiness of the night before.

'You look pretty good,' he said.

'All things considered, you mean.' She smiled bleakly. 'Come on, I look like shit.'

'Time to worry is when you can do that and look normal.' He placed the coffee on the table in front of her. His hands were sooty and roughened from making the fire. She reached for her mug and then unexpectedly took his right hand in both of hers and turned it over and inspected it.

'Surgeon's hands,' she said. 'You should take care of them.' She let his hand go and met his eyes. 'I said some stuff last night – about your wife. I shouldn't have. I'm sorry.'

'Don't worry about it.'

'It won't happen again.' She sipped her coffee. 'I know I can't let it happen again.'

'Fair enough.' He went back to the bench top and filled his own cup. 'Do you want some breakfast?'

She grimaced and swallowed.

'Me neither,' he said. He looked out of the window. Fred and Freya were coming out of the barn with the chickenfeed and moving towards the outhouses at the back. The girl did not quite skip, but there was a lightness in her step he had not seen before.

'You know, Sam,' Lauren was speaking into her

coffee cup, 'I don't suppose we'll ever like one another much–'

'But we don't have to be enemies?'

She glanced up at him in surprise. 'That's right,' she said. 'We don't.'

He held her eyes uncertainly for a moment. 'Look, Lauren '

'Sam,' she spoke in a rush, cutting him off, 'I think I need some help.'

'That's good.'

'Good?' She gave a wry laugh. 'It doesn't feel good.'

'We're talking about the drink here, are we?'

'You need to ask?'

'I wanted to hear you say it.'

She paused. 'Yes, I'm talking about the drink.' She lifted her chin at him a little defensively. 'I wasn't always this way.'

'You don't have to tell me.'

'I know I don't have to, Sam. I just want you to know that.'

He watched her for a while, then nodded.

'Will you see someone? I can help you to get to see someone.'

This seemed to catch her off guard. 'That wasn't really what I was asking for.'

'You asked for help.'

'I meant–'

'I'm not talking about anything heavy but there are controlled drinking programmes. Informal groups. Just to give you a bit of support.'

She laughed, and he discovered that this hurt him. 'What's so funny?'

'You're such a policeman, Sam. I ask for directions to the station and you call in a SWAT team and helicopters.' She saw his confusion and leaned towards him, smiling. 'I'm sorry. Look, I won't promise anything. But if you send me some stuff, I'll look at it.'

'You will?'

'Yes. And I'll even say thank you.'

In the yard the child and the old man moved across to the henhouse door. Fred opened the shutters and a small explosion of feathers and straw puffed out over both of them and for the first time Cobb saw Freya laugh. He wished he could have heard it. He said: 'Bring her here whenever you want, Lauren.'

He put his cup down on the counter and opened the door and walked out of the room without looking back.

Cobb crossed to the barn and collected his spade and mattock and fork and carried them across the pasture to the back of the orchard. He sank the fork into the ground and hung his anorak over it, then unhooked the string from the marker peg and traced the line of the ditch on the frosted soil with the corner of the spade. He stretched, feeling the knots click in his back, and breathed deeply. It was a raw white morning and the mist still lay in the hollows of the folded ground down towards the river. He began to dig.

He worked for an hour, chopping the heavy soil and

turning it up in dark slabs on the edge of the ditch. A couple of times he rang the steel of the spade on chert, and once struck a spark which jarred his wrist, but mostly the soil was soft and rich, the product of a century of leaf litter which had drifted into the old ditch. Cobb liked digging ditches. The rhythmic labour settled his mind. He liked too the secret world of the soil: the fibrous roots which tore like calico when he lifted the spade, and glossy pink worms which whipped in the bright air as the blade exposed them and trickled away again into the dark earth.

A glint of chestnut caught his eye and he set aside the spade and knelt and felt in the loam with his fingers until he found it, a conker-brown chrysalis, two inches long. It was undamaged, still nestling in the dry matted chamber the pupating caterpillar had built for itself four months before. He lifted it out carefully and rolled it in the palm of his hand. It kicked against the warmth of his skin, an indignant jerk, as if it was tetchy at being disturbed from its sleep too soon. The sensation reminded him of his childhood, when he had searched for hours for these fat shiny pupae and treasured them like unearthed gems.

'What's that?' Freya asked him. He had not heard her approach. She stood behind the mound of soil he had turned up. Standing straight in her red anorak with her hands behind her back, she reminded him of a toy soldier. 'In your hand. What is it?'

'Here.' He held out his hand and when she did the same tipped the chrysalis into her palm. It almost filled her hand. He gently closed her fingers around it. 'Careful with it, now. It's alive.' The chrysalis kicked her and he saw her start and open her eyes, but she did not drop it. Instead she uncurled her fingers and examined it. 'It's a chrysalis,' he said.

'I know that,' she said with some scorn. 'They're what butterflies come out of. I've never seen one this big, though.'

'That one's a moth. A great big fat hawk moth. The caterpillars eat the leaves on the apple trees all summer. It drives my dad wild, but he can't reach them and I pretend not to notice.'

She stroked the pupa with the tip of her finger. He regretted mentioning his father, but perhaps the reference had given her an opening she had sought, for she suddenly asked: 'What should I call you?'

'Me, Princess? Call me what you like.'

'No.' She looked up at him. 'You have to say. You're the grown-up.'

Cobb felt that he had been put in his place, and justifiably. 'OK, so call me Sam. I'd like that.'

'Sam.' She tried the name out. 'That's good. I didn't want you to be an uncle. Not like Uncle Tommy.'

'He's only trying to help, Freya. Your mum could use some help at the moment. We all need it sometimes.'

She watched him expressionlessly, stroking the pupa. But she did not take the bait. With a quick gesture she handed the chrysalis back to him. 'Will it die, now you've dug it up?'

'No. Tell you what, we'll put it in some sand in a box

in the barn. That way the birds won't get it. You might even get to see it hatch out.' He laid the chrysalis on the ground near the ditch and covered it with some loose leaf litter and marked the place with a stick. 'I used to go looking for these things when I was a kid, just so I could keep them safe through the winter and watch them hatch out in the spring. I never got tired of it.'

She stared at him solemnly, at the ground where the chrysalis lay hidden, and then down into the sheer-sided ditch he had dug.

'That's what will happen to Goodie,' she announced. 'She'll stay in that little hard box until it's safe outside and then she'll hatch out.' She looked up at him, challenging. 'Do you think?'

'Yes, Freya.' He sat down on the edge of the ditch. 'I think you're absolutely right.'

She nodded, apparently satisfied that the question was settled. She pointed at the chrysalis. 'When will it hatch out?'

'Oh, about March. A couple of months.'

'Am I coming here in March?'

'It's up to your mum, of course. But as far as we're concerned, Princess, you can come whenever you want.'

She was quiet for a moment.

'Why did you invite me?' she demanded suddenly.

'You wanted to come, didn't you?'

'Yes. But why did you ask me?'

'I asked you because I thought you deserved a break.

It was your mum's idea first.'

'Nobody ever asked me anywhere before.'

'Come on, Freya! You must have been invited lots of places.'

'Not me. Me and Goodie. Usually people asked Goodie, really.'

'Maybe she just said yes first.'

She considered that. Then she said: 'Are you very clever, Sam?'

'Like most people I'm pretty clever about some things and very stupid about others.'

She looked at him suspiciously, as if this might be a trick answer, the sort of slick response adults use to deflect questions from children. After a while she said: 'Are you clever enough to find Daddy?'

'I'm not sure anyone's that clever, Freya,' he said carefully, uncertain what she had been told and what she believed, 'but I'm going to keep looking. It's my job to keep looking.'

She looked at the earth, and then back up at him.

'Do you think he's died?'

He held her gaze. 'I think so, Freya. I think he'd be with you if he hadn't.'

'Mummy doesn't think he's died.'

'I know that's what she says. But she's very upset right now. She may come to see things differently later.'

'She's only upset because she made him go away,' the girl said fiercely, lifting her chin. Despite the force of her words, though, there was something slightly false about her delivery, and Cobb had the impression she was trying the attitude on, like a piece of armour.

'It's not as simple as that, Princess. It's never as simple as that.'

Freya looked down at the ground, a little shame-faced, perhaps. 'I can't remember what happened,' she said, in a smaller voice. 'I can't remember any of it.'

'Don't try.'

'I've got to try! She says he's a really bad person for what he did, and I was there and I can't remember any of it.'

'Ah, I see.' Cobb stretched across and stroked her arm. He was not sure whether he should do this and was simultaneously awkward and annoyed with himself for his awkwardness. 'But, you know, Freya – he did whatever he did, whether you can remember it or not. You don't have any responsibility for that. He does.'

'You think he was a bad person too, don't you?' she accused him, but did not move away from his touch.

'I tell you what, Freya. I think he was a really, really stupid one.'

33

Silver looked up as Maggie Turpin pushed the door open and clambered into the half-built flat. The breath hissed out of him in spurts as he pumped against the boards, and sweat ran through his bristled hair and down his scarred face. Eight he'd managed this morning. Three repetitions of eight push-ups. It gave him a certain savage triumph. When he had started, just ten days ago, he had been unable to lift his thin frame off the floor more than twice.

He became aware that she had not moved, standing in the doorway with the bulging white Tesco bags, wheezing with the effort of climbing the stairs.

'What's up, Maggie?'

'If you're so fighting bloody fit, you can fetch your own!' she shouted, and dumped the plastic bags on the floor so that they spilled fruit and tins across the boards. 'You bloody eat it all, anyway! I feel like a bleeding cuckoo, fetching and carrying for you, day in, day out.'

It was the first time she had ever shouted at him, and in that moment he realised Maggie Turpin was afraid of him. It had never occurred to him before, and the sudden knowledge caught him off balance. Perhaps it surprised her too, for she stood panting in the doorway, looking away from him, as if embarrassed at her outburst. He rolled over into a sitting position and blocked a trundling orange with his foot.

'What's your problem, Maggie?'

'My problem?' She advanced into the room, the colour rising again in her raddled face. 'I'll tell you what my problem is, Mr Joe Hill!' She stood fuming in front of him, with her hands opening and closing like claws.

'Well?'

'You plan on staying up here like bloody Quasimodo for the rest of your life while I wait on you?'

He stood up and stooped to gather the groceries, dropping scattered items back into their bags. 'Is it the money?'

'Yes! Yes, it's the money. The money and—'

Silver walked across the room and pushed aside the sacking that hung across the woman's sleeping space under the angle of the roof. From beneath the tangled blankets he pulled out a battered McVitie's biscuit tin.

' 'Ere!' she cried in sudden alarm. 'What you doing with that, Joe Hill? That's private, that is.'

Silver opened the lid and took out the entire wad of notes and tossed the tin aside so that it clattered on the boards. He weighed the money in his hand without glancing at it. 'How much is left, Maggie?'

She looked truculently at him. 'Near enough three grand, I s'pose. It ain't gone to waste, Joe Hill, unless you count Stevie's boozing. You can't accuse me of nothing.'

He thrust the wad out to her. 'Take it.'

'What?'

'Take it and get out.'

He pushed the money into her hand and turned away, lugging the bags of groceries over to the ancient fridge. He began stacking the food inside. When he looked up she was still there.

'Don't fool yourself, Joe,' she said in a different voice. 'You can't just smash things up and stick them back together again and expect them to work.'

'What are you talking about?' When she still didn't move he grew impatient. 'Look. You know that's all there is. You've had plenty of chance to count it.'

'Yes,' she said. 'Plenty of chance.'

'Don't give me the cow eyes, Maggie,' he scoffed. 'You've done all right. Now you've got the last of it. There's enough there to trade in that old heap of yours and buy something halfway decent and just drive away.'

'Away where?'

He went back to stacking the fridge. 'What does it matter, Maggie? None of us is going anywhere.'

'You know, Joe,' she said to his bent back, 'while you was dead to the world in there I could have took all of it any time. Bought meself a bleeding Merc if I'd had a mind, and let you rot.'

'So why didn't you?'

She stared at him and shook her head. 'Be buggered if I know.'

When he looked up again she was gone.

Later, Silver lay with his hands locked behind his head

and listened to chucking out time in the bar below. He was used to hearing the routine and knew they were worse than usual tonight, even for a Saturday. He had never seen George, the barman, but knew his name and his Drill Sergeant's voice, as he might know a character in a radio play. George was roaring now at some drunk. George roared a good deal at his customers, and Silver could now tell the precise moment at which he moved from bark to bite.

'Davey,' George boomed, 'I fuckin' told you twice already. Now you're going through that door, and you better open the fucker 'cos I won't.'

Then the bang of the counter flap going back. The bar babble stilled for a moment, a chair clattering over and a man shouting, then the street door was banging hard against its stops and someone's shoes were scuffing the pavement in flight. Silver smiled to himself. It was his first night alone and he savoured the solitude. Not that old Maggie had ever said anything much. She would just be there, every evening, in the partitioned off space she called her room, while Stevie was out drinking.

Silver got to his feet and paced through the empty loft, now all his. He pushed aside the curtain she had pinned across the doorframe. The bed was a stained mattress. Beside it lay a pile of women's magazines, an overflowing glass ashtray, a nest of brown ale bottles. Silver regretted a little having given her the rest of the money. Yet there was a certain poetic balance to it. The money had belonged to another man, and that man was dead now. He walked back through the attic room to his own curtained space. He felt behind the fibre-board and pulled out a grubby manila envelope and slid out the newspaper cutting it contained. The photo had been over-enlarged from some old library shot, so that Freya's image was misty and indistinct. He smoothed the soft paper and pinned the cutting up on a beam where he could see it from anywhere in the room.

The stair door banged.

'Oi, you up there?' George's voice boomed up from below. 'Joe, or whatever your name is?' Without waiting for an answer, the barman came pounding up the stairs and stood peering in the dim light, one hand shading his eyes from the glare of the bare bulb.

Silver said: 'I'm here.'

George made to step forward and pulled up short as he saw Silver's face. 'Gawd, fuck me rigid.' He sucked his teeth. 'Jesus, they done a job on you.'

'What do you want?'

The brusque challenge of Silver's question pulled George up short and he bristled. 'Want? I want you out of here, mate. That's what I want.'

'Oh?'

'I seen Maggie earlier. Took that old shitbox car of hers and that drunk she hangs around with and pissed off. You have a barney with the old cow, did you?'

'It doesn't matter.'

'It bloody well does, mate. I only let you lot stop up here as a favour to old Mags. Shouldn't be here at all, by rights.'

'You got paid, didn't you?'

'Only up to the end of the month. That's Tuesday. I'll give you till then, but that's it. You're out.'

'I'll pay,' Silver said.

And only when he formed these words and uttered them aloud did it come home to him that he could not pay, that he had no money, that giving the last of it to Maggie was not a quixotic gesture but a form of castration. He did not have the money to buy a cup of tea or a sandwich or a bus ticket. Not enough to make a phone call or buy a paper.

He said: 'I'll work.'

'You what?'

'I can work. I'm fit. I'm getting fit.'

'Yeah, but . . .' George looked at him doubtfully. 'You ever work a bar before?'

'Do you need a PhD to pull beer these days?'

'No offence, mate, but you'd scare me customers half to death.'

'Maybe some of them could do with it.'

George hesitated. Silver could see greed flicker across his fat beery face. George said, slyly: 'You got a problem with the law?'

'Not the way you think.'

'Because I don't want no trouble, you hear me? I might look like I went out with yesterday's garbage but I was at Goose Green, mate. Me and five thousand fucking Argies. I can still sort out a stick of celery like you.'

'I just want some peace and quiet for a while and a few quid every now and then.'

'Peace and quiet.' George nodded, his lip curling. 'That's the way I like it.'

The stairs opened on to a bare concrete passage crowded with steel beer kegs and smelling of piss. At the far end of the passage Silver could see the car park, a gap-toothed paling fence, and beyond that the silhouette of a gasometer against the night sky. It occurred to him he did not know where he was – London, presumably, but which part, which side of the river, he could not even guess. It made him feel oddly lightheaded. The sensation was not entirely unpleasant. Silver followed George's stertorous breathing through a back door into the bar. The place had been closed for an hour, but a blue fug of smoke still hung under the low ceiling and the shoddy room stank of stale beer. A long old-fashioned bar shone with spilled drink.

'I'm on me own here,' George complained. He slung the dregs out of a used glass and pulled himself a pint in it. 'Fucking brewery'll close it before long. They don't give me any help, the tight bastards.' He drank, looking at Silver over the rim of his glass. 'So I help myself now and then.'

'I'm going to need some money,' Silver told him.

'Fuck off!' George banged his drink down. 'You ain't even started yet.'

'I'll start now.'

Silver stepped into the room, righted a couple of chairs, took a cloth from the bar and wiped tables. He found a plastic rubbish bag under the sink and moved around the tables emptying ashtrays and collecting litter. A faint twist of floating ash rose like smoke from the bag as he worked. George watched him suspiciously.

'What's your game, then?'

'Game?'

'Come in here, with your up-yer-arse accent . . .'

Silver glanced at him. He had never been aware that he had an accent. 'No game, George. I just need a little money from time to time, that's all. Just enough to live.' He collected glasses, stacked them on the bar, found washing-up liquid and ran warm water in the sink. He could feel the man's eyes on him. He stopped and looked back. 'Have you got kids, George?'

'Two. Idle bastards. What of it?'

'I've got a daughter.' Silver clunked the glasses into the hot water. 'I need to see her. Just see her, that's all. I won't cause any trouble.'

'Bloody right you won't. Not here, anyway.' George refilled his empty glass. 'I was at Goose Green, y'know.' He seemed to remember he had already said this, and stopped. Instead he punched the till and when it opened, groped inside and slapped a ten-pound note on the wet bar in front of Silver. 'That's a float, right? I'll see how you work out before there's any more.' He tapped the till with his knuckle. 'And you can keep your sticky fingers out of there, too. The brewery might not know what goes in and out, but I fucking well do.'

'I won't touch it, George.'

'And another thing.' He pushed his whiskered face close to Silver's. 'I don't want to know nothing about you, OK? I don't know who you are and I don't give a toss, so long as you do your work and remember who's in charge.'

'I understand.'

George straightened, pulled down the hem of his greasy knitted jerkin and drank off the second pint. When he had finished it, he waved at the washing up with his empty glass.

'You can do that tomorrow.'

'It's OK. I'll do it now.'

34

Silver worked in the run-down pub all week, finding tasks for himself in its warren of dingy rooms. He gradually grew used to activity: lifting, cleaning, mopping floors, rolling kegs, pulling beer – moving in new ways.

He had not realised how thoroughly wasted his body had become, and at first the simplest acts left him dizzy and spent. On the Tuesday morning it took him two hours to sweep the floor of the bar, a job that should probably have taken twenty minutes. Stacking chairs on tables was an extreme test of his strength. Not that George noticed. He slept until mid-morning, drank half-a-dozen pints with whoever chanced in at lunchtime, and then slept again until the six o'clock opening. While Silver worked he could hear the fat publican snoring upstairs in his room under the front gable.

George was too slovenly to be strict, and Silver worked at his own pace while he learned what his body would and would not do for him. He discovered that his left knee pained him if he flexed it too far and, though he could walk well enough, his leg dragged slightly. Any sharp lifting movement caused a badly healed rib to jab him like a dagger in the centre of his back. The stump of his missing finger throbbed maddeningly in either hot or cold water, and sometimes the ghost finger itself hurt him fiercely. Silver felt he had woken up in someone else's brokendown body, and had been given the task of learning to use it.

Yet the toil was comforting. The jobs he set himself were simple and repetitive – cleaning up, washing glasses, restocking the shelves – and he could feel himself growing stronger as he tackled them. At night he would serve a few drinks, if George needed him to, although the Battle of the Nile was almost empty during the week. Only an occasional off-duty bus driver came in from the depot across the road, or a few of the day-shift packers from Tesco's. They sometimes watched him as he worked, but were neither curious nor unfriendly and nobody asked him any questions. After closing Silver would climb back up to the attic, so weary that he had to force himself to eat from the remnants of Maggie's last shopping foray – fruit, stale bread, tinned fish straight from the can. There was a one-ring camping gas stove in the corner of the loft and a few battered aluminium pots, but though Silver boiled a couple of eggs he had nothing else worth cooking, and most of the time he lacked the energy.

By Thursday of that week he could feel his body beginning to respond to this routine. Already it was less draining to move the tables in the bar, and he could use the plunger in the constantly clogged gents' toilet for two or three minutes at a stretch without his shoulder muscles screaming at him. He knew that soon he would be able to risk walking out in the street, and the prospect filled him with a strange excitement. His body began to crave food at the thought of it and he hoarded George's ten-pound note jealously, like a small boy with his pocket money, and fantasised about what it would buy him to eat. He did not think. He worked. He ate little. He dreamed of eating more. He slept. He had no clear idea at first what he was building up to, and between work and weariness barely had the energy to ask himself. But every night the child's eyes looked defiantly out at him from the newspaper cutting pinned to the beam above his head. She would make him ask the question, he knew. And, soon enough, she would force him to find an answer to it.

It was Saturday morning. Silver followed the track up through the beech trees above the children's play-ground, climbing steadily. The suburban park had looked tiny on George's dog-eared A-Z, but now he was here it surprised him how broad and green it was. He had not realised how far he still was from full fitness and the walk from the pub had exhausted him. His calf muscles ached and his breath came in laboured gulps. He concentrated on this discomfort. It distracted him. Otherwise, the strangeness of it all threatened to engulf him. There had been a moment, as he crossed the open expanse of the football pitch, when he had felt the depth of the soft grey sky above pulling him, as if he might lose his grip on the earth like a spider dropping off a ceiling and spin off into infinity. He had been cooped up among the rafters for too long to cope with the limitless vault of the sky.

At first he felt acutely out of place among the ordinary people there – people with their children and dogs, their raincoats and umbrellas and frisbees and newspapers. He pictured himself through their eyes: a gaunt disfigured man with convict hair and shabby clothes. He had caught two or three of them glancing at him as he passed. Perhaps they were just curious about his face, perhaps not. He could feel them recoil, fall silent as he passed, nervously smile, mutter among themselves. He would have turned back but he was afraid to give in now. He continued up the track. At the top of the ridge the beeches stood in a double line like the columns in a cathedral, and the track wandered among them away to his right, soft underfoot with beechmast. There was a wooden bench a few yards ahead, commanding a view southwestwards over the grey derelict dockland with a mercury flash of the river beyond. Silver took up station there.

Perhaps it was the glimpse of the distant river that did it. Silver could feel it coming but was powerless to stop it, like a man at the edge of a whirlpool, tugged inwards and down. He made to rise and found that his knees would not bear his weight. He shuffled to the end of the bench and leaned against the beech tree which grew there, rubbing his face against the rough bark for animal reassurance while the world lurched, and the crying of gulls and the distant laughter of children spun away to a roaring blackness, and he glimpsed again the beast with its lunatic eyes, diving down away from him and carrying his soul with it.

'Are you ill?' The boy's voice was hesitant. He was about twelve, wearing a grey school pullover. He stood back at a safe distance, hauling on his labrador's lead as if the dog might catch some contagion if it approached too close to this ragged man. Silver felt the chill of sweat cooling on him: he could hear it dripping from his chin, ticking on the leaves below. The dog's eyes came into focus first: curious, sympathetic eyes. Then a switching golden tail. Then the boy, wary, uncomfortable, leaning away from him on the lead.

'Shall I get someone?'

Silver stared at him.

'There's a man down there with a mobile,' the boy persisted. 'I'll get him to call someone.'

Silver sat up slowly, the sweat drying on his skin. He brushed crumbs of moss from his face.

'I'm going to get someone,' the boy said, and with sudden resolve hauled his dog round.

'No.' Silver forced himself to speak. 'I get these turns. It's nothing.'

The boy looked unconvinced, but Silver could tell he was relieved not to have to act. Silver stood up as quickly as he dared and spread his arms as if displaying his vigour. 'There. Right as rain.'

The boy tugged the dog away and retreated, glancing back as he went. Silver brushed himself down and walked away as quickly as he could manage, down the path. He could feel the boy's eyes on him as he went.

* * *

'Where the fuck have you been?' George stopped the steel keg with one meaty thigh as the driver rolled it down the planks from the back of the truck. The evening was cold but George was red in the face with exertion and blowing like a walrus through his whiskers. 'We open at five Saturdays. Remember?'

'I'm sorry.' Silver slung off his jacket and took hold of the rim of one of the kegs.

'Let go of that, you soft bugger. You couldn't bleeding lift that if you tried. Piss off inside and get the bar open. See if you can do something right.'

Silver pushed through the old-fashioned frosted glass doors into the bar. He was breathing quickly and realised the encounter had scared him. It came to him that he needed George, he needed this buffoon with his beery jowls and his ridiculous whiskers. The idea left him confused and nervous. He lifted the flap and moved quickly behind the bar and sheltered there, furiously polishing and repolishing glasses, calming himself with work.

'How's this sound?' The girl's amplified voice boomed across the room. Silver looked round sharply. He had not realised anyone was inside the pub and for a moment he thought the question was for him. The voice sounded familiar. 'One. Two. Three. Mary had a little lamb . . .'

He realised she was testing a microphone. She was in the dim far corner of the room standing in a tangle of leads, with an old amplifier at her feet. The amplifier was strapped together with electrician's tape. A Yamaha twelve-string guitar leaned over it, a cheap chrome pick-up screwed into the soundhole. The girl had lurid blue hair cut short, an old black Megadeth T-shirt worn loose over frayed jeans, and huge clodhopping army boots, gaping at the laces. A blue jewelled stud was set precisely in the middle of her left cheek, which was something even Silver had never seen before. He thought she was perhaps seventeen. She fixed the mike on its stand and, glancing up, saw him watching her.

'What are you looking at, Scarface?' The insult was so casual that it was comradely. It seemed she was leaving it up to him whether to take offence or not, and didn't much care either way.

He said: 'Who are you?'

'I'm Jit. I'm here every Saturday.'

He placed the voice at last. 'You're the Joan Baez girl.'

'Yeah, yeah.' She waved him away, too busy, losing interest. She shouldered the guitar strap and hunkered down to adjust the amplifier. 'How's this sound, Nugget?'

Silver saw a solid man of around thirty-five leaning on the bar with a pint standing in front of him. The man wore a black shirt and his forearms under the rolled-up sleeves were thick and brown. He nodded across at Silver and raised his glass slightly in greeting. Silver saw steel-rimmed spectacles and the flash of intelligent blue eyes behind them, a broad powerful face, prematurely grey iron-filing hair. The man tapped

his glass. 'The money's on the fridge,' he said cryptic-
ally. He had an Australian accent. He stuck out a big
bony hand. 'Bob Nugent. They all call me Nugget.'
Silver took the hand warily, and when he didn't speak
Nugent prompted him: 'And you?'

'Joe. Joe Hill.' For the first time Silver noticed the
man's dog collar.

The girl struck a chord which rang like a bell around
the dim bar, then she ran her left hand quickly up the
fretboard in a long liquid arpeggio. 'Sound OK,
Nugget? Not too loud?'

Nugent said: 'Sounds great, Jit.'

Silver heard himself say: 'The second string's out.'

The girl damped the strings with the flat of her
hand. 'You say something, Scarface?'

'One of your B strings is out,' Silver said, more
loudly. 'Flat by half a tone.'

'Don't talk shite,' she scoffed.

Silver shrugged and moved away. Nugent was
suddenly interested, and put out a hand to detain him.
'You know a bit about music, Joe?'

'No.'

Silver kept moving, unstacking chairs, wiping down
tables, collecting stray glasses. He ignored the girl, but
he noted that when his back was turned Jit quietly
tuned the off-key B string. He moved behind the bar
and emptied the dishwasher, restacked it and put it on
for a new cycle, then cleaned the counter top, staying
away from Nugent's end of the bar, avoiding conversation. Jit was setting up her sheet music,

practice-whispering lyrics to herself, running through chord progressions. Silver could tell he had unsettled her and when she executed a knuckle-breaking blues sequence he suspected she had done it to re-establish her primacy as the musician in the room.

'How d'you like that, Nugget?' she called. 'That last one's a major seventh. I only just learnt it.' She played it again, a sobbing, plaintive chord. 'Isn't it great?'

Silver polished a pint sleeve and stacked it with the others in a glittering pyramid. He said: 'It's a major ninth.'

'Get outa here!' the girl cried, using the microphone to amplify her contempt.

Silver glanced over his shoulder at her.

'It's C major ninth,' he said.

'If you know so bloody much, why don't you come up here and play the thing yourself?' He ignored her and went on polishing glasses. 'Get outa here,' she said again, but with fading confidence.

The doors crashed open again and George barged through, beetroot red and sweating. He banged back the counter flap and marched up the length of the bar, trapping Silver at the far end. 'I want a word with you.'

'It won't happen again.'

'I'll say it won't bleeding happen again.' George's shirt was open to the waist and coiled grey hair sprouted out: the sour smell of his body was over-powering. 'I been out there sweating my balls off for two hours waiting for you. You want this bleeding job or don't you?'

Silver looked away. 'I want it.'

'Well, Rule Bleeding One, sunshine,' he prodded Silver hard in the ribs with a blunt forefinger. 'Rule Bleeding One is that you get here on time or you're down the bleeding road.'

'OK. I'm sorry.'

Behind the publican's shoulder Silver caught sight of Nugent, theatrically examining his empty glass. 'George! Any danger of another beer?'

'Right with you, padre,' George said, without taking his eyes off Silver's, refusing to be deflected. 'Just a little disciplinary matter here.'

Silver said: 'I've got the message, George.'

George relaxed a little, backed off a step. 'I dunno where you come from, Joe Hill, and I tell you straight, I don't much like the look of you. But while you work here, don't you never forget who wears the stripes.'

'Not your bloody stripes again, George,' Nugent groaned. 'You've got more stripes than the Esso tiger.'

George swung away from Silver to take this new bait, as Nugent had intended him to do. 'I was at Goose Green, padre. A bloody RSM, I was, with two 'undred scared schoolboys-in-uniform under me—'

'— and five thousand screaming Argies in front,' the priest completed the line. 'George, you're a bloody star. Now pull me a beer, for Chrissake.'

By seven the pub was packed. The priest left after two pints and Silver deliberately ignored his departure. He did not want to attract the man's attention. He knew he had tweaked Nugent's curiosity, and was annoyed with himself for not keeping his mouth shut.

With Nugent gone there was some relief to be found in the dark and crowded pub. Here he was the barman, nothing more. He caught a couple of customers eyeing him oddly, but it was merely freakshow interest in his scarred face and they looked away quickly when he met their eyes. Most of the drinkers were a down-at-heel lot: tattooed ex-dockers, long retired; London Transport workers coming off shift; half-a-dozen unemployed loafers from the council estate with their shapeless women in tow. The only colourful characters were an old man with long white hair and bare feet, whom everyone seemed to know, and a grossly fat woman with two greyhounds which sat under her bar stool, taut as piano wire, daring people to pat them. Nobody did.

The girl who called herself Jit played on as the babble and the smoke and the smell of spilled beer rose through the evening. No one paid much attention. The Battle of the Nile was a drinkers' pub, and beyond an occasional patter of applause they ignored her. Silver wondered why she bothered. She was untutored but she was too good for this place. That pure voice kept drawing his attention. Her choice of music was eclectic, a mixture of middle-of-the-road folk, some unplugged Clapton, and a handful of strange and haunting songs he did not recognise.

He found he didn't mind washing up. He did not need to concentrate on orders and change. It left his mind free to work on other things. He took the first of the pint glasses and plunged them into the soapy water, rinsing them together under the greasy surface. Soon he was into a soporific rhythm of washing and rinsing and drying which lasted him for two hours or more, while the girl's clear song played through his mind like a breeze.

'Oi! I'm *talkin*' to you, clothears!'

Silver started. He had not heard George's summons. He steeled himself for another confrontation, but six or eight pints had drowned George's earlier aggression, and transformed him into a blustering and jovial bully, showing off to a group of his cronies across the bar. 'See that? He's off with the bleeding fairies – eh, Joe, my son! Ain't that right?'

'Sorry, George.' Silver dried his hands.

'Sorry, George,' the landlord mimicked for his friends. 'Ring me up four pints of half-and-half and a lager, like I've been telling you for the last ten minutes.'

'Right.' Silver stepped to the till but fumbled the entry. He tried again, fumbled it. George, sensing there was more fun to be had, stepped up behind him.

'What's up, sunshine? Can't count to ten, eh?' He grabbed Silver's left wrist and held up the mutilated hand for his cronies to see. 'No wonder. His bleeding calculator only goes up to nine!'

George bellowed with laughter until they joined in, his red face thrown back and his black and stumpy teeth exposed. For just a second Silver saw the room swim, had a sickening glimpse of all the bullies and buffoons, all the Georges, who now had power over him.

'You got to keep a sense of 'umour. See, Joe?' George kept an over-firm grip on Silver's left hand, and with his own free one gently cuffed the side of Silver's head, as if he were a naughty boy in class. 'That's Rule Bleeding Two.'

He turned away and in a moment was drinking with his mates, his dominance re-established. Silver emptied the sink, unloaded the dishwasher and reloaded it again, pulled more pints. He did it all mechanically, using the simple actions to calm himself. He knew he would have to learn how to deal with this. He knew this would not be the last time.

'It's a pity the Argies didn't shoot the old bastard.' Up close her bright blue hair was shocking against the line of shabby jackets along the bar. He had not seen her come to the bar and turned away, but she called him back. 'Joe – get us a rum and Coke while you're here.' He made the drink, set it down, uncertain of the house rules. She saw his hesitation. 'It's OK. Nugget'll fix it up when he gets back.' He turned away again. 'What's your hurry, Joe? I just wanted to say I was sorry about that crack. You know –' she mimicked her own challenge with a funny voice '– "come up here and play it yourself, buster". I didn't know about the hand.'

'It doesn't matter.'

'How did it happen? Car accident?'

'I'm busy.'

'How was I?'

'What?'

'Come on, Joe. I've been singing for three hours. How was I?'

'I didn't notice.'

'No, of course not.' She smiled. 'That's why I could see you listening. You knew all of them, didn't you, Joe? Every note. Except the ones I wrote myself, of course.' Silver looked up quickly and she smiled, the jewel in her cheek flashing kingfisher blue. 'Ah, that got you, didn't it? Well, it's true. I wrote the middle set. What do you think of them?' He stared stonily past her. 'You can't fool me, Joe. You know about music, I can tell.'

'My father used to make instruments. I picked up a bit from him, that's all.'

'That's cool. What instruments did he make?'

'Violins and cellos. Things like that.' He gathered glasses noisily from under her nose.

'Can you do that?' she asked eagerly. 'Make things?'

He stared at her stonily. 'It was a long time ago.'

She was a little ruffled by this. Finally she picked up her drink and slipped down from her bar stool. 'OK, Joe. Have it your own way.'

He watched as she bent down for her bag, turned her back, took a step away.

'It's nothing personal,' he said, and she halted and looked at him over her shoulder. He found it impossible to avoid the question in her eyes. 'You're pretty good,' he said, and felt it come out in a rush, the need to make contact, the need to be useful, the gratitude at being asked something, anything. 'And if you wrote that middle set, you might be very good. Very good indeed.'

She turned back, surprised and flattered, cocking her head so that her brilliant hair glittered. 'Well, thanks.'

He walked away quickly to the far end of the bar and lost himself in serving a group of Irish roadworkers raucously entering the fourth hour of celebrating a birthday. After a while he saw Jit pack up her gear and a minute or two later the Australian priest reappeared and helped her carry her stuff out to a waiting van.

35

It was Sunday, but Cobb was on duty in the office to take the call.

'Inspector Cobb, sir? It's Dennis McBean.'

'Sergeant McBean. I see you're enjoying your weekend, like me.'

'Thing is, Mr Cobb, I'm sitting here doing Sunday roster, and I get talking to a mate of mine over at Rotherhithe about an hour ago. I think they've found Silver's wallet.'

Cobb sat up. 'What?'

'I called the Duty Sergeant there, sir, a bloke called Gornall. He says it's not positive yet, but it sounds like it must be Silver's. Credit cards and all.'

'I hadn't heard about this.'

'It only happened this morning. One of those treasure hunter types – blokes with metal detectors? – found it in the mud down there. I told Gornall I'd give you a buzz about it direct.'

'Kind of you, Sergeant.'

'Knew you'd be interested, sir.' McBean seemed to be waiting for something, reluctant to end the conversation.

'Do you fancy a trip to Rotherhithe, Sergeant?'

'Meet you there in half-an-hour, sir.'

★ ★ ★

Cobb slid the waterlogged wallet out of the plastic evidence bag on to the table and poked it with a pencil the Duty Sergeant handed him. Sergeant Gornall was a hard man of sixty with a weatherbeaten face who disapproved of having his evidence prodded about. The wallet was black and clogged with mud and it stank of the river. The contents had evidently been removed once already by Gornall's people and were loosely fitted back inside the leather pockets. Cobb shook them out again on to the surface and separated them with the pencil. A platinum AMEX card, the first Cobb had ever seen, glittered through the grime.

'We cleaned that one off a bit to get the ID, sir,' Gornall said. 'You won't find much else in there except more cards. Your bloke wasn't short of credit. Of course we'll get forensic to have a proper look at it.'

Cobb nodded. He separated the plastic cards on the tabletop. Visa, Diner's, a fancy membership card for an exclusive country club in Kent, three £50 notes and half-a-dozen French 100-franc notes, the remains of a boarding pass, and a flat metallic security card. Cobb assumed this was what the detector had picked up. There was one other item, a square of disintegrating paper. Cobb peered at it.

'It's a photo, sir,' Gornall said. 'Wife and kids, I suppose. You can just see the outlines under the light.' He turned to McBean. 'He did have two kids, didn't he?'

'Yes,' McBean said. 'He had two.'

Cobb stood up from the table. He felt curiously let down. He was not sure what he had expected, but the wallet did not speak to him. It had been a slim wallet and, before the Thames had stained it, would have been a sleek, elegant item, hardly used. But it was a sterile thing, the possession of a man who travelled light and carried little. Cobb's own wallet was bulging with scribbled notes and dockets, receipts, other people's business cards, expired tickets, driving licence, warrant card, security pass, loose stamps. This wallet belonged to a rich man, one who would not sign for anything himself, and if he did, would certainly not trouble to keep the receipt. It carried Silver's name, but not his identity.

Cobb would probably have thanked Gornall at that point and left, disappointed, but as he stood back from the table, McBean moved forward and opened a penknife. He lifted the sodden photograph on the blade and turned it under the light.

'You won't see much,' Gornall said. 'We've been squinting at it for the last half-hour before you got here. Just the outline. See?'

It was clear that the decaying photograph had no secrets to reveal, but McBean's interest in it rekindled Cobb's own. He remembered the icy morning on the bridge and the black Sergeant's distress and for some reason this memory brought the smudged silhouettes to life for him.

'You say some character with a metal detector found it?'

'That's it, Mr Cobb. He handed it in about eight this morning. Never even knew whose it was.' Gornall gently slid the wallet and photograph back into the evidence bag and sealed it. 'Funny, ain't it? A bloke spends his Sunday mornings poking round in the mud looking for Queen Victoria farthings or whatnot, but when he finds a wallet with a hundred and fifty quid in it, he doesn't even open it.'

'Maybe he was superstitious,' Cobb said.

'Maybe he was honest,' McBean said.

Gornall guffawed. 'That's a new one! What was that word again?'

Gornall parked the squad car in what had been the entrance to the warehouse car park. The roadway was drifted with litter and scattered with broken glass and the chain-link fence had been twisted aside in several places. All around stood the skeletons of derelict buildings, a few redbrick Victorian piles recalling the great days of the docklands but most of them low and ugly breeze-block hangars from the fifties. Now their windowframes were sagging and weeds had broken up the tarmac of the car parks.

'Supposed to be redeveloped, this is,' Gornall sniffed. 'New bleeding Canary Wharf on the south bank. Mind you, they've been saying that for twenty-odd years.'

They ducked through a gap in the wire fencing. An enamel sign bearing the stylised picture of a guard dog, fangs bared, lay rusting on the ground in a litter of beer cans. They crossed the forecourt and walked down beside an abandoned warehouse towards the river. The warehouse was set back a little with a dock area in front of it. The dock was incised with curving arcs of tramlines, half swallowed in the crumbling surface. The lines led to a loading dock with an old steel crane bolted to it on massive castings, jutting out over the water. The crane was seized up and rusted, but the name of the Manchester firm which had built it was still visible.

'Just after the war they built this place,' Gornall said, shaking his head. 'Used to send out sheet metal from here, in barges and lighters and stuff. It's all containerised now. They should've seen it coming.'

Cobb walked to the edge of the dock and rested one foot on an iron bollard. Below him a flight of stone steps led down ten feet to the mud of the foreshore, exposed now at low tide. Greenish rocks and an old truck tyre showed through dull grey slime. The blackened stumps of some ancient wharf marched out into the opaque water. The plodding line of searchers had passed the old wharf and were dragging with agonising slowness through the foul mud. There were a dozen of them, all Cobb could muster on a Sunday afternoon at an hour's notice, grim men in waders and oilskins. They avoided his eyes. Cobb didn't blame them for their sullenness. It would be miserable out there, thigh-deep in stinking slime. The searcher at the extreme end of the line was half in the river itself, the water almost up to his waist. As Cobb watched, the man stumbled and fell full-length and came up cursing and spluttering.

Beside him, Gornall laughed shortly. 'You won't be on that bloke's Christmas card list, sir. It'll be the stomach pump for him.' Cobb said nothing and after a moment Gornall went on, with satisfaction: 'Tide's making. If they ain't found him by now, he ain't there to be found. Fact.'

'Thank you, Sergeant,' Cobb said sharply. 'Why don't you go and chase up some coffee for these men?'

Gornall looked at him. 'Sir.' He sauntered off with calculated insolence.

Cobb gazed out over the Thames. It was a soft February afternoon, and a diffuse and pearly light fell across the quarter-mile expanse of river that stretched in front of him. The water looked like beaten pewter. He could hear it muttering against the beach a few feet below him. Away to his left he could see the fairy castle spires of Tower Bridge and on the far side of the river the City's steel and glass business blocks. Beyond that, London was lost in a soft white haze. A tug thumped up against the current in midstream a hundred yards away, towing three tarpaulin-covered barges. As Cobb watched, a crewman came out of the cabin and emptied a teapot over the side. The breeze out on the river whipped the tea dregs away in a spiral behind the boat. A brace of curious gulls planed above the tug's funnel, watching for scraps, and when they didn't appear, soared away into the white air.

The line of the treasure hunter's footprints was

visible in the mud for several yards downstream, stopping in a mess of churned filth just below the steps and perhaps six feet out from the wall. Cobb looked at them for a while and then turned away. A police canteen truck had arrived and Gornall stood with his hands behind his back, watching as the canteen was readied for use, flaps opening, gas jets lit. Cobb was fairly sure that the Sergeant would be in line for the first mug of coffee that was handed through the hatch. He walked up beside the man.

'You know the river, Sergeant. Could that wallet float here, all the way from Lambeth Bridge?'

Gornall jerked up his chin. 'Leather and plastic? It wouldn't float at all, sir. Even before it got waterlogged it would sink. I'd say it'd just roll deeper and deeper into the river. No special reason for it to fetch up here.'

'So what does that mean?' McBean demanded, walking up between them. Cobb recognised in his voice the same impatience he felt himself, a sense that they had been cheated, that they had come here for a solution and found only more confusion.

'It doesn't mean much,' Gornall said mildly. 'Maybe your Mr Silver was washed in here, and rolled along the bottom until the wallet fell out of his pocket. Maybe he's stuck in the mud right now, just below the tideline there. We aren't going to drain the Thames to find out. But most likely he just drifted out again on the next tide and left his wallet behind to fox us.'

'Let's get this straight,' Cobb said. 'In your opinion, you don't see anybody getting out of the river here after floating all the way down from Lambeth?'

'Getting out alive, you mean?' Gornall smiled, the idea beyond serious consideration. 'My opinion, sir? Your boy's crab food. He's down on some mudbank off Canvey Island right now, rotting nicely. That's my opinion.'

'And what are the chances of ever finding what's left of him?'

'People forget this old river's a quarter-mile wide here. It's six miles wide at Southend. Twenty-five miles at the mouth. There's shoals and channels and marshes and tidal islands and all sorts, all the way down. That's a lot of nowhere to find one poor little stiff in.'

'Great,' McBean said. 'That's just great.'

Gornall shrugged again, losing interest. He knew the facts. It wasn't his fault if other people didn't choose to accept them. 'I'll be over in the car when you need me, sir,' he said, and walked away with ponderous dignity in the direction of the fence.

Cobb watched him go. After a while he looked down at the churned grey mud and at the trail of footprints up the steps, and then gazed out again over the sliding river. A thin sun broke through momentarily and for a few seconds the Thames shone like a polished shield. It was indeed a great deal of water, Cobb thought. Beside him McBean kicked a loose stone savagely and it cannoned over the river and fell far out with a white plume of spray. A gull appeared from nowhere and hung on the wind above the splash, cocking its head to one side to see if this might be something to scavenge.

The sight of its greedy beak triggered in Cobb's mind an image of Silver's collapsing body crucified on a mudflat somewhere in this vast estuary, amid acre upon acre of shining water, attended by the gulls and the crabs and the larvae which squirmed in the silt. The hieroglyphs printed on the grey mud by the wading birds would be his epitaph. Beside him, McBean kicked another stone.

'What exactly did you expect, Sergeant?' Cobb asked him, and then, to take the challenge out of it, added: 'Really. I'm interested.'

'Closure. Put this thing to bed.' Belligerently McBean stuffed his hands into the pockets of his uniform anorak. 'It's Dennis, sir. Everyone calls me Den.'

Cobb nodded in acknowledgement. He said: 'Well, Den, that's what I want too. Closure.'

'Ever since that night, this one's been on my mind. Mine and Jayce's. Hayward, sir, that is. You get involved. It feels kind of personal. Know what I mean?'

'Yes.'

'I hear the wife doesn't believe he's gone, sir. Would that be right?'

'That's right.'

'Hubby marches out like that with the kids. Breaks your life up. And then there's no corpse. No end to it. You feel sort of sorry for her.'

'Yes.'

'I suppose she'll come to believe it in the end, sir. Only–'

Cobb looked across at him, and completed the thought for him. 'Only you're not so sure either. Are you?'

The Sergeant met his eye, held it appraisingly. It was as if he was considering whether to confide in Cobb. McBean looked out across the river to the far bank. 'I saw that little kiddie come up out of that water, like she was inside a big bubble. Like one of those membrane things babies are born in sometimes, or kittens. What d'you call it?' Cobb shook his head. He couldn't remember either. 'Anyway, like she was just born on to the surface in one of those. This sounds crazy, right?'

'No.' Cobb watched him: he knew that McBean had never told anybody this before, and he felt privileged.

'Well, sir. It shook me. That I'd nearly missed it, I mean. If it hadn't been for Hayward, that little girl would be dead now, like her sister. I can't get it out of my mind how certain I was. And I was wrong, wasn't I?'

Cobb stared up at the white sky. Bruised clouds were blowing in from the sea. It was growing cold. Soon it would rain. The first of the police searchers clambered up the steps and on to the concrete apron not far from them, plastered in grey filth. A Constable had run out a hose and now played it on the man, who stood there swearing as the slime slid off him, leaving his oilskins slick and black. The river mud stank as it pooled around his feet.

'Let's walk,' Cobb said at last.

They walked, slowly and in silence, across the concrete apron towards the abandoned warehouse. A cold breeze freshened from the river. A faded blue lager can rolled across their path with a desolate clatter.

'There's no way that wallet got into the mud out there unless it arrived in his pocket,' McBean said, suddenly emphatic. 'So he was here, wasn't he? Whether he was alive or not. We know that much.'

'It probably happened the way Gornall says.'

'What? The body floats in here, drops the wallet, and floats away again?'

Cobb faced him. 'So what's your explanation? This far downstream from the crash he just feels like getting out? Oh, and then tosses his wallet back in, with a hundred and fifty quid still in it?' But as he said this, a thought struck him and he stopped.

'What?' McBean demanded, sensing an opening.

'Lauren Silver said he pocketed the cash she was going to take away with her. We didn't find it in the car.'

'Oh? How much?'

'Six thousand.'

'Six! In cash?' McBean whistled. 'With six grand in his pocket he didn't need a wallet.'

'For God's sake, Den,' Cobb laughed. 'Why are you so keen to prove he's alive?'

'Why are you so keen to prove he isn't?'

Cobb froze with his hand on the handle of the sliding door. It started to spit with rain but for a second he still did not move.

'Did I say something, sir?'

'No. No.' Cobb shook himself and wrenched the door open, grinding against its runners. He stepped inside. 'And call me Sam.'

The chill cavern of the warehouse smelled of mould and bird droppings. The open door threw a broad wedge of light across the concrete floor. Steel pillars rose an immense height to a metal roof with filthy translucent panels set in it. Cobb could hear pigeons chortling high up among the steel rafters. The floor was speckled with their droppings, cemented in ridges following the line of transverse girders high above. Against the far wall was a clutter of steel shelving and a pile of old wooden pallets. One or two of the pallets had been dragged from the pile and lay scattered and broken around the warehouse. The floor was littered with rotting newspapers, flattened cardboard cartons, and dry twigs fallen from the pigeons' nests above. Whitish bird down floated in the cold air.

They stood just inside the door for a couple of minutes, shrugging themselves deeper into their coats, while the rain grew heavier outside, stippling the river. As his eyes grew accustomed to the gloom, Cobb made out a semi-circle of plastic milk crates over to the right of the door, and a mound of what looked like ash. He walked across to it and McBean followed. The fire had been built against the front wall of the warehouse and the milk crates were arranged on either side of it, presumably as makeshift seats. Against the metal wall was a small nest of garbage: a dozen beer bottles, polystyrene cups, food cartons, cigarette packets. Wooden pallets lay in pairs to form three low platforms on the open sides of the fire. Soiled blankets, a sleeping bag and stacks of newspapers lay abandoned around the pallets.

'Welcome to the Hotel California,' McBean sniffed, stirring a blanket with the toe of his boot. 'They left in a hurry.'

Cobb lifted one of the newspapers, then another and another, peering in the dim light at the mastheads.

'They're two months old,' he said, looking up. 'All of them. Just before Christmas.'

'Yeah?' McBean was suddenly alert.

'If you were a bum, out sleeping rough,' Cobb said, 'why would you leave all your blankets behind?'

'If six grand had just floated into my lap,' McBean said carefully, 'maybe I wouldn't need blankets.'

36

On impulse Lauren bent over the bed and kissed her daughter lightly on the forehead. She had grown so unused to doing this that she moved clumsily, like a teenage girl kissing a boy for the first time. Freya watched her gravely as she did it. She did not move her face away, but she did not respond.

'Haven't you got a goodnight kiss for me, sweetheart?' Lauren said, without much hope. 'Not even one?'

Freya breathed out and looked at the wall, and then back at her mother. 'When can we go to the farm again?'

Lauren stood up. 'It was only two weekends ago,' she said. 'We don't want to wear out our welcome.'

'Uncle Fred said I could go any time,' Freya said truculently. Lauren knew that she was intended to notice the exclusion, and she did.

'Other people have their lives to live too, Frey,' she said wearily. 'We can't go down and stay with people just when we feel like it.'

Freya turned away from her in the bed and stared at the wall. 'I hate it here.'

'I know you do, Frey. It's not much fun for me either.'

'Why do we stay here, then? With that stupid man.'

'Please don't talk like that, Frey. Uncle Tommy's done so much for us. We need his help.'

'I don't want his help!' Freya rolled back to face her mother and her eyes were hot. 'Why do I have to stay in this place? It's all horrible now.'

'Yes, it is.'

Lauren rubbed her own temples hard with her knuckles. Her head ached and her mouth was dry. She wanted to say that for her it had all been horrible and worse than horrible for years, but there seemed no point. Instead, she said: 'I expect it will get better. Eventually.'

'It won't ever get better.' Freya's voice was full of contempt, and Lauren could not summon the conviction to contradict her.

She said: 'I could really use that kiss, sweetheart.'

'No. You smell of that *stuff*. You said you'd stop drinking that *stuff*. You promised.'

Lauren sighed. 'I'm doing the best I can, Freya.' When her daughter did not respond she stood up and moved to the door. 'I'm really trying. Can't you see how hard I'm trying?' But she said this softly and the hunched figure in the bedclothes did not stir. Perhaps her daughter had not heard. Or perhaps, Lauren reflected, she just wasn't trying hard enough. She turned off the light and trod heavily downstairs.

She crossed to the bar and poured herself a vodka, not troubling with ice or tonic. She supposed she should not, but it could hardly make things any worse.

She drank the first half-inch of warm spirit at one swallow and topped it up at once. Tommy Hudson, working at the walnut desk in the corner of the big room, pretended not to notice. He knew she had been with Freya and, since the outcome was always the same, he knew roughly what had happened. But Hudson was bad at pretence. The very angle of his head, the determined way he refused to look up from his papers, conveyed both concern and disapproval. She was not sure which of the two dominated, and did not much care. Finally, when she refused to speak and then when she topped her glass up for a second time, he laid his half-moon glasses on the desk and looked up at her.

'It'll take time, Laurie,' he said. 'I s'pose that's not much help.'

'No, it isn't.'

He tried again. 'She's been better since the farm. You must admit.'

'Yes. So the counsellor says.' She took her drink and sat staring out over the black garden through the great span of French windows. 'Now she tells me I stink of booze.'

'Oh.' Hudson was shocked, but at a loss to know how he should respond. He looked at the desktop then said stupidly: 'Vodka doesn't smell.'

'That's supposed to make me feel better?'

He shut up then, and after a few moments he perched the glasses back on his nose and went back to frowning at his papers. She finished her drink in morose silence. In a few minutes the warmth of the alcohol spread through her blood and numbed her a little and comforted her and allowed her thoughts to form some pattern. She knew well enough why Freya hated it. The place was a tomb, an expensively furnished tomb. In the old days, whenever Matthew was in residence, the house had been like a royal court, full of colour and noise and music, packed with actors, musicians, agents, hangers-on – flamboyant characters who did absurd and dangerous things. Once, a dancer from Colombia had tried to castrate his gay lover with Lauren's carving knife. Typically, it was Tommy Hudson who had disarmed him. Another time the dreary finance officer of a music company, coaxed into trying cocaine for the first time, had driven his Mercedes into the outdoor swimming pool of the wealthy diamond merchant next door.

Not that Freya and Gudrun had seen much of all this, but they had certainly heard the revelry, and on a hundred mornings-after they had seen the thrilling and destructive results of their parents' lifestyle. The sense of drama and excitement had been palpable when Matthew was home, and often even when he wasn't. Lauren had journalists, society friends and business people in the place at all times. TV companies made shows about her house, her garden, her cooking, her way of life. High-ranking sales people from the world's fashion houses queued to get in to see her.

Tommy Hudson was always there. Lauren could not recall a single gathering which had excluded him. She knew that, whatever Freya might think, in business

terms there was nothing stupid about Hudson. The
world thought of him as Matt Silver's right-hand man,
part bodyguard, part campaigning veteran from the
hard old days before fame had come shining down on
them all. Lauren knew better. She knew that without
him there would have been no fame shining down on
any of them. Matthew was mercury, but Hudson was
iron. Matthew was creator, but Tommy Hudson was
builder.

'I need some money, Tommy. I had a call from the
bank today.'

'Sure.' He sounded pleased to be able to do something. 'Five grand OK?'

'That's fine.'

Hudson slid open a drawer, took out a chequebook
and used his gold fountain pen to write a cheque, then
brought it over to her, waving it to dry the ink. 'I'll set
up a regular transfer for you tomorrow.'

He flopped on to the gold brocade couch and put
his feet up on the arm and rubbed his broad face. He
wore elastic-sided boots and had not troubled to
remove them. Lauren watched him over the rim of her
glass. At that moment the sight of his big brown boots
against the brocade suddenly struck her as strange,
even threatening. She wondered if he had ever done
this before, and for some reason it worried her. In the
old days Hudson would always remove his shoes at
the door, as though the house were a Japanese shrine.
When had he stopped doing that? When had he started
to feel relaxed enough to sprawl around with his boots

on as if he owned the place? It seemed to her that it mattered. She glanced down at the cheque he had handed her.

'But this is a personal cheque, Tommy.'

'Think of it as a loan.'

'I don't want a bloody loan,' she shouted, feeling a rising sense of panic which she could not define. 'I want my own money.'

Hudson swung his feet off the sofa, and leaned forward earnestly towards her.

'It's just temporary. I don't want you to worry, Laurie. I said I'd take care of things, and I will.' He leaned across and put his big hand over hers. 'Tommy'll take care of everything. He always does, don't he?'

Despite her anxiety it moved her to see him so worried for her, and at once she felt guilty for shouting at him. She got a grip on herself and after a moment patted his scarred knuckles contritely. 'I'm sorry, Tommy. It's just that I hadn't given a thought to money for years.'

'And you shouldn't have to be bothered with it, neither,' he said, indignant on her behalf. He sat back and took a pull of his beer. 'You know I loved Mattie like a brother, for all his faults. But I'm really angry at him that he didn't take better care of you, I've got to say that.'

She looked away, embarrassed by this confidence.

'But you know something, Laurie? One thing I do know is that Mattie would've wanted me to take care of all this. For you. He'd have wanted me to look after you.'

His voice had grown hoarse and although she looked away she knew that he was staring at her, trying to gaze into her eyes, uncomfortably close. She pulled her hand away as gently as she could. 'Tommy–'

'How about we get away this weekend, Laurie? I'll take you somewhere nice. Find a bit of sun, p'raps? Lisbon or Naples or somewhere. Find somewhere for Freya to stay, with some friends or whatever. Do you good, get away.'

'Tommy–'

'No strings,' he said, wide-eyed, horrified at the thought. 'Oh, no, no. Nothing like that. But maybe we could just talk a bit. In a funny way, we never really knew one another, did we, Laurie? I mean, Mattie was always there. Always a threesome. But maybe we could start to get to know one another a bit now.'

'But we're already going away,' she blurted. 'Freya and me. To the farm.'

'Oh.' Hudson sat back. 'I didn't know about that.'

'I'm so sorry, Tommy. Old Mr Cobb invited us especially.'

'Well,' Hudson said in a different voice, 'that's that, then.'

The room was ink black, so black that she had to blink hard before she could convince herself her eyes were really open. She felt a stab of claustrophobia, as if the velvet darkness might smother her. At least that meant she was in her own bed. Two or three times recently she had come round after daylight, on the couch downstairs, with Merilda hoovering in the next room. That was humiliating enough, but nothing could compare with waking in the desolate wastes of the night, dusty with thirst, her tongue glued to the roof of her mouth. There were so many hours of darkness left to drag herself through.

She wondered what in particular had awakened her this time. The money, she supposed. It had never occurred to her that money would be a problem. Matthew had made so much, surely it couldn't be a problem. Yet apparently it was. Apparently he could still reach out to screw up their lives, what was left of them, even now. Lying in the darkness she felt a wave of loathing and anger that made her stomach clench. She rolled out of bed and the room spun. A lurch of nausea made her grope for support: the dressing table jingled. She moved unsteadily into the bathroom and sat down on the toilet until her heart stopped thudding.

She urinated, swallowed three painkillers with tapwater. Her stomach churned a couple of times as the cold water hit it, but then it settled. On impulse she got into the shower and turned it on full, and gradually the warmth of it began to make her feel better. Her reflection trembled in the mirror as the steaming water sluiced across her body. She looked at herself critically for the first time in months, examining her body as a horse dealer might inspect a mare, turning from one side to the other. There was no point pretending she was still attractive. She hadn't troubled with her hair for weeks and it lay plastered across her shoulders and breasts like seaweed on a drowned woman. It would be an unruly blonde tangle when it dried. Her skin was dull and there were charcoal smudges under her eyes. Her body was whippet thin and she could count her ribs.

She hooked her hands over the top of the shower cubicle and leaned into the water with her eyes screwed shut, letting the heat blast against her head, willing the pain away. She knew what this was about, and it wasn't about money. She supposed she should have seen it coming. A romantic weekend in Majorca or wherever with Tommy Hudson? Her spirit groaned at the thought. Why he would be interested in this wasted body was beyond her understanding, but it had to come to this in the end, and she realised now that she had always known that it would. For a moment she thought about asking him to move out, before it was too late. But this was dreamtime stuff: she knew she simply could not manage life without him yet.

Lauren knew quite well she would not have survived even this far without him. She would never have found the strength, and Freya would be alone in a hostile world. Poor Tommy. He would be easily enough satisfied, after all. She pictured his lovemaking – clumsy, unimaginative, a bit rough. She had a sudden vision of him fumbling into her with his blunt fingers. Her stomach turned over and she sat down with a thud in the shower and threw up pills and tapwater into the vortex over the drain.

When the spasm had spent itself, she got up and wrapped a towel around herself and walked shakily into the bedroom and sat on the edge of the bed. She was hollow and trembling and could feel cold sweat gathering on her face. So this was what she had come to, despite her resolutions. Her own daughter refused even to kiss her. And Tommy Hudson assumed it was only a matter of time before she would come across. The thought made her stomach churn again, but she controlled it with an effort and breathed deeply until she was steady.

'This has got to stop,' she said aloud into the darkness. The frailty of her voice almost made her laugh, but the quaint Victorian ring of the phrase had a certain solidity and gave her comfort. It reminded her of the sort of thing Cobb would have said, and she repeated: 'This has got to stop.'

When she had asked him for help at the farm some part of her mind had believed that asking alone would be enough to clean the slate, like an act of contrition. She had thought him well-meaning but too formal, too mechanical in his response. She had accused him of calling in SWAT teams and helicopters. When he had sent her the promised names and addresses she had put them aside, a little scornful of his concern. But he had been right. Alone, she would not be able to overcome. He had seen this and she had not. The realisation made her feel as if he had seen her naked.

Even as she sat shivering on the bed she felt herself blush.

'Mummy?' The door opened a crack and Freya stood in the rhomboid of light. 'Mummy, I heard you. Are you all right?'

'Not really, Freya,' Lauren replied. Then she drew herself up. 'But I will be.' The clarity of her own voice surprised her. 'Yes, I will be.'

37

Cobb left the flat early the following morning and, though he chose to walk to work, he was in the office before eight. He greeted a couple of other early risers, took his Prêt à Manger coffee across to his desk and settled himself there while his computer booted up.

It had nagged at him all night, yesterday's business of the wallet and the dead fire in the warehouse. He felt that he was close to something, to some form of resolution. For the first time he could begin to guess what had happened. Someone had seen the body, had even touched it, had rifled through the wet pockets while the white eyes stared at the moon. That someone had found the bundle of money, and in panic had thrown the incriminating wallet away and pushed the body back out into the ebbing tide. Gornall was certainly right: Matt Silver was food for crabs. But somebody had seen him first, some drop-out sleeping rough, Cobb was almost sure. He decided to raise it at the task force briefing later in the morning. He could imagine the team's reaction, bored and derisive. But if they could find that witness, whoever it was who had seen Silver's body, that would be enough to close the whole thing off. The prospect of doing that made him feel good.

'Hey, Cobby,' Sykes shouted from behind him. Cobb started and spun in his chair. Sykes grinned demonically. 'First time I've seen you with an untidy desk. You must be busy, for once.'

'Something like that, sir.'

To cover his surprise, Cobb shuffled papers aside and cleared a space for his coffee then set it down. It annoyed him that Sykes had caught him unawares, and he was resentful that the Detective Chief Super, as always, made him feel like a boy found smoking behind the toilets. But Sykes was right about his desk. It was littered with papers and files. The pegboard partition which screened his workstation was pinned with photographs of Silver, and of Gudrun, and of the damaged Jaguar, along with cuttings and photocopies and scribbled notes and yellow stickers. Sykes grabbed a chair from a neighbouring desk and banged it down facing Cobb.

'Matt Silver,' he said. 'Developments?'

Cobb talked him through the investigation as succinctly as he could. It surprised him that Sykes was interested. He had not commented on any of Cobb's progress reports before and had seemed content to let him get on with the investigation, such as it was. Cobb finished speaking.

'Right.' Sykes grinned savagely. 'Pull the plug on it.'

'What?' Cobb could not hide his surprise.

'The Matt Silver Task Force is disbanded as of now. What's up, Cobby? Thought you'd be pleased.'

'But this business down at Rotherhithe yesterday, sir . . .'

'Doesn't prove bugger all. We've still got no body.'

'No, sir. But I was going to send a couple of lads round to liaise with Gornall's people. Maybe one of the local dossers got rich about Christmas.'

'Fair enough,' Sykes said, indifferent. 'But frankly, if some drunk found the stiff in the river and lifted six grand from it, I'd say it went to a good home. And Silver's just as dead either way, right?' He looked narrowly at Cobb. 'That is right, isn't it?'

'Sir.'

Sykes nodded, then sucked the inside of his cheek for a while. 'Wait. I'll tell you what, Cobby. Keep tabs on it till the inquest. When is it, by the way?'

'Three weeks, sir. March the eleventh.'

'OK. Until then. Put out a release after the inquest too, and announce we've closed down the task force, if anyone's still listening.' Sykes stood up. 'And after that we might find you some real work to do. That is,' he grinned so hard his eyes disappeared, 'if you're going to stay around long enough?'

Without giving Cobb time to answer, he replaced his chair with a clatter and strode away across the CID room, tossing jokes and insults at anyone who caught his eye, and grinning his piranha grin as he went.

Cobb rescued his coffee and sipped it. It was tepid, but he drank it anyway. He reflected that all his encounters with Sykes had this whirlwind quality. The man appeared out of nowhere, uprooted everything in a burst of destructive energy, and was gone again before the dust had settled. It was disturbing, but in some ways Cobb found that he was glad. It had brought matters to a head. He had not realised, for example, how far back he had pushed the idea of resignation. Somehow his original promise to hold on for two weeks had come to mean holding on until the Silver case was closed. Perhaps the dead Matt Silver had given him some direction at a crucial time. Cobb was not sure how he would feel after the inquest. He decided to wait and see.

At the same time he was oddly disappointed by Sykes's announcement. Of course it was right to close the case. But in the past two months Cobb had spent so much time talking to people about Silver, reading about Silver, thinking about Silver, that this ending seemed brutal. He finished his coffee and while he did so let his glance wander over the pegboard with its curling newspaper cuttings and its photographs. He put the cup down and unpinned the photograph of the wrecked car and flattened it on his desk. All through his patient explanations to Lauren, all through his arguments with McBean, something had niggled in his mind. He could feel again the upward twist in the metal channels as Maxey's fingers guided his own around the edge of the Jaguar's sunroof.

Well, Cobb thought. Some things in every investigation remained unanswered. He tossed his empty coffee cup into the bin and switched his phone off voicemail. Instantly it buzzed at him.

'Sam? I'm sorry to call you at work.' Lauren sounded ill at ease. She had never worried about calling him at work before, and it put him on his guard.

'No problem.'

'I really need to come down to the farm this weekend. It's quite important to me. That will be all right, won't it?'

It was not a question. That did not surprise him, but the form of the demand did. He could not identify at first what was different about it, then realised she had spoken in the first person singular.

'That's fine. I'll be out Saturday night at a reunion, but there's no reason why that should make any difference. You're welcome any time. Both of you.'

'Thank you.' She sounded relieved. He could hear the tension go out of her.

He left a gap for her to fill with some kind of explanation, but she did not, and eventually he asked: 'Is Freya OK?'

'Freya? Oh, yes, of course.' She caught herself. 'Well, no. Not really. The farm did help her, though. Anyway, the therapist tells me she's making progress. Please tell your father that, too. I know he'll be pleased.'

Her tone puzzled him. The form of her sentences seemed oddly conventional, as if they were two distantly acquainted middle-class professionals discussing a dinner party. 'Lauren, are you sure everything's all right?'

'All right?' Instantly the edge was back in her voice. 'Oh, yes. Everything's fabulous, Sam. Just fabulous.'

He was almost relieved at this more familiar tone. He changed hands with the phone to make notes. 'I'm off duty Friday. I'll be going down Friday morning. But you turn up whenever you want. Tommy's bringing you, is he?'

She hesitated for just one beat but he registered it.

'Tommy can't bring us this time,' she said evenly. 'He's going to be away on business. I'll come on the train with Freya on Friday. She's got half term.'

Cobb thought about it briefly and came to a decision. 'Why don't I pick you up? I virtually drive past your place anyway.' She didn't answer at once. 'Well, only if it suits you, of course.'

'It's not that.' Her voice changed in a way that silenced him. 'I go down to the church at Leighford every Friday. To Gudrun. I'm taking Freya this time. We couldn't come until after that.'

'Ah.'

'It's kind of a ritual. We couldn't miss it.'

'Of course not.' He drummed his fingers on the handset and then realised that she could hear that and stopped. 'Look, Lauren, if it's any use to you, it's not much of a detour. I mean, I'd be happy to drive you to the church. Drop you off there and pick you up an hour later, or whatever. It's no trouble.' She was silent for so long that he thought they had been cut off. 'Lauren?'

'Yes,' she said in a flat voice. 'Pick us up here at nine.' She hung up without waiting for him to confirm.

It was only much later in the morning that he

realised he had forgotten to tell her about the wallet. It would keep until Friday, he decided. Perhaps by then there would be more to tell. Perhaps it didn't matter anyway.

38

Silver worked quietly and with mounting strength through the following week. There was a little more money from George, and he had a minor windfall on the Tuesday night when a party of council workers came in after work to mark a retirement and stayed for a lock-in. George, purple and paralytic, stumbled upstairs to bed at midnight and left Silver in charge of the half-dozen remaining boozers in the bar. They stayed until nearly three, ribald, hilarious and increasingly openhanded. They forced drinks on him and he accepted the first one and after that took the money. As he let them out of the pub's back door the group's leader, swaying on his feet, pressed a note into Silver's hand which he may have thought was five pounds. It was twenty. By the end of the night he had nearly £50 in cash. He counted it like a miser in his dim chamber among the roofbeams, and felt like a rich man. It would be just enough.

From then on he used his half-healed body carefully, husbanding it. He slipped out every afternoon to fuel himself at some cheap café, picked up newspapers discarded by the customers and read them all. There was nothing. He seemed to have evaporated. How long had that taken? A few weeks. He supposed they must have looked for him. Presumably that had stopped now. He did not exist. On his way back to the pub one afternoon he passed a discount music store and saw Matt Silver CDs set out on a stand in the street. He nearly walked past without noticing. The upthrown exultant face on the sleeve seemed no more than faintly familiar, hardly more so than the faces on the other CD boxes – Gallagher, and Clapton, and even Presley – artists alive or dead, but all in another universe. He was a ghost.

By the following Friday morning he was ready. He had picked up an old black coat from the Oxfam shop, which would at least cover his shabby shirt and jeans. He stood for a long time looking at the twisted and stubbled face in the shard of mirror before deciding. But finally he began, dragging the razor down the line of his jaw and between the grooved scars. It was a cheap plastic razor from Boots, and he was so unpractised with it that he nicked the raised welts of skin four or five times. When he had finished, the scars stood out in livid ridges against his white skin. The beard had at least given him some protection. Now he was stripped bare, and at first this unnerved him. But as he gazed at the ruined reflected face, something fell into place within him. He went quickly downstairs before he could change his mind. He told George he would miss the lunchtime opening and left the pub, walking at first, then taking a bus to the City and a tube out to the western suburbs of London. He got off at Kew and walked some more.

He took up his position on a bench just across the road. From a newsagent's he had bought a packet of limp sandwiches and a paper as props, but he could neither eat nor read. His heart banged painfully and he felt nauseous with apprehension. He had arrived early in his nervousness and now fought the desperate desire to leave again, to convince himself that this could wait another week. But he knew it could not. He tried a corner of the sandwich but it was like sawdust in his mouth. He looked at the paper and found he was holding it upside down. The weather had changed since he had set out an hour before, clouding over and threatening a bleak day. Now it started to rain, heavy drops slapping through the bare branches of the trees in the park and marking the path with big grey medallions. He didn't care about the rain but he would have to move or he would look conspicuous. It had never occurred to him before how suspicious it was for a man merely to *be* somewhere. His mind raced. Absurdly, he began to recall the phrases policemen used in old movies – 'What's your business here, then?' and 'Move along, now' – as if there always had to be business, always somewhere to move along to. The rain strengthened.

The air chilled and he smelled the dankness of rotting leaves, stirred by the rain. People hurried past him towards shelter, crouching under umbrellas. Water trickled down his face and despite the cold he could taste his own salt sweat as it ran into the corners of his mouth. He must go. He rose to his feet. He saw her.

She was impossibly real, impossibly solid. He had dreamed about her for so long that it was hard to accept she had an independent flesh and blood existence outside his own mind. But she did. In the clatter of the children's shoes on the playground was the clatter of her shoes; her voice was one of those seagull voices squealing in protest at the driving rain. She reached the arched gateway of school and paused there with a band of other girls, sheltering, solemn as ever, her glasses flashing, her yellow slicker shining. Silver walked towards her helplessly, walked until he crossed the flowerbeds and collided with the iron railings of the park, and but for the railings he would have walked on blindly across the road to her and taken her in his arms and felt that warm puppy weight of her and felt the soft breath against his cheek, no matter what the cost. His newspaper and sandwiches slipped from his hand and fell in the mud of the flowerbed at his feet.

She turned her head and he saw her through the throng of parents and umbrellas and the grey rain driving down and clung to the railings as if crucified. Her head came round a fraction towards him – a doe catching the first hint of a scent – and in a second she would see the gaunt figure clinging to the railings fifty feet away, the scarred face and outstretched arms. But in that second a black London cab pulled up between them and a blonde woman he did not recognise ran across the kerb and hugged the child in her arms and hurried her into the back of the taxi. The woman's face was pale in the gloom, and her hair was tightly gathered, and though she smiled at the child the smile was full of sadness, and though she hugged the child, the child did not return her embrace. Silver realised that the woman he did not recognise was his wife and it was pain that made her unrecognisable to him.

He turned away from the railings and stumped back across the wet earth to the bench. For a while the world shrank mercifully away from him. If the boy had not trodden on his foot as he was feeling through Silver's coat pocket, he might not have discovered until later that he had been robbed. He opened his eyes and saw the circle of their faces around him, boys of sixteen or so in bomber jackets and baseball caps, hunched in the rain, anxious to look tough.

'Get on with it, Marty,' one of them hissed. Half conscious, Silver saw the furtive looks around the empty park, felt the hand groping into his jacket, smelled the boy's beer breath on his face.

'He's sick,' another voice said uneasily from the back of the group. 'Let's move.'

'He's not sick,' muttered the first boy contemptuously, almost in Silver's ear. 'He's just some wino.' He saw Silver's eyes flicker, and sensing they would meet no resistance from him, he jeered softly: 'Ain't you, mate? Just some old drunk.' At that moment his fingers found the fold of money. He jerked it out without looking at it and they were gone, walking away quickly, huddled over the spoils.

After a while, Silver got wearily to his feet and left the park and walked away down the wet street. The mud from the gardens clumped under his heels and bled across the pavement in ochre streaks. He kept walking blindly until the light began to fade and then, when a bus pulled up beside him, he climbed aboard.

'It is not a personal matter.' The Sikh bus driver wagged his turban. 'It is specifically an issue of the rules.'

'But I have to get into the city,' Silver repeated stupidly. He had been in another world, bleaker even than the grey rain-spattered one beyond the throbbing windows of the bus. A woman behind him in the queue clicked her tongue and dumped her shopping bags with unnecessary force on the pavement.

'You don't have a ticket, you don't have a travelcard, and you don't have money. How is it I can permit you to ride?'

Silver swayed unsteadily on the platform of the bus. It came to him that he was naked, powerless, unable to affect the outcome not just of this situation, but of any situation. He had seen the agony of his wife and child. And there was nothing he could do now to relieve it. Nothing. How could he? He could not even buy a bus ticket.

'I'll lose my job,' he said at last. In his own ears his voice was pathetic, pleading. He could not understand why he was saying these words. What did it matter if he lost his job? What job? Yet some cringing reflex made him beg, just as if it did matter.

'You forget your money, or what precisely is the problem?' the driver offered, seeing his despair and taking pity, anxious to provide him with an excuse. Silver stared at the man's soft brown eyes, and felt his mouth open and shut a couple of times. Finally the driver sighed and hit a button so that the ticket came buzzing out. When Silver still didn't move, the man tore off the scroll of paper and thrust it at him. 'You don't do it again, please. It will cost me my employment.'

Silver stumbled up the length of the bus, avoiding passengers' eyes. He heard the driver muttering apologies to the people waiting behind him. An explanation too, perhaps – released too early into the community, not his fault, unfortunate gentleman. A hiss of shared laughter. Silver screwed the ticket up in his fists and stared at the floor as the bus pulled out into the traffic and at last the attention of the other passengers began to drift away from him again.

Later, he lay stretched on the mattress under the luminous rectangle of his window. It was midnight, winter midnight on a Friday in London with the cold rain sluicing in from the estuary. Through the window he could see the cloud base as thick and grey as an army blanket over the rooftops, lit dull red by the glare of the city. The foul weather must have kept the drinkers away because downstairs it was quiet in the bar. George had not come bawling for him: perhaps the fat publican had seen his face when he came in, soaked and shivering, and had thought better of it. In the middle distance Silver could hear the traffic on Commercial Road. Two police sirens, their wailing notes plaiting together into a discordant thread, climbed in pitch and then faded away. From a block of council flats across the High Street he heard shouted laughter and thumping bass notes from a party, surging up in volume and down again as a door was opened and closed. A glass shattered; a shriek of laughter. A two-stroke motorcycle drew up and stood popping at the kerb while change jingled and the smell of pizza drifted up to him. Then the bike puttered away and the party started again. He could hear empty beer cans tossed clattering down basement steps.

The image would not leave him alone. The moment he closed his eyes he saw their faces swim back into focus. Lauren, pale and jagged, stretched to the point of fracture, like a woman in physical pain. Freya, squinting against the rain through her big flashing glasses, jostling in her yellow slicker with her school-friends. He could see that she was among them but not of them. He saw the faces of those schoolgirls, the polite and kindly faces of well-mannered children, careful with his daughter. And yet they maintained a distance, as if her tragedy marked her. There was a space around her like a force field, almost as if they needed to leave room for the larger, more vivid personality now extinguished, and of which she was not much more than a shadow. He saw this vision of her and it stabbed him. He saw himself, too, gripping the park railings, like a Somme soldier hanging on the wire. How could she ever be like any other little girl now? She could never be. And this was his fault.

Such was the cipher written into his survival. He saw that he had been spared only so that he could break the code for himself, read for himself the hateful message it concealed. That he had failed when he had the chance to succeed. That he had sucked beauty and warmth out of the world, instead of pouring it in. That he was guilty. He stared out through the dirty glass at the weirdly lit blanket of cloud. The wind muttered among the chimney stacks, rattling a TV aerial, slinging rain like gravel against the glass.

When he looked again the clouds were gone and a sky of rinsed pearl had replaced it and his stomach was telling him it was empty and somehow a day had passed. He was not conscious of having slept, and perhaps he had not. Perhaps his mind had simply shut down under the weight of thought and vision. His clothes were still slightly damp on him and his bladder was full. He got up stiffly and hobbled to the makeshift bathroom and urinated and stared into the shard of mirror at his branded face, stubbled and hanging with fatigue. At least this was the last time he would have to look at it. He felt neither calm nor rested, but at least his course was clear now and he found himself able to plan it with dispassionate precision.

He crossed to the upturned tea chest which served as a table and emptied his pockets. A twenty-pence piece, a scatter of smaller coins. He remembered staring in stupefaction at the same pitiful handful of change as he stood on the platform of the bus under the sad brown gaze of the Sikh. Who would take pity on him now? It was one thing not to have the money for a bus fare, another not even to be able to afford to die. For he would need enough to get back to Lambeth Bridge on the far side of London. Go back to the beginning, to where all this had started, replay it, and make no mistake this time. It was absurd to be cheated of eternity for lack of a ticket on the tube. He could almost have laughed.

The stair door banged open below and George's beery parade-ground voice came booming up. 'Joe? You up there, you idle bastard?'

'I'm sick.'

'Sick be buggered. It's gone four. You want this fucking job or don't yer?'

Silver straightened his back. His joints felt swollen and tight. He could feel his sinuses and the back of his throat burn with the itch of infection. So he really was sick. Well, he thought, it didn't matter much now. If he could get through tonight and beg, borrow or steal just a little cash . . . maybe he could help himself to a half bottle of Scotch – something to take the chill off that dreadful black water – and then he could quietly slip away.

'Give me five minutes, George.'

He heard the man grunt, walrus-like, and the door slammed. He found a hard cube of cheese in the fridge and silenced his stomach with it. Then he shovelled his handful of coins into his pocket and moved stiffly down the stairs.

George held a glass up to the light, squinted at it, buffed it on his sleeve, squinted again. A banknote lay on the bar.

'Take it or leave it, my son. This ain't the Royal Bleeding Mint. And you been skiving off. You're lucky I give you that. Where you been, anyway?' It almost sounded as if he cared.

'I was sick, George. Flu.' Silver smoothed the crumpled note against the wood. It was derisory by way of payment, but under the circumstances it didn't seem worth arguing about. It would probably be enough for his purposes. George put the glass down and picked up another, repeated the polishing ritual. He seemed to want to talk.

'What you saving up for anyway, Joe?'

Silver stared down at the money. It was the sort of sum he used to give to cab drivers as a tip, and yet he had worked all week in this grubby drinking hole for it. 'I'm saving for the future, George.'

'The future, eh?' George snorted. 'Well, my son, good bleeding luck.' He made to move off down the bar then changed his mind and turned back, pushing his whiskers into Silver's face, bunching his shirt in his fist. 'But you just watch your step, sunshine. You got something going on and I don't trust you.' A drinking crony shouted a greeting and George released Silver's shirt and walked away.

'It's Saturday night and I just got paid.' Nugent swung himself up on to a bar stool, leaned across and with his fingertip prodded the banknote which Silver was still smoothing mindlessly against the bar. 'A pot of your finest ale there, tapster.'

Silver stared blankly at him. On the far side of the room the girl called Jit was setting up mike stand and amplifier. Saturday night. Music. He had forgotten. Silver found that it was taking him time to make obvious connections: his throat felt hot and he was feverish. He wished suddenly that it was later, that he could get on with it.

Nugent said: 'Do we have a problem?'

'No.' Silver crushed the note into his pocket and pulled a pint. Nugent took the beer, sipped it.

'You want to talk about it, Joe?'

'Do you think I want your advice?'

'I don't know what you want,' Nugent said mildly. 'Do you?'

'I'm working.'

'Me too,' the Australian said, deadpan, 'I'm about my father's business. But maybe you didn't notice. I've never been much good at this love thy neighbour stuff. It's not that I care much about you, Joe. I couldn't really give a fat rat's arse. It's just we're supposed to ask.' He drank, leaned his elbows on the bar top. 'You know, it's funny – old George is a real shithead, but in a way I'm a bit like him. Rule Bleeding One, Rule Bleeding Two. All that makes sense to me, cause and effect. It's good Old Testament stuff.'

'If you're trying to tell me something, I'm not interested,' Silver said, but he did not move away.

He seemed to lack the energy.

'I'm just wondering what cause has the effect of bringing you here, Joe. A bloke with a lot of new scars, with the remains of a thousand-quid leather jacket on his back, with one of those halfway educated Pommie accents. And here you are in this bloodhouse, taking pocket money from an old bastard like George. Fair go. It'd have to make you curious.'

'It doesn't matter,' Silver said, meeting the Australian's eyes for the first time and silencing him. 'Trust me. It doesn't matter now.'

He turned away and moved down the bar. He could feel the priest's look following him as he went.

Silver worked in a haze, dragging himself down the hours towards closing time, at one remove from the noisy bar. Pulling beer, washing glasses, stocking shelves, cleaning tables, pulling more beer: it was an endless wearisome toil. Perhaps it was only the girl's singing which made it bearable. He clung to the rhythms of her songs as marching soldiers once stepped out to the fife and drum, drawing courage from the music long after their native strength had dwindled away. And she was singing beautifully tonight. He seemed to hear her through a mild delirium, a cool, pure voice that soothed him. Sometimes he caught himself idling, just listening to it, and once he glanced up at her, unable to credit that this scruffy urchin in laceless boots could be the source of anything so fine. She saw him looking and made a funny face at him without faltering in her song, as if mocking herself simply for being in this smoky dungeon. He looked away quickly.

He set himself 11 p.m. as his target. It would be easy enough to cross London then, and quiet enough by the time he reached Lambeth Bridge. He watched as the hands of the big wall clock above the fireplace crawled towards the end of his life, and willed them to move faster.

At ten-fifty the bar was packed, busier than he had ever known it. George was out of the way for the moment, packed into a circle of rowdy boozers at the far end of the bar. Jit was finishing up with one of her Joan Baez favourites and singing with such confidence that, for once, she had the attention of almost the whole room. Drinkers turned their backs to the bar to listen, leaving their empty glasses on the countertop.

Silver seized his chance, dodging down the steps into the cellar storeroom. He found a half-bottle of Bell's in its cardboard carton, broke the seal and drank some of the hot spirit, then slipped the flat bottle into the inside pocket of his jacket. He came back up the steps and quietly opened the bar flap. Jit finished a song to an unusually generous burst of applause, some glass-banging and a couple of encouraging shouts.

He might have done it then, simply pushed through the bar and out through the old frosted glass doors and into the night. But the room had suddenly fallen silent, listening while Jit went through some end-of-performance patter. Someone shouted cheerfully at her to go on, to give them one more, and the call was taken

up by half-a-dozen others. Flattered, she laughed into
the mike, and struck a chord, and Silver stopped in the
act of lifting the bar flap. She hit the chord again, then
a fresh one, a plaintive, keening sound. Silver froze. He
saw the pattern of the finger positions in his mind and
he knew, before she played it, what would come next.
And then she was singing:

> *You people climbing on that Narrow Way*
> *Can climb from cradle up to Judgement Day*

Stunned, Silver heard the song through. He found that
he was unable to move. A couple of people asked him
for drinks while she sang. He ignored them. There
were some muttered complaints and someone tapped
sharply on the bartop with a coin. Across the bar he
saw George's coarse and florid face lift in his direction.
But he could not move. And then it was over. There
was more applause, more good-natured catcalls, and
Jit's shouted goodnight through the mike. Silver closed
the bar flap behind him, saw George look at him and
slide down from his stool, suddenly suspicious. Silver
took three steps through the crowd towards the doors,
feeling the bottle in his pocket knock against his chest.

'Joe?' Jit appeared right in his path, her face shining
with pleasure at her small triumph. 'Was I good, or
what?'

'Great.' He tried to move past her.

'Well, don't go overboard.' She looked disappointed
at his reaction, but stood her ground. 'Look, give me a

hand with the gear, will you? Nugget's gone to get the van.'

'I can't.'

She squared up, hands on her hips. 'What do you mean, you can't?'

'There's something I've got to do, Jit, that's all. Something important.'

'What's so bloody important you can't give me a hand with my gear for five minutes, you miserable sod?'

'Jit—'

'All right, sunshine,' George said, shouldering her aside. 'What's your hurry, then?' He flipped open Silver's jacket and in a surprisingly dexterous move extracted the Scotch, looked at it, smiling at his own cleverness. 'I just knew you was—'

Afterwards, Silver could only remember snatches of it: the splintering of the girl's amplifier as he pushed George hard in the chest and the fat barman tripped backwards over the equipment, the girl's indignant shout. He remembered turning to run and a mass of bodies blocking him, dragging at him. Then someone had him in a bearhug and the breath was crushed out of him and he felt George's wiry whiskers scrub against his cheek and his sour beer breath in his face.

'That's you finished, sunshine.' The hissing voice, so close to his ear, was oddly intimate. He struggled but what fight he had was gone out of him: he allowed himself to be pushed, half-crushed, towards the doors, one of his badly mended ribs jabbing him like a dagger.

His knees hit the doors and they shuddered open on to the rainslick car park shining under the night sky. George got his boot into Silver's back and sent him skidding over the tarmac so that his knees burned and his chin bounced and his jaw clacked shut on the edge of his tongue. He rolled over and George stood towering and bristling at the door. 'Don't try coming back here, Joe Hill. You got any stuff upstairs you'll find it out by the bins in the morning. I don't want to see your ugly face again.' He turned to go in, swung back, pointing, triumphant. 'I knew you was trouble from the start. Knew it.'

George pushed out his chest, tugged down his waistcoat and swaggered back into the bar. Silver sat up in the rain and hugged his knees until the pain died down, his eyes screwed shut. After a moment he heard the door open and swing closed again, and he thought George had come back to reinforce his lesson, but he no longer cared enough even to look. An arm was hooked under his and dragged him to his feet.

'One of the problems with this job,' Nugent said, 'is I have to be nice to arseholes like you.'

39

'I suppose you've got nowhere to go.' Nugent made no attempt to hide his disgust. He rammed the van down a gear and took a corner so sharply that the back wheels skidded a little on the wet tarmac. 'I suppose we've got to bloody give you a roof for the night, with all the other derros.'

'Dump him right here, Nugget,' the girl shouted from the back. 'He's wrecked my amp.' She leaned forward and prodded Silver hard in the collarbone. 'What got into you, you crazy bastard? What have I ever done to you?'

He stared out dully at drab streets flicking past in the night. Were these part of his capital? He didn't know any of them. Parades of shabby shops, some derelict, their windows gaptoothed, grimy redbrick gables, litter blowing down the gutter. Mean blocks of council flats with car bodies on blocks outside them and knots of hard-eyed kids, hunched against the rain.

'I'm sorry,' he said finally.

'Sorry? What good's that? How am I going to get another gig without an amp?' She was almost in tears, and her voice abruptly dropped an octave. 'And I was doing good tonight.'

He rubbed his head. He felt ill. He felt like death.

The thought formed into words in his mind and he was caught for a second between laughter and tears. He felt too ill to die; it was too much effort tonight. Right now he would take the easiest option going, whatever it was. He heard himself say: 'I'll fix the amp.'

'You can't fix that!' she cried. 'It's totally fucked. Totally!'

'I can fix it. I can fix things.'

'Is that so, now, Joe?' Nugent said, with new interest. 'Is that a fact?'

After a few minutes he drove through a maze of crumbling backstreets and into a square of narrow Edwardian terraces. Several were boarded up. The façade of one was blackened by fire. The tiny front gardens were overgrown with grass and tangled shrubs and piled with litter. On an island in the centre of the square crouched a grey stone church with a hall of black corrugated iron beside it. Nugent turned in through a rutted driveway and pulled up. Jit got out without a word and slammed the car door behind her. Silver could see gravestones and a withered palisade of cast-iron fencing beyond. He climbed out. His knees were stiff and stung as he moved. He leaned against the van and rubbed them and his hands came away wet.

Nugent led Silver round to the front of the little hall. Now that he was close to it, Silver could see the place was barely holding itself upright, the rusting iron curling away in sheets from its rivets. Nugent pushed the door open and stepped inside. 'Hi, Phil. How's it going?'

'No trouble at all, Father.' A portly man with horn-rimmed glasses and a maroon knitted cardigan sat at a trestle table inside the door, reading from a New English Bible. He smiled peacefully at Silver, took in his tattered clothes. 'Another guest, Father?'

'For tonight, maybe,' Nugent replied over his shoulder, striding the length of the room with Silver in his wake.

The hall was dark and chilly and Silver could see the glimmer of the night sky through rivet and rust holes above his head. He became aware of half-a-dozen huddled shapes on beds around him, folding beds laid out barrack-wise, feet to the central aisle. The dark shapes stirred and muttered as they passed. The air was tainted with the smell of urine and unwashed bodies. Someone – a woman – cried out, a despairing sound. A male voice cursed in reply.

'The diocese doesn't like it much,' Nugent said, 'but there you go.' He stopped, peered into the darkness. 'Spider?'

A voice answered, sepulchrally: 'The Demons of Beelzebub, Father. They're after me again.'

'I'll be bloody after you tomorrow, Spider. You're not taking your medication, are you?'

'It seems ineffective against Beelzebub, Father.'

'Rest easy, Spider. Not even Beelzebub will get past Fat Phil.'

'No, Father.' Doubtfully. 'Thank you, Father.'

There was a small stage at one end of the hall and Nugent led Silver round it and through to a space that apparently served as some sort of combined changing room and kitchen. He flicked on a light and closed the door behind them. There were three sinks in a row against the far wall, an old gas cooker, a doorless cupboard with oversize aluminium saucepans in it, and in the middle of the room a kitchen table and five unmatched chairs. The space under the stage, which formed one wall, was packed with boxes of tinned and bottled food, plastic sacks of clothing, battered children's toys. Nugent put the kettle on the gas, rinsed out some mugs, spoke over his shoulder.

'Clean up that gravel rash. There's some Dettol and stuff in the cupboard on the wall there. Use the kitchen towel.'

Silver looked down and saw for the first time that his jeans were torn through and that both his knees were grazed and bleeding. He had not noticed. 'It's nothing.'

'Just do it,' Nugent told him impatiently. 'I can't stand fucking heroes. And when you've done that, sling your duds in the bin and dig around in those sacks for something that fits. You might as well pull out anything else you can get into while you're at it.'

Silver was too tired to argue and did as he was told, stripping off his ruined jeans and dabbing antiseptic on the raw flesh until it screamed at him. Then he dragged over a couple of the plastic sacks and broke them open and rummaged through them on the floor. He had worked through the first sack twice before he realised he had forgotten what he was looking for. He tried again and then stopped, too weary and ill to go on, bent over in his threadbare underpants, his hands buried in the thrown-out clothing. The room tilted a little and he sat down on the floor with a thump. He felt Nugent's strong hand grip the nape of his neck and his head was roughly pushed forward.

'Breathe,' the priest told him, as he tried to straighten up. 'Breathe. You can't pass out here. You've got to keep Beelzebub off Spider's back yet.' Nugent took his hand off Silver's neck and let him sit up. He handed Silver a mug of tea. 'Try that. There's enough sugar in it to stand the spoon up in. And these.' He shook out a couple of white pills and pushed them into Silver's hand.

He sipped the tea. It was sickeningly sweet but the sugar jumped straight into his blood and he felt some of his strength return at once. He sipped again and then again. He looked up after a while through the steam and saw Nugent reclining on one kitchen chair with his feet up on another, watching him.

'Well, Joe. Look at you now. Going through the rag basket for cast-offs, taking charity tea. Getting all ready to bed down on the floor with a dozen drunks and misfits and a couple of total copperbottomed lunatics.' Nugent drank some of his tea, surveying Silver almost with amusement. 'You got no job. You got no home. You haven't even got your own name any more.'

'My name's Joe Hill.'

'And I'm Joan Baez.' The priest stretched back so that the chair creaked. 'No, Joe. I don't know who you are and I'm not going to ask. But I guess you're just about as low as you'll ever get. Wouldn't you say?'

'I'll move on tomorrow.'

Nugent shook his head. 'We ought to call the police right now. You couldn't be any worse off.' Silver stared at him stonily and after a while Nugent set his mug on the table and swung his feet off the chair. 'I'm not going to do that, Joe. Not because I like you much, but because it's not part of my brief. There's supposed to be somewhere to go when there isn't anywhere to go, and this is supposed to be it. All the same, it isn't a bolthole for crims who probably ought to be locked up.'

'I'm not a criminal. Not the way you think.'

'Whatever you are, Joe, you can stay here tonight.' Nugent stood up. 'After that, you pay your way.'

'I'll be gone tomorrow.'

'We'll see.' Nugent leaned over and hooked from the heap of clothes a pair of khaki trousers, a couple of shirts, socks, underwear, and piled them on the kitchen table. 'We'll see.'

40

Silver came awake with a jolt. Nugent was standing over his cot in the morning light, kicking him lightly on the leg. The priest clutched bulging plastic sacks in his arms. He looked at Silver over the top of them and lightly kicked him again.

'Wakey, wakey. Hands off snakey.' Nugent set one of his sacks down, opened it and tossed a bread roll on to Silver's blanket. It was still warm. 'Breakfast. Wonderful what the bakers will give you if you threaten them with hellfire. Now get a wriggle on.' He marched off towards the kitchen, still shouting instructions to Silver over his shoulder. 'There's a shower out the back in the shed, but leave that till later. Give a hand in the kitchen.'

Silver sat up on the end of the bed and yawned and shivered in the cool, trying to wake up. His breathing was thick and his throat was sore. From the slight tenderness of his skin he supposed he did indeed have flu. But his body felt so restored by sleep that compared to the night before these things were insignificant. He had slept like a dead man. The night was a pit of unbroken blackness behind him and he had no re-collection of anything since he had rolled into the bed, not a cry or a whimper from the others in the room. He had rested in so deep a chasm of sleep that it took him some moments to pull all the pieces back together: some crazy talk of Beelzebub, an image of a kindly pompous man in a burgundy cardigan, a drive across unfamiliar stretches of London. His memory reached back: the pub, George's pig bristles in his ear, the girl's amplifier. Freya. Freya. Freya.

The rich aroma of the hot bread made his stomach gurgle and he nibbled at the roll, then devoured it in two wolfish bites, surprising himself. The food thrust energy directly into him and he sat up and swung his legs out. The healing skin on his knees cracked and stung and he winced, sitting on the bed for a moment with his feet on the warm boards. All around him other sleepers were all already up, rolling sleeping bags, folding their beds and stacking them to one side in some practised routine to which only they knew the movements. Taking charge was a fit-looking young man with a pony tail and a yellow T-shirt, restacking the beds, bullying them along, clapping his hands and shouting orders at them. He ignored Silver, perhaps giving him a few moments to recover.

Silver stared around him. There was not much talking. He supposed these lost strangers must have been sleeping all around him in the darkness. It was an odd discovery, knowing he had been at his most vulnerable among them. Had they watched him in the night? Plotted against him while he slept? He could not understand why it should matter, why he should care. And yet it seemed to, and he did.

In the daylight, they seemed to have little in common

with one another. A big soft boy in a lovingly home-knitted sweater, mumbling to himself. A pair of grizzled old soldiers in Army surplus coats. A lanky man in a crumpled suit, who looked like a college lecturer and stared shiftily at the floor, never meeting anyone's eye. A jolly woman in dirty pink stretchpants. Two teenagers, a boy and a girl, both with the stringy, desiccated look of heroin addiction.

The room was cold and bleak in the morning. Silver could see daylight in half-a-dozen places through the tin roof and there were damp patches on the floor below. Seated on a cot on the far side an old man was coughing volcanically on the raw air, choking and hacking, until the youth in the T-shirt shouted at him. Then the old man shuffled to the door and hung on to the frame and Silver could hear him hawking and spitting into the gutter outside, over and over again. It made his stomach churn.

A small neat man clicking an amber rosary appeared at Silver's elbow. He wore shiny black trousers and a surprisingly clean white shirt, which made him look a little like a Spanish waiter. Silver avoided his eyes and busied himself with tugging on his unfamiliar clothes, hoping the little man would disappear again. Silver discovered that the new pants were too big for him but the soft overwashed texture of them was luxurious.

The neat man hovered. At last he said: 'I don't think it's Fat Phil who keeps him off.'

Silver ignored him, shrugged on his shirt, shook out

the blanket, fumbled under the fold-up bed for the release catch.

The man moved closer. 'I don't think the Prince of Darkness is afraid of Fat Phil.'

Silver groped under the bed. If he could only fold the damn thing up he could get away from this madman.

'No, my friend. I believe it's you who kept me safe.'

Silver stared at him, too surprised to move away even when the stranger leaned forward and gently touched his face with his fingertips.

'I believe Beelzebub saw your battle scars, and knew you were too much for him.'

The man bent down and slipped the catch on the folding bed for him and expertly collapsed the jangling frame. Then he turned away and joined the breakfast queue. Silver was still staring at his narrow back when Nugent shouted from the door.

'Don't stand there like a stunned mullet, Joe. Get your arse into gear.'

The jolly woman in pink stretchpants shuffled past into the line. She smiled kindly at him. 'First time?' She patted Silver reassuringly on the elbow. 'You'll get used to it, dear.'

He avoided the queue and walked quickly up to the kitchen door where Nugent was stationed. The priest was supervising the breakfast hand-outs like a Quarter-master Sergeant, bawling at the slow or greedy, shouting instructions, cracking crude jokes and laughing at them himself. Perhaps he did not see Silver approach, or perhaps he simply ignored him, but Silver found himself waiting like a schoolboy to be noticed. He could see over Nugent's shoulder into the kitchen beyond, where a band of women toiled in clouds of steam and smoke and a jabber of voices. They were mostly elderly, irreverent characters making a great game of frying bacon, buttering bread, pouring tea. Through it all they shouted insults at Nugent, who tossed back coarse rejoinders of his own. The coarser they were, the more the women shrieked with laughter.

Silver was mesmerised by their good humour. Somehow he found it hard to remember what he had come to say. The hall began to fill with the savour of frying onions and bacon. The boy in the knitted sweater reached the head of the queue beside him and walked back with a plate of food which glistened with hot fat. Silver swallowed hard. He did not think he had ever been so hungry.

Nugent said: 'We struck lucky with the local mini-market. Freezer broke down and they were going to dump it all. We took it off their hands.'

Silver did not reply, watching as more food was carried past him.

'Still, there's not much point in wasting it on you, Joe, if you're going to jump off a bridge.'

Silver looked up at him stupidly.

'That's what you came up here to tell me, right? "Can't stay, Nugget, thanks for everything, just going to slip out and top myself." Huh?'

Silver tried to concentrate. He felt weak and faint.

He coughed hard a couple of times and the effort made him see stars.

Nugent said: 'You sick?'

'It's just a virus.'

Nugent thought about it, then relented. 'If you're going to live long enough to wash up after it, I guess we can waste a breakfast on you.' He pointed to the small table near the door where Fat Phil had sat the night before. 'Go sit. I'll bring it over.'

Silver walked to the table and sat down heavily. The door of the hall was ajar and through it he could see the soft grey sky shining above terraced houses of ochre brick. A clean breeze blew in around him. It was pleasantly cool and it seemed to Silver that it carried with it some barely definable promise, something like woodsmoke, the faintest change in the chemistry of the air. The first hint of winter unlocking into spring. He stared out at the soft morning, suddenly fascinated by it.

Nugent came striding across the hall with a plate of food and set it down with a clatter. 'Eat.'

Silver did so, ravenously, without even looking up to thank or acknowledge the man, tearing at bread, cramming bacon into his mouth, egg bursting and running down his chin. At the end of it he was breathless with the effort of eating, and the food sat warm in his belly. He became aware that Nugent was watching him, amused, across the table.

The priest was toying with a matchstick between his teeth, rolling it thoughtfully from one side of his mouth to the other. Nugent tapped his own face, nodded at Silver's. 'That was punishment, was it?'

'You could call it that.'

'You upset somebody important?'

'Yes.' Silver looked at his plate. 'Apparently.'

'And is that finished? The punishment?'

Silver frowned at him. 'Finished? How could it ever be finished?'

Nugent lifted his chin in acknowledgement, flicking the toothpick around his mouth. 'That wasn't quite what I meant, but as an answer it'll play.' He sucked the match for a moment. 'You weren't stealing that Scotch last night, were you, Joe?'

'Not the way George thought.'

'You were going to do it then, right? Slip out and pop a few pills, wash them down with the booze. Draw a line under it.'

'Something like that.'

'Well, I'll tell you what, Joe.' Nugent leaned across the table and picked up Silver's knife and rang the blade against his empty plate. 'For a bloke who's so keen on dying, you show a powerful will to live.' He got up. 'It's not my job to stop you topping yourself. Call the Samaritans for that. But I'll tell you this much: guilt is debt, right? To get free of debt, you've got to start paying it off. And as George would say, that's Rule Bleeding Three. Now you can go and kill your stupid bloody self if you want.' He took a couple of steps away, then turned back. 'But wash up first.'

After a while Silver took his plate across the hall to

the kitchen. He had not seen the other inmates go. He had not been paying attention, seated in a daze by the door, sleepy from the food. Now he rather missed them. The speed and orderliness of their departure suggested that some rule governed it, and the fact that he did not know this rule made him feel very alone in the echoing hall, like a child left behind by a school outing.

As he walked into the kitchen he was just in time to see the back door shut and through the glass he watched the last of the cooks – a West Indian woman with a blue hat – shout at someone to wait for her. She clapped her hand to her hat to keep it on in the wind and, laughing, ran down the steps and out of his sight. A door banged and a car drove off. Silver walked across to the sink and ran water and slowly washed his plate and cutlery, then dried them and found a drawer and put them away.

When he had done this he put his hands on the edge of the sink and leaned on them and stared out through the dirty glass of the kitchen window into the churchyard. The kitchen was a shabby pleasant place, smelling of soap and pine cleaner, and warm from cooking. It seemed to hold within it the echo of the women's energetic chatter. The view over the church-yard was pleasant too, with a skittish wind silvering the grass between the gravestones, and the soft light glowing and dimming again as the winter sun tried to break through the clouds. He felt that his strength and will would take him no further than here, a disfigured man with a dose of the flu, leaning on a sink, gazing out over a winter graveyard.

'You going to stand there all bloody day?' Jit crashed into the room, backing through the door, her arms around the remains of her amplifier, its cabinet canted into a parallelogram, its fabric split. 'Well, give me a hand then, you dozy bugger.'

Silver stepped forward and took the debris from her and set it on the table.

'And you reckon you can fix that?' she said, challenging him. He lifted the torn fabric and poked around inside. His movements were vague.

'I don't know.' He could not for a moment remember why he was looking at this broken heap of junk. 'I suppose I could.'

'You suppose you could?' she mimicked. 'You've changed your tune, Mr Bloody Fixit.'

'Have I?' He frowned and looked more closely, handling the ruptured speakers, tugging at soldered wires to test them. The inside of the cabinet was filthy with dust. He said: 'This thing's a wreck.'

'I know it's a wreck!' she shouted, hands on hips. 'You wrecked it! You made that fat fart George sit on it. My bloody amp!'

'Uh-huh.'

He would need a few things: some timber, new fabric, some decent flex, and, of course, two new speakers. Wood glue. Tools. Solder. He got a grip on the chipboard top and wrenched it off, creaking against the nails that held it together. She looked theatrically at the ceiling.

'Thanks. Now you've totally stuffed it.'

With the top removed the guts of the cabinet lay exposed: components badly fixed with insulating tape and flapping loose, tangled wiring, a litter of dead flies, bottletops and cigarette ends.

'It's a wonder this thing ever worked at all,' he said. He held up a length of electrical flex, its insulation crumbling with age and the copper wires showing through. 'Look at that. You're lucky you didn't kill yourself.'

She opened her mouth to fire off a reply, but at that moment seemed to hear what he had said and caught herself. And then abruptly she started to laugh. He watched her in amazement. Seeing him stare, she clutched at the furniture for support and shrieked and pointed at him with tears running down her cheeks. Finally she sat down at the table and howled, slapping the Formica, her brilliant blue hair shivering in the light.

'I'm sorry, Joe,' she gulped, regaining control for a second. But seeing him still standing there foolishly set her off again. 'But . . . I'm lucky I didn't kill myself?' She got a grip and breathed hard, holding on to the edges of the table. 'Don't you think that's about the funniest thing ever, coming from you? Nugget told me –' She rested her blue head on the table and her shoulders shook silently.

Silver was astonished to discover that his dignity was offended, astonished because he did not think he had any dignity left to offend. This girl didn't think he was tragic. She thought he was ridiculous. She thought the whole thing was hilarious. For one crazy second, trembling on the edge of hysteria, he thought so too.

'I'll need tools,' he said, with such desperate seriousness that she stopped laughing at once and looked up at him, wiping her eyes.

'Nugget keeps them under the stage. I'll show you.'

She stood up and took him to the rear of the kitchen where Nugent had piled up the bags of charity clothing. She moved some of them out of the way. An old wooden toolbox, the size of a small coffin, had been pushed deep into the cavern under the stage. Silver shifted papier mâché animal masks and a tangle of lighting equipment and dragged the toolbox out and opened it. They were fine old tools, and they had belonged to a craftsman. Silver, who knew about tools, could tell that at once. Some of them were half-a-century old or more, bearing the marks of English and Scottish manufacturers, marks he had not seen since his childhood in his father's workshop. He sat cross-legged in front of the box and took the tools out, and turned them in his hands. It calmed him. The touch of cool walnut, the weight of them, the smell of oiled steel settled him, grounded him.

He asked: 'Are these Nugget's?' It seemed important to know.

'I guess they are now. They belonged to the guy who had St Mark's before him, Nugget said. Some old geezer who was here forever.'

Silver nodded. He began to take them out of the

box and laid them reverently on the floor around him: wood chisels, screwdrivers, folding rule, hammer. She watched him curiously.

'These mean something to you, Joe?'

'My father had tools like these,' he said. Plane, clamps, mallet, a Senior Service tin full of washers.

'Oh, yeah. He made violins and stuff. You said.' She put her head on one side to watch him, and the jewel in her cheek flashed like a turning fish.

'Yes. Violins. He made violins. And dulcimers. And lutes. Anything with strings.' Silver smiled to himself. 'Except guitars. That's why I had to have one.' A jacknife with a gnarled bone grip. Cold chisels. Pliers. A fat carpenter's pencil. A set of non-metric spanners which would fit nothing made for thirty years past.

'So you do play,' she said. 'I thought so.'

He brought his head up quickly. 'I can fix the amp. Come back in a couple of hours.'

This might have been a dignified dismissal, but the dust under the stage got into his nose and he sneezed violently, six or seven times.

'Nugget said you had the flu,' she said, stepping back. 'You taking anything for it?'

'No.'

'He's a bit of a tough nut, is Nugget. It isn't all show. But he won't throw you out while you're sick.'

'It's not important.'

'It bloody well is until you fix my amp. Besides,' she jerked her thumb upwards as rain started to drum on to the tin roof of the hall, 'you don't want to go out in this. You'd catch your death.' She met his eye for a fraction of a second and he could see her mirth bubbling up again and she fled, banging the back door behind her and running down the side passage through the downpour. He could hear her laughing as she ran.

It was satisfying to have his hands occupied again. Even his injured left hand worked well enough, automatically compensating for the missing finger, relearning movements. His little finger took its place for most operations, and he could feel it gaining in dexterity as he worked. Every few minutes he had to stop and massage the flesh at the base of the finger, aching from its unaccustomed use, but it grew easier as he worked on.

He worked quietly at the job for over an hour. Nobody interrupted him. Nobody seemed to know he was even there. He could hear occasional noises from the street: a car turning, a drift of music, the slap and bounce of a soccer ball kicked against a back wall. Sunday morning noises. He had forgotten that it was Sunday. Newspapers and coffee. Idly intellectual radio programmes presented by people with quizzical BBC accents. His mind drifted as he worked. His throat was raw and the back of his soft palate itched. But he was beating the virus. He was beating the virus and his hand was recovering and he was fixing something. He let that line of thinking rest. For the moment, his mind and eyes and hands were occupied with the intricacy of his work, and it was enough just to be.

Silver touched a final globe of solder on to the back of the jack socket and watched it cool and glaze as it hardened. He straightened his spine luxuriously, and then sat for a minute or two examining his handiwork.

'Not bad,' Nugent said for him. He was standing by the door into the hall and Silver had not heard him approach. 'So you really can fix things.'

'It's not done yet. I need to get hold of a couple of cheap speakers.'

'Piece of piss,' Nugent said. 'You'll find some down the Mile End Road tomorrow.'

Silver looked at the priest but the remark was neither a plea nor an offer. It was simply a statement of fact, and Silver could either take it or leave it. He said nothing. Nugent beckoned to him. 'Come with me a minute, Joe.'

Silver followed him out of the kitchen into the fresh air. It was cold outside but it was no longer raining and the yard was washed with a pale pellucid light. The area between the hall and the flint wall of the church was littered with old engine parts, rotting timber, two halves of a 44-gallon oil drum, filled with rusty water.

'Keep meaning to clear this place up,' Nugent said. 'Always something better to do.' He led Silver around the corner of the kitchen and across the bushy turf of the churchyard. Against the back wall of the hall was a brick double garage with collapsing wooden doors, overgrown by bramble and privet. Nugent felt on his key ring and unlocked the doors and dragged one of them open, its bottom edge leaving a groove in the muddy soil.

'There you go, Joe Fixit,' he said, standing back. 'Think you can fix that?'

The Ford minibus stood at an odd angle, with its offside tyres flat. Silver could see it was filthy and rusting. It was blue, and reminded him at once of one of the long series of battered vans and trucks and minibuses in which he and the band had limped around the country a quarter of a century or more ago, travelling from gig to gig.

'How old is it?' he asked, poking around it. The windows were cobwebbed and through them he could see up-ended seats, balled newspapers, milk cartons, a leather shoe green with mould. Pigeons had nested in the roofrack and the top of the vehicle was concreted with guano.

'Never mind how old it is. Can you fix it?'

'What's wrong with it?'

'Beats me,' Nugent said. 'Heaven and hell I can manage, but cars are a mystery to me.' He was growing impatient with Silver's slow inspection. 'Look, it doesn't go, that's what's wrong with it. Hasn't gone since I got here. But Father Lewis had it running before my time, and we could really use it now. Can you fix it or not?'

'I can fix cars. Used to be able to.'

'How are you with drains?'

'What?'

'Boilers? Leaking roofs? Wiring? You name it, it needs fixing around here.'

But Nugent's questions were rhetorical now and he no longer expected an answer. He waved Silver out of the garage and closed the door behind him and locked it.

'Listen, Joe,' he said. 'You suit yourself. But I'll give you a roof and a meal so long as you're useful to me here. Up to you.' In a pattern that was becoming familiar to Silver, he took a couple of steps away and then swung back. 'You still sick?'

'No,' Silver said. 'No, I'm OK.'

Nugent nodded and looked at his watch. 'Then get to work or get out by five. I've got Communion.'

41

Lauren lit her fourth cigarette of the morning. She usually made some effort not to smoke in the same room as Freya: she had never smoked at all in the old days. Perhaps she could put this right too. But on Fridays she had to cut herself some slack. She suspected she would never get used to Fridays, and in a way she hoped she would not. As long as the pain stayed with her she knew she was still alive, and that meant she was still effective, after a fashion. But this morning it was worse than usual. She felt anxious and volatile, and it was more than the ritual visit to Gudrun's grave which made her feel this way. She was not sure but she thought she regretted accepting Cobb's offer. The idea of sharing a car with him made her edgy. Despite their truce there was a sternness about him which made her feel he was sitting in judgement on her, no matter how correct and courteous he was. She did not know why she should care whether he was judgemental or not. When she thought about that it made her edgier still.

Freya grunted with the effort of beheading her egg. Lauren screwed up her eyes to watch this performance through the smoke of her cigarette, but she knew better than to offer to help. Freya would not permit it, she knew, and for once this was not hostility. Freya would never let anyone do this particular job for her and she tackled it with grim intensity, pursing her lips and scattering shards of shell around the table. Gudrun, Lauren remembered, had simply refused to eat boiled eggs once she found that getting into them involved even an elementary level of skill. That was not Freya's style. Lauren was not sure she had ever noticed this before. She was still considering the question when Hudson barrelled into the kitchen.

'Hey there, Frey. You're making a right pig's ear of that. Let me.'

'Go away,' Freya told him icily.

His broad friendly face fell. 'Well, that's nice, that is.' He walked to the stove and poured himself coffee and sat at the far end of the table, visibly hurt. Lauren wondered if he would ever learn. It did not seem likely. She checked her watch impatiently. Another ten minutes. She grew all the more certain that this was a bad idea. Hudson's presence reminded her that she had lied to him about the weekend. She disliked lying. It reminded her of how dependent she was. She felt a rush of resentment: she should not need to lie, should not need to make that effort too. Not on top of everything else.

'So, Frey,' Hudson boomed, renewing his charm offensive, 'down to the farm again.'

Lauren closed her eyes. Freya had her egg in two pieces and was eviscerating each half with great precision. She did not answer.

Undaunted, he went on: 'Second time in two weeks. Not wearing out your welcome a bit, are you?'

'If she were I wouldn't take her,' Lauren snapped.

'Hey. OK. Take it easy.' He pulled a face. 'You all got out of bed the wrong side, didn't you?'

'I'm sorry.' She fumbled out a cigarette and lit it. 'I'd better get ready. Sam will be here in a minute–'

'Sam,' Hudson said, trying the name on his tongue. Suddenly Lauren knew where he was coming from.

'I can't very well call him "Inspector Cobb" when we're staying at his house, Tommy,' she said, and realised how defensive that sounded.

'Marvellous old bloke, the father,' Hudson mused, too casually, 'but your Sam's a bit of a cold fish. Real polite and all that. But a cold fish. That's what I reckon, anyway.'

Lauren said nothing. Freya finished her egg, and fitted the two halves of the shell back together and reassembled them in the eggcup. When she had finished this she smiled brightly up at Hudson. 'You're just jealous,' she told him.

Lauren felt her heart bump. Hudson swung his head slowly to face the child.

'And you're so bleeding sharp, young lady,' he said with undisguised malice, 'that one day you'll cut yourself.'

A rocket went off in Lauren's brain and she was on her feet yelling, her coffee cup bouncing across the table. 'Don't you ever talk to her like that, Tommy! Do you hear me? Not ever!'

Hudson looked up at her and for a second his eyes were stones. Then he relaxed and smiled and spread his hands. 'Hey, come on, Laurie. You know I didn't mean nothing.' At that moment the security buzzer sounded. Hudson, still smiling, nodded towards the door. 'Your chauffeur's arrived. Better hurry.'

As Cobb pulled up and climbed out of the Saab, Lauren was already leading Freya out of the front door and across the gravel towards him. Before he could speak she said: 'Can we go right now? I like to get there early.'

'Sure.'

Her urgency surprised him, but he saw her clenched face and knew better than to comment. Instead he walked around the car and opened the door for her and held it while she settled Freya in the back. He made a funny face at the child over her mother's shoulder, but she did not respond. Her eyes shifted past him and as he followed her line of sight he caught a glimpse of Hudson standing inside the house, at the window beside the front door, watching them. It puzzled him that Hudson had not come out to see them off. It puzzled him, now he came to think about it, that Hudson was there at all. There had been something about a business trip. Cobb climbed in and put the car into gear and drove slowly past the house, half-expecting Lauren to wave at the big man, but she stared rigidly ahead, the muscles tight along the line of her jaw. Some instinct warned Cobb not to ask. He drove out through the gates, lifting a forefinger in acknowledgement to the security guard.

They motored on in tense silence, through the wealthy suburbs and south through the brown and bare winter countryside. Cobb made some small talk about a short cut, about a prettier drive avoiding the motorway, but when she did not answer he left it alone. After ten minutes she reached for her bag and pulled out a gold cigarette case and put it ostentatiously on her lap. He recognised it as the one he had seen her use in the hospital. That seemed a long time ago now. He remembered doubting then that she could survive for long. She had seemed so peculiarly ill-equipped for survival. Now, glancing across at the strained woman beside him, he supposed he had to admit that she had come through so far, against any odds he would have given her. She had a sterner spirit than he could have imagined. Looking at her again, he realised she was still a handsome woman, despite everything. He wondered why he should notice this now, and it occurred to him that she seemed just a shade more in control today. She did not strike him as hopeless. Had she made some progress, crossed some frontier? He guessed she had argued with Hudson, and wondered if this had anything to do with it. He did not know why he should think that, but for some reason the idea pleased him. Cobb found himself wishing with sudden urgency that he could do something for her. Anyone would feel the same, he told himself.

She took a cigarette out of the case but did not light

it. Instead she rolled the white cylinder nervously between her fingers.

'Light up, if you want,' he said.

'You don't mind? In the car?' The cigarette was already halfway to her lips.

'I don't make any rules that can't be broken,' he said lightly. He lowered the window an inch for her. But at his words she stopped with the cigarette between her lips and her lighter lifted.

'You mean that?'

He glanced at her, puzzled at her intensity. 'Yes, of course.'

'Good,' she said, and some of the tension went out of her. She stroked a flame out of the lighter and looked at it for a moment. 'Ah, to hell with it,' she said, and flicked the unlit cigarette out through the crack of the open window.

Cobb caught a glimpse of Freya's eyes in the rearview mirror, fixed solemnly not on her mother but on him. When he looked at Lauren again she was curled away from him on the leather seat, asleep.

Cobb drove quietly down through Surrey and turned off into the steep lanes to the west of Guildford. He threaded the car deeper and deeper into the country through pretty villages with cricket greens and pubs and clapboard mill buildings but she did not wake, even when he stopped to let a herd of cows shoulder past the car in a narrow lane. The beasts were massive and lowered their heads to look mournfully into the car. He turned in his seat and smiled at Freya but she stared impassively past him through the windscreen. Even the shuffle and clop of the cows' hooves and the sound of their bellows breath could not move her. When the herd had passed he drove on.

He rounded a final bend in a lane so narrow and steep-sided that it was almost a tunnel, and the poplars around the church were suddenly just ahead. Lauren was awake at once, stretching in her seat. He pulled up in the lay-by opposite the church but left the motor running.

'I'll park at the Cross Keys and grab a coffee,' he said. 'You take your time.'

'We won't be long.' She hesitated. 'Why don't you come to the church in about twenty minutes? You can walk across from the car park.'

He felt she was trying to include him a little, or at least trying not to exclude him, and was grateful. 'Fine. Twenty minutes then.'

She climbed out and helped the child out of the back seat then leaned back into the car. 'I'm sorry, Sam. We're a miserable bloody bunch today.'

She closed the door. He sat there for a moment, the engine murmuring, and watched the sullen child and the faded woman as they walked towards the squat little church. Then he drove quietly up to the pub at the end of the lane.

The Cross Keys was not open yet and he sat in the parked car next to the wall of the churchyard in the exact spot where he had parked on the day of the funeral. It gave him a vantage point across to the church and out over the moist downland. Gudrun's grave was close to the corner of the church. He saw the two distant figures standing there for a moment before they moved away between the tilted gravestones.

He realised now he should have called Lauren about the wallet earlier. It would be difficult to tell her today, and he should have foreseen that. He stretched back in the car with his hands behind his neck and loosened his shoulder muscles. But then, it hardly mattered. The fact was that the man was gone, one way or the other. As he watched, the two figures re-emerged into the churchyard and Freya broke free of her mother's hand and ran away between the headstones to the far fence. Even from this distance he could see Lauren's shoulders sag at this small rejection. She stood undecided for a moment and then turned aside and sat heavily on a stone bench up against the church wall. Let Matt Silver rest, Cobb thought with a spurt of anger. Let him rest and let him rot. He got out of the car and crossed the stile and walked across the field towards the church.

The rough grass was wet and hung with dewy cobwebs and it soaked the bottoms of his trousers. He walked around Gudrun's small neat grave to stand beside Lauren. 'Am I too early?'

She shook her head, patted the bench, inviting him to sit. He did so. Gudrun's grave was bright with the flowers they had brought. Beyond the grave and out of earshot Freya was at the fence. She had made friends with a pair of ponies and was feeding them with torn-up grass, stroking their velvet muzzles.

'She blames me. Herself too,' Lauren said. 'Especially when we come here.'

Cobb could think of nothing useful to say. He ripped up a strand of wet grass and plucked at it.

'You never had children, Sam?'

'No.'

'Why?'

'We forgot.' He tossed the stalk away and plucked another. 'We were too busy, and then all of a sudden it was too late.'

'You regret that?'

He did not know any way to answer the question. The woman who asked it had a warm living child and a cold dead one within a few feet of where they sat. Whatever answer he gave had to be wrong. Finally he turned to her and said: 'I don't regret missing what you're going through, Lauren. I don't regret that at all. I could never have done it.'

She nodded. 'There was a while there when I thought I was dead myself, and it was just Freya who kept me from lying down. Her and Matthew. And don't give me one of those looks, Sam.' She lit a cigarette and leaned back against the stone and blew smoke. 'Do you think he's still alive?'

'No, Lauren. I never did think that.'

'How come he won't let me go, then?'

'You sure it's not the other way round?'

She shrugged. 'What does it matter? He's there. I'm not strong enough to put a stop to him.'

'I wish I could have put him to rest for you, Lauren. I know that was my job.'

'Yes, I wanted you to find him. I thought you would if anyone could. But inside I think I knew it wouldn't be as easy as that.'

'They're taking me off the case,' he said abruptly. 'They're closing down the investigation.'

'When?'

'After the eleventh,' he said, avoiding the word.

'Gudrun's inquest.'

'Yes.'

'Will you be giving evidence?'

'I'll probably be called, yes.'

'Good. That seems right.'

'You know you'll be called too, Lauren. They'll want you to go through it again. It won't be a very good day for anyone.'

'What difference will it make,' she said, 'after all this?'

They were silent for a while. He noticed that the snowdrops were already up in white clusters under the yew tree, and down by the fence, where Freya was still stroking the horses, dark green clumps of daffodils and jonquils were pushing up through the soil.

'It'll be spring soon,' he said, and as he said it, he could taste spring in the air. 'There'll be some lambing this weekend if we're lucky.'

'Lambing?' she almost laughed. 'You really go in for this country squire stuff, don't you?'

'Me? I'm useless. The only thing I'm any good at is digging ditches. Until last year I thought wool grew on trees. You know, like macaroni.' This time she did laugh, the first time he had heard her do so. 'But I like to watch the lambing.'

'It'll be this weekend?'

'We can't actually schedule it. We have to ask the ewes to cooperate. But it's been a mild winter. They probably started during the week.'

'Frey will enjoy seeing that.'

'Of course she will. So will you.'

Lauren examined the end of her cigarette for a moment and then flicked it with a jerk of her wrist so that it flew in a long arc into the wet grass. 'Why should you care, Sam?' She made no attempt to soften her tone. 'When it comes right down to it, it's none of your business.'

'No, it's not. I guess it's because I've been part of the way there myself.' He stared up at the poplars against the pale sky. There was a patch of blue beyond the bare branches. As he watched the crows came beating back across the farmland, jeering as they flew, the way they had jeered on the day of the funeral. Against the brighter sky the birds seemed less sinister than they had seemed that day, mischievous clowns rather than lost souls.

'What was she like?' she asked suddenly. 'Your Clea?'

'Like?' The question wrongfooted him.

'Tall? Short? Smart? Dumb?'

'She was dark,' he began at random. 'She wasn't tall. She was thirty-six. She was from New England. She was as bright as a new penny.'

'And?'

He stood up. 'And she got cancer. And she died.'

'And you couldn't help, right?'

'She had cancer, for Chrissake.' He swung on her. 'How could I help?'

She silenced him with her raised hand, holding up her palm to get his attention, and when he was quiet again, repeated, very deliberately: 'And you couldn't help. Right?'

'That's right.' He looked away.

'Some things you just can't help, Sam,' she told him. 'Some things just run their course.' She leaned forward and patted his hand quickly, as if touching a hot plate, one-two. 'Let's go.'

42

Cobb drove thoughtfully back across country, winding up through Berkshire and skirting Oxford. No one spoke much, though the earlier tension relaxed the further they got from the church. Once or twice as they neared the farm he caught a glimpse of Freya's face in the mirror, and saw, he thought, a new light in it, a new animation.

It was strange to be driving this woman and her child away for a weekend in the country. It seemed such a conventional thing to be doing. Cobb tried to imagine what a casual onlooker would make of them: a professional couple and their only child, people with decent left-of-centre politics and a cottage in France they were too busy to visit. People with full, ordered, comfortable lives.

He smiled to himself at that. Presumably behind the calm façade of every ordinary couple lurked tragedy and passion in some measure, but he doubted the truth was ever much further from appearances than in this case. And yet something of the comfortable ordinariness of the day worked its way into his soul. The woman beside him held the road atlas upside down and frowned when she couldn't read it that way. She sang out the names of villages and towns – Streatley and

Pangbourne and Thame – and they seemed to him to be a song composed from the milestones which led to his home. The child asked about animals on his farm as if they were family, as if she had grown up with them all her short life.

By the time Cobb had carried their bags into the garden room, Fred was allowing himself to be dragged around the yard by Freya on a tour of inspection. Cobb watched them for a moment through the French windows. The old man was happy to be with the child. His very stance spoke of his pleasure. To his surprise, Cobb found that this relieved him of a certain pressure. He had not been aware that any pressure existed, but now that it was lifted he saw that Freya had taken from him the responsibility of being the sole focus of his father's attention, and even of his love.

Cobb checked that the radiator was working and opened the window a fraction. He heard Lauren moving in the living room, back in the centre of the house. She was about some small chore, choosing a book or tending the fire, perhaps. And here too the sense that she felt sufficiently at ease to do these things relieved him. It was as if the life of the farm ran like a large old-fashioned clock, and as if increasingly he had become the mainspring of it. Now these two new personalities, if only by a little, were helping to drive the ramshackle mechanism along. So far from disturbing the farm's tranquillity, Cobb found that the sight and sound of mother and child busy about the place increased the sense of peacefulness he felt here.

Lauren appeared in the doorway of the garden room as he was about to leave it. She glanced at her watch. 'Don't you have to go soon? This reunion thing?'

'It's a lot of nonsense, but I did promise.' He realised as he said it that he did not want to go now. And yet he had wanted to go. He had looked forward to it as a step back into the world. Now it seemed an imposition.

'Well, don't mind us,' she said, unpacking clothes from her bag. He noticed that this time she knew which cupboards and drawers to use and what to put in each. He liked to see that. He felt he could have watched her do this for some time. She went on: 'It's not part of the deal that we should screw up your plans.'

'I'll be back tomorrow morning anyway.'

She put aside her unpacking. 'We can look after ourselves, you know, Sam.'

'Sure.' He moved to the door. 'I'll get going, then.'

'You do that.'

'Right.'

Cobb changed, made himself a sandwich and, when he had delayed as long as possible, finally drove out of the farm track in mid-afternoon, just as the winter light was beginning to fail. John Piggott's choice of venue this time was a restored country pub outside Winchester. Cobb had never been there, but he knew the kind of place it would be: dark, comfortable and expensive, with good food and unobtrusive service. Piggott always chose venues like that, coaching inns and country clubs, heavy, masculine places. Hearty male get-togethers weren't Cobb's style, and it was only because of the particular care which Piggott put into organising these reunions that Cobb had ever troubled to go at all.

He did not look back with much warmth on his two short years in the Army, and had made few close friends there. He had never gone to an official regimental function. But he had missed the last two of John Piggott's reunions since Clea's death, and had not had the heart to refuse this one. Good food, a little too much to drink, the company of people who shared some of his history. There were worse ways to spend an evening, and he was angry with himself that he resented the obligation. He told himself he was annoyed because the evening interrupted his weekend routine at the farm, and lectured himself about this as he drove south down the darkening A34. It only went to show how important it was to get out now and again. He was, as Fred kept telling him, becoming too set in his ways. Maybe he was getting old.

But none of this helped. His irritation grew steadily stronger and by the time he pulled up outside the hotel he knew it had been a mistake to come. Piggott had attracted twenty guests this time, all of them men, and nearly all now retired from the service. Cobb found them in possession of the saloon bar, where most of them had evidently been since before lunch – fleshy men in their forties and fifties, red-faced and loud. He vaguely recognised about half of them but could see no immediate sign of Piggott. He walked into a ragged roar of greeting though only a handful of these men knew who he was and he doubted if any of them cared. There were some catcalls about his late arrival and shouted demands for him to buy a round by way of forfeit. He moved to the bar and ordered with as much grace as he could muster. At least it meant he did not have to sit down among them yet.

He stood at the bar waiting for the drinks to arrive and surveyed the crowded room. It struck him that these men had grown suddenly older in the three years since the last reunion he had attended. And it came to him also that he did not much like their slack bodies and their loud voices and their clubby complacency, and that he did not want to be one of their number. As the drinks were loaded onto a tray in front of him, he began to wonder how he was supposed to get through the evening.

At that moment, Piggott padded up beside him like a large pink bear. He held out his hand and Cobb took it. 'Sorry, Sam, I was at the heads. I didn't see you arrive.'

'The heads, for Chrissake. You've been in the bloody Navy too long.'

'Quite right.' Piggott's pink face was flushed, but he was not drunk. He was serious about his duties as host and organiser and generally stayed out of the more raucous revelry. 'It's good to see you here again, Sam.'

'Well.' Cobb passed a beer to Piggott and lifted his own glass. He liked Piggott and was glad to see him, and he wondered if perhaps the evening might improve if he just relaxed a little. 'Cheers, anyway.'

'I wasn't sure we'd get you back after Clea died,' Piggott persisted, without returning the toast.

'Me neither.' Cobb hesitated, surprised that Piggott would mention this so directly.

'But you know, Sam, it's at times like that a man needs his friends and loved ones about him.'

Cobb stared at him, his glass raised but untouched. He had the clear impression Piggott was trying to tell him something important, something about Piggott's own loneliness and need. Cobb lowered his glass slowly and set it back on the tray. He looked around the room again. Someone at the far end of the table knocked over a mug and the surface was suddenly swilling with beer and men were jumping back to avoid it and tripping over their chairs and the room was full of cursing and laughter and bawling for the barmaid.

Cobb said: 'I'm sorry, John. Truly.' He put a twenty on the bar and turned and walked out of the room, collecting his bag at reception as he went. When he pushed open the door he glanced back and saw Piggott standing pensively where he had left him. It seemed to Cobb that he did not look surprised.

Cobb drove back slowly to the farm and arrived just before eight. As he pulled up he noticed that the lights were out in the house, except for the one they always left on in the kitchen, and then he saw that Fred's Land Rover was missing. Cobb was pleased at the prospect of having the house to himself for an hour or two. He parked the Saab in the barn and closed the door on it and let himself into the kitchen through the back door.

'You're early,' Lauren said, startling him. 'I didn't expect you till tomorrow.'

'No.' He hung up his coat, a little thrown by her presence. She was in what he now thought of as her familiar place, seated at the end of the big scrubbed pine table. There was a tumbler in front of her with half-an-inch of gin in it.

'I left the bottle in the cupboard this time,' she said, interpreting his look. 'Didn't want to risk breaking another one.' He realised she was trying to deflect his disapproval by making a joke of it, and the thought that she cared about his disapproval flattered him. She said: 'Fred's taken Frey to the movies in Oxford. *The Prince of Egypt*. She's seen it about eight times. I couldn't face it again.'

'Good move.'

'Can you imagine your dear old father sitting through two hours of technoDisney with five hundred screaming kids?'

He smiled at her. He went to the cabinet and poured a Scotch and also brought the gin bottle back with him and showed it to her.

Her eyebrows lifted in amusement and she looked from the bottle to his face. 'It's OK. I've got plenty.'

He nodded and replaced the gin in the cupboard.

She laughed aloud. 'Well, Sam – did I pass that little test?'

'Yes.'

'Good. Let's drink to that.' She tilted the glass archly at him and drank a little, and he returned the toast. She said: 'I've booked into one of those courses. The stuff you sent me?'

'That's great, Lauren.' He was surprised by how much this pleased him. 'I'm sure that's the right decision. I really am.'

She lifted her glass mischievously. 'So I figured I'd better get a couple of snorts in before they dry me out.'

Cobb knew she was teasing him but he didn't care. 'Good idea. Let's both have another.'

This time she let him pour her a small one and they sat in companionable silence for a minute or two, pleased with one another. At length, Lauren stretched back and locked her hands behind her head.

'So tell me, Sam: why did you leave your boys' party so early?'

He looked into his Scotch for a while before answering. 'I discovered I preferred to be here.'

Lauren made big mocking eyes at him. 'And I prefer it too.'

She placed her palms flat on the table and stood up. She walked past him and crossed to the window to stare out into the night. 'Do you see her at all, Sam?' she said abruptly, turning to face him. For a moment Cobb thought she meant that someone was in the yard and followed her gaze. The outside light above the door threw inky shadows over the cobbles, still slick from the rain. She went on: 'Clea, I mean. Is she still around for you?' She stood with her back to the glass.

Cobb waited a while before answering. 'There was a time, just after she died. She'd had a lot of pain, you see.' He paused. 'For a while I used to hear her. At night, sometimes. But after a time, after a few weeks, it seemed as if she simply left.' He looked up at her. 'And I stayed.'

'It's like that for me with Gudrun. I wondered if I was strange or something. No one ever tells you.'

'You're not strange.'

'Do you know, the other day I went an entire hour without thinking of her. Isn't that dreadful?'

'No.'

'When I realised it had happened, I had this agony of guilt.'

'You don't need to feel guilty. You heal whether you want to or not. Sometimes it does seem disloyal.'

'You told me that once. I didn't believe you.'

The outside lamp on the porch blazed into her hair through the glass behind her. She closed her eyes. 'It'll never be over for me, Sam. But one thing you said is true: Goodie's gone. Wherever she is, it's a different place. And I'm still here. More or less. I can't help it.'

Cobb sipped his drink, rolled the tumbler between his palms. 'And Matthew?' he said. 'Is he still here?'

Her eyes sprang open. 'Please don't crowd me, Sam,' she said, as though he had asked quite another question.

43

Cobb woke at five and lay listening to the sparrows fussing in the eaves while the square of his window paled. The secret chitter of the nesting birds, just a few inches away from him behind the boards, always swept him back in time.

Fred had sold their London flat and taken over the farm when Cobb was just fifteen. That year, the first year after his wife had left, Fred took long leave and brought his younger son home from overseas so that they could be together. Cobb could see now that it was his father's way of starting again, of launching a new life built around the two of them. At the time, Cobb had known only that the spring of that year and the long summer which followed it had been in some way pregnant, and that the slow rhythms of the farm, so new to him then, masked some wild and pagan energy which trembled on the point of bursting out. Life ran like electricity through his fifteen-year-old body. He had felt weightless, quick, nervous, desperate: his lungs seemed cavernous, but could not hold enough oxygen to charge his blood.

He could remember waking in this very room more than thirty years before, hearing the sparrows squabbling above him, just as they did now, while he lay lashed by the pitiless lust of adolescence. He smiled to himself at the memory and rolled out of bed. The sound of the sparrows always did it to him. He waited a couple of minutes before he could tug his jeans on, then grabbed his shirt and moved through the sleeping house to the kitchen. He stopped in surprise at the door.

'Well, it's young Princess Freya, up with the lark.'

She sat upright at the table on one of the kitchen stools, with her hands curled round a Bart Simpson mug. She eyed him severely through her spectacles. 'You look like you've been dragged through a hedge,' Freya told him. 'Backwards.'

'Not forwards? Definitely backwards?'

'Definitely.'

'Well, it's nothing that a pot of coffee won't fix.' She tried to hide it, but Cobb could see her face fall. He put the pot back on the shelf. 'Bugger the coffee. Let's go and see the lambs.'

She skipped ahead of him across the yard while he dragged on his sweater. The air was sharp and clean, cool enough for their breath to steam. Pale spokes of light lay flat across the morning fields. There was already activity in the yard and in the barn. The ewes were crowded into one corner of the field, a few of them nursing new lambs dropped during the night. A gangling boy was moving among them, spreading his arms to keep the animals bunched together. Arthur Riordan, in gumboots and rainjacket, was leaning on the rail, shouting to the boy to cut out this one or that one from the flock.

'Well, if it isn't the Laughing Policeman,' Riordan called across to Cobb. He looked ostentatiously at his watch. 'Putting in a half-day, are you, Sam?'

'Give me a break, Arthur. I did bring an extra hand.'

'So you did. Well, I'm sure she'll be more use than you are.'

'What a rude man,' Freya said loftily. Cobb laughed and took her hand and led her into the barn.

'Don't mind Arthur,' he told her. 'These are mostly his ewes. He just boards them here. That way we get to see them, and he has to feed them. Let's have a look at some of his new arrivals.'

The barn had been partitioned off into a series of stalls, one ewe in each, some already suckling their newborn lambs, others on their bellies in the straw, panting, waiting for delivery. Riordan's two horsey daughters and a young vet who looked like an accountant were working among the sheep. In the centre of the barn a flock of uneasy ewes milled, bleating, some scratching at the ground.

'We only have half-a-dozen of our own. Just for fun. That's why Arthur takes the mickey out of me.'

'Which ones are yours?'

'Well, I guess it doesn't matter much. They're all pretty much the same.'

Freya frowned at that. 'I bet their mummies think they're different.'

''Course they do, Princess.' He tugged the hood of her anorak down over her eyes, mocking her gravity. 'That's what mummies are for.'

'Birth isn't a spectator sport, Sam,' Riordan called, dragging in another ewe. 'Time to get your hands dirty.'

'Me? I don't know one end from another.'

'You'll soon work that out, my lad. And your little sidekick can help too, if she wants.'

'All right,' Freya said at once.

Cobb hadn't expected this. 'It's a bit messy,' he warned her.

'Of course it's *messy*,' the child said with withering scorn. 'They're having babies.'

By the time Lauren arrived, around mid-morning, Cobb was helping to deliver his sixth lamb.

'Get your hand right up there,' Riordan shouted at him, holding the ewe's head. 'Get hold of it and pull.'

'Go on, Sam,' Freya told him, picking up one of Riordan's phrases: 'Pull it – don't tickle it.'

Cobb, kneeling in the straw and caught between effort and laughter, groped inside the animal, felt the unborn lamb jerk under his fingers, warm and slippery. The ewe pushed forward a foot, bleating in protest, and dragged Cobb over on to his elbows in the straw. The movement freed the lamb, which was suddenly born in a rush in his arms, slimy and bloody.

'It's a boy!' he shouted in triumph, rolling in the dirt with the warm wet bundle. He could hear Freya clapping and squealing with excitement. Riordan took the lamb by its back legs and laid it on the straw. It looked like a drowned rabbit.

'Is it going to be all right?' Freya asked.

'Oh, it'll be fine,' Riordan said. 'A perfect delivery. The mother might be a bit sore, though.' He lifted the lamb's black little leg. 'And by the way, Sam, it's a girl. See that the mother suckles it, now.' He released the ewe and left the stall, leaving Cobb still sitting in the straw.

'Pleased with yourself, huh?' Lauren said, from the rail of the walkway.

Cobb looked up at her and raised his filthy hands. 'Surgeon's hands,' he said.

'Sam's delivered six of them!' Freya shouted to her mother, jumping with excitement. 'Six little lambs!' Lauren stared at her daughter, speechless for a moment. It was as if she didn't recognise this joyful, noisy child.

'Freya helped with all of them,' Cobb said, coming to her rescue. 'We did it together.'

'Great,' Lauren said, feeling for her cigarettes. 'That's great.'

'Mustn't do that in here, Mummy,' Freya cried, 'you'll give the baby lambs passive smoking.'

Lauren put the cigarettes away again. She looked dazed at the change in her daughter, and Cobb felt a pang of pity for her confusion. He looked away to give her a chance to recover, fussing with the newborn lamb, standing it up as he had seen the others doing. It was too soon, and he let the animal rest back on the straw. It was then that he noticed the ewe had not moved. She lay on her side, still panting.

Freya followed his eyes. 'What's the matter with her, Sam? Isn't she very well?'

Arthur Riordan struggled past, manhandling another ewe towards the yard. He glanced down as he went by. 'She's got another one in there, Sam. Better do your midwife bit again.'

'Arthur–'

'Too busy. Sorry!' And he was gone.

It only took five minutes, though it seemed longer. Five minutes of groping inside the struggling animal with one arm while trying to hold it still with the other. When it was over and the dead lamb lay on the straw at the girl's feet, there was a moment when Cobb could have murdered Arthur Riordan. Maybe he might have saved it, and then Freya would still be bouncing and noisy with joy. He glanced up at the rail but Lauren avoided his eyes. She stared out dully over the barn.

Cobb wiped his hand on his jeans and touched Freya's arm. 'Well, we saved one of them, Princess. Didn't we?'

'Yes.' She hugged the surviving lamb but her eyes were fixed on the dead one, a pathetic bedraggled bundle cooling in the straw. Cobb knew the live lamb ought to go to its mother but he let it ride for the moment. Suddenly she said: 'They'd have been twins. Twin sisters.'

He felt the busy sounds of the barn shrink away; the bleating, the shouting, the stamping of hooves on the wooden floor, all retreated behind a glass dome that contained only him and Freya and Lauren. He saw

Lauren's head turn and knew she was watching him. 'Yes, Freya,' he said clearly. 'They'd have been twins.'

'Why did she die?' the girl said. She was looking at the dead lamb, but Cobb knew better.

'I don't know. Nobody does. Don't let anyone tell you they do.'

'It isn't fair.'

'No, it's just the way things happen, Freya. It's nobody's fault.'

She looked at him steadily. 'It was Daddy's fault.'

'Maybe that's true, Princess. I only know it wasn't your fault. And it wasn't your mum's either.' She stared at him, hugging the lamb, rocking it. Cobb put out his hand and stroked the lamb's warm head. 'Why don't you keep her?'

'I can?'

'Of course. She's one of ours.'

'How do you know?'

'Oh, I can always tell.'

After a while she got up quietly, struggling under the small weight of the lamb, and staggered past him out of the stall. He watched as she went, edging round the wooden partitions, unnoticed by the bleating sheep and the working men and women. She climbed the three steps at the end of the barn, bringing one foot up next to the other one on each step until she reached the top. Then she walked back along the gallery above Cobb and sat down next to her mother, hugging her lamb, hot-eyed, her mouth turned down. She hesitated there for just a moment. Then, in a sudden and convulsive movement, she clutched in against her mother's side and turned her face into her mother's body and Cobb saw Lauren's arm lock quickly around the child and her head come down so that he could not see the girl for her mother's protective hair, falling across both their faces.

Cobb looked away and busied himself by gathering up the dead lamb in a mat of stained straw. Arthur Riordan struggled past, manhandling another ewe, nodding to the burden in Cobb's arms.

'Where you taking that?'

'I'm going to bury her, Arthur.'

'Bloody waste. Be good with new potatoes, that'd be.'

'No, I'm going to bury her.'

Riorden shook his head in mocking disbelief. 'Bury *her*, indeed.'

'That's right. And you know what, Arthur? We're going to put up one of those tacky wooden crosses over her grave, saying "RIP Lucy the Lamb". Or something.'

Riordan propped the helpless sheep against his knee and with his free hand pushed up his tweed hat. He gave Cobb a knowing look. 'You know something, Sam? You've gone a bit strange since those females arrived.'

'Get stuffed, Arthur,' Cobb said.

44

Silver worked on the dismantled engine for most of the morning, hand-grinding the pitted valve seats down to matt grey steel, checking the guides, replacing worn valve springs. He enjoyed machines. Precision and power pleased him, in machinery as in music.

He had learned most of his skills on the road, in the years when the band's transport was his first priority, ranking way ahead of food, drink or even dope. Without transport they were literally nowhere. The only vehicles they could afford were big old brutes, and Silver remembered every one of them. There was a converted Bedford hamburger wagon that stank of onions when the motor heated up. There was a surprisingly spruce Volkswagen camper, which turned out to be stolen, so that the police repossessed it. An ex-US Army ambulance – a veteran of the Normandy landings – lasted them until the drummer succeeded where the Panzers had failed and destroyed it against a bridge on the M6. For a few weeks they used a retired hearse, but travelling in it so unnerved the keyboard player that he jumped ship in Liverpool and never came back.

And finally for nearly two years there was a beaten-up Ford Transit not unlike this one. Silver remembered the Ford particularly because it had lasted right up until his first major recording contract. He remembered it too because of Lauren. He would not forget that morning. He had taken his leave of her upstairs in her bare little cube of a student flat just a few minutes earlier. He would have liked to have left while she still slept – that would have felt more Bohemian – but she was in his sleeping bag (real goosedown from Milletts) and he couldn't afford to part with it. So instead he had left her with her legs curled under her on the bare boards and a poncho thrown around her shoulders, hunched over a cup of instant coffee. She was still blurred with sleep and sex. And then, ten minutes later, she arrived uninvited as they were loading up outside, a shining, tight-bodied blonde of nineteen, quivering with the promise of adventure. She burned like a flame in the chill grey street.

He wondered what sixth sense had marked him out for her from the hundreds of other poet-radical longhairs who drifted across the university scene in those days. He wondered too why no similar sense had warned him about her. For surely the fateful chain started there on that raw morning in Leeds. Even then he had thought of telling her, gently enough, to run along home. She was not much more than a schoolgirl, with her too-new rucksack and her wide and eager blue eyes, and he could not find the heart to do it. There had been something else too, a kind of exultation about her, that he could not deny. It came to Silver suddenly that she really had loved him then. He paused in his work and a great wash of pity for them both flooded through him. Whatever had happened since, whatever pain they had caused one another, Lauren really had loved him then. He wondered if he had ever truly loved her.

It seemed to him now that it had all taken place in another universe, in another dimension. Silver straightened his back and began to tidy up. He was as methodical as a surgeon, cleaning the tools and putting them carefully away. He covered the gleaming open pots of the engine with plastic sheeting, and unpopped the bonnet support and closed the bonnet over the plastic. He covered the dismantled valves and pistons on the benchtop with more plastic and weighed the sheeting down with a couple of heavy spanners, and stood regarding his work while he rubbed at the grease on his hands with a crumpled newspaper.

It had been over a week. He did not know quite where the time had gone. It did not take this long to get the head off an engine and regrind the valves, but every time he started to make progress, Nugent would appear with some new task. Silver had been sent to fix a loose step in the hall, to dig out the drain, to climb up on the roof and wire into place one of the sheets of corrugated which had blown off in the night. The demands appeared to be random, but he was coming to realise that he was deliberately being kept busy – not perhaps solely out of concern for his welfare, but in order to get the most out of him while the opportunity was there. He did not resent that. It seemed like a fair exchange to him. He could not deny that each day he achieved something, however small, and that this felt good. Nor could he deny that it was something to be recognised in the breakfast line-up, to have the cheerful volunteer women call him 'dear', and to have the other drop-outs and rough sleepers accept him into their erratic society whenever they appeared for the second or third time. He did not know where this was leading. For the moment it was enough to live each day at a time.

He stood at the door of the garage and looked out. It was the first day of March, someone had told him at breakfast, as if this were significant. He felt in some ill-defined way that it might be. He had assumed that the winter, that winter, would never end. It had not really occurred to him that it could end. And yet now there was some pale sunlight falling between the gravestones. A few early daffodils were open already. Something had happened. Wherever he stood now, something had happened around him. The air was still cool and Silver hugged himself and beat his arms around him to warm up. He could feel the firm slap of his own flesh. He was putting on a little weight.

He had worked for three hours this morning undisturbed. He pulled the garage doors across and moved into the kitchen to make himself a coffee. As soon as he opened the door he could hear someone moving in the body of the hall, and after a moment she began to sing in a high and plangent voice. It gave him a peculiar pleasure to hear it. She had been gone for a week, visiting relatives, as Nugent put it, which seemed to

Silver an unlikely explanation. He found it impossible to imagine Jit with relatives. It was like trying to visualise Tinkerbell's mother. Wherever she had been, he was glad she was back.

He walked softly to the back of the stage and stood listening quietly. He wondered if she knew that he was there, and instinctively felt that she did. He had only heard her sing in the closed space of the public bar, over a hubbub of laughing and drinking and the coughing of the slot machine. Here in the hall her voice swooped among the high girders like a released bird. She sang unaccompanied for a while, and then with the twelve-string, some Joni Mitchell, some traditional folk, and some more of the strangely haunting songs he now knew were her own. He walked into the hall.

'Don't stop.'

But she did stop, looking down at him uncertainly from the stage, the blue jewel winking in her cheek.

He fumbled for something to say. 'I've fixed the amp, more or less.'

'You have?' She sounded surprised.

'Nugget got you a couple of new speakers and I fitted them yesterday. The old ones were shot anyway.'

'They were after you finished with them.'

'Well, it works fine now.' He made to walk away then changed his mind. 'Play some more. Please.'

She kept her eyes on him as she hefted the strap of the big guitar on to her shoulder and began to sing: an old Lightnin' Hopkins twelve-bar, then some Bessie

Smith, two more of her own, a bluesy version of *Hotel California*, and finally a slow treatment of John Lennon's *Imagine*. Somewhere in the middle of this he found an old canvas-backed chair and sat in the body of the hall, and after a while he closed his eyes and let go. He drifted up among the rusty girders with her voice, swinging like a swallow between the fans of light that fell through the gaps in the corrugated iron, hovering there and gazing out over the lightwashed vista of the city, creamy in the morning, clean in the morning.

'You know about this stuff,' she said. She had stopped playing and had come down from the stage and was standing in front of him with the guitar held across her. 'It touches you.'

'Yes.'

'When you used to play, before you lost the finger, you were good. Weren't you?'

'Yes.'

'I know – just by watching you – when I'm going wrong.'

He straightened in his chair, cleared his throat. 'You sing a little flat in the top register. That's mainly confidence. Breathing and confidence. That can be fixed. But your guitar technique is pretty average. You spend too much time on open strings up near the nut–'

'You could teach me. No one ever taught me.'

'Did you ever see a nine-fingered guitar teacher?'

She shrugged. 'Django Reinhardt only had eight.'

He stared at her. She put her hands on her hips and stared back. 'Jesus, Joe, you're a defeatist.' When he still didn't speak she said: 'I've got my brother's old six-string up in the room. You could have that. It'd be a challenge, wouldn't it?'

He looked hard at her. 'What are you doing here, Jit?'

'Nugget brought me here.' She said it as though it were obvious, as if this were an answer in itself. When she saw he didn't understand she went on, with a touch of impatience: 'I'd come down from Nottingham with Jake. My brother. I was kind of looking after him. He was on a methadone program, but he'd been selling it for crack. He's OK now.'

'He is?'

'Sure. He's a New Age traveller now. In a camp out near Northampton. But at the time he'd done his head in a bit and he sort of left me with nothing up at Euston Station. That was a bit severe. I was sleeping rough near King's Cross and doing some busking in the tunnel at Euston tube when Nugget picked me up one night. I was pretty low. Now I sort of work for him here. Half-a-dozen of us do, on and off. Just for board. The church owns a couple of the houses in the street. We have rooms there. Bedsits, sort of.'

It seemed to Silver that there was something child-like about the way she described her wastrel life. Not childlike, perhaps. Fey. Charmed. As if her spirit could not be broken, because she had no expectations beyond the day she lived in.

'And now you're going to be a star,' he said.

'I'm already a star, Joe.' She smiled, impish under her brilliant blue hair. 'Want me to bring Jake's guitar over?' He sat massaging the stump of his severed ring finger, frowning at it. She waited for a moment and when he stayed silent, she spoke again. 'Do you like my rock, Joe?' He looked up, puzzled at the apparent irrelevance of the question, and she touched the glittering stud in her cheek. 'Everyone notices it.'

'I'll bet.'

'You know why I had it done?' He shook his head. 'Well, one night last summer in a pub in Goodge Street, this bloke belted me. I don't know why. Just hauled off and belted me. He had this big ring on and it cut right through my cheek here. It left this scar, like a bullet-hole. It was really ugly.' He stared at her.

'That's it?'

'Sure. It was ugly and I made it pretty.' She seemed to find his bewilderment funny. 'God, you're slow.'

The back door of the kitchen banged and Nugent's voice rang out in the hall. 'Joe? Hell are you?' The priest walked through into the hall, saw Silver. 'What are you sitting around here for? The bloody heater in the church is stuffed again. Come and take a look at it.' He noticed Jit for the first time. 'Oh. You're back.'

'Joe's going to teach me music,' she told the priest.

Silver made to protest but she went on: 'He's a gypsy. Did you know that?' She talked to Nugent over Silver's head. 'Oh, yes. He was the best gypsy guitarist in the world, and in love with the beautiful Esmeralda.

410

And then one day his deadly rival Vargas burst into his caravan and did that to his face and cut off one of his fingers so he couldn't play any more.'

'Oh yeah,' Nugent said, checking his watch. 'Sounds fair.'

'And then Vargas left him for dead, and now it's Vargas who lives with Esmeralda. Joe's been plotting revenge ever since. It's dead romantic.'

'Right.' Nugent looked at Silver. 'Now piss off and fix the central heating.'

'I'll take a look.' He walked to the door.

'Wait,' Nugent said. 'You doing that folk club gig tonight, Jit?'

'Every Tuesday.'

Nugent nodded to Silver. 'Why don't you go with her? Give her a few tips if you know something about this stuff.'

Silver said: 'Nugget, look—'

'Take the van.' The priest tossed the keys to Jit. 'I'll be glad of a Tuesday night without listening to those hairy bastards caterwauling.'

45

Despite its grand name, the Duke's Head Music Room was merely a long dim chamber above the saloon bar. Ranks of plastic chairs, a tiny triangular bar cutting off one corner, hunting prints on the walls – horses with all four legs outstretched like greyhounds. Jit liked it, she told him, because here she had a real audience, people who had come specifically to hear singing – hers among others – and not simply a casual crowd of drinkers in some beer-stinking bar. But in reality it was only half a step up from the fug-filled folk clubs where Silver himself had first performed a generation before.

He let her buy him a pint and then slipped away from her to the back of the room. He took a corner seat in the shadows and watched as the place filled up. Jit sat up at the end of the second row, chatting easily to people who could not keep their eyes off her brilliant blue hair and the stud in her face. She caught his eye for a second through the swelling crowd and winked conspiratorially at him. The amateur musicians who would perform the first couple of sets were joking too loudly in their nervousness and fussing with the tuning of their fiddles and banjos and guitars. Knots of over-hearty people were greeting one another at the door, recalling previous meetings at Glastonbury or the

Arundel Festival. New people arrived every few moments, backing into the room with trays crowded with pints of bitter.

They were the usual mix, Silver could see, middle-class radicals and earnest folk zealots and grey-bearded rejects from the sixties. There was much fussing with curtains and windows and heaters and a rising babble of laughter and talk. Comfortable blue smoke began to stack in layers against the ceiling. He caught the bonfire tang of it – something harmless and herbal. Silver had seen it all before. Such places had always generated in him a sense of alienation, as if everyone present belonged to a secret society from which he was excluded. Whenever he had performed in them in his youth, he would be earnestly admonished by some bearded folkie for playing too many encores, or for using an amplifier, or for changing the words of some traditional song.

There was a burst of applause and some cheering and a neat, bald man who might have been a bank manager took the floor. He carried a banjo. He was joined by a squat woman with long grey hair and a dress of brown Indian cotton. Finally a second man shuffled to a dim spot just on the edge of the audience, staring fiercely at the floor while he adjusted the straps of the accordion over his shoulder. After a moment of nervous patter the grey-haired woman began to sing *The Lark in the Morning* and the two men came in raggedly on the second line, the accordionist in particular playing clumsily and with savage concentration.

They were not very good. The woman must once have been told she had a beautiful voice, Silver guessed, but sadly this was untrue. She sang in a reedy contralto which twice cracked on the high notes. The banjo player was competent but played with all the passion of a metronome. The accordionist was locked in battle with pathological shyness and it must have been torture for him to perform at all. Silver found it torture to watch.

The woman finished her song and an astonishing storm of applause and cheering and whistling swept over her. She seemed to expect it for she stood there basking in the glow of it, beaming, with her head back and her arms spread. But Silver did not expect it. He did not expect the upturned shining faces, the people on their feet shouting for more – and Jit among them, he saw, her lurid head jumping up and down in the front row. He hunted the faces for an answer. Did they really think this woman was good? Had he missed something?

She was starting again, a lugubrious version of *Edward* this time, and her audience clung to every phrase. They loved her, for some reason that was hidden from him. Maybe she was some kind of a local saint. Maybe she had just been diagnosed with cancer and they were being kind. But he knew that none of this was so. The truth was that she was simply one of them. In applauding her they were applauding themselves, with all their own imperfections. They liked her because she made it easy for them to do that. Silver sat back on the bench in the gloom and hunched over his warming beer. And he was suddenly overcome with a great sadness. Yes, he had missed something, all right. He had missed a turning, and he had missed it long, long ago. At about the time that he had come to backstreet singalongs like these, and sneered at their amateurism, and prickled at their small pretensions. He heard his sixteen-year-old voice, defiant in Dr Gottschalk's dim basement study, ringing out over the shuddering of the hot water pipes.

'But I want to be the best!' he had cried, raging against the heavy shabbiness of the room, the awful grey suburban life outside the streaked windows.

And the old man had stroked his nicotine-stained moustache and softly asked: 'Why?'

Silver got up quickly and put the unfinished beer on a ledge and pushed roughly out of the room while the woman was still warbling her uncertain way through the Middle Ages.

He walked the black streets blindly for two hours until cold and exhaustion forced him back to the church. It was close to midnight – the worst time at the refuge, he had already learned, when the pubs turned out and the police patrols grew tired and edgy. It had started to rain and this always drove in the more desperate ones from sleeping rough on park benches and in shop doorways. Somehow Fat Phil had been left alone on duty at the hall. As Silver approached he could see that two elderly drunks were fighting in the gutter outside the church. Phil was vainly attempting to separate them, tugging at the collar of the topmost one, his voice beginning to plead. Silver hesitated, on the point of walking past and finding his cot as he had done for the last twelve nights.

'Joe!' Fat Phil looked up at him with evident relief. 'Could you possibly give me a hand?'

And in that instant Silver saw that his role here had changed. Then a backflung elbow caught Fat Phil in the face and his thick glasses cracked and fell on the pavement and he staggered back. Without thinking Silver grabbed the topmost man by the hair and wrenched him away hard enough to hurt him and stamped very hard on the one below so that he gasped and rolled over and puked on the pavement. He loomed over the old men so that they huddled together on the wet tarmac, blinking at him, shocked into timidity.

'You get out of here until you can behave yourselves,' he told them, surprised both at the threat and at the command in his voice. 'Go on. Piss off.'

The men stood up shakily and, forgetting they had been at one another's throats a second ago, linked arms and stumbled off up the dark street in the rain like some ungainly quadruped.

'Poor chaps,' Fat Phil sighed, rubbing his bruised face. 'Poor helpless souls.' But he could not quite keep the satisfaction out of his voice. Silver grunted. He found the pieces of Phil's glasses and handed them to him.

'You all right?'

'Oh! It comes with the territory, you know. This sort of thing.'

Silver had learned during the week that Fat Phil was a wedding photographer in Shoreditch by day, a man with a modest but comfortable living. Silver found it hard to imagine what drove him to exchange that territory for this. The question was uncomfortable and confusing, and to avoid it he walked away into the hall.

He expected to find refuge here, as he had on every other night, a dark place where he could claim his bedspace on the floor and shut out the night. But somehow the hall had been infected with the night's anarchy. All the lights were on and the room was full of noise. Someone had upended a couple of the beds and the room was disordered and untidy. The fleshy boy he remembered from his first morning was wandering the room, talking loudly to himself. A raddled woman he did not recognise was sitting on Fat Phil's desk by the door and smoking. An old man was weeping noisily on his bed. Silver could hear noises from the back of the hall and saw that a stringy youth had got into the kitchen area and was rummaging through the shelves like a foraging rat.

Silver stood and looked at it all for a second. Then he snatched up the woman's cigarettes and tossed them out into the wet street. When she squawked in protest he shoved her out after them and turned his back as she stood in the rain shrilling obscenities at him. The room fell quiet at once and Silver marched between the cots to the kitchen area. The stringy youth looked up at him mildly from the sink into which he had emptied the tea and coffee canisters.

'Don't waste your time, mate,' the boy said. 'They got bugger all here.'

Silver wrenched open the back door and grabbed the boy by the collar and the back of his belt and pitched him into the mud, so quickly that he had no time even to shout. Then he walked out and prodded him with his boot until he rolled over, rubbing his elbow. 'You come back here and I'll break your neck,' Silver said, and felt a savage pleasure in saying it.

'What's your problem?' squeaked the boy. 'You think you own the fucking place, or what?'

Then he scuttled off into the night. Silver went back into the kitchen. Fat Phil was re-establishing some order in the hall and Silver left him to it. He cleared up the kitchen, tidying the tins and boxes and cutlery and crockery and allowing the work to calm him. He was glad of the activity. The lights were going down in the hall now, but he did not feel like sleep. He worked for an hour. When he had finished he pulled up a chair and sat down and waited.

Jit opened the kitchen door and startled him. Perhaps he had dozed off after all. He had not heard the van's engine, over the drumming of the rain on the tin roof, nor her steps up the side path.

'Hi, Joe. Still up?'

She rested her guitar against the wall and shook the rain off her bright blue hair. It glittered like gaudy nylon, like a kewpie doll's hair. She pushed the door shut behind her and pulled out a couple of the clothing sacks and sat on them with her knees drawn up and rummaged in her shoulder bag.

'You left early.'

'You didn't need me, Jit. No contest in that place.'

'I didn't know it was a competition.'

She lit up and closed her eyes and inhaled hard and the aromatic smoke rose in a blue mushroom, then flattened and slid out sideways under the door beside her.

'You'll get busted carrying that stuff about,' he told her. 'You're asking for trouble.'

'You sound like my dad.' She leaned back, at ease. 'Why didn't you stay till the end?' She handed him the joint. He took it, drew on it, passed it back.

'Reasons.'

'I did some Baez for an encore. Thought it would keep the folkies sweet. They loved it.' She paused. 'I am good, aren't I, Joe?'

'Too good for that place.' But this wasn't the answer she wanted.

'I made twenty quid,' she protested. 'If I could do that every night I'd be OK.'

'You could do better.'

'Like what?'

'Theatre restaurants, nightclubs . . .'

'I don't want all that!' she laughed. 'All those rich wankers perving at me!'

'You prefer poor wankers perving at you?'

She smoked in silence for a while, a little hurt. Then she said: 'Brought you a present.' She reached across to the guitar case and flicked it open. He realised for the first time that it was not her own twelve-string guitar but a Yamaha six-string. 'It's Jake's. The one I told you about. I said you could have it.' He straightened and looked at it. She smiled at him puckishly so that the blue stone in her cheek winked. 'So now you can be king of the gypsy guitarists again and win back the beautiful Esmeralda.'

'From the evil Vargas,' he said. Part of him was troubled by the gift, but it was impossible not to respond to her good humour.

'You got it.' She drew on her joint again and handed it back to him, and then stood up, watching his face.

'Won't your brother want it back?'

'Jake? No. He's too busy becoming a real gypsy.'

'You can't just become a gypsy, Jit.'

'Sure you can. You can become anything you want.' She closed the guitar case and fastened the clasps and leaned it up against the table next to him. 'Get stuck into some practice, Joe. Because I want you to teach me.'

'Jit–'

But she was gone, waggling her fingers over her shoulder at him in farewell.

46

Lauren pulled up opposite the school and, to her relief, spotted a parking space almost at once. There was a bright blue coach parked directly outside the gates, sparkling in the spring sunshine. A small knot of people had already gathered at the foot of the steps: a woman with a clipboard, a handful of fussing parents, a driver with a cap.

'There you go, sweetheart,' Lauren said, as brightly as she could manage. 'Looks like you're going to have fun.'

Freya stared silently out of the car window at the bus and said nothing while her mother backed the car into the space. Lauren had not driven for three months and she felt awkward behind the wheel. Hudson had disapproved. They both knew the last time she had planned to drive anywhere was the night she was going to escape. In fact the little Citroën had been standing for so long that it had failed to start when she tested it the afternoon before, and she had had to get Hudson to charge the battery overnight. Even this he did resentfully.

'This is stupid, Laurie,' he had told her. 'I'll drive you. You're not ready.' But when she had pressed him he had not been able to say what she was unready for.

'I've had a licence for twenty years, Tommy,' she had told him haughtily, and felt her confidence rise as she said it. 'And I'm sober. And I'm perfectly capable of taking my own daughter to school in my own car.'

She knew the truth. She was nervous about driving again: by some twist of association in her mind, it was somehow bound up with her wider independence. Confident, assertive, positive people drove well. Defeated, negative ones drove poorly. She badly wanted to show Freya the right Lauren Silver today.

'I don't think I really want to go,' the girl said, staring miserably out at the sunlit street.

Lauren leaned across and pulled her daughter against her and kissed her. 'I know it's difficult, sweetheart.'

'The camp won't be the same without Goodie.'

'Of course it won't. How could it be?'

'She always won everything at camp,' Freya said, and thought about this for a moment. And then: 'Everyone's going to ask me where she is.'

'They'll all know, love.' Lauren hugged her. 'We've told everyone who didn't know already.'

'Not all the girls from the other schools. Not all of them will know.'

'No, I expect not all of them will know.' Lauren tossed her hair back and looked out through the windscreen. 'It'll be hard no matter what we do. Life is.'

'I should stay here with you,' Freya said, suddenly fierce, pulling free to face her, and Lauren could see at last what really troubled her daughter. Freya said: 'You need me.'

'Yes, I need you, Frey. But not for this. It's an inquest. It's not some big ceremony you have to be there for.'

'*You* have to be there.'

'Yes, but you've told them everything you know, and there's no need to go through it again. It's just an official thing, that's all. A kind of signing off.'

'Will Sam be there?'

'Yes,' Lauren replied, surprised at the question. 'As a matter of fact he will be.'

The answer seemed to satisfy the girl. She nodded. 'That's all right, then.'

'It is, yes,' Lauren said. 'In a way.'

'I can't remember what happened,' Freya said suddenly, and looked at her lap. 'I've tried and I've tried.'

'You're not expected to, Frey. People often can't remember that kind of thing. It's good they can't. It's a defence.'

'Will I ever remember?'

'It won't matter, sweetheart. I think we know what happened anyway, don't we?'

They were silent for a while. Across the road the footpath was growing crowded with parents and children and teachers. The luggage compartments of the big shiny bus were open and bags were being pushed in, sports bags and holdalls and camping equipment, while a teacher tried to keep track of it all and tick it off a list.

They were only going for five days, and only to South Wales at that, Lauren reflected, yet it looked as if they were preparing to farewell a liner. For a second she felt cynical. But then Freya moved against her and the jagged moment fell away, and she thought: This is how ordinary people live life. Silly and excited, warm and trivial, and messy and undignified and funny. And as deep as the deep blue sea and just as constant. This is how it went on before Gudrun died, how it has been going on ever since, and how it will go on in the future.

'I've not been a good mother to you, Frey,' she said, staring out at the bright scene.

'Not very good,' the girl agreed. 'But you're the one I got.'

Then in an uncharacteristically impulsive gesture she wrapped her arms around her mother's neck and kissed her.

'See you Saturday,' she said, and before Lauren had time to respond she had grabbed her bag from the back seat and was lugging it across the road into the crowd of excited children.

47

Silver was head down under the bonnet and did not hear the priest until the last moment.

'You're singing, Joe,' Nugent observed. Silver started, then levered himself up out of the engine compartment. He was filthy with grease, and his knuckles were chipped, and his hands and forearms ached after four hours of work on the engine. But it was true. He had been singing.

'Is singing against the rules?'

'My oath! This is a Christian establishment. You're supposed to suffer.' Nugent looked relaxed in a sweater and slacks and was drinking from a tall can of lager. He lifted the can to Silver, winked and drained it. He walked around the old minibus, stroking the bodywork affectionately. 'You reckon you'll ever get this thing going? You've been on it for weeks.'

'You should've got me a reconned engine, like I asked.'

'Money, Joseph,' the Australian said easily. 'Besides, I needed to keep you for fixing the drains and mending the roof and scrubbing off the graffiti. Which reminds me, that needs doing again.'

'Why do you bother, Nugget?' Silver slid down from the bus and found some paper towel to wipe his hands.

'Twenty-four hours and there's a new lot.'

Nugent pulled up a crate and sat on it, leaning back against the fence in a patch of afternoon sunlight. The weather was beginning to warm perceptibly now and as Silver stretched his knotted muscles he could hear the birds singing for the first time.

'At least it keeps you off the streets for a while,' Nugent said. 'Which may be a benefit to the community.' He rolled his head and squinted up at Silver. 'Is it, Joe?'

'Is it what?'

'A benefit to the community?'

Silver took a feeler gauge from the bench and cleaned packed grime from under his nails with it. 'I do what I'm told around here, Nugget. What more do you want?'

'Oh, you're a regular saint, you are. Three weeks of cleaning up after the bedwetters, digging out the cess pit, saving Fat Phil's hide, keeping Beelzebub off Spider. And sleeping on the floor among the bums while you do it. Better watch out. We'll start to think you like it.'

'Is this what I get for humming a tune?'

Nugent crushed the beer can in his fist and tossed it deftly through the open back window of the bus, where it clattered among the litter and upturned seats. He stood up. 'I wouldn't want you to get too happy, Joe.'

'Thanks.'

'I wouldn't want you to think you could stay here for ever. This can only be a halfway house for people like you.'

426

'Who are people like me?'

Nugent held his eyes. 'There's nothing much wrong with you, Joe. You're a first-class asset among all these liabilities. But one day I'll have to ask why you're still here.'

'Are you throwing me out?'

'You should want to get out. I wonder why you don't.' He looked steadily at Silver. 'Maybe you're still getting your head together. But I wouldn't want to think you had another agenda.'

Silver moved across to the workbench and tipped fresh petrol from a can over a clutter of greasy components in a tin dish, shaking them in the fuel as if panning for gold until the grease and dirt dropped away and revealed the bright steel. He glanced up at Nugent.

'Do you want this motor finished or not?'

'Sooner or later you're going to have to look beyond here and get a life,' Nugent said. Silver concentrated fiercely on his work: he swilled the fuel again so that the heady reek of it filled the warm afternoon. 'You'll have to face it, Joe, sooner or later.'

Silver set down the tray, stared down into it, said nothing. Nugent took a couple of steps out into the sunshine and stretched, opening his arms to the slight heat of it, embracing it. He let his arms drop to his sides.

'Jit says you're playing again.'

'With nine fingers? What do you think?'

'She says you're already better with nine fingers than she is with ten.'

'I just fumble around. I haven't played since I was a kid.'

Nugent smiled slowly and Silver saw that this was a lie too far.

'That's not what Jit says. She says you must have been bloody excellent once. She also says you can teach her a lot.'

'I've got nothing to teach anyone.'

'I've got this theory, you see, Joe,' Nugent continued as if Silver had not spoken. 'Everyone gets shut in the cellar at one time or another. It's dark and lonely in that cellar. Sometimes they get out real easy. They find a torch or a key in their pocket. Sometimes someone else has to let them out. Sometimes it takes a while.'

'Meaning?'

'Music is Jit's way out. But she needs guidance.'

'I'm not in the guidance business.'

'Oh, I'm sure you'll learn to be, Joe. Because you want this.' The Australian tossed him a key with a wooden tag. 'Second floor in number seventeen, across the street. Young Andy's moved out.'

Silver rolled the key in his hands. The houses were half derelict and little more than tenements. They were all condemned. But they belonged to the diocese, and if Nugent put him in there he could have some peace and some small space to himself.

'Thanks, Nugget.'

'Now you listen, Joe. To you it's a cell, right? Not like a prison. Like a worker bee has. I'll give you a few quid a week. But it's not a cheap apartment or a bolthole. I put you in it because I want your work. And while you live in it you do what anyone here tells you to do.'

'Understood.'

'Anyone. And that includes Jit.' Silver stiffened and Nugent saw it. 'That's right, Joe. She wants to learn, you teach her. Otherwise, it's been nice knowing you.' He turned and sauntered away round the corner of the hall. Almost at once he stuck his head back into the garage. 'And that's Rule Bleeding Four.'

It was a bare cube with a single shadeless bulb, a couple of chairs and a split foam mattress. He pulled the door to behind him. Then he moved one of the hardbacked chairs around and sat on it. The room was no more than a partitioned-off box in what must originally have been a front bedroom. The plasterboard partition cut the window vertically in half. His half looked out over the ugly little church in the centre of the square. The lowering afternoon sun gave a gilding of life and colour even to this shabby pocket of East London. Three black children were playing in a weed-choked goldfish pond in the front yard of one of the terraces. The dusty foliage beside the church's north wall had erupted into an explosion of purple and white lilac. Someone in an upstairs room was practising scales on an out-of-tune piano. The sound of that stumbling pianist, picking away at stained ivory in a backstreet tenement gave him a sad pleasure he could not define, a pleasure which troubled him.

'Hi, neighbour.' Jit pushed open the unlatched door. She had brought her guitar and now stood it against the wall. He said nothing and she moved around the little space, inspecting it. With her fingertip she tested a shelf for dust, looked at it absently. 'I cleaned the place up a bit for you. It was such a tip. Andy was a nice enough guy, but let's face it, he was a bit of a dreg.'

Silver recalled an intense young man with a beard who spoke with a Geordie accent, when he spoke at all. Silver remembered that he fastened every button on his shirt right up to the Adam's apple and down to both cuffs.

'Where did he go?'

'Dried out, got himself together, got a job.'

'That's good, I suppose.'

'Oh, he'll be back in two or three months. Nugget will pick him up off some park bench, and away we go again.'

Silver looked out again over the square, the squat church, the corrugated iron hall, the laughing children flinging jewels of water over one another. In his mind he saw the taciturn, buttoned-up Andy, his beard matted and his dull clothes stained, brought in again in the back of Nugent's little van, as hopeless and as referenceless as before. Coming from nowhere. Going nowhere.

Jit idly ran her finger along the bass string of her guitar so that it buzzed like a wasp in a jar. 'Three months clean is better than nothing. Who wants to be a gutter junkie all year round?'

Silver was about to argue but somehow did not have the spirit for it. Drifting in on the cool air came the sound of the piano, the beginner still picking out notes every bit as clumsily as before. Jit lit a joint with elaborate care. When it was under way she drew on it, and drawled through the smoke.

'I've got a gig at the Rum Jungle Club Thursday week.'

'The what club?'

'It's in Stepney Green. It's not much, but at least it's a real night club. Maybe you brought me luck, Joe.'

'That'd be a first.'

'I've written this new song for it. Listen.'

She handed him the joint and took up the guitar and began to play. He drew on the spliff and sat back against the wall to listen. He was not sure how the connection was made. Perhaps it was because she looked so very young at that moment, the sparkling stone in her cheek, her head at first cocked in concentration over the strings and then lifted to sing, projecting that pure voice like a shaft of light, a haunting song of pain and loss, like so much she wrote. It seemed to illuminate something in his mind. Whatever the reason, suddenly he knew that he was strong enough to face the pain again, that he had to see Freya once more.

'Put you to sleep, did I?' she accused him. 'Well, that's a great bloody compliment.'

He shook himself, concentrated. 'The song's great,' he said. 'You'll do fine.'

'Is that your idea of constructive criticism?'

He was stung by her persistence, and sat up on the bed.

'Look, Jit, you want criticism? Well, I'll tell you. They'll all love you because you look sweet and gamine and you sound like a Sunday school teacher. But technically you're nowhere.'

'Well, don't beat about the bush, Joe. Come right out and say it.'

'You've got to do what I tell you and move down the fretboard more. I told you that before. All this C, F, G7 twelve-bar stuff won't do for an audience that knows what it's listening to. You need to put some grunt into it.' He found himself warming to this. 'You'll always sell yourself on your voice, that's obvious. But you need to do a lot more with the axe—'

'The what?'

'The guitar. Christ, don't you know anything? Here, give it to me.'

He handed her back the joint and took the guitar and cradled it. Perhaps it was the dope. This time his left hand found the positions on the fretboard with a speed that was almost fluid. It was not remotely like anything he could once have done, but it was still a leap ahead of where he had been just a couple of days earlier. A dammed stream was overspilling, carving a new channel to his remaining fingers. In his surprise at this returning power he did not realise what riff he was playing. She rolled her head back against the wall, eyes closed, and whisper-sung the words:

'You people climbing on that Narrow Way—'

He clapped his hand hard over the strings, killing the song dead.

She opened her eyes and pulled a face at him, mocking him. 'You were playing it, pal.' She sat up and handed the joint back to him and waited while he drew on it, watching him. 'You did something bad, didn't you, Joe?'

'Yes.'

'Really bad?'

'Yes.'

She took back the spliff and inhaled, studied the glowing tip of it. 'Can you put it right?' Her voice was matter-of-fact, entirely without drama.

'No,' he said, but he realised that he had hesitated, and that she had sensed this.

She looked at him through the smoke. 'Well, can you make it any better than it is?'

'Jit, I don't want to talk about it.'

'You don't?'

'No.'

'You want a fuck, then?'

He jerked his head up and stared at her in such frank astonishment that she laughed aloud.

'Yes, with me, Joe. Do you see anyone else here?'

'Give me a break, Jit.'

'You're shocked! You really are shocked!'

She was vastly amused. She held the joint up away from her and rolled against the wall and laughed louder.

'Hey, Joe – I'm not that bad, am I?'

'I'm three times your age, Jit.'

She regained some control with an effort, wiped her eyes, assumed a serious expression. 'You can still get it up, can't you, Joe?'

He stared at her in confusion and her self-control exploded in a cloud of smoke. 'Christ, Joe – don't look at me like that! I can't stand it.' She stood up with an effort, pushing the heels of her hands into her eyes. 'I'm sorry, Joe. I mean, look, if you don't want it, you don't have to have it. But did you think I was some sort of little nun?'

The idea of this doubled her over again and she groped for her guitar and pulled the door open. At the last minute she turned, handed him the rest of the joint. 'Here. Maybe you need this more than I do.'

Silver could hear her joyful laughter ringing all the way up the stairs. It was a curiously innocent sound.

48

McBean shifted the phone to his other ear to block out the noise of Hayward eating. He had grown used to doing this because Hayward was almost always eating. The car smelled like a different restaurant every day. Today it was Chinese.

The sound of Hayward munching meant that it took McBean a moment to identify the gruff voice on the phone, and he had to ask the man to repeat his name.

'Gornall. From Rotherhithe. Couple of weeks back.'

'Sergeant Gornall?' McBean had virtually given up on him. The sound of his voice now made McBean's pulse quicker. He waved Hayward to silence so that the Constable stopped in mid-mouthful, his cheeks bulging like an oversized hamster. McBean said: 'Sorry. There was bit of interference this end. What can I do for you, Sergeant?' It was strangely formal to be calling Gornall 'Sergeant' but he did not know his first name and Gornall was not the kind of man to volunteer it.

'It might be that I can do something for you, Sergeant.'

McBean lifted a finger as a signal that Hayward should listen.

'You mean about the Silver business?'

'I do. I put the word out, to see if any of our local

435

yobbos had got rich quick. Like we agreed.'

'Yes?'

'Well, no luck. Or I'd've called.'

'But?'

Gornall paused, relishing his moment of drama. 'If you hang on a minute, Sergeant, I'll tell you. I just had a call from Newington. There's an old tom called Maggie Turpin who used to hang around the pubs up our way from time to time. Not a local. From up East somewhere. We haven't seen her around here for a few weeks. And now she's just turned up dead in this flat in Newington, not far off your patch. Now the thing is, they found a lot of cash on the bloke who's with her.'

'A lot?'

'About fifteen hundred quid. Not all that much but a lot more than he would have seen in a very long time. I thought you might like to shoot round there. Get in first and score a couple of points with that tight-arsed boss of yours.'

McBean laughed. 'Cobb? He's not so bad.'

'Anyway, thought you'd like to know.' Gornall read out the address and Hayward took it down. Then Gornall said: 'Look, I wouldn't go jumping to any conclusions. This probably doesn't mean much. Get round there and see for yourself, I would. The lads are still there.'

McBean's favourite uncle had lived in Newington and he knew the area well. He even knew the street. Flats and maisonettes with a railway line running across the bottom of the estate, ragged privet beside concrete drives. He swung the car around and flicked on the siren.

The area south of London Bridge was rundown and nondescript when McBean had stayed at his uncle's, twenty years before. He remembered pebbledashed 1930s houses, car repair workshops in backstreets, railway arches boarded up to make furniture stores. Since then London's boom had launched the district violently upmarket. Flower baskets hung in the High Street outside glossy new shopping malls. The railway arches now sheltered boutique restaurants and antique stores with BMWs parked outside them. Dennis McBean did not much like the changes but despite them he could not suppress a sense of homecoming. His uncle, an upright Jamaican who had served in the RAF, had been good to him.

McBean found the street and parked behind a squad car and an ambulance. He and Hayward climbed out and moved through the huddle of neighbours gathered on the public side of the tape. Here, away from the High Street, nothing had changed much. This end of the street was flanked by square redbrick blocks of flats, eight to a block, neat enough but charmless. There was a police car, an ambulance and a shiny black mortuary van outside the place. McBean recognised the Sergeant who met them at the front door, a tall and angular man called Crick. He had a beaky nose and a permanent stoop and reminded McBean of a stork.

'You're a bit off your ground, Den. Not enough trouble for you in Clapham?'

'We can't resist your magnetic personality, Birdy, that's all.'

'Ho, ho, ho.'

Crick led McBean and Hayward through the cramped hallway of the flat and turned right through the kitchen-diner. It was a bare, underfurnished room. The bench surfaces were empty and uncluttered, but there was a faint smell of spoiled food. McBean saw that the fridge door was open and had been that way for some time, for a yellowing cabbage lay draped over the top shelf. The oven door was open too, and McBean thought he could still detect the faintest whiff of gas although the room's windows had been flung wide. From a bedroom the other side of the hallway came a sudden explosion of obscenities, a man's voice, a ripped, drunken voice which spiked up, roaring, and then faded feebly away. Crick followed McBean's glance.

'The other half. We can't get much sense out of him. You can have a go later.'

A man in a white labcoat was on his knees on the floor in front of the open oven, minutely checking the linoleum.

Crick said: 'My bet is he came in pissed, found the old duck in here, and then put her to bed, like.' He ushered them through into the bedroom and made a courtly gesture of introduction.

The bulky figures bending over the bed made her body look as frail as a sparrow's. The woman was a husk. The flesh was grey, her hair yellow-white on the pillow. The heavy chemical smell of death was gradually dispersing through the opened window. She had been placed with some care, the blankets pulled up to her chin and her sticklike arms laid outside the covers. McBean, peering between the photographer and the paramedics, could not convince himself that she looked peaceful. She merely looked absent. He glanced around the bedroom. It was surprisingly pleasant in a cheap and chintzy fashion. Clearly she had tried hard to make it cheerful, and this immediately brought her to life for him. McBean knew a good deal about making the best of shabby flats.

A vase of flowers stood on the window ledge, the wilted blooms stirring as the cheap print curtains shifted in the air. It was the sort of posy that might be picked from a suburban garden while the owner wasn't watching. Colourful photos cut from magazines were taped to the walls – a view of Lake Windermere, a Dutch windmill in a sea of tulips, a smiling picture of the Queen.

'Poor old biddy,' Hayward said from beside him.

McBean leafed through the papers.

'It says here you were a sailor, Stevie.' The documents were crumpled and stained and they smelled of the man's bonemeal body odour. 'Long ago, was that?'

Stevens's eyes drifted to meet McBean's. He had washed-out blue eyes with a hard white ring around the pupils. He was filthy and he stank of excrement and of some raw spirit, and had a crusted cut over his temple which should have been stitched. McBean thought he might be about fifty. He gained the impression of a violent and stupid man who had once been immensely powerful. Now he looked feverish and ill. McBean wondered how long it had been since Stevens had eaten.

'Open that window, Jayce,' he said, then loudly: 'Where are you from, Stevie? No one around here seems to know you.'

'I been in the East.' The voice was vague. 'The Nile and all.'

'The Nile, Stevie?' McBean pulled a comic face. 'And it says here you were born in Deptford.'

Stevens stared through him.

'Had to be somewhere *nice*, Maggie says.' Stevens flipped his hand contemptuously at the flat. The emptiness behind his eyes was expanding. McBean sensed that in a moment he would lose him altogether into some other even more hopeless universe. 'For once, she says. *Respectable*, she says.' Stevens leaned forward, remembering, and his voice became thoughtful. 'Just like she was sleeping, it was.'

'So you put her to bed, is that it, Stevie?'

Stevens peered at him, as if noticing McBean's dark skin for the first time.

'Don't they sleep in beds where you come from, then?' Someone near the door laughed. Stevens gazed in wonder around the cheap room, as if he had not seen it before. 'She blew nearly the whole wad, renting *this*.'

'What wad?' Hayward said. 'Where did you get all this money, Stevie?'

Stevens ignored him.

' "Stevie," she says. "Stevie, you go out and get yourself a few beers." She give me a twenty. 'Course, I knew then.'

'Where did you get the money, Stevie?'

But the man had left, his face slack and the focus of his eyes drifting.

Outside the door McBean handed Stevens's Merchant Navy discharge papers to Birdy Crick and shook his head.

'We won't get much out of him.'

Crick shrugged. There was a sudden commotion in the bedroom and Stevens appeared in the doorway, purple in the face and bellowing, two Constables struggling to hold him back.

'Shoulda left him!' he roared, thrashing against their grip. 'Shoulda let him just float away!' A policeman's cap came bouncing into the hallway. 'Him and his fucking money!' Stevens came halfway back to sanity for a moment, stopped fighting and fixed McBean with a look of such crazed despair that it was as much as he could do not to recoil. 'It was so cold,' Stevens said in an entirely rational voice. Then his eyes rolled up and he slipped through the policemen's grip to the floor and there was shouting and a rush of paramedics and McBean was pushed back against the wall.

'Well, thanks a lot, Den.' Crick idly picked his large nose. One of Stevens's arms jerked uselessly, again and again, as the resuscitator fired. 'Is this a patented interviewing technique, or can we all try it?'

It was the end of their shift and they drove back to the station in silence. They still had not spoken ten minutes later when they took seats opposite one another across the canteen table. Hayward created an Olympic logo with rings of spilled tea on the Formica, using his mug as a stamp. He spent a great deal of care on this, frowning with concentration as he worked. Finally he said: 'I know what you're thinking.'

'How do you know I'm thinking about anything?'

'Because you're always such a miserable sod when you're thinking, Sergeant.'

Hayward was right about this, and McBean was quiet for a moment.

'It just got to me, that's all,' he said at last. 'That old tart, trying to make the place *nice*.'

'That's not what got to you, Sergeant. I mean, that's not all of it.' Hayward completed the Olympic sign and sat back to admire the pattern. 'You're thinking Stevie pulled Matt Silver out of the river. You're thinking maybe Silver wasn't dead when he did that. And now Stevie's gone to the big meths tank in the sky, and we don't even know where to look.'

McBean stroked his lower lip. 'The man didn't know what day it was, Jayce. He thought he was still in Cairo or somewhere, in the Navy.'

'He said it was cold.'

'And all that stuff about the Nile?'

'It's the Curse of Tutankhamun's tomb,' Hayward said, daringly. 'That explains everything.'

McBean lifted his china mug off the table and swirled it, staring at the vortex of tepid brown liquid in the bottom.

'I guess it doesn't matter now,' he said. 'They're closing the book on it after the inquest.'

'It matters,' Hayward said decisively. Then added in a rush: 'I keep thinking of his wife and the little girl. It's funny, I feel kind of responsible. Maybe they just need to know for sure.'

McBean was quiet for some time, rolling his warm mug between his palms. Eventually both men got up and returned their mugs to the counter.

It was not until Hayward was pushing open the door of the canteen that he spoke again. 'You know, Sarge, it's a funny thing . . . Where I grew up, there was a pub. Queen of the Nile, it was, or Hero of the Nile or something. Everyone just called it "The Nile". Think there are any pubs called that, up East?'

McBean looked at him. 'Tell me something. How did you get a name like Jason? You an argonaut or something?'

'No, Sarge.' Hayward looked a little shocked. 'We're Methodists, we are.'

49

Cobb dismissed them and watched them file out of the incident room for the last time. They seemed happy enough to go, even without a result, and shuffled out smiling and joking and calling the odd cheerful farewell to him. He could hardly say he had welded the Matt Silver Task Force into the Met's dream team during the three-month investigation but he had grown strangely fond of his unlikely crew. He thought he might even miss them.

Cobb closed the door behind the last of them and walked back into the untidy little room and let his gaze wander around the pinned photos and the scribbled whiteboard and the reports in their stacked marbled folders.

All this had been for nothing. Owens's constantly redrawn maps of 'most likely sites' worked out with the River Police. The fat file of witness statements from security men and street sweepers and night-owls who had seen the crash. The endless doorknocking around Rotherhithe. The pathology reports PC Carlow had chased up, the examination by Sergeant Maxey and his team from Accident Investigation. All the kilograms of paper, all the megabytes of computer memory, all the square metres of glossy photographic print. Nothing new in all of it.

Cobb supposed he should feel bitter or frustrated at their failure. But he did not. They had looked everywhere there was to look, and no one could have done more. The door opened behind him and he turned.

Sykes said: 'That's it, then, Cobby? Lord Dismiss us with Thy Blessing, and all that.'

'I suppose it is, sir.'

Sykes reached up and jerked a photograph free from the noticeboard so that the coloured pins flicked across the room. It was the pathologist's picture of Gudrun Silver, much as Cobb had seen her on that first morning nearly three months ago. The noticeboard caught the afternoon sun now that the days were growing longer, and the photo had curled a little. 'Tomorrow, is it? The inquest?'

'Two o'clock.'

'Accidental death. Formality.' Sykes tossed the warped photo back on to the table. 'Over in twenty minutes. Pity they can't do the father at the same time.'

'Yes.'

'Come back here after the inquest. Take all this stuff down. Put it in the bin. Lousy fucking job. All PR, no policing.' Sykes looked up at him. 'But you done all right with it, Sam.'

It took Cobb a moment to register that this was the first time Sykes had ever used his Christian name.

'If you still want to move on,' Sykes continued, 'maybe we should transfer you to Public Affairs.' He saw Cobb's expression and grinned savagely. 'That's by way of a witticism. Maybe you didn't recognise it.'

Cobb relaxed. 'It was very droll. Sir.'

'I thought so.' Sykes turned away and reached for the door handle. 'Superintendent Parris at Regional Crime's got an opening, Sam. Nominated you.' He waited. 'I expect you mean "Thank you, Mr Sykes".'

'Yes. Yes, I do.'

'It's got to be better than chasing dead rock stars.'

'Yes, it has to be. Thank you.'

'One snag – Parris is away for a few weeks. You got any leave owing?'

'Leave? A couple of weeks, sir.'

'Take it, Sam. Make a clean break with all this.'

'I'll need to clear up a few things, sir.'

'Come in and do it next week.'

'Sir.'

Sykes indicated the photographs and cuttings and notes with a jerky sweep of his hand. 'Dump it all, Sam. It's over.'

Cobb watched him swagger away across the big open-plan office, leering at the women in the room, jeering at the men, grinning his Pan grin. He felt as he had occasionally felt before in his life, that he had completed some sort of apprenticeship, or come through some initiation. Or perhaps it was a re-habilitation. Whatever the truth of it, Cobb knew that Sykes had opened a door for him. For two years his career had been sliding. His life, indeed, had been sliding. He had known and he had hardly cared. Sykes had shown some faith in him by waiting while he got his balance back. He was grateful.

Cobb had a sudden sense of things coming together, of new beginnings. His hand touched the curling photograph on his desktop and he picked it up and looked at it. It was fading so soon, the grainy image of that dead child, white skin and grey steel. He was momentarily annoyed with himself for forgetting that tomorrow would be a grim day for this child's sister, for her mother. But then it came to him that the two issues were interlocked, as endings and beginnings always are. 'It's over,' Sykes had said. Yes. In a way. Cobb was filled with an irrational sense of protectiveness. It was inappropriate, probably. But he crossed to his own desk and dialled her number, and when she answered, he said: 'Come down to the farm this weekend.'

'Sam?' Lauren sounded surprised. And something else. Cautious. 'You know what tomorrow is?'

'Of course I do. That's why.'

She did not answer directly. 'I sent Frey on a school camp. To Wales. I wanted her away from here this week.'

'Good idea. When does she get back?'

'Saturday morning.'

'So get them to drop her off at Oxford. We'll pick her up. It'll do you both good.' When she didn't answer, he said: 'I planned a bit of a surprise for her. Take her mind off things.'

If she guessed he was lying, or at best improvising, she did not betray it. But her voice was still uneasy. 'All right. I'll come up on Saturday.' She stopped. 'Sam, you know I'm not going to be a bundle of laughs this weekend.'

'That's not what it's about.'

'No,' she said, doubtfully. 'I know it's not.'

50

Lauren replaced the receiver quietly in its cradle and stood looking at it for a while, thinking. She stood for so long that Hudson asked, too casually: 'Cobb again?'

'Yes.'

Hudson, seated at the antique desk in the corner of the room, jerked up his chin a fraction and turned back to his work. 'An Inspector calls,' he murmured, as if to himself.

Lauren registered what he had said. 'What do you mean, "again"?'

He looked up, innocently. 'Sorry?'

'You said "again". Cobb "again". What do you mean by that?'

'All right, Laurie. All right.' He spread his hands. 'I just meant–'

'Why don't you just mind your own business, Tommy?' she snapped.

She instantly felt sorry. Hudson looked so pained whenever she hit out at him. He was a little pathetic, she thought, crammed into the impossibly delicate Regency chair, hunched over his papers, fat fingers stumbling over his calculator. She wondered what he did there all day. Something she should have been doing, probably. Something she should have dealt with.

He sighed, then turned towards her and laid his half-moon glasses on the desk. The chair groaned under him. She wondered if he had any idea how much Matthew had paid for it. He said: 'I understand, Laurie. It'll be better after tomorrow. You'll see.'

But for some reason his doleful sympathy only sparked her irritation afresh. 'Fuck off, Tommy,' she shouted at him. 'Just fuck off, for Chrissake.'

She turned and stalked out of the room, banging the door hard behind her, shocked at her own outburst.

She found a jacket in the hall and slung it over her shoulders and marched blindly through the dim corridors of the house until she reached the kitchen. She pushed open the swing doors. It was not dim here. Merilda was crooning along with a Latin radio station, all guitars and passion, and at the same time cooking energetically – even acrobatically – with garlic and tomatoes and basil, something that smelled of sunshine and hot stones and spat like a cat in the pan. As Lauren came through the kitchen Merilda stopped singing and stared at her: neither of them could remember when she had been here before. Lauren forced a smile and waved at her to go on, meaning that she should go on with everything: with the noise, and the smells and the colour and the life of it all. Then she walked through to the back door and opened it and went out into the evening garden.

Her trajectory ended here. She wasn't sure why she had come and did not know where to go next. There was an old set of wooden garden furniture outside the back door. She sat down there. It was cool, but the last of the spring sun fell at an angle through the larch trees and across the lawn and filled the corner where the table was placed, so that the wood was warm and the angle of the wall was sunlit. Lauren saw that an unwashed coffee cup lay on the table in front of her, and an opened blue aerogram form with a Portuguese stamp on it. She realised that this was Merilda's private space and the discovery embarrassed her. She made to rise but at that moment Merilda came sweeping out of the kitchen, beaming at her. Lauren could see she was flattered by her visit, flattered and perhaps pleased on Lauren's account too. Lauren wondered if she had somehow overheard her exchange with Hudson, or at least guessed at it. Lauren had the feeling that this would have given Merilda grim satisfaction.

With a practised flourish Merilda gathered up the letter and the empty cup, and set fresh coffee in front of Lauren. She tapped the hot rim of Lauren's cup with her fingertip, making no attempt at subtlety.

'More better, Mrs Silver,' she said kindly. 'Coffee more better than wine in bad times.'

Then she swept away again, singing to her own music.

Lauren smiled to herself. Merilda was right, but all the same at this moment part of her would have dearly loved a drink. Confrontation always made her feel like this. That was something she had learned at the counselling sessions, and was glad to have learned it, because knowing it made it easier to handle. Besides, a drink was out of the question. It would have meant retreating back into the dim heart of the house, where Hudson would still be hunched over his papers. She could picture him, gazing at her reproachfully over the top of his glasses. The thought of him made her feel obscurely ashamed. He had been good to her, in his fashion. She was, after all, still living on the loan he had made her.

And that was the least of it. He would do anything for her. He was always ready to drive her anywhere – resented it if she refused. He dealt with all the finances, from the accountants to the funeral expenses, handling everything so that all she had to do was sign the cheques or the forms. She had not seen a bill for months. He had fielded every single phone call, every pestering reporter, every threat to her security and privacy, until she had had her new private line put in. He had protected her like a medieval champion. And he had asked little enough in return, in all conscience. Only to be useful. Only to be around her. Only to be given the merest flicker of hope.

Oh yes, she thought guiltily. That was it. That was why she felt ashamed. She pulled her jacket close around her and pushed his mournful heavy face out of her mind. She should have done something about it before now. But not tonight. Not tonight of all nights. She was entitled to a little peace, a little space to gather her strength. Perhaps poor Tommy was right in a way he did not yet understand. It would all be different tomorrow.

It was good to see the sun again, this primrose spring sun. She remembered that Cobb had said something about this: that one day she would feel the sun on her skin and discover that it still felt good. Something like that. She sipped her coffee. That was good too. She felt the tension go out of her shoulders. The sun fell behind the rim of the earth and a blackbird sang as the light faded, a long bubbling trill. It evoked in her the faintest echo of summers past, long evenings by a tennis court, the soft bop of a struck ball and midges swinging in swarms under the darkling trees. It would all come back again. Gudrun would not come back, but summer would. She felt as if she had spied it through a keyhole: an illicit glimpse of an enchanted world, golden and aromatic, lyrical with birdsong.

She caught herself. It was growing cold. She heard the blackbird chirr away in the gathering darkness. Perhaps after tomorrow she might allow herself another peep through the keyhole. After tomorrow.

51

The motor started at a touch and purred like a sewing machine. Silver had known that it would but his sense of achievement was overwhelming just the same. He left the engine on tickover and walked around the bus, stroking it, listening to the murmur of the bearings he had refitted, the valves he had reground, the tappets he had adjusted. All that bright metal, spinning and pumping, opening and closing, all at unimaginable speed. And it was all running like a big watch, precisely, powerfully, quietly, because he had made it do so.

'Hey, that's neat.' Jit stuck her blue head out of the rear window. 'It goes.'

'Of course it goes,' Silver grunted. 'I fixed it so it would go.'

'It'd make a great gypsy caravan. Stacks of room. Couple of bunks in here, cooker in there.'

'Gypsy bloody caravan,' he said.

She made a face at him and went back to work. She had dragged all the rubbish, loose seats and fittings out of the bus. He was surprised at how practical she was and how resourceful, finding spanners and screwdrivers for herself, unbolting brackets. She seemed to treat the old van like a big Lego set, so that dismantling it was not a chore but a game. She sang constantly while she worked. Now she started on the burst plastic seats, so that the garage was filled with the smell of pine cleaner and the sound of scrubbing. Silver doubted the van had ever been cleaned before.

'Pride's a sin, Joe,' Nugent said. The priest was watching him from the door. 'One of the seven deadlics.'

'So I'm a sinner.' He could not keep the satisfaction out of his voice.

'Not much doubt about that.'

Nugent looked tired. It was Tuesday morning and Silver knew the priest had been out most of the night, ferrying the homeless, taking some to refuges, some back to the institutions from which they had wandered, some to casualty. Monday was not a bad night, but Nugent had less help than on the weekends. The priest said: 'This was supposed to be occupational therapy. I never thought you'd actually get the bloody thing to work.'

'Now you can collect three times as many dossers.'

'Bloody right.' It was unclear whether or not Nugent thought this was a joke. He walked round the minibus, touching it, obviously impressed.

'It's not finished yet,' Silver said. 'We need a couple of new tyres. And the battery's shot. But apart from that she's OK.'

Nugent nodded. Jit clambered out of the rear doors with a plastic bucket and walked away into the kitchen for fresh water. When she was gone, Nugent said: 'Take it down to Danny at Triple-A Motors in Bow Road.

Make sure you tell him it's for me. He'll put it on the slate.'

'Right.'

'New battery and a couple of tyres. Just to make it legal, OK? No more than that. I'll sort out the registration later.'

'Right.'

Nugent stood looking at the old vehicle for a while longer. 'And then you'd better get ready to move out.'

'What?'

'Truck's fixed. You're fixed. And we need the room.' Nugent saw Silver's face and snapped: 'Wise up, Joe. You knew you'd have to face it one fine day.'

Silver stood silent for a time. Nugent was right: he had known that he would have to face this some day. The idea of leaving did not surprise him. It did surprise him, though, that now the prospect had been raised, he was not more frightened by it. He was not sure what he felt, but it was not the fear he had expected.

'When, Nugget?'

'No rush. Jit's got this gig coming up, hasn't she?'

'The Rum Jungle. That's next week.'

'I want you there for that.'

'She doesn't need me there.'

'She needs you there,' Nugent said. 'After that, I don't know, maybe the two of you can sort something out. You seem to get on.'

'Me and Jit?'

Nugent yawned, too tired to argue. 'Mate, I don't care what your deal is with her,' he said. 'You take help

456

where you can find it in this world.' He yawned again and then took a step forward and peered into the open engine compartment, poked experimentally at the high-tension leads which carried spark to the purring motor. When he got tired of this he wiped his fingers on a rag on the bench. He looked up at Silver. 'You've done some good things here, Joe. For Jit. For yourself.'

Silver raised his eyebrows. 'But?'

'But debts don't get cancelled, Joe. I told you before. They have to be paid. Maybe it's time you thought about that.'

Jit lugged her steaming bucket into the garage and set it down hard in front of Nugent so that it slopped on the concrete floor and over the priest's shoes. 'Why should he think about it, Nugget?' The defiance in her tone made Silver glance at her. Something in what she had overheard had touched her on the raw. She said: 'No one can go back. Why tell him he can?'

'He can do what he wants, Jit,' Nugent said. 'I'm not his keeper.'

'No,' she said. 'You're not mine either.'

'You can finish this later,' Silver said to her, walking between them and unlatching the bonnet support. 'I'm going to get the battery.'

He edged the minibus out of the driveway and drove hesitantly the couple of miles to the garage in Bow Road. The trip took all his concentration. He had not been behind a wheel for months, and the bus was slower and more cumbersome than anything he had driven for the last twenty years. At the garage the mechanic called Danny took the keys from him and parked the old Ford outside the workshop and told him the work would take an hour. It was late-morning and Silver discovered that he was hungry. He crossed the road to a cheap cafe and ordered a bacon sandwich and a tea. They seemed normal things to order. The greasy smells of the cafe were normal too, and so were the other customers – shop assistants and bus drivers and housewives and electricity repairmen and a cabbie and a couple of pensioners. And outside, the buses and cabs and a flower stall and the snarled traffic and a sudden spring rainstorm stippling the windows and turning the tarmac to ebony and people hurrying under umbrellas through the grey. All normal. Reassuringly normal.

Could he ever be part of it again? He could feel the bulge of the wallet in his back pocket. That was money, the few pounds Nugent gave him every week. Not big money, of course. But real money. Enough to pay for this ordinary, greasy, beautiful sandwich. Enough to buy a couple of movie tickets, a few pints in a pub, a bus pass. And, if it kept coming in, why not enough eventually for a beaten-up old van like this one, for a decent Gibson guitar, for a few books, a cheap stereo, some CDs? It wasn't much. It wouldn't ever be much. But it could be a life. A place of his own – perhaps even legitimately rented – his name on the statements. And what after that? A bank account, maybe? Nugget would give him references of a sort. Was there a way to get a National Insurance number, a driving licence, a passport even? Could such things be fixed, if a man had a small income, a place to live, an identity? He had heard that they could.

He finished his food, paid and left the cafe, and stood for a moment outside in the rainslick road, hunched into his jacket while the cars hissed by. An identity? What kind of fool was he to be thinking this way?

He crossed the road to the garage. He took the keys back from the mechanic, climbed in, started up. He nosed the bus out into the traffic, signalling left, back down Bow Road the way he had come. A truck stopped for him and flashed its lights to let him out. He hesitated, then wrenched the wheel the other way and cut across both lanes and pulled away fast in the opposite direction.

It took him over an hour. He drove south and west, cutting across the motorway, out through the suburbs and the stockbroker belt, winding cross-country with the wipers sighing. He drove through the village, drab in the rain, and up the steep-sided lane beyond. He parked in a lay-by cut into the bank and left the van there, climbing the last two hundred yards on foot. The rain ran in a shining track down the gravelled roadway between its hedged banks and he splashed up it, the water filling his shoes, his head down.

The churchyard was unkempt, overdue for its first mowing of the year, and the gravestones stood in banks of cow parsley and nettle. But hers was clear, a rectangle of dark earth with a simple grey marble marker above it. The letters of her name were sharply cut into the stone: Gudrun. Just her first name. He did not blame Lauren for that. He did not blame anyone for anything any more.

His knees gave and his body crumpled on to the grassed mound beside her grave. The rain fell solidly over him from a white sky, the clouds so close that the blunt tower of the church was lost in them. He reached out and tore up a handful of yellow ragwort, an early spike of bluebells, and arranged them carefully on the raw wet earth beside him. The rain ran down the groove of his spine and along the ridges of his face, and fell on the flowers as he laid them down.

52

It was a high 1930s courtroom and the sun fell in dusty bars from the tall windows across the benches and chairs. It reminded Cobb of his schooldays. Outside, the capricious spring weather was breaking up. He could hear the March wind leaning on the windows and the light dimmed and brightened and dimmed again as clouds were driven across the sun and then were blasted clear.

For Cobb, now that he was here, a curious sense of unreality surrounded it all, as if he were watching it on a stage. He had been to a hundred inquests, and testified at many of them, and he was so familiar with the routine that for minutes on end it carried him along in its flow. But these dramas were not supposed to be personal, and he experienced a fresh sense of shock each time he realised that characters in the cast or in the audience were people he knew. He had forgotten about Phil Latimer the police doctor, and about Sergeant Maxey from Accident Investigation, about McBean and Hayward. Even about Tommy Hudson. He supposed he must have known they would all be here, but on one level he still had not expected it. Seeing them was a little like attending a reunion of people with whom he had once shared a lifeboat. They seemed out of context here in their neat clothes and on their best behaviour. No, he had not expected to see them. He had only expected to see Lauren.

Yet Cobb avoided looking at her. He was glad they were separated by the width of the room and by the measured formality of the proceedings. It disturbed him to see her. She had regained some of the strained pallor of the weeks after the accident. Until he saw this, he had not realised how far she had moved from that fragile state, and perhaps she had not realised it either. Her white skin against her black suit reminded him of the night she had come to his Baron's Court flat. He had thought her crazy then, he remembered with a touch of shame, beyond hope or help. He did not feel that way any more, though this had not been clear to him before now.

And then he was called, and his automatic professionalism took over and he stood up before the court and spoke clearly and concisely and answered the coroner's questions in full, just as if he had been talking about any little girl, any child's sister, any woman's daughter.

After that it went very quickly indeed. Lauren was called briefly and spoke in a low voice about Silver's state of mind when he left her, taking Gudrun away for the last time. There was some stirring of interest among the handful of journalists seated behind Cobb, but, if she heard it, she ignored it, and spoke directly and almost intimately to the coroner and seemed to see no one else in the room. When she had sat down again, others were called in rapid succession. The coroner was old, kindly and competent beneath the deceptively bland façade. He hurried them through, paused only to praise Hayward's courage and quick action – Cobb saw the gawky boy stiffen and blush – muttered a few words of sympathy, and recorded Accidental Death. Then the seats were clattering and the doors swinging and sounds ringing in from the corridor, and the inquest of Gudrun Silver, nine years old and never to see ten, was over.

Cobb waited until the court was empty, then packed his battered legal case and followed the last of the stragglers out through the swing doors. He did not want to meet Lauren face to face. It would be grotesque to make small talk about travel arrangements and train timetables. For a moment he regretted extending the invitation. He knew he had pressured her. But there were times when someone had to take the initiative, he reminded himself, and it was hard to expect her to do so. He nodded to himself. It would do her and Freya no harm to be away from London this weekend of all weekends. After all, that was why he had suggested it.

And then he did catch a glimpse of her, Hudson's broad back ushering her through the street doors, a swirl of black coat, a flash of the fitful sun on her hair. Yes, that was why he had suggested it. Surely.

53

Lauren let Tommy Hudson guide her out across the pavement to the waiting limousine, shouldering people aside with unnecessary aggression. He pulled open the door for her and she ducked in, but before he could climb in after her she closed it in his face. Hudson hesitated outside the car and then slid into the front passenger seat. Lauren heard him grunt a command at the driver and the car shot away from the kerb and forced its way into the traffic with a blare of its horn.

Hudson slid back the glass partition and turned to face her. 'All right there, Lozz?'

'Don't call me that,' she told him. Lozz? When had he started doing that? 'And tell him not to drive like a maniac. We're not going to Maternity.'

Hudson gave her a knowing, long-suffering look but he signalled to the driver and she felt the pressure of the car's acceleration ease slightly and release her from the upholstery. He said: 'I want to get you home as quick as poss, darlin'. That's all.'

She closed her eyes and massaged the bridge of her nose. This was ridiculous. The very sound of his voice was beginning to grate on her. The smothering protective tone of it made her feel stifled and airless. She felt a headache begin to tap at her temple. She had an urge to stop the car, get out, find her own way back through the windswept city. 'Just leave me be for a while, Tommy. Huh?'

'It's only that–'

'Tommy!' she shouted. And then more quietly: 'Please.'

He twisted his mouth in disapproval but finally slid the partition closed and faced the front. With his broad face turned away Lauren felt an instant release. She lowered the window an inch and cold air sluiced through the car and she drank it greedily and the tension faded from her at once. The sky was a thin blue above Westminster, ribbed by cirrus, and the streets were scrubbed by the March wind until they glittered. She realised all at once that they were following the southern bank of the river, and that here – just here – was Lambeth Bridge, off to her right, with the broad stretch of water sparkling beneath it and the ochre pinnacles of the Houses of Parliament standing above on the far shore, postcard bright. There the heavy iron railings of the bridge. There the flat ramp of the embankment where the ambulances had parked. There the steps down to the ferry wharf where that child-Constable had floundered in. That was how it must have been.

She said: 'Stop the car.'

Hudson twisted urgently in his seat. 'We can't stop here, Lozz. It's–'

'Stop the fucking car right *now*!' Lauren smacked the glass partition hard with the flat of her hand, again

and again, until the driver pulled over. A storm of
protest – car horns, shouted insults and a short squeal
of brakes. Somewhere behind she heard the crump of
a collision and glass tinkled. She pushed open the door
and slid out and ran across the road through the
gridlocked traffic. Glancing back she saw Hudson
struggle out of the car, but then he was lost to view
behind a red doubledecker.

She slowed to a walk and crossed to the eastern
footpath. Trailing her hand along the smooth iron
capping of the railings, she walked towards the mid-
point of the bridge. Just short of halfway she stopped.
Here. It had been here. With her fingertip she traced
the joint between the sections of railing. She placed
her palms on the parapet and went up on tiptoe to see
the sliding water below. This place. These railings. That
water. She tried to feel horror. And yet it was such a
very fine day. The river sparkled at her. The pinnacles
of Westminster shone in the sunlight. It came to her
that no one was going to declare Lambeth Bridge a
national monument because Gudrun had died there.
People would walk and drive across it just the way they
always had. Ferries would chug over the spot where
her daughter had died. Tourists would take their
pictures of Westminster just as they always had, clowning and pulling funny faces and leaning over this
parapet, just as if Matthew Silver had not driven
through it one insane night in December.

She felt for her wallet and opened it and slid out the
photograph. It had never worked, trying to get the two

of them in the same shot. Gudrun so thoroughly eclipsed her sister. Yet this was the picture she had carried. She gazed at it for a while. Then she folded it and tore it gently across. She lifted the torn square of paper and kissed it and then let it flutter from her hand, a fleck of confetti flickering down towards the river until the wind caught it and sucked it away under the bridge and out of her sight. When it had vanished she looked down at the other half of the photograph. 'Hello, Freya,' she said. Then she opened her coat to the keen wind that pushed up along the river and let it billow behind her and let the cold air squeeze tears from her eyes.

His heavy steps clattered towards her. 'Christ, Lozz! You gimme such a fright.' He was red in the face and panting. 'Come back now, darlin'. Come back.'

She let him lead her back to the car, now pulled up high on to the footpath. She climbed in and they drew smoothly away. She turned in her seat, but though she craned to see, the scene withdrew from her and quickly it was left behind. In a little while the bridge was lost to her sight.

There was a cabinet of burr walnut behind the driver's seat and she leaned forward and opened it and made herself a drink. This one at least she could allow herself. She sensed Hudson stir and glance back at her, as if to register that he had noticed, but she ignored him and sat back with her vodka and nursed it as the southwestern suburbs slipped by. In spacious gardens the cherries and willows were coming into leaf and the verges of the streets were brilliant with daffodils. Over. She played with the word in her mind. Over. No, of course it was not over. It would never be over. But things went on anyway. That was the point. Whether you wanted them to or not. They passed a park, a blaze of green and gold, gone in an instant. But in that instant, momentary though it was, her mind and eye registered a series of snapshot images, brilliant as icons. An old man with his hand on his cap, leaning against the wind. Young mothers clustered around the swings, their colorful clothes blown like the plumage of parrots. A girl of Freya's age, towed at a run over the fat spring grass by two madly grinning Labradors. It was possible to go on, Lauren saw. People did it all the time. It was possible to find a new way, to shoulder the burden and go on anyway. In a sense it was impossible not to.

Lauren knew what held her back. She realised that she had not thought of him, not even in anger or in hate, for days now. Longer, perhaps. But even when she did not think of him, it was Matthew who held her back. If it had been his inquest today, and not their daughter's, how much simpler it would have been. She shut out reality for a second and let the thought take flight and was surprised where it led her. For it seemed to her that she could see herself as an old woman, talking about him to someone – a grandchild, maybe. Talking to this young person, turning an old photograph in wrinkled hands, telling the story. The story of the pain he had brought her, which had so nearly destroyed her. The story of her grief and her bitterness and of the blind animal hatred for him she had nursed like a cancer, in the bleak wasteland of the weeks after Gudrun was gone. But telling another story too. The story of his reckless buccaneer spirit, of his dazzling talent. Of the sheer perilous glamour of loving him. Loving *him*. Not just the daredevil faithless pirate, but the whole of him. The man with music in his soul, the man with the child inside him who, in the way of children, knew instinctively so much about people, and so very little about himself.

She was no longer sure what she believed. But she knew that if she could only be sure that he was gone, gone for ever, she could move on. If she could only be sure, then one day she could tell that story. And perhaps grant the two of them some absolution at last.

She pressed the button so that the window whispered down and the glassy air bucketed into the car, and she flung her untouched drink out into the sunlight.

She must have slept then, for she was next aware of the car swinging down the gravel drive and they were back at the house. Merilda was at the front door and Lauren could see she had been weeping again, affected by the gravity of the day and by sympathy for her. As Lauren passed, she briefly put her arms around the woman and hugged her before walking on. It was something she had never done before and she found that the contact gave her an unexpected surge of strength. She climbed the stairs to her room and shut the door behind her, aware somehow that Tommy Hudson was standing at the foot of the staircase, watching her, troubled by her strange new assertiveness.

She stripped and ran the shower and got in and let it hose over her, as hot as she could stand it. Tommy *would* be troubled, she thought. Despite what she planned to do, and perhaps partly because of that, she found it impossible not to feel sorry for the big man. On another occasion not so very long ago he had stood at the foot of those same stairs and listened to her running the shower up here. That time he had rightly guessed that it was a trick to buy her time. She could imagine him standing there that night, with his eyes narrowed in suspicion, like a big dog given a command he did not entirely trust.

Well, he could trust it now, she thought. This time the noise of her running the shower meant just what it sounded like. She no longer needed him to come bounding up the stairs to break open the door with his teak shoulder. She no longer needed to be saved. It was sad in a way. He would not understand.

She stepped out of the shower and towelled herself dry and dressed slowly in jeans and sweater. When she could put it off no longer, she walked out of her room and down the stairs. He was in his familiar seat by the antique writing desk. The half-moon glasses made him look studious and even gentle. For a moment she thought her spirit might quail, and she spoke quickly, before it could do so.

'Tommy, I want you to move out.'

He did not seem to hear. 'How's that?'

'You've been a real friend in need, Tommy. I want you to understand that. But I think you've done your duty by Matthew and me.'

'What are you on about?' He laid his glasses on top of the papers and without them she saw what she already knew, that he was neither studious nor gentle.

'I mean it, Tommy. I should have said something earlier. Of course there's no rush at all, it's just–'

He smiled. 'Don't fool yourself, Lozz. You couldn't cope without me.'

'Please don't call me that,' she said, and all at once she was angry. 'Just don't call me that, all right?'

'Hey, hey.' Hudson spread his broad hands, smiling, conciliatory.

'For God's sake, Tommy!' She swept an ashtray off the bar top with a jerk of her arm so that the glass dish bounced among the furniture. 'Will you stop smirking at me and listen?'

'All right.' He stopped smiling, folded his hands in his lap. 'All right, Laurie. But there's no need for this. We all know it's been a shit of a day for you. For me too.'

'I understand that, Tommy.' She controlled herself with an effort. 'I know you loved Goodie too.'

'Not just Goodie,' he said.

'Oh, Christ, Tommy, don't make this any harder than it has to be.'

'It doesn't have to be hard at all. You just give yourself a couple of days to settle down, and we'll be back to normal. Right as ninepence.'

'I'm sorry, Tommy.' She straightened her spine against the bar. 'I want you to leave. I appreciate everything you've done, but I can stand on my own feet now.'

He looked at her for so long that it made her uneasy. Finally he said: 'Are you fucking that copper?'

For a second she could not believe that these words had been spoken. She screwed up her eyes and stared at him in utter outrage. '*What?*' she demanded. '*What* did you say to me?'

He put his head on one side, pursed his lips. 'Just a thought,' he said.

'Tommy, you pack your bags and get out of here right now. Tonight. I mean it.'

He did not stir. He looked as calm and immovable as if they had been discussing the weather. 'Think you'll be able to manage this big old place without me, Laurie?' he asked.

'Not that it's any of your business, I'm going to sell it,' she said, flinging across the room, still stunned by his suggestion and not entirely sure why it had rocked her so profoundly. 'Sell it. Sell everything in it. I'm going to put this whole business behind me. Behind us. Behind me and Freya.'

'How are you planning to do that?' His calm was unsettling. 'I mean, it's not like you own the place.'

Lauren stopped. Through her shock it came to her that this was a thing unacknowledged, a thing dreaded, and yet a thing not entirely undreamed of. She turned to face him but found herself backing up against the

472

wall. He watched her, then he rose and went to the bar and poured himself a Scotch. He dropped the ice cubes in one by one, punctuating his words.

'I took over the payments on this place weeks ago, Laurie.' Clunk. 'And the kid's schooling.' Clunk. 'And every other bill that came in.' Clunk. 'You should be bloody grateful.'

'I won't live on your charity, Tommy. Not on yours or on anyone else's.'

Hudson's face darkened. 'Oh? And how *are* you going to live, then, Laurie? What you going to do? Take in washing?'

She fought hard to concentrate. 'This is ridiculous. They'll release Matthew's money to me in the end. I'm his wife. His widow.'

'Understand this, Lozz. You can't get hold of Mattie's money until he's officially dead. Without a body, that takes for bloody ever.' He took a sip of his drink. 'Oh, you can try if you like. You might even work it out. After a few months of arguing. You up to that?'

'There are people—'

'No, Laurie, there aren't *people*!' he shouted. Then, hearing himself, he lowered his voice. 'There isn't anyone, Laurie. There's just me. Mattie didn't know nothing about money. And he didn't know nothing about friends.' He tossed back his Scotch and breathed out hard. 'There was only me.'

She felt some of her spirit return. 'That doesn't make me your responsibility.'

'Oh, yes,' he said with quiet certainty. 'Yes, it does.'

She pushed herself away from the wall. 'I'll find somewhere to live. I'll get a lawyer.'

He put his empty glass down and walked across the room to her. There was something stricken in his face. He reached out and took her shoulders in his hands. 'Laurie, I been straight. All those times I come here when Mattie was away, and fixed things for you and the kids, and done things Mattie forgot to do. But he's gone now.'

'Take your hands off me, Tommy,' she told him.

His eyes faltered but he stayed where he was. 'Laurie, you don't understand. You never did understand. I'd do anything for you. Anything.'

'Then let me go.'

His breath was in her face and she rolled her head away from him. The connecting door banged open.

'Everything is all right, Mrs Silver?' Merilda called to her in a Sergeant-Major voice.

'Fuck off,' Hudson told the woman without turning.

'I speak Mrs Silver,' Merilda replied haughtily, without trying to disguise her contempt. 'I don't speak you.'

Lauren took the opportunity the woman gave her and ducked under Hudson's arm and walked away from him. She could feel herself trembling but it gave her strength to see Merilda's plump defiant face lifted in her defence. 'It's OK, Merilda,' she said, and added pointedly: 'I'll call if I need you.'

Merilda waited for a moment longer, then tossed her head disdainfully at Hudson and turned away and stumped off through the house. Lauren felt in her bag, found cigarettes and lit one.

'Tommy, we have to work this out. We have to be sensible about this.' She drew in a shaky lungful of smoke. 'I'm not going to live here as your house guest. Or whatever you expected.' She looked at him. 'You couldn't have thought that.'

'In the end you'll do what you have to do to get by, like the rest of us,' he said with bleak certainty.

'What does that mean?'

'You were just Matt Silver's wife, Laurie, when all's said and done. You'd've been nothing without him. What gives you the right to be so damn choosy?'

She stared at him. 'I'm not staying here to listen to this.'

He shrugged, walked across to the bar and poured himself another drink, then took a seat with his back to her and facing the television. He pointedly put his boots up on the brocade sofa and flicked the remote so that the television sprang on and the room was raucous with the sound of a soccer crowd. She hesitated for just a moment. Then she ground her cigarette out in the ashtray and ran up the stairs to her room and threw clothes in a bag without looking and came back downstairs and walked across the room to the front door. Her hand was on the latch before he turned.

'Where d'you think you're going, Laurie?' His voice sounded weary. 'Don't be bloody stupid.'

She looked at him for a moment but could see nothing in the bovine face that gave her hope. Nothing, in fact, that she recognised. 'I've just got to get away, Tommy,' she said.

His eyes hardened and he flung out an arm and pointed at her over the top of the sofa. 'No one'll take care of you like I will, Laurie. You remember that.'

'I don't need anyone to take care of me, Tommy. Not any more.'

He let his arm drop and turned back to the television. 'You'll be back,' he said to the screen.

She tugged open the front door and half ran across the gravel to her car.

54

She drove blindly at first, simply following roads that looked familiar. She asked herself no questions. For the moment it was enough to be in the safe cocoon of her car, away from him, out of the house, away from the confrontation. She let the rhythm of driving calm her, glad that the remaining light in the sky made it easy. It wasn't until she reached Guildford that she realised where her unconscious mind had been taking her. It surprised her, but did not seem inappropriate, and for a while she was calm and focused, knowing where she was going, not needing to think beyond that.

It was almost dark by the time she got there. Lauren pulled up beside the churchyard wall and climbed out. A gold band of light lay along the western horizon to mark the end of the spring day. The church was a squat black mound and the darkness was chill and damp. She realised she had not brought a coat. She hugged herself and walked around the church to the grave. She was not sure what she had expected: some mystical infusion of courage, some sense of bold new direction. She did not get it. Something was wrong. Not wrong, out of place. The flowers she and Freya had brought on their last visit lay wilting on the wet soil. But they had been moved. Just a few inches, but moved aside. And beside them a ragged bunch of wildflowers had been laid. The blooms glowed in the failing light, yellow and blue. A well-wisher, maybe? The vicar, touched by the newness of the child's grave? She leaned forward and touched them with her fingertips. The flowers were fresh, perhaps a day old, even less. As she straightened she noticed a flattened hollow in the rank grass beside the grave, as if some animal had rested here, had sought sanctuary here. She frowned. The dark hedgerow stirred in the press of moist air from the downland and a few drops of rain struck her face and arms. Lights came on in the twilit countryside beyond the church-yard wall and she felt all at once cold, miserable and alone.

She walked back to the car and sat behind the wheel. She realised she had no idea what to do next. She turned the radio on for company, but it made a poor echo of real companionship and somehow accentuated her loneliness and she switched it off again. For a moment she had an overwhelming urge to be with Freya and it even crossed her mind to drive to South Wales right now and go to the camp and fetch her daughter. But for what? So that she could hug her and feel better for a few minutes? And what then? She gripped the wheel so that her knuckles glowed white. She was to see Freya tomorrow anyway at Oxford. There was some momentary relief in that. The weekend at the farm would at least give her two days' grace. But what then? What then? And for that matter – what now?

She saw Hudson's heavy face in her mind. His expression was weary, tired of her play acting. 'You'll be back,' he had said, as though she were a teenager threatening to leave home after a tantrum. Remembering it, she was filled with a frustration and fury so bitter that she cried out and the force of her grip flexed the wheel between her hands. She would not let him be right. She would find a way, whatever it cost. But when the spasm of outrage had passed, she could still see his bored face, waiting for her to come to her senses. Waiting for her to realise that, when it came down to it, people did what they had to do, made the compromises they had to make. She was no longer Matt Silver's wife. She wasn't anybody. If she wanted things for herself and her child, she would ultimately have to pay for them like other women did, with whatever currency she could scrape together. She wasn't strong enough to do it any other way.

The lights of the Cross Keys pub sprang on beyond the far wall of the churchyard. She watched the lit sign swinging in the wind. After a while she started the engine and drove up the lane and parked outside the pub, locked the car and went in. She was the first customer. The lounge bar seemed cavernous and she felt conspicuous. She crossed the empty room and leaned on the bar, not knowing quite what she was doing here, and yet knowing quite well. The landlord came through the connecting door from the public bar. He was setting out fresh coasters and ashtrays and at first did not notice her.

'I'm sorry, madam. Didn't see you there.'

'It's OK. No hurry.' That was true enough, she reflected. She had nowhere to hurry to. A sudden surge of panic swept over her, and she thought: To hell with it, and ordered a vodka. If she couldn't have one tonight, when could she?

She took the drink to a table in one of the window bays and sat on the padded window seat where she could feel herself protected by the angle of the wall. She began to relax. It was comforting to watch the landlord busying himself around the room, riddling the grate and polishing off the blackboard which announced the bar snacks. These were normal, domestic activities. The man looked up once or twice from his work and passed a few comments about the weather, but when she merely smiled in reply he didn't push it. Still she was glad of the sound of his voice, glad of the sound of him humming to himself as he went about his routine chores.

The vodka warmed her and she went back to the bar and ordered another. She was halfway through the second drink when the landlord opened the back door and let an old boxer dog into the room. The dog trotted up and inspected her, decided she was acceptable and twitched its docked tail once or twice before moving on to find itself a place in front of the fire. With a rush of yearning she thought of the farm and of the old dog there and of the fire, and of Cobb and Fred. A sane

and tranquil place where she and Freya were treated
with respect, with gentleness. Treated even with affection. She realised how completely she had shut them
out of her mind tonight, and she wondered why. She
stared for a long time into her drink. If she left now,
she could be there in – what? – an hour and a half.
That seemed incredible. The farm was in another
galaxy, separated from her world. Yet if she walked out
now and got in her car, she would get there before this
newly laid fire needed more logs. Possibly before the
boxer dog had moved from his comfortable position in
front of the flames. Uneasily, she rolled her glass
between her palms.

It wasn't as simple as that. At the start, she had
needed to beg for permission to go there. She had
promised not to go there uninvited, and even now she
felt that to do so would somehow be against the rules.
She told herself that this was ridiculous and tipped
back the last of her vodka. She desperately wanted
another, though she knew that if she had one more
drink, she would be over the limit. She thought of her
controlled drinking group, the circle of friendly, sincere
faces every Thursday night. Two drinks a day was
supposed to be her limit. She felt a real pang at the
thought of letting the group down. It would be her
first lapse. But then, they'd forgive her. It wasn't every
day you went to your daughter's inquest – and walked
out of your home with nowhere else to go to. They'd
forgive her all right. But of course she'd be over the
legal limit too if she drank any more, and that might

matter if she had to drive all the way to Oxford on a night like this. To go or not to go? Lauren remembered suddenly the last time she had had this argument with herself. It was not action which had been fatal then, but lack of it. She stood up quickly.

'Same again, madam?' called the landlord cheerfully. By the time she had registered his question, he had taken her silence for assent and was already pouring another double. Well, she thought, she didn't have to drink it. Just pay, avoid any tension, thank the man and go. She walked to the bar, found some crumpled notes in her bag.

'Staying in the village?' the man said, taking the money.

'I don't think so.'

He was at the till but she saw his eyebrows lift. 'Oh, I thought you'd probably come down for the wedding.' He brought her the change. 'The Ashtons? Big local family. They'll all be down here soon, I expect, drunk as lords. If they ever get out of the reception.'

'I'm just passing through.' It was impossible to move away from his affability, from the warmth of the bar. She found she had started on the fresh drink. She could not decide why she still lingered here. She was expected tomorrow morning anyway. They couldn't possibly take it amiss if she turned up twelve hours early. Could they?

'We used to do rooms here, you know,' the landlord droned on. 'But there's nothing in it for us, really, and then when we had Caroline . . .'

She shut his voice out of her mind. She could always ring the Cobbs. That would be the courteous thing to do. The landlord would let her use the phone. But somehow she could not bring herself to do this. She searched her mind for a reason. She realised that she was afraid she would get Cobb and not his father on the end of the line. She did not want to listen to those long serious pauses, that measured, judgemental tone he adopted whenever she caught him unawares. At least she supposed it was judgemental. That was how she always took it. She tossed back the drink.

'And have you got far to go, then, madam?'

'Oxford,' she said with sudden decision. 'Near Oxford.'

'Oh,' he said, a little taken aback. He sucked his lower lip, avoided looking at her empty glass. 'Well, take care, won't you.'

'Too late for that,' Lauren said.

55

Cobb settled back in his seat and realised that he felt good. He realised too that he had not felt this way for a long time. On impulse he flipped up the armrest and felt through the compartment with his left hand. He only had one Matt Silver CD and he played it now, winding up the volume so that the music filled the dim cabin of the car as night fell – angular, driving blues, howling treble on the guitar, and a big, aggressive voice, a diamond-hard voice.

He had watched a dozen videos of this man during the last few weeks, and he could put the movements precisely to the music: the strutting lupine walk, the upthrust chin, the whipping black hair with sweat flying in the lights. It was impossible not to respond to the relentless power of this music, of this man. What must it have been like to love a man like Matt Silver? Dangerous, he thought. Doomed. And, almost certainly, irresistible. His mind flicked back to the inquest and to scenes that had built up to it. To Lauren, drawn as tight as a bowstring; to the blue-white face of her dead child; to the hurt and incomprehension that her living daughter struggled so hard to conceal. He jabbed the eject button, cutting Silver off in mid-phrase, and savoured the rushing silence for a few seconds. Then he tossed the CD carelessly aside.

By 8.30 he was bouncing the Saab down the unsurfaced track to the farm. He went into the house and spent a couple of minutes watching the news headlines with Fred, then changed and went back out to the barn and got to work.

He had been there a little under an hour and was close to finishing. It was cold in the barn, and he was beginning to get tired and hungry, but despite that his sense of contentment grew steadily. He had forgotten how satisfactory practical work could be, even a trivial task like this one. But he knew it was more than that. It was because he was working at a job which had no point to it whatever except to bring another person pleasure. Because the farm would be populated tomorrow, and with people he cared about. He put down his paintbrush and stretched and walked to the barn door. He found his pipe and packed it inexpertly and lit up. He had only recently started smoking a pipe – he felt it fitted the country squire image Lauren had poked fun at – but he found that it gave him a calm satisfaction. He blew smoke into the cool night and leaned against the ancient beams of the barn. The kitchen light was on still but the body of the house was in darkness. The place was still and quiet under a hazy moon with skeins of cloud streaming across it. Out in the copse a vixen coughed and snarled, calling for a mate, an ugly and imperious sound. It occurred to Cobb that he should tell his father the foxes were getting bolder. But then the old man would nag him until he shot one, and

Cobb did not want to do that. He decided to keep quiet.

He saw a car's lights flicker through the trees on the road above the farm. The car slowed and turned through the gate, then came bouncing down the track towards him. He frowned: he did not recognise it at first and he did not feel like visitors. He noticed that one of the headlights was badly askew. He glanced at his watch. It was late, whoever it was. On impulse he stepped back into the barn, put away his pipe, banged the lid tight onto the paintpot, tidied up briefly and turned the light off.

As he came back out into the yard she was climbing out of the car, pulling her bag from the back seat. She had not seen him and he hesitated in the darkness, confused at the sight of her. It made him apprehensive. It did not fit that she should be here now: she was ahead of her cue. He knew something had happened and it worried him to speculate on what it might be. As he stepped forward, she reached the farmhouse's front door. Lights sprang on in the house and the door was opened to her. He heard Fred's cry of welcome and her low reply, and then she was ushered into the house.

He crossed the cobbled yard, pausing to look at the car. The offside wing was badly scraped, with bare metal gleaming, and the headlight assembly hung loose. By the time he got to the kitchen Fred was already setting the kettle on the stove. He wore a ratty old dressing gown knotted over electric blue pyjamas and was fussing over Lauren, plainly delighted by her arrival. She was seated at the kitchen table, pale and tired and a little crumpled. She looked, Cobb thought as she lifted her eyes to him, strained and apologetic and defensive, all at once, as if she feared that arriving unannounced had been a mistake.

Fred gestured with the teapot. 'Samuel, my boy. I was just coming to call you. What are you doing out there, anyway?'

'I'm sorry to barge in like this, Sam,' Lauren said, cutting across the old man. 'So late. So early, I suppose.'

'What happened to the car?' he said at once, his concern making him brusque.

She blinked at the force of the question but did not rise to it. Instead she nodded at his flecked hands. 'You should try Dawn Blush. Hot Coral does nothing for you.'

'It's paint,' he said, foolishly. 'And I asked you what happened to the car.'

'Nothing much. I had a bit of an argument with a crash barrier on the M40, that's all.'

'Are you all right?'

'Yes, I'm *all right*, Sam,' she said with a flash of irritation. 'Don't make a fuss.'

Fred walked between them, cutting their eye contact. 'Get Lauren a drink, Samuel, would you?'

'A drink?'

'That's what I said, Samuel,' Fred said sweetly. 'I have a feeling she needs one.'

Cobb hesitated and then did as he was told. When he set the gin down in front of her he could smell the alcohol on her breath and see the faint trembling of her hand when she reached for the glass. 'What's happened, Lauren?'

'Happened?' She shrugged with theatrical unconcern. 'Nothing's happened. I bent the car a little, that's all.'

'Perhaps this can wait, Samuel?' Fred said quickly.

'Were you drinking before you drove here?'

'For God's sake, Sam.' She set her glass down hard. 'Don't be such a fucking policeman. Do you want to see my tax disc too?'

'Why didn't you call me, Lauren?'

'Maybe because I thought I'd get a reaction like this.' The room fell silent for a couple of beats. She stood up suddenly. 'I knew this was a dumb move.'

'Lauren, you know I'd have picked you up.'

'I don't need "picking up", Sam. I don't need to be in by midnight. I don't need nursemaiding. Jesus! Why don't the lot of you just leave it alone?' She grabbed the bottle of gin by the neck and turned her back on Cobb and faced Fred. 'Excuse me, Fred. I'm going to bed.'

'And you need that?' Cobb nodded at the bottle.

'Yes. Right now, I need this. And you're not making me need it any less.'

Fred stepped between them. 'My dear, I'm sure we can—'

'I'm sorry. I knew I shouldn't have come.' She stuffed the bottle under her arm and with her free hand gathered up her bag and walked to the corridor that led to the garden room. 'I'd drive away again, except that Inspector Morse here would probably confiscate my keys.' She marched the few steps down the corridor, barged into the bedroom and banged the door behind her.

Cobb stared after her and let his heartbeat slow.

'I bloody would have, too,' he said, half to himself.

'You know, Samuel,' Fred set the unused teapot back on its stand and regarded the beams of the ceiling. 'There are times when I'm quite glad you didn't follow me into the Diplomatic Service.'

Lauren lay fully clothed on the bed for twenty minutes, listening to the sounds in the house, waiting for her pulse to slow. She was furiously angry, angrier than she remembered being since the world had changed, angrier than she thought she still had the capacity to be.

She realised she had left her glass out on the table and so she lay in the darkness and drank from the bottle. This gave her a savage and childish pleasure – *that* would show him. After a while she began to feel foolish and put the bottle on the bedside table. She had not drunk so much in some weeks and it made her feel tearful and belligerent by turns. Her hand touched the edge of the frame of Clea's picture. It was face down on the table, as if Cobb had been looking at it and had meant to tuck it away in its usual position in the drawer but had been distracted. Lauren lifted the photo and turned it to catch the starlight. She had glanced at it when she was last here but had little recollection of the face: perhaps it had simply meant less to her then. This time she saw a woman in her thirties with a strong, square face, humorous and relaxed. She wasn't pretty but she had bold eyes and Lauren instinctively knew she would have been fun to know. Ironically, for the photo must have been taken only a couple of years before her death, she looked unusually healthy, the kind of woman who would have played a lot of tennis, spent a lot of time at the pool. She was, Lauren thought, utterly unlike herself. She replaced the photo on the bedside table, and stood it up in its proper position.

Muffled noises from the house drifted through to her. Fred was talking and Cobb answered in monosyllables. She could not make out the words. There was the rattle of the poker in the fireplace, the clink of cutlery, and some bumpy, cheerful classical music: she thought it was Elgar. Perhaps Fred had put it on to lighten the atmosphere. One of the two men moved into the kitchen and made something to eat, taking exaggerated care to be as quiet as possible. He coughed softly and she knew it was Cobb. For a second her anger flared up again, and she was ready for another fight, but then he softly closed the kitchen door behind him and she felt cheated. Over the diminished music she could faintly hear the sound of chess pieces knocking on a board in the living room. From this she knew she had so disturbed the harmony of the place that the old man could not sleep. She heard Fred's grunt of annoyance as he lost a piece, and once the murmur of Cobb's voice, and loneliness ran through her like a sword.

She was next aware of coming fully awake, wretched, cold and hung over, to the sound of his footsteps in the passageway. Lauren sat up and her brain shifted painfully inside her skull. She put her forehead in her hand and gasped. Perhaps this was audible, for the footsteps outside faltered, and for some reason that maddened her. She got up and marched across to the door and wrenched it open and hurled her spite and her pain into the dark corridor: 'Look – why don't you just fuck off. OK?'

'I'm not sure it would be good for me, my dear. At my age.'

'Oh my God.' She turned away and sat on the end of the bed and put her head in her hands again. 'Fred, I'm so sorry.'

'I hoped to catch you before you fell asleep. It seems I did.' He hesitated. 'May I step in for a second?'

She realised the old man had not followed her through the door and would not do so without being invited. 'Of course, Fred. Of course.' She made to get up and find him a chair but he waved her away.

'Please don't trouble, my dear. I'm quite content to stand. I shan't detain you a moment.' He moved in front of the French windows and faced her. 'You are . . . all right, are you?'

'No,' she said.

He nodded. 'I thought not.' He stood in silence for

a while. 'However, the darkness is rather restful.'

She thought for a moment this might be a hint that he wanted her to switch the lamp on but when she moved her hand towards the button he stopped her with a gesture.

'No, no. There's plenty of light from the sky, even at night, don't you think?'

She realised that she was crumpled and unkempt and that this was his way of sparing her. 'Yes, Fred, there's plenty of light.'

He turned in profile against the window and she could see his white hair stir as he moved. He sighed. 'I'm so very sorry about that.' He waved his hand towards the kitchen. She wanted to answer sharply, but it was impossible in the face of his antique charm.

'Fred, I won't say it doesn't matter. But it's not your fault.'

'You mean it's not my business, and of course you are quite right. Although in a sense it is. My business, I mean.'

It seemed to her that she was being reprimanded for conducting a shouting match in his home, and the thought that she had offended him shamed her into contrition. 'I'm sorry, Fred. It wasn't very dignified.'

'No, it wasn't. But I didn't mean that.'

'What then?'

She had a sudden image of him as a courtly old herald between two armed camps. Fred walked to the door, opened it, stood looking down the corridor.

'He cares, my dear,' he said at last in a different

voice. 'My son. Cares for people. He tries very hard
not to. That makes him . . . clumsy.'

He stepped out of the room and closed the door
behind him. She lay back on the bed and stared for a
long time at the streaked night sky beyond the windows
before she fell asleep.

56

A sky of luminous pearl lay over the dawn fields by the
time Cobb reached the buried village. The climb
burned off most of the heaviness of the uneasy night.
He settled in his favourite spot against the oak growing
from the buried churchyard wall. Baskerville blundered
away among the green hummocks, his muzzle ploughing the long wet grass for the scent of rabbits he would
never catch. It was very still and Cobb could tell from
the sky that it would be a gauzy day, the kind of day
Turner might have painted, with mist already filling
the river valley below. It was good to be out in the cool
air among the birdsong, high above the farm, high
above the argument. He hoped it would give him some
perspective. He took his pipe from his pocket and
played with it for a while, filling it and tamping the
tobacco and trying the stem between his teeth. Finally
he put it away unlit. He had thought it might help him
think but now it seemed childish, a distracting toy.

He played through the scene again and again, but
could find no other way that it could have come out. It
might have been delayed, he supposed, but not avoided.
It did give him a twinge of conscience that he had not
been gentler with her yesterday of all days. But
ultimately they were going to come up against these

same issues. Sooner or later they would have to be faced, and all his instincts demanded it should be sooner. He could not have her bucketing around the countryside drunk, erratic, unpredictable. Turning up unannounced in the middle of the night, and dodging death on the motorway to do it. He had believed her when she said she was getting on top of things and now he felt a fool. It was the first lie of every addict. He felt disappointed in her. He felt betrayed.

He heard the thought as if he had spoken it and the patronising sound of it gave him pause. He supposed he had no right to think like that and for a moment his certainty wavered. She had, after all, given him no licence at all. But then his sense of justice came down like a portcullis across his doubt. Maybe he had dealt with things badly. Clumsily, as his father had told him. But all the same, they still had to be dealt with, and somebody had to take responsibility.

Lauren stood at the kitchen window and cradled her coffee cup in both hands. Her head felt dull and the smell of Fred's fried breakfast made her slightly nauseous. She had stayed in her room until she heard the old man go out to start his rounds about the farm. She knew his ritual: he would spend an hour or more feeding the animals, and then come back in and clean up the kitchen. That hour was her space. Cobb had left much earlier, presumably to climb to his eyrie up at the old village. She was safe from both of them for the moment. She thought maybe she ought to do the washing up for Fred – she still blushed as she remembered last night – but she could not face the greasy sink right now.

She drank some coffee and waited for it to make her feel better. As she waited she saw a movement in the gorse on the flank of the distant hill. It was the old dog wallowing through the yellow brush, his brown back breaking the rough carpet of colour. And there was his master, a hundred yards further up, striding down the slope, a dark, square figure moving easily over the steep ground. She watched him through the steam of her coffee, glad that he could not see her. He wore a black fleece windbreaker over khaki work pants. He looked stern even in outdoor clothes, she thought. There was something self-consciously formal about him, something almost military, even out here on the farm. It was hard to imagine him ever wearing bright colours or clothes that were anything but functional. She had thought maybe this was a kind of mourning but she could see now that he was never quite out of uniform. In better times she might have teased him about this, making a game of his seriousness. As he drew closer and swung over the last stile into the farmyard she could see his face. It was as stern as his bearing. More than stern, the downturned face was grim. Well, she felt pretty grim herself. But at the same time she was as nervous as an adolescent about facing him. She didn't want to fight with him again. She so badly wanted not to fight with him now.

She turned away from the window so that he would

not see her as he came nearer. In turning, she saw that she had left the gin bottle standing in full view on the kitchen table when she had brought it out of the bedroom. She moved now to put it back in the cabinet. She was anxious that Cobb should not walk in and see the bottle there at this time in the morning. She was also angry with herself for caring what he thought. She lifted the square bottle and saw that the inch or two of gin inside it was quivering with her tension. She rammed the bottle into the cabinet with the others, and had actually closed the doors on it before she turned back and pulled it out again. The spirit tasted vile and for a second she almost choked on it. But it gave her a spike of energy, and drinking raffishly from the bottle she was able to rekindle a spark of the same schoolgirl defiance she had felt the night before. She replaced the bottle steadily, closed the cabinet and walked back to the window. She could have more whenever she wanted, and to hell with him.

When he did not come marching in through the kitchen door as she expected she looked out of the window again. He was standing a few yards away, outside the barn, knocking the mud off his boots. He had been working on something in the barn, she knew, something to do with Freya, and all at once the thought of his kindness to the child softened her, left her weak and confused again. She leaned her forehead against the cold glass. The gin was acid in her stomach and she felt hollow and giddy. She wondered if she should get another drink right away to settle herself. In a moment, she told herself. In just a moment. Soon they would fetch Freya from Oxford. Maybe Freya would make the difference and things would come right again. Surely she would make the difference. As she watched, Fred appeared at the corner of the barn and spoke to his son, and she saw Cobb nod, answer his father, and then laugh unexpectedly at something the old man said. And the smile lit his face like a flame.

Perhaps, if he had walked in at that moment. But instead he stepped out of sight into the barn without even glancing at the window where she stood, and pulled the door to behind him. Lauren stepped back from the window and watched her breath fade from the glass. She could not seem to find her earlier defiance. Instead, anxiety began to grow in her again. This was all on the point of going horribly wrong, just at the moment she most needed it not to. It came to her that when Freya arrived she would have to tell her that they had nowhere to go after tomorrow. Or worse still, she would have to decide not to tell Freya anything, and she would be forced to do just as Tommy Hudson had predicted she would do. Because no one would look after her like he would. She felt her stomach clench. She poured her coffee down the sink and went back to the cabinet.

Cobb worked on in the barn, glad to be occupied. A little delicate sun was breaking through over the fields. He checked his watch. It was close to nine. In half-an-hour or so they would need to take Lauren to Oxford and pick up Freya. He sat on one of the feed boxes near the door of the barn and felt for his pipe and this time he did light up. He puffed a cloud of blue smoke at the dry timbers above him. He hated the thought of another argument.

'Thought we might all go and pick the little one up,' Fred called from the door, and Cobb could see the old man was excited. 'It's a little early, I know.'

'I'll leave you to it, Dad,' Cobb said. 'You and Lauren. I want to finish up in here. Get everything ready.'

'Oh.' Fred hesitated. 'Not being just a little . . . prickly, are you, Samuel?'

'I just thought I'd keep a low profile for a while.'

'Well, I imagine you know best,' Fred said. 'Not that you ever did before.'

An hour later Cobb heard the Land Rover pull up outside and the banging of the car's doors and the child's excited voice and the dog's asthmatic bark of greeting. He waited for a moment longer. When he had heard them all go into the house he knocked out his pipe and followed them across the yard.

The moment he opened the kitchen door his eyes met Lauren's and he knew how it would end. She sat at the head of the table, somehow apart from the old man and from her daughter. There was about her the jaggedness Cobb remembered from the first time he had seen her. Her skin had the same unnatural pallor he had seen then, with streaks of high colour along the cheekbones. He clothes were slovenly and her hair was roughly bundled up into a faded blue scarf. He saw she already had a fresh drink in front of her. Her eyes disturbed him most. They seemed to carry both accusation and defiance.

'Hello, Sam!' Freya cried and ran across to him and hugged his legs. He ruffled her hair.

'Hi there, Princess. Back from the wilds of Welsh Wales?'

'You'll never guess what I did!' she shouted at him, bouncing back to her seat at the table.

'I think you're going to tell me.'

'I played rounders,' Freya said, banging the kitchen table for emphasis. '*And* I played hockey. *And* I played soccer.' She sat back. 'There.'

'Soccer?' Fred looked bewildered.

'Girls play soccer these days, Dad,' Cobb explained.

'Do they really? Good Lord.'

'Of course they do, Uncle Fred!' Freya cried, laughing. 'Girls can do anything!'

'Well, if you say so, Freya my sweet. Astonishing, isn't it?' Fred turned to Cobb. 'They'll give them the vote next.'

'*And* –' the child shouted, slapping at her mother's arm for attention.

'Frey,' Lauren smiled tightly, 'easy on the decibels.'

'– but the best bit – *listen*, Sam!'

Cobb had been watching Lauren again, noting her struggle for concentration and for control. He said: 'I am listening, Princess. What's the best bit?'

'Wait!' Freya commanded and slipped down from

the table and ran out of the room.

'Well, she seems to have had a wonderful time,' Fred boomed, trying to fill the widening gulf with his cheerfulness. 'Splendid! Splendid!' He clapped his hands and rubbed them together.

Cobb sat back and crossed his arms, then realised that this betrayed the gathering darkness of his mood, and uncrossed them again. He had hoped, and the phrase kept playing over and over in his mind, he had hoped that at least she might have let the child enjoy her moment in the sun. She might at least have stayed sober long enough to greet her own daughter. He felt desperately let down by her on Freya's account and on his own. Obviously nothing was going to change. The cycle of destruction and pain would go on unrelenting. He watched her as she rose with elaborate nonchalance and fetched herself yet another drink. He supposed he should not blame her. And yet it was so very hard not to.

Freya returned with a packet of instant-print photos and a rolled certificate tied with red ribbon. She pulled the ribbon loose and let the cartridge paper spring open. She spread it reverently on the table, sucking at her teeth in concentration. As she worked at this she passed the photos to Cobb. 'You can look at those.'

They were prints of children, boys and girls of about Freya's age, paddling open canoes on a peaceful river fringed by willows. The sun was shining. The children were bundled into blue life jackets which made them look intrepid, like miniature commandos, though Cobb guessed that the water was probably two feet deep.

'There!' Freya said.

She had weighted the certificate down with cutlery. Cobb leaned across her so that he could see the document's impressive copperplate script, and he read it aloud: ' "Freya Silver. Admiral of the Blue". Wow! Sounds great, Princess.'

'Admiral,' Lauren repeated slowly. She was standing behind her daughter now, frowning over the child's shoulder at the certificate. Cobb saw her face cloud as if she were having trouble coming to terms with this news. 'Did they really make you Admiral this year, Frey? You?'

'It says so there, doesn't it?' Freya rapped the cartridge paper indignantly. 'Admiral of the Blue. See?' She turned to Cobb, her face shining with triumph. 'And *I've* never even been in a canoe before!'

And then, as if a switch had been thrown, she laid her head on her arms on her outspread diploma and burst into tears.

The room froze. Cobb instinctively looked to Lauren to act and their eyes met: perhaps a moment later she would have moved, but he did not see this. He saw her standing rigid and useless, her eyes hot and defensive, glaring at him while her daughter wept between them. Cobb took his eyes from her with an effort and moved forward, but Fred was quicker and swept the child up into his arms.

'Push them a little too hard at these camps, I think,' the old man said gruffly, rocking Freya against him.

'Little over-tired. Only a tot, after all.' He hefted the girl against his shoulder and carried her across the room, nodding to Cobb to open the door. Cobb did so and his father carried his burden out into the farmyard.

Cobb closed the door behind them and watched them go for a few paces. Then he turned back into the room and crossed to the table and rolled up Freya's certificate and retied the ribbon. He did not look directly at Lauren but he saw that she had not moved.

'Don't you try to lay this on me, Sam Cobb!' she cried suddenly.

He stood up to face her. He tried to look bewildered but he could not bring conviction to this attempt, for he did blame her, and he knew that this showed in his face, and he knew that she read it there. Even so, her gathering ferocity surprised him. He said, as evenly as he could manage: 'I thought maybe all this was behind us. Behind you.'

She dragged out a chair and banged it down on the flagstones. 'Christ! You think you're so smart.' She seemed to have trouble knowing where to stand or how to hold her arms. She pointed out into the yard, her outstretched finger following Fred and her daughter. 'You think that was my fault?'

'Lauren—'

'Well, let me tell you what that was about! Gudrun was Admiral of the Blue for the last three years. *Gudrun* was. It was Gudrun's job. Freya always watched from the bank.'

He sat down and looked at her. 'I see.'

'You see,' she sneered. She prowled the width of the room, the ice jingling in her glass. 'You've got all the answers, haven't you?'

'I'm going to get you some help, Lauren,' he said, speaking softly. 'I'm going to call some people for you.'

'Help?' She swung to face him. 'I've got all the help I need. Thank you.'

'You mean Tommy Hudson?' He felt blood begin to thump in his temples. 'He must be pretty bloody good, if he sits by and watches you drink yourself to death.'

'Tommy doesn't *let* me do anything.' She rested the heels of her hands on the table to push her face towards him. 'I don't need permission, Sam. Not from him. Not from you. From anyone. For anything.'

'Lauren, look at yourself. You don't want to be like this.'

'Why can't you get this straight, Sam? I don't need some bearded shrink telling me I'm fucked up.'

'So what's your alternative?' He put his fists on the table and found he could not unbunch them. 'Are you planning to play the tragic heroine from here on in? Would you call that a solution?'

'Where do you get off, talking to me like that, Sam? What the hell's it got to do with you what I plan to do?'

'And how long do you think you can go on like this? Or maybe you'll kill yourself in the car next time and speed things up.' A gyroscope was beginning to spin off-balance in his mind. He tried to control it but he could feel it make him rash and eloquent. 'Maybe that doesn't matter to you. But maybe next time you won't be alone.'

'Will you get off my case? I am not your responsibility.'

'In this house you are.'

'Is that the price of coming here?'

'You know there isn't a price.'

'Oh, yes, there's always a price. You have to control everything. That's the price.'

He took a deep breath. 'I care about you, Lauren. I don't want to see you do this.'

The confession cost him something and, once spoken, he expected it to defuse the tension a little. Instead it seemed to infuriate her.

'Go on!' she spat at him, thrusting her blotched face towards him. 'Now offer to take care of me, why don't you? That's all I need.' The venom in her voice shocked both of them into silence. After a moment she backed away a little. 'You know this whole thing isn't about me anyway. It's about Freya. She's all that matters.'

'We all matter, Lauren. Whether you like it or not. Freya and you and me, and my old man. Everyone connected with us.'

She pushed her hair wearily out of her face but didn't answer.

'I didn't want you around here in the first place,' he went on. 'I didn't want anything to do with you and this whole tragic mess. But now you're here I can't ignore you.'

'Why not?' she said. 'I can ignore you.' But the

brutality was a reflex. She was spent. She pulled out her chair and slumped into it with her elbows on the table.

'Because we're real people, Lauren, that's why. When it comes down to it we have to look out for each other. That's what real people do.' He got up, walked around the kitchen in a circle, trying to get his focus back. Finally he came back to the table. 'Lauren, you're ill. It's natural. Everyone understands that.'

'Great. What a relief.' Contemptuously she tossed off her drink. She refilled her glass. 'Sam, just because you've had your own little loss in life doesn't make you an expert on everyone else's.'

He rocked back a little at that. He said: 'This can't go on, Lauren. We both know that. I'm not going to sit back and watch this happen and do nothing about it.'

'I don't want your help,' she said, staring into her glass. 'I didn't ask for it.'

'Yes, you did, Lauren.'

'My Christ, you're a self-righteous bastard.' She stood up clumsily, pushing the table back. 'Why can't you just leave me alone?'

Freya opened the back door and stood in the doorway, staring at them. After a second the bewilderment in her face hardened. 'You were shouting so loudly,' she said, 'I thought Daddy had come back.'

'Me too,' Lauren said bitterly. She pushed both hands through her hair, an exhausted gesture, and the fight went out of her. Cobb thought he had never seen her look so defeated. Almost sadly, she said: 'Freya, we'd better go.'

'Go?' the child repeated, puzzled. 'Go where?'

'You don't have to go,' Cobb said. 'That's not necessary.'

'Oh, don't worry, Sam,' Lauren said with bleak sarcasm, 'I'm not planning on driving anywhere.'

Fred stepped into the room past the child. 'Lauren, there's no need. Everyone's upset this weekend. That's natural. Now we'll have a bite of lunch and cool off a little—'

'It's best we go, Fred. Truly. It's not your fault.'

'But we can't go now,' Freya cried, with an edge of desperation. 'My surprise is in the barn. Uncle Fred told me.'

'By Jove, that's right,' Fred pounced on this. 'I almost forgot. Samuel – you'd better take young Freya over there and show her what it is, hadn't you?' When Cobb didn't move, Fred repeated very loudly: 'Hadn't you, Samuel?'

Fred waved the girl out into the yard, then he grabbed Cobb's arm and turned him with painful strength towards the door and pushed him through it so hard that he stumbled on the step. As he did so Fred hissed in his ear. 'You'd better think of something. And pretty damned quickly.'

Then Cobb was moving mechanically across the yard and Freya was pleading with him, catching at his hand.

'What's happening, Sam? Why do we have to go?'

The sight of the child's distress forced Cobb to get a grip on himself. 'I can't answer you, Princess. Your mum's very upset at the moment. I suppose we all are.'

'Have I done something wrong?'

'No,' he said fiercely. He stopped and looked down at her, and said again: 'No. You're about the one person who hasn't.'

'I don't want to go back there, Sam,' she said. 'Back to our house. And I don't care what Mummy says, she doesn't want to go either.'

He looked at her. 'I'm afraid she's going anyway, Princess.'

She stared at the ground, and kicked the dirt with the toe of her shoe, and his heart fell like a shot bird. He knelt down to face her. 'Freya, you're not going anywhere just yet. Not until you've had your surprise, anyway.'

He stood up and pushed open the door to the barn and ushered her in. It was gloomy inside and he snapped on the light.

'What's in here?' Freya asked, peering around at the closed stalls.

'Well, Mrs Buckets is in here, for one thing.'

On cue, the cow stuck her head over the half door of her stall and gazed mildly at them. The child's bright reflection rode in the dark pool of the beast's eye.

'I know that,' Freya said, a touch of renewed disappointment in her voice: she had been expecting more. 'Mrs Buckets *lives* in here.'

'Oh, Mrs Buckets isn't the surprise,' Cobb said. 'This is.'

He swung the stable door open. A five foot dinosaur in shocking pink sat grinning from a nest of straw, with six pink beachball eggs at its feet. 'I told you they come here in the spring.'

'It's my dinosaur!' Freya's voice was awed. 'Can I touch her?'

'She's yours, Princess.'

'Is she? Is she really?' Freya ran into the stall and put her arms around the fat pink beast. It was bigger than she was, but she could just lift it off the ground with one arm hooked under its tail. She hugged the grinning creature. 'She's beautiful! I love her!'

'Sam.'

Cobb spun on his heel. Lauren was leaning against the doorpost, silhouetted against the light.

'Sam,' she said again, and her voice was lost and desolate, like the call of a nightbird.

Freya caught sight of her mother and opened her mouth to speak, then thought better of it. The child stood cuddling her huge pink dinosaur, swinging it gently from side to side as she looked in silence from Cobb to Lauren and back again. She said carefully: 'Can I take my dinosaur to show Uncle Fred?'

'Go on, then, Princess,' Cobb said, without taking his eyes from Lauren's. 'Don't run.'

She staggered out into the yard, almost smothered by the stuffed animal, its moonface leering over her shoulder. When she had gone Cobb latched the door. Lauren was leaning against the edge of the stall with her back to him, staring at the pink eggs in the straw.

She had untied her hair and the blue scarf hung from one hand. Without it her hair was a blonde tangle. She pushed against the edge of the half door and her knuckles were white against the wood as she gripped it.

'You stupid bastard,' she said, without turning.

'Hell of a job to paint the eggs,' he said, suddenly awkward with her.

She still did not turn to face him. 'You stupid, crazy bastard.'

There was a catch in her voice. She began to laugh, softly at first and then louder, her head thrown back. For a moment he was glad she was laughing. And then she wasn't laughing any more but sobbing with huge tearing sobs that shook her and shook the wooden door she clung to. The cow gazed at her sympathetically from the next stall.

'Lauren. Don't.'

He moved forward and touched her shoulder and she turned, rolling against the door to face him, her face crumpled and wet, the sobs heaving helplessly out of her so that her thin body shuddered. He took the scarf from her hand and wiped her face with it as if she were a child, murmuring to her, knowing he was lost. Then the length of her body was against the length of his, hip and thigh and breast, and her arms were clutched convulsively around his neck, and his face was in her tangled hair.

57

Cobb felt her stir beside him and was awake at once. She was propped on one elbow and in the chrome light of the afternoon she was studying herself in the dressing table mirror.

She caught his eye in the glass and her reflection made a rueful face at him. 'Jesus. Look at the state of me.' Still watching herself in the glass, she ran her fingers down her thin bare ribs and around the ridges of her eyesockets. 'I used to be a bit beautiful, I think,' she said. 'At least, everybody said so.' She turned to him. 'What are we going to do, Sam? What's going to happen to us?'

'One day at a time.' He brushed the backs of his fingers along the curve of her throat.

'Sam, you know I can't go back.'

'Who can?' He touched each of her fingers in turn, flexing them under his thumb, examining them minutely, as if he had never seen them before.

'No, I meant . . .' She took a deep breath. 'We'll have to stay here for a while, Sam. At the farm. Freya and me.'

He looked at her. 'That's a problem?'

She laughed a little and put her arm around his neck. 'I thought it was.' She kissed him. 'I thought it was a big problem.'

'Well, there you go.' The curve of her ear fascinated him now. He traced it with his forefinger.

'Is it strange?' she asked. 'In this room?'

He stopped, rested on one elbow. 'It's as day follows night.' He slid his arm under her head so that she lay back against his shoulder, cushioned on her hair. She rolled her head a little against his arm. She said: 'That's good. You can do that.'

He felt her open beside him and he moved into her as naturally and gently as breathing. Her fingers followed the curve of his waist and he felt his own flank shiver like a horse's flank. Then he was away somewhere in a world where the only sound was the tap-tapping of a thrush against an anvil outside, again and again, and then her face went taut and then slack beneath him and she breathed out one long breath and he lifted the weight of her head against his shoulder and rocked her there for a long while.

Afterwards Cobb lay for a time watching her rest. When he turned his head he could look out over the farm. He saw that a fragile spring sunlight lay over the fields. In the walled garden just outside the French windows the thrush was back, cracking a snailshell on its flint anvil near the edge of the pond. It was a big flint that looked something like a bullock's head in the pale afternoon light. It seemed odd to Cobb that he had forgotten the thrush and its strangely shaped anvil. He had lain here countless times, watching the bird, bold because it felt unobserved. He wondered if it could be the same bird. Could that be? Did thrushes live that long? Or maybe their offspring came back, generation after generation, to the same anvil.

She moved beside him. 'You know that if you tell me he's gone, I'll trust you,' she said.

He turned his head to look at her and her eyes were dark with intensity.

'You don't have to find him, Sam. You don't have to prove anything. Just tell me he's gone.'

He leaned forward to kiss her but she held him away with her fingertips.

'Tell me that, Sam.' Her voice became fierce. 'You must tell me that.'

'He's gone, Lauren,' Cobb said. 'He's gone and he won't ever come back.'

She watched his face as he said it, and finally nodded. 'That's good,' she said. 'That's very good.' She reached up her arms to him and kissed him. Then she rose and crossed to the dressing table and sat down and began to comb out her hair. After two or three strokes she stopped, tipping her head, examining herself again in the mirror. 'Maybe I could be beautiful again,' she said.

Cobb stood behind her and rested his hands on the yoke of her collarbone, then stroked his hands down over her breasts and let them stay there while her nipples rose against his palms like fingertips. He said: 'Time to make this official.'

He kissed the top of her head and moved away. He dressed quickly and left the bedroom, walking down the short passage into the kitchen. The room was filled with the hot savour of roasting meat and with a torrent of Elgar at his grandest. Fred, his back to Cobb as he worked at the Aga stove, was wearing an enormous white confection of a chef's hat and conducting the music with a carving fork. In the living room Cobb could see Freya perched on the sofa, fussing over her huge pink dinosaur. He walked through and pulled up a chair opposite the girl.

'We plan on staying here for a while, Princess,' he told her. 'How do you feel about that?'

Carefully she set aside the dinosaur and faced him, crossing her hands primly in her lap. 'You mean here at the farm?'

'For sure. Right here.'

She lifted her chin warily. 'Together?'

'Yes, Princess. Together.'

'And what about school?'

'We could stay at my flat during the week. It'll be a squeeze, but we'll work something out. Come down here on weekends.'

She thought about this. 'Squeeze is good,' she said finally.

Cobb heard Lauren move up beside him and he glanced around, and in that moment Freya flung her arms round his neck, clutching him, and he heard her hot voice hissing in his ear: 'Yes. Yes. Yes.'

Later, after the meal, Cobb watched as his father repaired the battlefield of the kitchen. He knew he would not be allowed to help and he was glad. It was late, and he felt heavy and comfortable and the wine sang in his blood. Lauren had already gone to bed but Cobb did not want to move yet. Dinner had developed into one of Fred's three-hour epics. There was something medieval about the litter of empty wine bottles and broken bread. Under the table Baskerville snored full length on the flagstones, a pig's knuckle between his front paws. That was strictly against house rules. Cobb knew that Freya had slipped the bone to the dog before she went to bed, and that Fred had pretended not to notice. He smiled at the memory of the old man's elaborate efforts not to see her transgression.

Fred bundled the cloth and brushed off the bare tabletop, emptied the sink and finally dried his hands. Then he set the Laphroaig bottle squarely on the table in front of Cobb. With a flourish he produced two shot glasses from his apron pocket. 'I think we should,' he said.

Cobb smiled. 'Mad if we don't.' He filled the glasses with the smoky spirit.

The old man lifted his drink and peered at the amber light which shone through it. 'I know I told you to think of something, Samuel.' The old man's moustache twitched as he fought back a smile. 'But you are such a very *literal* chap, aren't you?'

They clinked glasses.

'Sam?' The girl was standing in the doorway.

'Hey, Princess.' Cobb quickly set down his glass and crossed the room to her. 'What are you doing up?'

'Scarecrow Man.' She knuckled her eyes.

The words pricked him strangely. 'Who?' He shook himself, bent down and scooped her up. 'You want to tell me all about it?' He carried her through and sat her next to the grinning pink dinosaur on the settee. The fire had died to a glow in the dim room and he moved the guard and tossed on a log so that the flames sprang up again.

'It's a dream,' she said, her mouth turned down. 'It's dumb.'

'Dreams aren't dumb, Princess,' he said. 'But they aren't real either. You don't need to be scared of them.'

'Scarecrow Man's real,' she said. 'I've seen him.'

'Oh?' he said cautiously. 'And where have you seen this shady character?'

'At school. Over the road in the park. All the girls have seen him.'

'And what's he like, this Scarecrow Man?'

'He's like a scarecrow, silly.' She was fully awake now, and brave again as the room brightened in the firelight. 'He's thin and funny-looking and he wears this long horrible old coat and his face is all . . .' She twisted her face into a pantomime grimace and thrust it at him. The effect was so grotesque that Cobb only just stopped himself from flinching.

'And you've seen him?'

'Well,' she looked down, 'not really. I sort of caught a glimpse of him once. The other girls told me the rest. But he was there.'

'Sure he was, Princess.'

Cobb heard the door open behind him and Lauren moved into the circle of light.

'What are you up to, young lady? Frightening the poor man with your stories? Come on. It's time we were all in bed.' She took the child's hand and led her away. But at the door Freya turned back to Cobb.

'He won't come here, will he, Sam? Scarecrow Man?'

'No, Princess. I promise you he won't come here.'

For a while after they got to bed the incident troubled him. He lay watching the starlight fall over the midnight fields, trying to remember what it had been like to be a child and to be afraid of nameless horrors.

He said: 'Are you awake?'

'Is that your idea of foreplay?' Lauren started to giggle.

'What's this Scarecrow Man stuff?'

'Oh, that.' She stopped laughing and rolled to face him. 'It's something the girls at school go on about. I think they've got a bit of a thing about some drunk in the park over the road. Someone christened him Scarecrow Man. You know how it is.' She nestled against him.

'No. Tell me how it is.'

'Oh, stories about ghosts and ghouls and things that go bump in the night. The older girls tell the younger ones creepy stories. It doesn't mean anything.'

'Has it been going on long?'

'Since the Stone Age, I should think. Oh, I see. I don't know. A month or two.'

'And it's getting to her?'

'A bit. She's had a few bad nights.' She sat up. 'You've got to remember what she's been through, Sam. She's not the ice maiden she makes out.'

'I know that. But–'

'Look, don't worry. Frankly, I'm glad they're scared of dirty old men, aren't you?'

'Does the school know about it?'

'Of course the school knows about it. And the Parents Teachers Association. And the local police.'

'Good. That's good. I'll check with them when I get back.'

'You're such a Mr Plod, Sam,' she said, touched and amused by his concern. 'It's just some harmless old drunk. Besides, there's a security guard. And the girls aren't allowed outside the gate alone. Not ever.' She kissed him. 'It'll be at least ninety per cent make-believe, trust me. Ghost stories. You know how kids are.'

'No, I don't.'

'Well,' she sighed, moving the length of her body against him, 'I guess you're finding out.'

58

Cobb came awake slowly. The windows were slate grey with the dawn. It was raining softly outside: he could hear the water running in the gutters. Lifting his head, he could see the stippled surface of the pond outside the French windows. Lauren was curled away from him in the bed, breathing deeply. He checked his watch. It was not yet six but he found himself seized with a restless energy which would not let him sleep. He rolled silently out of bed, threw on a bathrobe and left the room, closing the door gently behind him.

He padded through into the kitchen with his clothes bundled under one arm, and stopped there, the ancient flagstones stinging his feet. Baskerville, in his basket beside the potbelly stove, smacked the blanket a couple of times with his tail and stayed where he was. Cobb felt the silent weight of the sleeping house around him. In the yard, just beyond the back door, the gargoyle at the end of the stone gutter was spouting rainwater on to the cobbles.

He waited for a moment, scenting the air, aware of a strange potency. Then he slid the bolts on the back door and swung it wide and let the robe fall away from him. He stood with the cold air and the birdsong rinsing over him while out across the fields the drizzle unfolded like skeins of muslin. He moved out on to the cobbles and, without pausing, stepped under the spouting water. His breath shuddered and he clapped his arms around himself and his flesh was as cold and as hard as marble under his hands. He spread his arms under the falling water and watched the blurred disc of the sun lift above the edge of the world and he thought maybe he would live for ever.

'Is this part of the deal?' she said from behind him. 'Cold showers at dawn? I'll have to rethink the whole thing.'

He stepped out of the water and faced her, smiling and unembarrassed. She was standing inside the door, swathed in a towel, hugging herself against the chill. He said: 'I thought you were asleep.'

'Not any more.' She paused. 'Were you going to stand there all day?'

'I've got to walk,' he said. He stepped back inside, towelling himself with the robe. 'Do you want to come along?'

'I'll grab some clothes.'

'Perhaps we both should.'

They walked in silence for half a mile up the sunken lane which ran from near the farm gate. It was a tunnel of dripping hawthorns under the drizzle, dim in the shadow of high banks. The mud was thick underfoot and a rivulet of water ran down the centre of the track, exposing the gravel below. Not fifty feet ahead a russet fox loped across the lane, stopped insolently halfway across to stare at them. Baskerville, shambling through the nettles under the hedgerow, did not notice. Cobb shouldered an imaginary gun and let fly at it, but the fox waited another few seconds before trotting disdainfully up the bank and into cover. They climbed the bank and crossed a stile into the upper pasture, a rough sheepbitten paddock on the flank of the hill, and followed the fieldpath diagonally across it. At the point where the muddy track reached the upper fence stood a wooden bench, commanding a view over the farm to the dark ribbon of trees bordering the river. Behind it the rough gorse hillside rose to the ruins of the old village, another quarter of a mile above. The rain had stopped and the sloping light lay across the fields and across the farm and they sat quietly for a while.

'Well, that's torn it,' Lauren said suddenly, and started to laugh.

'What has?' He wanted to hear her say it.

'Us.' She waved her arm. 'We've torn it. Haven't wc?'

'A bit,' he agreed. 'I suppose we have.'

He found his pipe and began to fill it.

She looked at him, still laughing. 'How did I ever get into this?'

He tamped the tobacco and lit it and blew smoke into the dawn. 'Just lucky, I guess.'

She shook her head as if to clear it. She got up and walked a few steps away from him down the hill. She stood gazing out over the land with the valley and the farm spread out before her. 'You know yesterday won't happen again, Sam. The drinking. Not like that. You know it won't, don't you?'

'I know.'

'But let's not fool ourselves. This isn't all going to come right just like that. No matter how good it feels now.'

'And?'

'And I don't want to give you anything too heavy, Sam. My life's a mess. You can still stay out of it.'

He looked at her. 'That's a joke, right?'

She held his look for a moment. 'I need to sort some things out,' she said. 'Tommy will take it hard. I've not handled that well.'

He took the pipe out of his mouth and examined it. 'I'll go and see him.'

'No,' she said. 'It's not your problem.'

'It is now,' he tamped the bowl of the pipe again and burned another match. 'It's no drama. I'll just go and see him and tell him how things are. That's only fair.'

'I don't care about fair,' she said. She looked out over the paling country and the breeze lifted her hair. 'But I'm going to see Tommy, Sam. Not you. And I'm going to see him today.'

'Today?'

She nodded. 'That's right. Put all that behind us.'

He stood up, knocked the pipe out on the edge of the bench. 'OK. Then I'll take you. I have to go to the office sometime this week anyway. Clear my desk.'

'No. I need to do it myself. You can drop me at Oxford and I'll get the train.'

'You've got this all worked out, haven't you?'

'Yes.'

'You know, you don't have to put yourself through this, Lauren.'

'Yes, I do. Listen to me, Sam.' She came up to him and put her hands on his shoulders. 'I'm not made of porcelain. I won't break. Not any more I won't.'

'If this is what you want, Lauren.'

'It's what I want. I'll meet you later at the flat if you like. We'll spend the night in town. Frey's not back at school till Tuesday. She can stay here till Monday night.' Then she shook her head and caught his hands and hung away from him, laughing. 'Give up, Sam. Whenever you try to look serious, I see you standing under that waterspout. I think I always will.'

Cobb dropped her at Oxford station just after midday. She kissed him quickly and left without a word and then trotted away up the steps, her bag bouncing jauntily against her hip. He watched her until she vanished through the glass doors, but she did not look back.

He drove on slowly, savouring his mood. He was taut, nervous, and exultant all at once. Like an adolescent, he reflected, an adolescent at forty-six. The thought of that made him smile as he drove. He took a cross-country route, avoiding the main roads. To him this was the heart of England: high banks of hawthorn, old oaks in the corners of irregular fields, churches dozing like ancient elephants in the spring light. The countryside was as dense and intricate to him as a medieval tapestry, and as rich in allegory. That peaceful meadow was a battlefield. At that innocent road junction a gallows had stood. Inside the quaint thatched cottages countless unknown people had loved and fought and given birth and died, all down the ages. Cobb was not deceived by the tranquillity of the countryside: something in him responded to its hidden paganism.

He stopped at a village somewhere near Watlington. It was a place with a stone bridge and a black-beamed pub which looked out across a patch of green. He bought a pint and took it outside and sat at a wooden table. The pub garden was lovingly tended, brilliant with spring flowers. The sun was warm enough to draw drops of golden resin from the timber. A drowsy queen wasp, attracted by the smell of the beer, blundered against his glass and fell stunned on to the table in front of him. He flicked it away into the long grass with his thumbnail. Cobb sipped his beer. He was aware that his world had wobbled from its orbit, and was already spinning away on some unguessable new path. It frightened and excited him. He realised he knew nothing about Lauren. What paper did she read? Did she like ice cream? Did she believe in God? He was amazed at the audacity of his assumptions, amazed and delighted with himself for making them. He felt his cautious mind prepare to lecture him about responsibility, about good sense, about pain and loss. To hell with it, he told the voice in his head. Give me a break for once. It's been so very long.

The phone squawked in his pocket. Cobb fumbled for it, spilling beer.

'It's McBean, Mr Cobb. Den McBean.'

Cobb tried to focus. He heard himself say stupidly: 'I'm on leave, Den.'

There was a stiff silence. 'I'm not.'

Cobb shook himself. 'I'm sorry. What's on your mind?'

'Something kind of strange has come up.'

'Oh?' Cobb felt his heartbeat quicken.

'Couple of weeks ago we found this old tom, Maggie Turpin, dead in a flat in Newington. Suicide. And some old wino she shacked up with. Bloke called Stevens. He's dead too, now. But the point is, sir, they had money on them.'

'In Newington? That wouldn't –'

'No. But we know they were from up East.'

'How much money?'

'Over a grand.'

Cobb said quickly: 'That doesn't mean anything. They could have got that anywhere.'

'That's what I thought. I wasn't going to bother you with it. But then I did some checking. And it seems they'd been throwing cash around for weeks.'

'So?'

'So there must have been quite a wad to start with.'

'And that's it?'

'Well . . .' McBean faltered. 'Well, yes. Except Hayward's got this theory about the Nile –'

'You did the right thing telling me, Sergeant,' Cobb said briskly. 'But we've closed this one off.'

'I knew that, sir. It's just that I thought –'

'Give it away, Dennis. Don't waste your time on it.'

'If you say so, Mr Cobb.'

'Yes, I do say so. But thanks again.' Cobb hung up and turned the phone off. He looked around quickly but in the bright spring sunshine the garden was as innocent as before.

59

The cab dropped Lauren at the gate. She paid the driver and watched him pull away. Then she took a deep breath and walked quickly between the tall pillars before she could change her mind. It was strange to be returning here like this. It had been her home for so long, and yet it seemed to her now that she might have been away for years, rather than just a few days. The house was, she supposed, handsome in its way, and the pale sun washed away some of its oppressive weight. But it did not seem to be hers any longer. She walked across the gravel to the front door past Hudson's black BMW. There was a movement behind the glass and the door opened as she reached it. Hudson was barefoot and wore a blue flowered shirt open over slacks, and as soon as their eyes met Lauren knew that he knew.

'Well, well,' he said. He was smoking the remains of a cigar and wore a pair of sunglasses pushed up on to his forehead. 'I wondered when you'd be back.'

'I'm not back, Tommy.'

Hudson looked at her for a moment and walked away into the house, leaving the door open behind him. Lauren followed the big man down the hallway. He waved the cigar stub over his shoulder as he walked. 'Sorry about the ciggie. I know you don't like it in the house. But then it didn't seem to matter any more.' He stopped and turned. 'That's what you've come to tell me, I expect? That it doesn't matter any more.'

'We need to talk, Tommy.'

'Yeah.' Hudson's big face closed at once. 'I thought so.' He waved her through into the main room, as though she might not know where it was.

'Drink?'

'Thanks, no.' She walked across the huge living room and took a seat on the gold brocade couch while Hudson took his time at the bar, pouring himself a beer.

At length he brought his drink over and sat opposite her. 'Funny, thing, y'know, Laurie,' he said, 'but I never liked this place much. All this . . . stuff.'

Lauren looked at the room's clutter of ostentatiously expensive furniture, the Indian rugs and the Chinese jade. 'Me neither, Tommy. But it was Matthew's pride and joy. I wonder what that says about the two of us.'

Hudson sipped his drink and put it down on the marble-topped coffee table, wiped the froth off his upper lip with his finger and then wiped the finger on the fleur-de-lys cushion beside him. He looked up at her. 'Any danger of us getting to the point, Laurie?'

'We're going to stay at the farm for a while, Tommy.'

Hudson sipped again. 'You have a reason for that?'

'I don't need a reason. But you can guess at one if you like.'

He held her gaze. 'Cobb didn't come with you?'

'I thought I'd spare him the scene.'

'You mean, I might give the cheeky sod a slap or two?' Hudson leaned forward with tension bunching the slabs of muscle along his upper arms. 'I might be over the hill but I could still knock him through that wall.'

'Let's not do it this way, Tommy.'

Hudson sat back a little and took a pull of his beer. After a moment he seemed to take a decision of some kind and moved his shoulders, as if to release the tension in them. He breathed out hard and drank a little more. He said: 'I worshipped you, Laurie. Swear to God. Still do.'

'I know, Tommy. I'm sorry.'

He pointed at her with his thick forefinger. 'And you led me on. Didn'tcha?'

'You wanted so badly to be led, Tommy.' Then she shook her head sharply and stood up. 'I didn't come here for this.'

'What did you come here for?'

'To get you out of my house. Out of my life. To take back control.'

He smiled unpleasantly. 'Want to get your hands on some of Mattie's money for your new boyfriend?'

'Tommy, do you really think I care about the money? But I won't leave you in charge any longer.'

'You'll never sort it out, Laurie. There won't be two quid left by the time the lawyers have finished taking their slices out of you.'

She lifted her head. 'At least it'll be my two quid. Mine and Freya's. We won't owe it to anyone.'

Hudson looked at her in silence for a long time. Finally, and without apparent relevance, he said: 'It was me made Mattie, you know.' His voice was soft. 'You think you did it. But he was my creation, Matt Silver was. It was me stuck with him when no one else did. I twisted a few arms – I even broke a few – to get him on stage, get him into recording studios. You don't know the half of it.'

'Maybe I don't, Tommy. But we're not talking about Matthew here. We're talking about me. And you.'

'And Mr Sam bloody Cobb.'

'No. Just about you and me.'

'That makes it sound simple, now doesn't it? But it's not simple. We're all tied up together. Matt and me, we was like Siamese twins. Joined. And you belonged to him.'

'I'm not a piece of furniture, Tommy.'

The big man turned away and gazed across to the bay windows which gave on to the sloping lawn and the willows on the riverbank beyond. 'You know something, Laurie? You can toss me away. I'm just a prick. But you won't get rid of Mattie that easy. Maybe neither of us ever will.'

'What does that mean?'

'Thing I was told early on,' Hudson said. 'Never punch above your weight. Should've learned that.' He turned to face her. 'P'raps we both should've learned that, Laurie. You and me.'

Lauren opened her mouth to speak and then thought better of it. There seemed no point. She started to walk away across the mosque-deep carpet.

'I'll be out of here by tomorrow,' he called after her, when she was almost at the door. 'There'll be nothing missing. I'll hand it all over. The papers. The deeds. All that.'

She stopped. 'Thank you, Tommy.'

'I never wanted none of it anyway.'

'I know you didn't.' She looked at the floor and then back at him. When he didn't speak she said: 'What will you do now?'

He lifted his battered face to her and shrugged. 'What does it matter?'

She left the room quietly and walked out of the front door into the sunshine.

60

'And what time d'you call this, my lad?' Nelson's Yorkshire accent boomed cheerfully around the office. His buttons blazed in the afternoon sun as it struck across the office.

Cobb cleared the last of the voicemail messages and emptied the bottom drawer of his desk into a black rubbish bag. 'I'm on leave, Horrie. I only came in to clean up.'

'Oh, yes. I did detect a certain bank holiday demeanour. However, my trained policeman's mind allows me to make other deductions too.'

Nelson sounded vastly pleased with himself. Cobb glanced at him. 'What's up, Horrie? Black pudding overdose?'

'I note, for example, that the subject, whilst casually attired, is not covered in pigshit, and for once does not require the changing facilities afforded by my office.'

'Uh-huh.' Cobb's heart sank. He could see where this was going. He wondered how much Nelson had heard and from whom. It was somehow typical of the Yorkshireman to reach the right conclusion with only half the facts.

'And furthermore, the subject exhibits a certain unexplained jauntiness. Indeed he appears to be – how shall we put it? – shagged out all to buggery.'

Cobb put down the rubbish bag.

Nelson lowered his voice to a stage whisper. 'You're tupping that Silver woman, aren't you, you sly dog?' He winked at his own cleverness.

Cobb was surprised how much he resented the casual crudity. He had to resist a ridiculous urge to defend her honour. He thought he might be blushing.

Nelson said: 'Oh, it's like that. No offence, I'm sure.'

'She has a name, Horrie. It's Lauren.'

Nelson cleared his throat, tugged down his tunic. 'Nice name. Very nice.' He spoke a little stiffly. 'Of course, strictly speaking it's against the rules, you know, Sam. File not long closed, and all that.'

'Horrie,' Cobb said. 'Shut up.'

'Right. Right.'

Nelson tapped his teeth with his silver pencil and studied the light fitting in the ceiling.

Cobb said: 'Was it just my sex life you wanted to speak to me about?'

'No.' Nelson sucked his lip. 'No. What I really wanted to say . . .'

'Well?'

'We're going to miss you round here, Sam.' Nelson stuck out his paw. 'That's all.'

Cobb took Nelson's hand in both of his, suddenly ashamed of himself. 'Thanks for everything, Horrie. You're a good man.' He felt sorry that he hadn't said this before. Perhaps even now he could take the big policeman out for a farewell drink: he could at least offer. But somehow he couldn't face it. A sense of unease was growing in him the longer he stayed. He wanted badly to get out of this office, to put it behind him, to start again. He said apologetically: 'I suppose I'd better get on, Horrie.'

'As you wish, Sam. You know you can always come to us if you need anything.'

'I do know that, Horrie. Thanks.'

Cobb tore down a handful of photographs from the pegboard partition and stuffed them in the bag. The dead child, the twisted car, beautiful, radiant Matt Silver. He quickly crushed down the black plastic over the prints, but Nelson had already seen.

'Now that reminds me,' he said, 'that darkie chap called. McBean or whatever.'

'He did?' Cobb straightened. 'When?'

'About midday.'

He relaxed a little. 'That's OK. I've spoken to him since. It was nothing.'

'Oh,' Nelson sounded surprised, 'he was pretty keen to reach you.'

'Well, he did reach me, Horrie. It was nothing.'

'Fair enough. Fair enough.' Nelson made to move away towards his own office but hesitated at the last moment. 'One last thing, Sam. You know Regional Crime really wanted a Chief Inspector on this team. You don't need to be bloody Einstein to see what that might mean.' He looked at Cobb significantly.

'I won't blow it, Horrie. Don't worry.'

'See that you don't.'

Cobb watched Nelson walk away across the room. Then he cleared the last of the litter from his desk, packed a few personal things into his bag and took the fire stairs two at a time. He almost made it across the front office.

'Young Cobb! A moment, if you please.'

Cobb closed his eyes and opened them again. 'Brigadier.'

The mad Brigadier's ramrod figure was half hidden in the shadows by the lifts. He looked furtively from right to left as Cobb walked up to him. 'Don't lower your guard, Cobb,' he said darkly. 'Not for an instant.'

His tone was unsettling and Cobb spoke more sharply than he intended. 'Against what?'

'Fifth column.' The Brigadier lifted one knowing eyebrow. 'The enemy within.'

'Brigadier,' Cobb said, 'why don't you just piss off and leave me alone?'

The old soldier narrowed his eyes as if this were some daring new strategy. 'Damn fine notion, young Cobb!' He rammed his stick up under his arm. 'About to suggest it m'self.' And he was gone, marching into the street, the stick brandished jauntily over his shoulder. 'Carry on!'

Cobb let himself into the flat and dumped his bags by the door.

'Hey,' she said, gladly, 'I didn't expect you until tonight.'

'I had to get out of there. How did it go with Tommy?'

'It was fine, Sam. Everything's going to be fine.'

He stood staring at her. She sat at the tiny dining table in a chute of sunlight. Dust danced gold in the light. A cup of coffee in front of her smoked into the radiance and a book lay open against the dark wood. She had tidied the flat and showered and she was wrapped in his threadbare bathrobe, and the room was fragrant with coffee and soap and beeswax.

'What?' she said. Then tilted her head and smiled.

Cobb was astonished by their lust. They made love hungrily, roughly, hilariously. They made love on the floor so that the boards creaked like a ship at sea, and pretended until the last moment that it was not desperately uncomfortable. Once, her outflung arm caught the flex of the reading lamp and sent it crashing to the floor, and they were nearly hysterical with laughter when a neighbour thumped the wall to protest at the noise. They moved to the sofa bed and made love again there with the stays twanging like harpstrings beneath them. Then Cobb found a bottle of wine in the fridge and they drank it – to hell with her controlled drinking programme and to hell with everything else. Their sex was playful, thrilling, explosive, volatile, dangerous.

But it was not enough.

He awoke at three in morning in the dark cube of the room. It was raining outside again, the water trembling in ropes down the window and the lights from the city warped and refracted through it. A drainpipe was blocked somewhere and he wondered if the gurgling of it had awakened him. His face was against her breast and he was aware of her finger moving against his shoulder. She was tracing a pattern lightly on his skin, something intricate and elliptical, like the design of a Celtic brooch. In his half waking mind he could see it, a jewelled strap of bronze twisted into a knot, and he knew beyond doubt that this was the device in her mind also. He lay still in the dark, feeling her finger trace its ghostly design, listening to the rain gust against the window, cocooned in the smell of her skin and her body.

'Sam?' She breathed his name in his ear. 'Do you think this could really work?' It was as if she feared the sound of her voice might trigger an avalanche of retribution for daring to hope so much.

'If they give us a chance.'

He did not know why he used this form of words, though he did know they echoed some tremor of fear deep in himself. He could not tell whether the fear was his alone, or whether he picked up the vibration from her, as he sensed the coiled pagan pattern in her mind. Or again, whether some ripple had fluttered through space and time to warn him.

He said: 'What was he like, Lauren?'

'You want to talk about Matthew.' It was not a question. There was a kind of resignation in her voice.

'I just meant . . . it can't always have been bad.'

'No. It wasn't always bad.' She rolled over on to her back. 'Don't do this, Sam.'

For perhaps a full minute she said nothing more and he thought she had drifted back to sleep. Then abruptly she swung her legs out of bed and sat up and reached in her bag and found a cigarette and lit it. It was the first cigarette she had lit for four days. The smoke roiled in a blue cloud against the shimmering window.

'It was a ride, Sam. A ride like you couldn't believe.'

'You don't have to say anything you don't want to.'

'Oh, yes.' She glanced back at him over her shoulder. 'Oh, yes, I do. You want to know what he was like?'

'I don't –'

'Well, I'll tell you. Beautiful. Brilliant. Funny. Exciting. Exciting? That isn't the word. He was like a natural force. A hurricane, maybe.'

'Lauren.'

She stood up and paced across to the window so that the blue light fell across the planes of her body. 'But what you really want to know is if he was better than you. You want to know if you can *compete*.'

'I didn't ask you that.'

'Yes, you did. You just didn't voice the question.'

'Lauren, I'm sorry.'

She tossed her head and smoke plumed in the darkness. 'It had to come up sometime. It always does.'

'Come back to bed.'

'Was he a better man than you? That's what you want to know. Well, of course he wasn't. But, you see, Sam, that wouldn't have made any difference.' She swung towards him in the darkness. 'Is that what you wanted to hear, Sam? Is it?'

Cobb stood. He could see the tears shining on her face.

'For weeks after the crash,' she said, and stopped. She gathered herself and started again. 'For weeks after Gudrun died, not a day passed – not an hour – when I didn't ask myself if I would still have taken him back that night. If he had just begged me once more.' She drew herself up and looked straight at him. 'But things are different now. You have to know that if Matthew walked in right now and begged me to take him back, I would tell him no.'

'Lauren –'

'You make sure you heard that right,' she said fiercely, her voice twisting, 'because I'm not going to say it again.'

Cobb stepped forward and slid his arms around her and lifted her body against his. He felt her breath and her tears hot against his skin.

'He's dead, Lauren.'

'It doesn't matter,' she said. 'It doesn't matter any more.'

He rocked her there for a while in the darkness. 'This is my fault.'

'Yes, it is.'

'I should keep my big mouth shut.'

Her voice changed. 'Why don't you, then?' She reached up and brushed her fingers over his lips. 'And I will too.'

In a rush he said: 'I can't face losing it all again, Lauren.'

'Then hold on.' She slipped her arms around his body and locked him fiercely in her grip. 'Hold on really, really tight.'

61

He was watching the child, feeding on the sight of her.
There was something different about her, he knew,
something indefinable. Was it a certain balance? Did
she somehow stand more squarely to the world? He
could not decide. She waited just inside the redbrick
pillars of the school gates with a crowd of friends. A
plane tree grew there, just coming into light green leaf.
The tree was ringed by a low brick wall and the girls
gathered around this wall instinctively, as if around a
village well. He had noticed that before, and because
he had noticed it, he was at length able to see what had
changed about her. It was the space which had somehow always been beside her, around her. It was gone
now. She had grown to fill it.

Silver felt a great regret. He had missed something,
he knew, some seminal event in her life, and she was
passing away from him. Whatever had happened to
her, he had not been the first person she'd told. He
would never be told, not about this or any of the other
changes that would form her life. He lifted the newspaper and hid his face behind it, pushing himself back
and down into the hard curve of the park bench. It
would be better in a moment. Silver had waited here in
the park four times now, and he knew it would be

better soon. And soon it was, and he lowered the paper and looked again.

Freya's face lit up and she ran out of the gates to meet them. The man's presence confused Silver, a square man in early middle life who walked beside Lauren. She had never brought anyone to the school before. Freya hugged her mother and Lauren bent to kiss her and then turned her head and looked at the man and there was the pride of possession in her look. And the man looked back the same way and bent to accept the child's kiss, and the three of them turned and walked away up the sunlit street to a parked car, the child between them, swinging from their hands, Lauren bending as she walked, Freya turning her face up so that even from this distance he could see her glasses shining.

Silver folded the paper and tossed it unread into a wastebin. They were just in sight still, climbing into a dark car: Lauren's blonde hair, Freya's light blue blazer. The car pulled out and drew slowly past him so that the driver's face was no more than a few yards from him. A regular face, perhaps even a pleasant one, if a little stern. Silver tried to memorise the features. It seemed to be important to know his wife's lover, his child's protector. For this, he knew, was how it was. The car rounded the corner and Silver could see them no longer. He stood up and walked a few yards. His body seemed not to work properly: he found it hard to coordinate his movements. He moved stiffly down the steps from the park into the street and his legs felt suddenly leaden. There was a low wall beside the bus stop and he sat down heavily on it. People in the queue glanced at him curiously and then looked determinedly away. A young woman hovered on the point of asking him if he needed help, but she had a child with her – a child from Freya's school – and he could see she shrank from approaching this shabby man with his ruined face.

Nothing had prepared him. Yet he knew what Nugget would have said. This was part of the price. Debts must be paid, even when there is no hope of meeting the bill. He lurched to his feet and began to walk away.

The Rum Jungle Club was built into the cellar of a multistorey car park in Stepney Green. It was after nine before Silver found it. He had alternated between buses and walking all the way from Barnes and he was bonesore and dispirited, and weariness sat like a sack of stones on his back. The sole of his right shoe had worn through just under the ball of his foot so that the skin had blistered. For some reason the small jabbing of this pain was the cruellest humiliation of all. He leaned on the railings in the street above and looked down at the basement doors of the club. The doors were painted Gauguin fashion with stylised palm trees. They were propped ajar and outside them a bouncer in a gorilla outfit stood guard, incongruously smoking. The outfit fitted him rather too well. For a second Silver wondered if he could face all this and hovered on the point of limping back to his own room to seek some peace there. He half closed his eyes and felt himself sway with weariness against the rails. The gorilla glanced suspiciously up at him.

Then a patter of applause from inside the club, the murmur of an introduction, more applause. And her voice came swooping out of the dim doorway to him, pure and light. He leaned back and listened, drinking it. It was a song he had taught her: *At Seventeen*. She was always best at these, plaintive songs of love and loss with a touch of raunchy blues to them. Those and the songs she wrote herself, haunting ballads full of betrayal and despair. Silver wondered where, at her age, she found the well from which she drew such a bitter draught, and it came to him as she sang that she was seventeen herself. That wasn't logical but it seemed to be an answer.

'All right there, sunshine?' the gorilla called up to him. It was a challenge and not a friendly enquiry.

Silver opened his eyes: he had been drifting. In another moment he would have been asleep where he stood. 'Sure. Sure.' He stood up straight, brushed down his jacket. 'Just listening.'

'Well, pay the money or piss off. Make the place untidy.'

Silver hesitated for a moment longer then went down the steps. The gorilla watched him narrowly all the way down, then, apparently satisfied, took Silver's money and marked the inside of his wrist with an inked rubber stamp.

'She's good, though, ain't she?' Now that Silver was

a paid-up patron the ape became comradely. He jerked his hairy thumb into the club. 'She'll do all right, that one.'

The Rum Jungle was a dark low-ceilinged place with rattan furniture intended to look tropical. Square concrete pillars were decorated with plastic jungle leaves and plastic lianas and lurid yellow plastic bunches of bananas. On a miniature stage at the far end of the room Jit glittered in the spotlights, the polished guitar flashing sheets of dazzle, her hair a blue flame. Silver waited just inside the door while she finished the song. From this close he could hear a tremor in her voice, a fumbled note or two in the last chorus. When she hit the final ringing chord he could almost taste her relief.

'Fuckin' lovely, that.' The gorilla beat his paws together in applause. 'Fuckin' lovely.'

The audience agreed with the ape. As Jit bowed and bobbed up smiling they clapped and whistled at her and shouted their approval. Silver crossed to the bar, found a stool and ordered a beer.

'I'll get it.' Nugent appeared out of the gloom, took the seat beside him, and paid for the drink. 'You cut it fine, Joe.'

Silver said nothing. On stage Jit was stumbling through a funny story to introduce her next number. The audience found her nervousness endearing and whenever they could find an excuse they laughed to encourage her. Silver drank. 'She's doing OK.'

'She's terrified.'

'She's supposed to be terrified.'

'She depends on you, Joe.' Nugent allowed his anger to flash like a blade. 'You understand that?'

'There's no point in anyone depending on me.' Silver turned away from the priest and looked back to the stage. She was still ploughing through her story, making a play of fine tuning a couple of strings while she talked. Silver noticed that she had placed his six-string on stage in its stand. He saw her eyes slide nervously towards the bar, trying to pierce the glare. Her anxiety was so obvious that Silver took pity on her. He leaned forward and half stood so that she could see him and raised a hand to her.

'Hey, Joe!' she cried into the microphone so that it boomed round the room. 'I knew you'd make it!'

Silver cursed and pulled himself back into the shadows while people in the audience craned to see him.

'You people out there!' Jit was calling out, all confidence now, working them. 'You want to hear a real guitar player?'

Silver saw what was coming and slid off the stool. Nugent's hand locked on his arm. And then she was calling his name and beckoning to him and the audience was baying for him and Nugent was shouting in his ear:

'You run out on her now, you deadshit, and you'll leave your arm behind.'

Silver would have shaken him off, but at that moment he caught a glimpse of her over the priest's shoulder. She was crucified in the spotlights, her eyes beseeching him, the kingfisher jewel sparking in her cheek, and as he held back he could see her confidence begin to crumble. Silver found himself walking easily past Nugent into the light.

And Jit was saying into the microphone: 'Come on, Joe! Bloody late, as usual,' and she was laughing as she said it.

And Silver was up on stage and the audience was half standing, half sitting, watching, and before they could decide anything Silver had swept up the six-string from its stand. He moved to the microphone and struck the chords she knew, the chords they all knew, and he said: 'Hit it.'

And she did. And she sang so that her pure voice filled the room and there could be no doubt of it any more.

> *You people climbing on that Narrow Way*
> *Can climb from cradle up to Judgement Day.*
> *You want to win, but first you gotta lose –*
> *That's what they call*
> *That's what they call*
> *Redemption Blues.*

It was past one in the morning before they left the club. Nugent helped them load the equipment and drove them back to the church. Silver sat in the back of the little van, dozing fitfully, hearing Jit chatter from the front seat but too tired to listen. The images flickered through his mind like the jerky frames of an old cartoon. Lauren bending, her blonde hair swinging, her hand on Freya's back, and the sun flashing on the child's glasses as she looked up. The bulk of the new man's shoulder through the car window, clad in some rough oatmeal jacket. The dazzle of the stagelights and the raw energy that pulsed up to him through the darkness, just as it had in the old days, before life had stopped. He wanted desperately to sleep. He thought perhaps tomorrow might shake things into some kind of order. Or maybe not. He no longer much cared.

Nugent dropped them by the door of the house and drove away to park the car and did not come back. Silver helped Jit lug her gear up to her room. Then he followed her downstairs again and into the tawdry kitchen at the back of the house. The drabness of the place only made her shine the brighter. She was alight with her triumph. He could see it spark from her, could feel the surge and warmth of it charge the shabby room.

'Let's have a drink, Joe.' She was pacing, tugging open cupboards, poking among the crumpled cornflake packets and the tinned food. 'I really need a drink.'

'You're just on a high, Jit. It's like that.'

'You feel it too, Joe.' She could not keep still. She opened the fridge and closed it again without looking inside. 'Come on, partner. It's easier once you admit it.'

He said nothing. But she was right. They had given it to him, just like the old days. That raw pulse of energy. The power. They had sent it to him.

She opened the fridge again. 'There's got to be some booze around here *somewhere*.'

Her excitement made her magnetic. It was too much of an effort for him to break out of her field just at the moment and drag himself up to his room. Out of habit he moved across to the sink and ran some water into the kettle.

'You're not making fucking *tea*,' she cried, incredulous. 'It's two in the morning on the first day of my life and he makes fucking *tea*! We need champagne.'

'We haven't got any champagne, Jit. Get a grip.'

'Hey! There's some Newcastle Amber upstairs. Andy left it. At least that's got bubbles.'

She left at a run to fetch the beer. He heard her bare feet pattering up the stairs, as light as a deer. The sound of it made him feel old and cumbersome. Before he had properly registered that she had gone she burst back into the kitchen. 'I'm a star, right?' she demanded. 'Now is that right or not?' She held up one finger like a signal and lifted her eyebrows, warning him not to give a wrong answer.

'That's right,' he said.

'Right,' she confirmed, clicking her finger down. 'But I couldn't have done it without you, partner.'

Apparently she was searching for an opener now, slamming open drawers and slamming them closed again so that the cutlery rolled and jingled. He gave up trying to keep up with her. Finally she smacked off the bottle's crown cap against the edge of the draining board, sucked the creamy foam and handed the bottle to him. Then she smacked open a second one for herself, clunked it hard against his, and tipped down a draught of warm beer that half-emptied the bottle. She set the bottle down with decision, wiped her mouth with the back of her hand, and breathed out long and hard.

'That,' she said, and he knew she meant the whole glittering triumphant evening, 'was fun.'

'It could be more than fun, Jit. For you.'

'Don't start that shit again.' She waved at him in good-natured dismissal. 'It was just fun.'

'I know what I'm talking about, Jit,' he said.

'Pah!' Her scorn scattered bright flecks of beer foam.

He'd seen them come and go in the old days, girls more talented than she was, with better voices, better looks, a hundred times more experience. But that wasn't how it worked. The alchemy was altogether more subtle than that. Put them in front of an audience and he could tell in five minutes. She was going to make it, if she wanted to. In a big way or a small way he didn't know, and it didn't matter: if the right people saw her, she would get her season in the sun. He felt somehow that it was his duty to tell her so, and despite everything her indifference nettled him.

She seemed to sense this and turned on him. 'When are you going to get it through your head, Joe? I don't want to be rich and famous. It's just not my scene.'

'You've got talent, Jit.'

'Don't tell me I've got a duty,' she scoffed. 'Please don't. I'll puke.'

'People should hear you.'

'People in pubs hear me. For Chrissake, Joe, why don't you get it? It's here and now. But you won't have that. You've got this mania for easy answers.'

'Easy?'

'Well, answers anyway. You want things to add up. You with your ton of guilt. Nugget with his crazy religion. Debt and payment. What are you? A lot of bloody accountants?'

'Life's not as simple as you make out, Jit.'

'Yes, it is, Joe.'

'What would you know?' he bridled. 'Standing there with your blue hair and your army boots and all of your seventeen little summers.'

'You mean I'm not smart, like you?'

He caught himself before he could answer. Instead he tipped the gassy beer into his throat. It was warm and revolting, but he was glad of the distraction.

'Let's get out of here, Joe,' she said suddenly, in a different voice. 'Nugget's giving you the elbow anyway. What's there to stay for?'

'There's a person I need to see sometimes,' he said sullenly. 'An important person.'

'Is that where you slide off to these afternoons? Well, I don't know where you go, Joe, but it busts you up every time. What's the future in that?'

'Anyway, where would I go?'

'I don't know.' She waved her beer bottle expansively,

banishing the shabby room. 'You could go and find the evil Vargas and win back the beautiful Esmeralda. Become the king of the gypsy guitarists again.'

He looked at her. 'Life must be wonderful for you, Jit.'

'It's not so hard, Joe. You just do it. If you want me to name a place for you, we'll go up to my brother Jake's people in Northamptonshire. He's got this great trailer–'

'The New Age gypsy? Jit, come on.'

'Why not, Joe?' She gripped his arm. 'We'd play in pubs. Make a few quid. Have an adventure. Have some fun.'

'And then what? After all this fun we're going to have?'

She shrugged. 'Then one day we'll get sick and die. What did you have in mind?'

62

The country was paintbox pretty under a duck-egg sky. They played Bach on the Saab's CD and wound back the sunroof and drove too fast all the way. At a little after nine they turned through the farm gate and down the track towards the house. The yard looked unusually busy. The Land Rover was parked in front of the house with its trailer attached. Fred was busy in the yard, trudging in and out of the barn with what looked to Cobb like bundles of tawny bedding which he dumped in a heap in the trailer. Something staccato about the way his father moved warned Cobb even before he rolled the car on to the cobbles that there was a problem. As he drew level, he stopped and lowered the window.

'Your bloody fox is responsible for this,' Fred snapped at him, before Cobb could speak. He was plainly furious. Cobb saw that the tawny bundles his father carried were dead chickens, torn and bloody.

'My fox?' he protested.

'You should have shot it weeks ago,' Fred accused him, brandishing a lifeless hen. 'Nasty destructive creatures. Five of my best Rhode Islands. Five! And the damned thing took two of the ducks on the way out. I'd've shot the bloody creature myself if it wasn't for this blasted arthritis.' The old man slung the chicken on to the heap and a cloud of loose brown feathers rose on the air. He bent down to the car again and spoke across at Lauren and Freya. 'I'm sorry, my dears. Not much of a welcome home. *Damned* foxes.'

'I'm so sorry, Fred,' Lauren said. 'Your beautiful chickens.' She made a sympathetic face at Cobb, then slid out of the car and escaped with Freya towards the back door.

He said: 'I'll have a pop at it this week.'

'A lot of good that'll do now,' the old man grunted. 'Should have done it weeks ago.'

'Didn't Baskerville hear anything?'

The dog sat in the sun by the back door, in an attitude which suggested he was vaguely aware something untoward had happened, and that he might bear some responsibility for it.

'Samuel, that damned dog is deafer than I am. Now put your flashy foreign car away and give me a hand.' Fred stumped off into the barn, muttering as he went.

Cobb garaged the car and carried their bags across the yard towards the house. He glanced at the slaughtered hens on the end of the trailer as he walked by. The soft down under their wings stirred in the air and a steady drip of blood fell through the slats to pool on the muddy cobbles, impossibly bright in the sun. The sight darkened his mood a little. He was not sure why. Perhaps because of his father's distress. Perhaps because he would have to try to kill the fox, and he disliked killing. Perhaps simply because this small savagery touched some animal echo in him. At the kitchen door the dog grinned up at him and slapped at him with his tongue. Cobb pulled himself together. He would not have a shadow cast over this weekend. He would not allow it.

Freya slipped down from her chair and ran across and hugged his legs.

He lifted the child up and kissed her.

'The fox killed all our chickens,' she said, turning down her mouth. 'Rotten fox.'

'Big disaster.' Lauren pulled a tragic face, glancing out towards the yard where Fred was still stamping about in his fury.

'Uncle Fred says you have to shoot the fox,' Freya said, gripping Cobb's hand and hanging back from it. 'Poor fox. I mean, poor chickens too. But poor fox.'

'Don't worry, Princess. I probably won't even see Mr Fox. And if I do I'll probably miss.' He winked at her. 'But I'll give him a good fright, so he won't come back.'

Fred came into the kitchen from the yard, still muttering darkly to himself. He crossed to the sink without speaking and stood there washing his hands savagely.

Lauren exchanged a glance with Cobb then called brightly to Freya: 'Come on, young lady. Get your coat. I want to see round the farm.'

When they had gone Fred turned off the tap and stood there silently as mother and child, hand in hand, crossed the sunlit yard outside the window. Baskerville shambled after them, his tail swinging. Freya turned to call the dog and Baskerville broke into an arthritic trot.

Cobb said: 'So what's on your mind, oldtimer? Other than the poor bloody chickens.'

'Oldtimer?' Fred's face wrinkled with distaste.

'It's from one of Freya's cartoons. Pesky Pecos Pete the Prospector. He's got these white whiskers and everyone calls him "oldtimer".'

'And you allow the child to watch such rubbish?'

'Not exactly. She plays championship chess while I watch it.'

Fred said nothing. He did not wish to be charmed. Cobb watched the set of his father's profile and tried to guess what he was thinking. He followed the old man's gaze and saw that Fred was watching the dog. Poor Baskerville had given up his pursuit of Freya and settled himself in the middle of the yard, gazing with longing at the child's receding figure. Cobb suddenly knew what his father was thinking: that the old dog embodied his own gathering weaknesses. It struck Cobb that he should go out one day this week and buy his father a new pup, something that would grow into a big cross-bred mongrel like Baskerville himself. Something with a skin that was two sizes too big for it. Something with enormous feet. That would keep both the old man and the old hound company. He said: 'Why don't we get another dog, Dad?'

'Because I'll die before it does,' Fred snapped. 'That must be obvious.'

Cobb said nothing. It had not been obvious, though presumably it should have been. A sturdy mutt like the one he had in mind would live ten or twelve years. But Fred had such a head start he would still win this last race. Cobb quickly cut off this line of thought. It was obscene to be measuring out his father's life in dog years, a reversal of the natural order of things. 'Dad, you're going to live for ever. And if you decide not to, I'll look after any dog you want to get. OK?'

'Assuming you stay here.'

So that was it.

'Yes, I was assuming that,' Cobb said quietly. After a moment he added: 'Do you want a drink?'

'A little early, isn't it?'

'Yes. Maybe it is.'

It seemed to Cobb that there was nothing more he could say. He rose and went into the centre of the house and opened the cellar door and found the light switch and went down the dank steps. He unlocked the steel gun cabinet and took out his father's shotgun and the cleaning kit, found a packet of twelve-bore cartridges, and carried them all back upstairs. Fred was still at the kitchen window and did not move. Cobb spread newspaper on the table, broke the weapon down and started to polish and clean it. He did not like guns. He disliked handling them and loathed using them, even against vermin. He hoped he would never even see the damned fox. But for the old man's sake he made an industrious show of his work.

Fred turned away from the window at last and

watched him for a moment. 'Put the bloody thing away and get me a drink.'

'Sure.' Cobb stood up. 'You want a beer?'

'No, damn it. Let's have a real one.'

Some of his father's fire seemed to have burned out and he sounded annoyed with himself. Cobb went to the oak dresser and found the Laphroaig and the shot glasses, set them on the kitchen table. He sat, waited until Fred sat too, and carefully poured the drinks. 'You want to talk about it?'

Fred looked down at the table. He played with his glass in silence for perhaps thirty seconds. Abruptly, he said: 'I'm a selfish old bastard, Samuel.'

'I'll drink to that,' Cobb laughed, and clinked his glass against Fred's. The spirit was smoky in his throat. On a sudden impulse he reached across and touched his father's hand. He did not remember ever doing this before. He was surprised how hard and warm the old man's skin felt, like an animal's hide. 'I'll keep us all safe this time, Dad. All of us together.'

His father lifted his head and returned his look sadly. 'I hope you can do better than I did, my boy.'

A little later Cobb locked the shotgun away again, changed into his farm clothes and walked across to the barn. He circled it from the outside until he came to the wire enclosure of the chicken run. The surviving hens were huddled in one corner of the run, making small timorous noises at him. The flattened earth was still scattered with feathers, and a shallow trough through the grit showed where the fox had dragged away one of its victims. Cobb could see at once where the predator had broken in. It had even left a couple of strands of chestnut hair hooked into a knot of the wire. He could see the scratched depression the fox had dug for itself before bellying under the wire. From there it had nudged aside the flap which was supposed to keep the birds safe in their henhouse. The fox had worked hard to do this, and the wood around the edge of the flap was scored by its teeth and claws. Cobb walked into the barn and opened the rear door of the henhouse. Blood-drabbled feathers and droppings lay in the grit. An entire wing was opened like a fan in the dirt.

Freya was seated on a high wooden stool at the workbench and for a moment Cobb could hardly make out her small figure in the gloom. 'Hey, Princess. I didn't know you were here.'

'Poor chickens,' she said.

'It happens.' Cobb closed the henhouse door and walked across to her. 'The old fox has got to eat too. It's just a pity he couldn't take one for his lunch and leave the rest.'

'Why didn't he do that, Sam?'

Cobb shrugged. 'It's the nature of the beast. He can't help it.'

She nodded, as if she had come to this conclusion too. He saw now that she was peering at something on the bench, her head on one side.

'What have you got there, Princess?'

'It's our hawk moth. He's hatching out, just like you said he would.'

'Well, so he is.' Cobb had forgotten about the chrysalis in its tray of sand. He bent over her to see. The moth's front legs and antennae were already clear of the pupa. It was resting now, hanging back from the rough side of the box, quivering slightly.

'Isn't he beautiful?' Freya asked him.

'He certainly is, Princess.'

He felt a fresh rush of affection for her. It took the eye of faith to see anything very beautiful about this damp leggy insect, as fat as a small cigar. But as a child he had felt the same way about moths. There was something magical about their metamorphosis, but it was more than that. It was as if they lived in a parallel nocturnal universe, and only a privileged few were allowed to glimpse them. The moth gave a convulsive heave. The chrysalis dropped clear, and the insect hung free with its bladders of wings bunched behind it.

Cobb said: 'In an hour or so he'll have two of the loveliest glossy wings you ever saw.' She did not reply and he wondered if somehow she had not heard. He tried again: 'Do you want to keep him? We can put him in a box. Otherwise he'll fly away tonight.'

'No,' Freya said finally. 'That wouldn't be fair.'

'That's my girl,' he said, and ruffled her hair. To his surprise she turned at his touch and put her arms around his neck and swung herself off the stool and clung to him like a monkey.

'I can remember, Sam,' she said into his ear.

'What?' His voice tightened. 'You can remember what?'

'I can remember.' She was quite calm. She let him go and slid back down to the stool.

'You don't have to remember anything, Princess.'

'Of course I have to.' She leaned over the box and breathed very gently on the moth so that its feelers trembled. 'I remember Daddy saved me.'

Cobb could hear his own pulse booming in his ears. He said nothing.

She sat up straight and faced him. 'I remembered when I saw the moth climb out.' She faltered. 'It was so dark.'

'Do you want to tell me?' He put his hand over hers on the bench.

'I remember him. Kicking. I could feel his legs. Kicking. Really hard. I couldn't see him. I couldn't see anything. I couldn't breathe. There was this awful roaring noise.'

'It's all right, Princess.' He stroked the small warm hand. 'It's all right now.'

'Then he grabbed me and sort of pushed me. Out. Through a hole. It hurt me.'

'The sunroof. He saved you. He kicked out the roof and he saved you.'

'Yes, that's right.' She frowned. 'There was glass around the edges. I felt it.' She looked up at him. 'Why didn't Daddy follow me, Sam?'

'I'm not sure why, Princess. Maybe he couldn't.' Cobb found his mouth was dry. 'The main thing is he got you out. That's all that matters.' He ran his fingers down the side of her face. 'Are you all right? You look a bit pale.'

'So do you,' she said. And then: 'Sam? Should I tell Mummy?'

He swallowed. 'Yes, Princess. You should.'

Lauren threw back her head and stared at the white sky, blinking hard. She could feel Freya's uncertain gaze on her and she longed to give the child reassurance, but for the moment her power of speech seemed to have deserted her. Instead she groped across for her daughter's hand and found it, took it between both of her own and rubbed hard, as if the child's fingers were cold and she could warm them.

'Does it make you sad?' Freya asked doubtfully.

'Sad?' With an effort Lauren faced her. Freya sat in her red parka with her feet swinging under the bench. Her glasses were flashing in the thin spring sunshine, and the corners of her mouth were pulled down. Lauren said, 'How could it make me sad that he helped to save you, sweetheart?'

'You look as if you're sad.'

'I suppose I do.' Lauren laughed and pushed her sleeve across her eyes. Her voice was locked in her throat, and she seemed unable to free it and to speak normally. 'I don't feel sad, Frey. But I do feel all sorts of other things.'

'What other things?'

For a second Lauren was on the point of gently

laughing the question off, of hugging the child hard against her and avoiding those large intelligent eyes behind their polished glasses. Then, perhaps, she could find some quiet place alone and sort out with herself just what it was she did feel. But something stopped her. Some edge of challenge in her daughter's voice, some invitation to enter a new relationship, to trust and be trusted. She turned to face the girl squarely and this time took both her hands in both of hers, as she might have done with an adult.

'I'll try to tell you what I feel, Freya,' she said with a new determination, and her voice came under control at once. 'I'm full of joy that your father could do such a thing. That anyone could. It gives me hope. And I'm full of anger with him for confusing me. It would be so much easier to be able to hate him.'

'But you don't hate him?'

'How can I hate him now? And yet it's so . . .' She screwed her eyes up and struggled to find what she wanted to say. 'It's so bloody *typical* of him to do something like this. Something wonderful and unexpected, just when we had all decided he was a bad man.'

Freya thought about this and nodded to herself. 'I think it's good not to hate him.'

'Yes it is, Frey,' Lauren said, and felt the sudden release of something which had been trapped within her. 'Hating won't get us anywhere. I think I always knew that, but I didn't want to face it.'

'Will you be able to face it now?'

'I'll just have to learn, won't I, sweetheart?'

Freya watched her mother's face gravely for a second or two, and then reached up her arms.

It was mid-afternoon. Cobb came quietly into the room and Lauren moved under the sheets to show him that she was not sleeping. He walked over and sat on the edge of the bed and took her hand. He saw without surprise that there were tears on her face. He said: 'She told you?'

'Yes.' Lauren brushed the edge of her hand across her eyes. 'It's a relief, isn't it? We don't have to go on wondering when it's going to come back to her.'

'And neither does she,' he said. 'Yes. It's good news.'

'This?' She indicated her own face, in response to something in his tone. 'This is nothing. Just brought it all back for a moment. This will happen sometimes.'

'Of course it will.' He kissed her face and tasted salt. 'So it should.' He worked his arms around her in the warm bed.

She looked at him and made a funny face. 'What are you doing in all that gear? Get it off at once.'

He stood and shrugged off his sweater and shirt in one movement and sat on the edge of the bed to unlace his shoes. He got one off and dropped it. She stroked his thigh through the material of his jeans. Cobb took a deep breath and concentrated on the other shoe.

'Listen, Sam. I know what's on your mind. But it's all right now. Trust me.'

'He saved her. He stayed in the car and saved her.'

'You didn't want to hear that, did you?' she said gently. 'You wanted him to be an evil bastard. Rotten to the core.'

'Yes.'

'Well, I didn't.' She pulled herself against him. 'I'm glad to hear something good of him. It . . . closes the circle. Now we can all rest in peace. Do you understand?' When he did not reply, she said, 'This doesn't change anything, Sam. Trust me. Good or bad, dead or alive, Matthew is in the past now.'

Cobb looked at her and the fear fell away from him. He pushed his hand up into her hair and lifted her face and kissed her.

His mobile phone squawked. Cobb breathed hard, looked at the ceiling. He said, 'This cannot be happening.'

It squawked again, more imperiously this time. Beside him in the bed she started to laugh softly. Cobb snatched up the phone and punched receive.

'What?' he shouted.

There was a pause. 'Is that you, sir?' McBean's voice was uncertain. 'Inspector Cobb?'

'McBean?' Something cold slid down Cobb's spine and fear made him angry. 'Jesus Christ! What do you want now?'

'I'm sorry if it's a bad time, sir,' McBean said levelly. 'It's important.'

Cobb stood up and took a couple of paces across the room and turned down the phone's volume. 'I told you we'd finished with this, Sergeant.'

'And I told you it's important. Sir.'

'Well, what is it?'

McBean hesitated, guessing, perhaps. 'Can you talk, where you are?'

'No, I can't.'

'Then I think you'd better get over here.'

'Over where?'

'I'm at the Battle of the Nile pub in Stepney.'

'For Chrissake, Sergeant. I'm at home. I'm on leave. I don't plan on going anywhere for two whole weeks.' He glanced across the room at Lauren. She was dressing. She smiled across at him sympathetically, as if determined not to influence his decision.

McBean said sharply: 'Get over here, Mr Cobb. I'll give you two hours, and then I'm calling the local division.' He rang off.

Lauren looked across at Cobb and smiled ruefully. 'I guess this will happen sometimes, too.'

'I'm really sorry, Lauren.'

She shrugged. 'The weekend had a bit of a rocky start. Get back as soon as you can and we'll begin again.' She straightened her hair. 'What's the drama anyway?'

'Something I left unfinished, like a fool.' Roughly he pulled his clothes back on. She put her arms around him and hugged him.

'Don't be angry, Sam.' She kissed him quickly. 'I'm not. Anyway, I'd better get used to it.'

He quickly left the room and found Fred in the living room, raking out the grate.

'I'm going to London,' he said. 'Something's come up.'

'I see.' Fred straightened, trying to disguise his surprise and disappointment. 'That's unfortunate.'

'Yes.' Cobb dug out his keys and tossed them on to the coffee table. 'I'm leaving the Saab here in case you and Lauren need it. Are the keys in yours?'

'Of course.'

Cobb walked towards the door.

'Samuel.'

His father's voice stopped him. He turned to face the old man.

'Samuel, are you telling me everything I should know?'

'No.'

'Is there any likelihood of your doing that in the near future, do you think?'

'No.'

Fred nodded, satisfied with this answer. 'Very well. In that case, please be very careful.'

Cobb nodded and, after a moment, left.

63

Cobb threaded the big old vehicle through the City and out into the half-abandoned Docklands. He drove badly and, once off the smooth lanes of the motorway, had to make a deliberate effort to concentrate on London's Saturday evening traffic.

He was shaken by how thoroughly the call had thrown him. If he had been able to talk properly to McBean, maybe he could have put some limits on his fear. Without those limits it was ballooning inside him. He grew furious with McBean, even while he knew this to be unfair. The Sergeant had been on an unauthorised digging expedition. If he had unearthed a mine it would be Cobb's world that was blown apart, not his own.

It was nearly six when he found the pub. It was on the corner of a sidestreet of terraced houses, still gaptoothed from the war, set back from a shabby parade of shops. Cobb saw a greasy spoon cafe with a Greek name, an Indian minimarket, a betting shop. The Battle of the Nile was a crumbling Victorian pub in sooty red brick with a crude sign swinging above it. The sign showed a ship of the line, belching orange flame. A derelict petrol station stood to one side of the pub and a gasometer filled the sky behind. The car park was dominated by a yellow skip overflowing with junk. A family of cats, picking delicately through the rubbish, stopped to watch him as he edged the Land Rover past them. A neatly kept Ford Sierra, not new, was parked by the far fence. Cobb switched off and climbed out, and as he did so McBean emerged from the Sierra and walked across to him. Out of uniform he was unexpectedly well dressed in a long fawn jacket over white rollneck sweater. Cobb, aware of his own rough outdoor clothes, found this disconcerting, as if their roles had been reversed.

'Sorry about this,' McBean said. But he did not sound apologetic. His eyes strayed over Cobb's shoulder to the mud-spattered Land Rover. The Sergeant seemed as edgy and ill at ease as Cobb was.

'Don't keep me in suspense, McBean. Have you found our man or what?'

'Found him? Not exactly, sir.'

Cobb felt a spurt of relief and fought to contain it, for he knew this was not all McBean had to tell him. The Sergeant's 'sir' had come out awkwardly, as if McBean too sensed that their roles were out of kilter. Cobb did not attempt to put them back on first name terms. 'So tell me.'

McBean concentrated on Cobb's eyes. 'Like I said, there was this dead tom, Maggie Turpin. And her old man, a dosser name of Stevens.'

'And?'

'Maybe it's nothing,' McBean said, 'but Stevens said some things. About pulling someone out of the river.'

'Alive?'

'Not clear. But he talked about this place. This pub. Or at least, that's what we worked out, me and Hayward. So I came here. Just to satisfy myself. And it seems this Turpin woman did bring a bloke here. He worked for a while behind the bar. Gave the name of Joe Hill.'

Cobb waited. When McBean said no more, he said: 'And that's all you've got?'

McBean shrugged.

Cobb said: 'So does this Joe Hill fit Silver's description, or what?'

McBean looked away. 'They say not. But he was about the right age, about the right height.'

'Well, where is he?'

'He's gone. Left weeks ago, apparently.'

'Wait a bit.' Cobb struggled to disguise the relief in his voice. 'Are you telling me you called me out here for this? And this Joe Hill character doesn't even look like Silver?'

'Sir.' McBean stared into space.

'I think you're getting a bit hung up on this, Sergeant. Wouldn't you say?'

McBean pursed his lips for a moment, then looked down at him. 'I think I've heard enough from you, Mr Cobb.'

'What did you say?'

'You shut up and listen. Do you think I don't know you've got every reason for wanting Matt Silver to stay vanished? Do you think I'm a complete bloody idiot, not to know what's going on with you and Lauren Silver? Half the bloody Met knows.'

Cobb said nothing. He found that he felt vaguely ashamed. On some level his bluff had been called and he had no answer.

McBean said: 'I'm not drawing any conclusions. I'm not on duty. I'm off my ground, I've never even been here and I'm only a dumb black Sergeant. But even *I* can work this one out. I think Matt Silver got pulled out of the river alive. I've always thought so. And I'll tell you something else: you've always thought so too.'

'Matt Silver's dead,' Cobb said, fighting to keep his voice level.

'If you say so, Mr Cobb. I'm not going to say different, I'll promise you that much. It's your call. You can go in there and ask more questions. Maybe you'll come up with some answers. But if you don't want to know, don't ask.'

McBean turned on his heel and strode away across the car park to his modest saloon. He drove past Cobb without looking up at him.

Cobb watched him go and stood for a full minute outside the mean pub. Through the frosted glass doors the lights had come on in the bar and gave the place a spurious air of warmth and welcome. Cobb did not find himself in an agony of indecision. He wished that he could have been. A knot of noisy men in London Transport jackets walked up the steps and pushed in through the bar doors. Cobb locked the Land Rover and followed them, catching the swinging door as he went.

It was a shabby and rundown bar. The low ceiling was jaundiced with cigarette smoke, and the unpolished boards underfoot were black with decades of trampled grime. The group of men he had followed took up seats around a table in one corner and argued loudly about whose round it was. At the bar, a very fat woman sat chainsmoking while two greyhounds lay coiled like springs beneath her stool. A big rawfaced landlord in a greasy sweater was polishing glasses. Cobb walked up to the bar. Before he could speak, both greyhounds bared their needle teeth and growled at him.

'He's a copper, George,' the fat woman said, without so much as glancing at Cobb.

'Oh, yeah?' George bristled at once, pulling himself up to his full height and setting down the glass as if to leave his hands free for action.

'Have you ever seen this man?' Cobb said. He flashed open his warrant card in George's face and then slid the black-and-white picture of Silver out of his wallet and laid it on the counter. George flicked his eyes disdainfully to the photograph and away, and then looked back sharply as the picture caught his attention.

'Him? He's been on TV, ain't he?'

'Is that Joe Hill?' Cobb said.

'What?' George laughed scornfully. 'Joe? That useless prick? He wasn't nothing like that.'

'Nothing at all like that?'

'Nah. Joe? He was all scarred up. A car smash or something.'

'So where is he now?' Cobb pocketed the photo.

'I told the black bloke. Your mate, was he, that flashy nigger? I should've known. If the dogs'd been in here then, they'd've picked him. Eh, Gladys? Coon and all.'

The fat woman jerked up her chin in agreement but did not speak or turn her head. The greyhounds rumbled on, watching Cobb, yearning.

'What did you tell my mate, George? Tell me.'

'I told him I'd chucked the tosser out. He was nicking stuff. Chucked him out in the street, thieving bastard. Weeks ago now.'

'Where did this Joe Hill stay when he worked here, George? Where did he sleep?'

George's eyes flickered towards him, suddenly defensive. 'I don't know, do I?' When Cobb didn't speak, George said urgently: 'He never stayed here. The brewery don't allow it. Anyway, I got no rooms.'

Cobb put away his wallet. 'I want to look round, George.'

'Don't you need a warrant?'

'Don't you need a licence?'

George stared at him for a moment with a hunted look. There were broken veins across his cheeks, and his breath began to come quickly. 'Look, Inspector, this is all I got, this place.' His jaw moved and he swallowed. He avoided Cobb's hard stare. 'I was at Goose Green, y'know. Just me and five thousand Argies . . .'

'Where did he sleep, George?' Cobb said, and then more gently, 'I don't give a stuff about the brewery. I just want to find Joe Hill.'

George chewed his whiskered lips for a moment then pulled up the barflap and opened the back door on to a passage stacked with kegs. Cobb could smell the urine of cats and men. George jerked his head upwards. 'Stairs at the end. The three of them dossed up top for a while.'

Cobb pushed past him.

'I took pity, like,' George called after him, desperately. 'Tried to do them a good turn, see? This is what I get for it.'

Cobb trotted up the stairs and ducked into the dim half-built attic. The light was failing outside and the evening threw only a grey wash through the skylight. He felt for a switch and found one. The bare bulb sprang on and it was instantly night outside. Off to his right was a clutter of blankets and bedding with a pile of women's magazines and an ashtray filled with butts. Rain had got in somewhere and the ashtray was awash with yellow worms of tobacco. He stirred the blankets with his foot. They were damp and green mould was beginning to fur the folds. In the angle under the roof was a nest of bottles, perhaps twenty of them.

He moved on, past a partition of plasterboard tacked over the studs. In a boarded-off space behind a curtain was a toilet bowl full of brown water which had stained the porcelain, and beside it a sink unit growing out of the wall on its own pipes. A shard of mirror hung from a beam. Cobb caught sight of his own face in it, and was shocked by its wild-eyed look of strain. There was a stale smell about the place, something beyond mould. A small fridge stood against one wall and he opened it. It still worked, evidently, for the light came on, but it had not been cleaned out for weeks. There was a bulging carton of milk on the top shelf and a sodden mass of collapsed vegetables in the chiller. Foul green liquor had begun to seep out through the fridge door and had soaked into the floorboards.

There was a cot on the far side of the room, he could see now, a folding bed of some sort laid out under the skylight. The bed had been roughly made up, the blankets pulled into place. Cobb could see no trace of personality or comfort about the sleeping space: no papers or books, no coffee cup or ashtray. It was as impersonal as a bed in a recovery ward. He stood in the low space and looked at it for a long time as if it might nevertheless give him some answer. When it did not, he turned to go, gripping the joist above the bed as he did so. His fingers touched something pinned there – a scrap of newspaper. He stopped and tore down the cutting and held it under the light, tilting it to make out the fuzzy photograph. Freya's eyes looked out at him solemnly, and finally there could be no more doubt in him. As he stood there it seemed that her gaze carried an accusation, as if he had promised her much but she knew he would now withhold it.

Cobb came back into the bar and lifted the flap to let himself out. The greyhounds rumbled warningly at him as soon as he reappeared. He leaned close to them and bellowed: 'Shut the fuck up!' The room fell instantly silent.

'Ooh, you've got a way with dogs, luvvie,' the fat woman said admiringly, turning to face him for the first time.

George hovered uncertainly halfway down the bar. Cobb got a grip on his voice. 'When did Joe Hill leave here?'

'About – what? – six weeks back. But I never–'

'Where did he go?'

'I dunno, do I? I just slung him out.' George was nearly frantic that he could not give a useful answer. 'Wait. I did hear that padre picked him up and dusted him off, like. Not that I hurt him, much, see–'

'What padre? A priest, you mean?'

'Aussie bloke. Not a bad type for a do-gooder. Used to come here with some tart with a guitar, Saturdays. I ain't seen neither of them since.'

'Which church?'

'I dunno,' George wailed.

'St Mark's,' the fat woman told Cobb amicably, as if she had been chatting to him all night. His doghandling prowess seemed to have impressed her. 'It's off the Mile End Road, dearie. You'll find it, clever chap like you.'

64

Cobb pulled up outside the church but did not turn off the engine. It was dark now and under the two or three sickly streetlights which still operated the narrow square looked bleak and threatening. A group of youths in baggy clothes were skateboarding up and down the kerbs. They moved with an insolent grace, pausing occasionally to stare at him with hostile curiosity. There were lights on in some of the tall terraces which flanked the square. The smells of cooking drifted on the air, and jagged rock music thumped out of a basement flat. The church was in darkness but a black corrugated iron hall stood next to it and the open door threw light on to the pavement. Cobb sat in the Land Rover, listening to the burble of the engine, reluctant to kill it. He was nauseous from tension and hunger. He realised he had not eaten all day. For a second he craved food but at once his stomach churned at the thought.

For the first time it occurred to him seriously that he still had a choice. He could back up, turn round and drive out of this cul-de-sac now and no one would be any the wiser: not Lauren, not Freya. He could go back to the farm and pick up his life where he had left it, on the brink of a new chapter. Yes, he thought. And perhaps he wouldn't jump every time the phone rang.

He cursed himself, turned the engine off and climbed out, banging the door behind him.

'You looking for me?' A solid grey-haired man in his mid-thirties was standing in the middle of the road, looking at him. The man had been walking up the street towards the church. He carried white plastic shopping bags bulging with bread rolls. Cobb saw light flash on steel-rimmed spectacles.

He took out his warrant card. 'Are you the priest here?'

'Bob Nugent, that's me. You?'

Cobb picked up the Australian accent this time, flat and wary. Nugent did not look at the warrant card in its important wallet but waited for Cobb to speak his name. 'I'm Sam Cobb. Inspector Sam Cobb.'

'You with the Council, Mr Cobb? You got me dead to rights if you are. Again.' Nugent did not seem too worried by this prospect.

'I'm with the police.'

'That kind of inspector? I thought it was the drains.' Nugent put down one clutch of bags, flexed his fingers where the plastic had cut into them and shook Cobb's hand. His grip was, as Cobb had expected, painfully firm. 'You've come a long way, Mr Cobb.'

'I'm sorry?'

' "Lower Durning Farm. Oxon".'

It took Cobb a moment to realise that the priest was reading the address from Fred's fancy script on the Land Rover's door.

'Bit off your patch, aren't you?'

'It's the family farm,' Cobb said. He felt this diminished his authority somehow, and added: 'I'm with the Met, Father Nugent. I'm looking for Joe Hill.'

'Are you now?' Nugent flexed his fingers again, then stooped to pick up his bags. 'Well, you'd better come in, then.'

He led Cobb across the street and through the door of the hall. Two young men and a girl were setting out folding beds and folded blankets in rows up the body of the hall, supervised by a plump man in a maroon cardigan. Cobb noticed that the plump man had horn-rimmed spectacles inexpertly mended in the middle with white tape. Nugent marched through the hall so fast that Cobb found it hard to keep up with him. 'Hi, Phil. Any takers yet?'

'Not yet, Father.' The fat man smiled at Cobb. 'Have you brought us a guest already?'

'This bloke?' Nugent shouted with laughter. 'Hardly. But he does look the part a bit, I'll grant you.' In a kitchen area behind the stage Nugent dumped his bags, gestured to Cobb to take a seat, and filled a kettle at the sink. 'So what do you want with Joe Hill, Mr Cobb?'

'You know him, then?'

'I've met him.'

'Is he here now?'

Nugent carried the kettle over to the cooker and looked stagily around the room. 'Doesn't look like it.'

'Please don't play games with me, Father.'

Nugent walked over to the table and pulled out a chair opposite Cobb's. He put his broad forearms on the tabletop and leaned forward. 'I'll do you a deal, Mr Cobb. I'll be straight with you, if you are with me. And I'll tell you upfront that I don't much like talking to you people about my people.'

'Have you ever seen this man?' Cobb laid the photo of Silver on the table.

Nugent turned it round and took off his glasses to study it. Without the glasses his eyes were gimlet sharp, an extraordinarily clear blue. 'No. Well, that is I've seen him on TV. That's Matt Silver, or his twin brother.'

'It's Matt Silver. Is it also Joe Hill?'

'You're joking, right?' Nugent put his hands behind his head and leaned back in his chair. 'Of course it isn't Joe Hill. Joe Hill was nothing at all like this man.'

'Was?'

'I picked Joe up one night when the fat bastard who runs the Battle of the Nile threw him out. I gave him a place to stay for a while. I do that with a lot of people. Hundreds.'

'That's it?'

'That's it.' The kettle sang and Nugent rose and crossed to it. 'Coffee?'

'No, thanks.'

'Have a bloody coffee, Mr Cobb. You look stuffed.'

Cobb said nothing while Nugent made the coffee and brought him a cup and set it down in front of him. He thought that in a perfect world he might like Bob Nugent, but right now he distrusted his intelligence and coolness. Cobb himself did not feel either intelligent or cool. He felt himself outfoxed. He cupped his hands around the mug and lifted it and noticed that his hands were shaking slightly. The coffee was very strong and very good.

'When was the last time you saw Joe Hill, Father?'

'He stayed a couple of nights. Drifted off. They all do.'

Cobb knew he was lying, and that Nugent knew that he knew. He could think of no way of outflanking the priest. Cornered, he set down the coffee. 'I could have this place turned over, Father Nugent.'

'Been there, Mr Cobb.' Nugent sat back again, at ease, looked at the ceiling. 'Done that. Got the T-shirt.'

'If you're protecting him—'

'Look, Mr Cobb.' Nugent let his chair fall forward heavily. 'Just see if you can get this straight. This man —' he tapped the photograph '– is not Joe Hill.'

'You mean, he's changed or found God or whatever? That's what you mean by not the same. That's not good enough.'

'You're beginning to sound desperate, Mr Cobb. He's not the same man. Period. That's what I said and that's what I meant.'

They sat in silence for perhaps thirty seconds. Eventually Nugent touched the picture again. 'What did this guy do again? I thought he was supposed to be dead. Wasn't there a car smash some months back?'

'He killed his child.' Cobb sipped at his coffee. He felt weary and defeated. 'Nine years old. Nearly killed her sister.'

'That's terrible.' Nugent shook his head. 'You mean,

he was driving and there was a crash and his own kid gets killed. That's terrible.' He looked innocently up at Cobb. 'So what do you want him for?' Cobb felt a nerve jump in his cheek but Nugent had not finished. 'Let me guess. You've been chasing him for four months so you can punish him. If that wasn't so bloody grotesque, it'd be funny.'

'I don't make the rules, Father.'

'No. You're just following orders, Mr Cobb. You British policemen are wonderful.' Nugent stood up. 'How's this for an idea? Why don't you drink your coffee and fuck off?'

A car's headlights swung across the windows and Cobb heard it pull up in the street outside. Cobb and Nugent faced one another in a tense standoff for a moment. Almost at once the car's engine restarted and they listened to it whine away again in urgent reverse up the length of the cul-de-sac. A second later the plump man put his head around the curtain and gave a little nod of apology. 'Excuse me, Father. I told the young woman that she was no longer welcome here after her behaviour last night. I'm afraid I was rather short with her. I hope I did right?'

'Quite right, Phil,' Nugent said, without taking his eyes off Cobb. He sat down again. 'Bless you, Phil.'

Cobb said. 'You know I have to find him.'

'Why? Who'll gain by it?'

'Not me, Father. Believe me.'

The priest's eyes narrowed. 'Have you got some personal angle in this, Cobb?'

'What do you mean?'

'Look at you. You're coming apart at the seams. Why is this so important to you? Do you think you'll be free of him when you find him?'

'Least of all then.'

'So why look?'

'Because you don't set the agenda here, and neither do I. There isn't one rule for him and one rule for everyone else.'

'So make one.'

'You might have that luxury.' Cobb stood up. 'I don't. I have to find Matt Silver because he's done wrong. And now I believe he's alive. I wish to Christ I didn't believe that.'

'Then don't. Faith is achieved, Mr Cobb, not granted.'

'That's a good trick if you can learn it.' Cobb tossed his business card on to the table. 'Thanks for the coffee.'

65

Silver waited in black shadow on the basement steps and watched Cobb walk across to the Land Rover. As he moved through the yellow pool of the streetlight Silver could clearly see his face. This was hardly the smiling, confident man he had seen outside Freya's school just days before: this man was drawn and unshaven, scruffy in an old windcheater. But there was no question that it was the same person. So he was the police. Silver felt a sense of inevitability. In a way he thought there was a certain crude poetry to it.

He waited while Cobb backed the Land Rover up over the kerb, its suspension groaning, and then drove off towards Mile End Road. Beside Silver among the garbage cans Jit was silent for once. Some part of the game had crossed over into real life. He took her arm and she let him do so unresisting. They moved quietly down between the church and the hall and Silver led her in through the back door. Nugent was at the table with his arms crossed before him, his steel-rimmed spectacles and the two empty coffee mugs on the pine surface in front of him. Silver had never seen the priest without his glasses, and was struck as Cobb had been by the sharpness of his blue eyes. Nugent looked something like a headmaster waiting in his study for someone to discipline. Silver said: 'Thanks, Nugget.'

'You don't know what I did yet.'

'I know what you did.' Silver crossed to the table and picked up Cobb's business card. He turned it in his hand, running his fingertip over the embossed Metropolitan Police crest. 'Inspector Sam Cobb,' he read. 'So that's who you are.'

'He knows you, Joe.'

'And I know him.' Silver made a short sound something like a laugh. He looked up at Nugent. 'So we all know each other now, don't we, Nugget?'

'You're Joe Hill,' Nugent said steadily. 'That's who you are. I don't know bugger all about anyone else.' Nugent stood up and fetched his coat. He took out his wallet, opened it and threw some notes on the table. 'You're out, Joe. That's all I've got on me. Take it and get out now. Take the Ford bus. I won't report it.'

'Take the bus?'

'Take it. Keep it. That big old heap's no use to me. I only wanted you to fix it so you wouldn't top yourself before you'd dug out the drains.'

'Nugget–'

'Just get out of here. Now.'

Jit said: 'I'll get our stuff.'

Silver turned to her. He had forgotten she was in the room.

'It's half my van anyway,' she went on, her chin coming up defiantly. 'I cleaned the bloody thing out.'

When she was gone Nugent pulled aside some of the plastic bags of charity clothes and reached under the stage and dragged out the ancient toolbox by its steel handle. 'Take that too,' he said. 'It's no good to me. You might make yourself a few bob somewhere.'

'Nugget—'

'Listen to me, Joe.' Nugent swung on him. 'I'm doing this because Joe Hill deserves a break. But I'll tell you this much: I don't believe Joe Hill has a hope in hell.' He tapped Cobb's card with his fingernail. 'This bloke is smart and tough and he will not give up. I know the type. More than that, he's driven. I don't know by what.'

'I do.'

'Whatever it is, you stay a very long way away from him.'

Silver smiled. 'And I thought you were the one who wanted me to pay my debts.'

'That was the other bloke,' Nugent said. 'He's dead.'

Ten minutes later Silver sat in the passenger seat of the Ford bus in the street outside the church. He glanced back into the body of the vehicle. A couple of bags, the wooden toolbox, two guitars, two rolled sleeping bags.

'Isn't this neat?' Jit said in delight. She clashed the gears noisily. 'Don't worry, I'll get the hang of it.'

She pulled away with a jerk, hauled the wheel round and drove up the cul-de-sac in a reasonably straight line. Glancing into the wing mirror Silver saw that Fat Phil and Nugent were both standing in the yellow light thrown out of the hall door. They stood there, dwindling in perspective as the bus drew away.

Jit pulled up at the end of the street. The main road was a stream of trucks and black cabs and red buses jostling for position, all of them urgently going somewhere on a late Saturday night in London. Silver stared at it all in sudden bewilderment. For a second he was seized with a feeling close to panic. 'But where are we going?'

She glanced at him and swung the minibus left into the traffic with aggressive confidence. She grinned and the jewel in her cheek caught the light and sparked kingfisher blue. 'We're going to join the gypsies, Joe.'

66

Cobb pulled up in a service area on the M25. He was bone weary. He wandered into the bright plastic palace of a restaurant and stood staring for a while at garish food under lamps in traffic light colours. He heard himself order something and took it away and slumped over it and forced himself to eat. When he had finished he could not remember what he had eaten but the warm bulk of the food restored something in him all the same. Before he could change his mind again he pulled out the mobile and made the call.

'Sam? Do you know what time it is?' Even in his annoyance, Nelson's thick Yorkshire accent was comforting and familiar.

'No, Horrie. I don't.'

'It's eleven-thirty on a Saturday night, Sam. I've got the family here. Everyone's in bed. Kiddies trying to sleep. This had better be good.'

'It isn't good,' Cobb said. He left out McBean's involvement but included everything else: Joe Hill, the crumpled photograph in the attic, the lying priest. He felt instantly better when he had finished, as if a boil had been lanced. The matter would move out of his hands now.

Nelson was quiet for a long time. Finally the

Yorkshireman said: 'Are you out of your mind, Sam?'

Cobb opened his mouth to speak. Closed it again.

'You listen to me, Sam Cobb. You've got nothing at all here.'

'Horrie, I can't dodge this any more. You know what this means?'

'This means nothing, Sam. Because you've got nothing. No witnesses. No one talking. Nothing. Just a newspaper photo pinned up in some loft. What do you think you're about?' Nelson's anger was stoking steadily. 'Don't you understand at all, Sam? You've moved on from here, thanks to Mr Sykes and me. A new start. Do you want to throw all that away? The Matt Silver file's closed. Good Lord, Sam, you shouldn't even be making enquiries.'

'Hold on, Horrie–'

'Nobody cares about this any more, Sam. Only you. And we know why *that* is.' Nelson cleared his throat and spoke more calmly. 'Sam, you must see you're on some kind of a vendetta here. And against a dead man at that. It's paranoid. It's unhealthy. You don't have to be Sigmund bloody Freud to see that.'

Cobb said: 'You've got this all wrong.'

'I don't think so, Sam. I don't think so at all. Now you listen. I'm going to forget this conversation ever happened. But if you choose to raise this officially I won't support you on it. It would look very bad for you all round, Sam. Think about it. You wouldn't have to dither about resigning, I'll tell you that.'

'Horrie–'

'I've bailed you out before, Sam. But not this time. You're on your own.'

He hung up.

It was past midnight when Cobb drove down the track to the farm. There were no lights on in the house and he turned the engine off and coasted the last few yards so as not to waken the place. He parked and climbed stiffly out. It was a clear, cold night, almost cold enough for a late frost. The farmyard and house formed a study in black and white. A scatter of stars lay across the sky behind the silhouettes of the trees, and a white moon threw ink shadows across the cobbles.

Cobb drank the clean air for a few moments in great lungfuls. Its very purity made him aware of how worn and depleted he was. Somehow it seemed to mock him, taunting him with his impossible choice. He crossed the yard towards the back porch and was startled by a sudden movement at his feet. 'Baskerville?' The old dog gazed up at him from the shadows of the porch with milky eyes. The long tail thumped twice against the side of his basket. Cobb knelt and fondled the dog's sleepwarm head. 'Are you on guard, old son?' Cobb laughed softly. 'He'd have to be a dozy bloody fox to let you catch him.' He sat on the step next to Baskerville's bed and the dog grunted and shifted his head and dropped it like a log in Cobb's lap. The warmth and weight of him was comforting. 'Fine couple of guardians we are,' Cobb said.

He must have slept a little then, cradling the dog,

for he came awake with a jolt and saw that the moon was tilted further down the sky than it had been. Out of nowhere a couplet came to him from an old ballad he had once heard:

> *Late, late yestreen I saw the new moon*
> *With the old moon in her arms,*

and its haunting echo of threat and loss seemed to resonate in him.

'Can you tell me about it?' Lauren said gently from beside him. She was sitting on the other end of the step, watching him. She was huddled into his old sweater, as she had been once before.

'Soon,' he said. 'But not right now.'

'Is it about us?'

'Yes.'

She nodded and looked away, looked up at the moon. 'Is it too much for you, all this? Are we too much?'

'It's not that.' He stretched out his hand and she took it and he could feel the ball of her thumb stroking the back of his fingers.

'Will you be able to handle it for us, Sam?'

'I hope so,' he said. 'But just at this moment I can't see how.'

She leaned across and kissed him. 'I trust you, Sam. I trust you to keep us all safe.' She rose. 'Come in to bed when you're ready.'

67

Silver took over the wheel as soon as they left the motorway and Jit was asleep the moment she settled into the passenger seat. He drove on through the dark country, moving from main roads to minor, edging first north and then west. As the lights of the town fell away, the brick-red glow of London filled the rear windows. The glow swung gradually to his left, until Jit's head was silhouetted against it, and then slowly it fell behind them once more.

A lay-by came up and he swung the minibus into it. The noisy ratchet of the handbrake woke Jit and she sat up, blinking. 'What time is it?'

'About two.'

She stretched and yawned. 'Christ, I'm hungry. You hungry?'

'No.'

'Well, I'm hungry.' She reached behind her, rummaged in a plastic bag and found an apple and bit into it. She peered through the windscreen down the black tunnel of the road. 'Where are we?'

He sat with the lights from the dashboard catching the angles of his face. 'We're nowhere, Jit.'

She stopped chewing and put the apple carefully

away in the glove box. She sat up straight and stared out into the night.

'You can't turn back time, Joe.'

He unclipped his seatbelt. 'You take the bus.'

'I don't know the way,' she said quietly.

'You'll find it. And then I'll know where to find you.' He leaned forward and rested his forehead on the cool rim of the wheel. 'Jit, you know why I've got to go.'

Finally she turned to face him. 'Of course I know.' She smiled so that her teeth and her eyes and her jewel shone in the thin light. She blinked twice. 'You've got to find the evil Vargas.'

Silver reached across and pushed his hand through the short pelt of her hair, feeling it bristle against the stump of his ring finger. She nuzzled briefly against his palm. He said: 'Maybe the evil Vargas is me.'

68

It grew cold. Finally Cobb lifted the dog's head out of his lap and quietly entered the house. In the kitchen he stopped to check his watch. It was 3.30 in the morning of Easter Sunday. He supposed he should go to bed but sleep felt nowhere close. He poured himself a fat Scotch and sat at the table, then felt cramped there and paced for a while around the kitchen, seeking reassurance in the sense of the dark house slumbering around him. But reassurance would not come.

At length he took his drink down the short corridor to the garden room and, entering, softly closed the door behind him. He stopped there. It had happened once before but this time the haunting familiarity was keener. The peaceful room, her warm sleeping form and rhythmic breathing – like the distant sound of the sea, he had always thought. He sat down where he had always sat, in the winged chair by the door, and watched over her. It could not be as bad as that last time, he told himself. Nothing could be as bad as that. And yet a worm of doubt had entered his mind and was already eating at his certainty. Surely he could lose this woman just as he had lost Clea? It was unthinkable, but being unthinkable did not mean it would not happen. If he had learned anything, he had learned that much. She had promised. But when she had promised she had thought her husband gone forever. How could he compete if Matt Silver were no longer a ghost after all? How could he compete? So he sat and watched her silently as the minutes crept by, watched her slipping out of his grasp all unknowing, as that other woman had slipped from his grasp two years before.

His head came up with a jerk. Freya's cry pulled him up from his half sleep like a hooked fish and he was instantly and completely awake. He stood up. It had been a small sound and Lauren had not stirred. He opened the bedroom door and stepped into the corridor, pulling the door closed behind him.

She stood in the kitchen, tiny and waif-like in her pyjamas, knuckling her eyes. 'Sam?'

He went to her and lifted her up on to a chair. 'What's wrong, Princess?'

'I had a bad dream.'

He could see that she was pale and frightened. He put his hands on her shoulders and rubbed her arms briskly. She trembled slightly under his palms. He found the sweater that Lauren had been wearing and wrapped her up in it. It swathed her twice round and she saw her own dumpy swaddled figure and managed a laugh at herself.

'That's better, Princess.'

'I heard something,' she said.

'You did? It's that fox again.' He got up and went to the window and looked out. The moon was low now and its bone light fell across the cobbled yard and across the dog, peacefully asleep in his basket. That, Cobb decided, did not prove much. He could not see anything in the moonshadow of the barn, but if the fox were around, this would be the time. Freya watched him with grave eyes, and he returned her look. He was seized with a wave of protectiveness, as fierce as it was impotent, and with it a great rush of pain flooded through him. 'I'll be right back,' he said.

He went to the cellar and unlocked the gun cabinet and brought out the shotgun and pocketed the cartridges and trotted back up the steps to the kitchen. She sat, still swaddled in the sweater, and fixed her great eyes on him.

'Is he going to take me away?' she asked quietly.

Cobb stopped, the gun broken over his forearm. 'Who?' he said, and a weird dread crept through him, as if she had seen into the darkness and turmoil of his mind.

'Scarecrow Man,' she said. 'It was Scarecrow Man.' She pointed to the moonlit yard. 'He was out there. I saw him. He saw me.' They were both silent for a long moment. 'You promised me he wouldn't come here, Sam.' She stared at the floor.

'So I did, Princess. So I did.' Cobb walked to the window. And, as he knew it would, the gaunt figure stepped out of the shadows, the night wind moving its long coat, its face twisted and white in acid moonlight. In a second it was gone. Cobb glanced back protectively at the child but she had seen nothing.

'It was a dream, wasn't it, Sam?'

'Yes, Princess. It was just a dream.'

'The fox woke me up in the middle of my dream,' she scolded herself for her silliness. 'That must've been what happened, Sam. D'you think?'

'That's what happened, Princess.' Cobb's heart began to trip with a deep, full rhythm and he felt raw power and decision flow through him as if they had been dammed. He walked across and bolted the back door. 'You stay in the house,' he told the child, and took up the shotgun. 'I'll get your fox for you.'

She was suddenly anxious. 'Will it hurt?' he heard her voice calling after him as he moved away through the dark rooms. 'Don't let it suffer, Sam.'

Cobb let himself out of the front door on to the patch of lawn there and moved silently around the farmhouse in the shadow of the hedgerow. The cover took him a little way up the track and from here he slipped across to the fence on the far side and then moved down it to where he could step into the moonshadow of the barn. From inside he could hear the hens muttering nervously to one another, sensing him. He kept against the wall of the barn and followed it all the way round, coming back to the door. Inside it was black and silent. One of the horses shuffled and stamped as he moved around the stalls, checking each one, but there was no other sound.

He emerged into the clean air of the yard and crossed the paddock to the sunken lane. It was a ghostly tunnel leading up through the night, the moonlight falling like scattered silver coins through the branches. He padded up the track, surefooted in his familiarity. He wanted a vantage point over the farm, some place high enough to show him the buildings picked out under the cold moon. He knew where he wanted to be. His brain was working frighteningly fast now, computer fast. He paused and thumbed two of the fat shells into the gun and closed the breech. The clack of the action spoke through the trees but it was the only noise he made.

It was then, in the moment that Cobb lifted his head to move on, that he saw him. Silver was making little attempt at concealment, climbing straight up the centre of the paddock two hundred yards to Cobb's left, visible through a gap in the hedge. He was following the track which led to the ruined village. Cobb watched him. It was as if, after a fabled quest, he had at last tracked down some mythical beast, a creature he had only half believed in. Even now he only half believed. Scarecrow Man. Tall and skeletal with a long flapping coat. He was toiling at the climb, dragging one leg slightly. Cobb thought suddenly: But I have not tracked him down. He has tracked me. He has tracked me to my home. And this thought sent violence leaping through him.

Cobb crossed to the far side of the lane and entered the field there and climbed on the soft turf. He crossed a stile and moved through a hazel spinney on the flank of the hill, and up beyond the trees into a dark sea of bracken, finding the thread of track which he knew led from here to the summit. He paused to still his breathing. The sky was paling behind him, slats of magenta along the eastern horizon. A wood pigeon called from a stand of beech to his left and another answered it from somewhere ahead.

He moved a few more yards and then the lumpy contour of the abandoned village was against the sky above him. He trod silently over the turf, keeping himself below the skyline, and finally edged up to the mound which marked the far wall of the buried churchyard. He could see his oak now against the sky, the oak against which he had rested so often. And here he stopped, sinking down behind the cover of the mound, the barrels resting on the mossy stones. He could see the dew forming on the steel. He waited.

'Hello, Sam,' Silver said from behind him. 'You've been looking for me, I think.'

Cobb rose and turned in one motion, the shotgun clamped so hard against his shoulder that it bruised him. The spider-thin silhouette stood against the western stars. Cobb's blood boomed in his ears and the cold air whistled through his teeth. He felt for the trigger.

Silver said gently: 'You could do it, Sam. No one would blame you.' The dawn light fell across his ruined face. 'No one would even know.'

Cobb took a half step back as the shotgun kicked his shoulder. The twin shattering explosions hurled flat echoes around the hills, reverberating all around like slammed doors. The wings of startled pigeons whirred and banged.

'I don't know what's so precious about this old life,' Silver said as the echoes died away, 'that neither of us seems to be able to end it.' He looked around the lightening sky. 'Now you've scared the birds away.'

Cobb dropped the gun on the turf and sat down heavily among the mossy rocks. 'Why couldn't you leave us alone? Why couldn't you stay dead?'

'I'm sorry about Freya. I only wanted to see her again. I never thought she'd see me.' Silver gathered his coat around him. 'You love them, don't you, Sam?'

'Yes.' Cobb looked hopelessly at the turf between his feet.

'So do I. I always did, really, only I was too stupid to know it.' Silver belted the coat. 'I watched you, Sam. I watched you out on the step there with my wife. I watched you through the window with my daughter. And I watched them with you.' He stepped over the graveyard wall. 'You couldn't love them more than I do, Sam. But I think you love them better.' Silver sought out his eyes and held his gaze. 'There's no need to tell them, Sam Cobb. You'll never see me again. None of you will.'

He turned and began to walk down the track on the far side of the hill, away from the farm. Cobb stared unbelieving at his retreating back. It took him all his strength to wrench himself upright, and when he did Silver was already twenty feet along the track, stumping steadily downwards. 'Wait!' Cobb shouted after him.

Silver turned and looked up at him, wordlessly. The thin gathering light lay along the twisted seams of his face.

'You saved her,' Cobb said. 'You stayed in the car and you got Freya out. Or they'd both have drowned. You remember that?'

'Nothing. I remember nothing.'

'It's the truth,' Cobb said. 'She told me. She remembers. She'd want you to know. They both would.'

Silver stood still for a long time. Then he nodded gravely, perhaps in awe, perhaps in gratitude, and walked away through the bracken, his head bowed.

Cobb stayed on the hilltop until the pale sun rose and burned away the pearl mist in the valleys. Then he came back down the hill, the gun hooked over his arm, across the wet paddocks and through the hedge into the sunken lane. Halfway down a tawny fox stepped out on pointed feet not five yards from him, stared at him, and tripped away silently among the hawthorns.

Somehow he had not expected them to be up but they were all in the kitchen. Fred, clattering about the stove, waved his spatula at him in greeting. Lauren, wrapped in his bathrobe, was nursing her first coffee at the kitchen table, sitting in the spot he had come to think of as hers. She glanced up anxiously at him as he pushed open the kitchen door but Freya spoke first.

'You shot the fox, Sam.' The child looked at him sadly. 'We heard the bang.'

'I believe I did, Princess.'

'Did he suffer much?'

'Oh, yes, Princess. I believe he suffered a great deal.'

And then the room and the world it contained were swimming, and the faces of the people he loved were trembling in it.

Lauren stood up and crossed to him quickly. 'Sam?'

He felt her arms come round him and her fingers lock in his hair.

Fred put his head on one side and gave him a quizzical look from under his chef's hat.

'Lot of fuss for a bloody fox,' he said.

Free
WEEKEND BREAK OFFER*
Worth up to £200
CONGRATULATIONS!

The voucher below is worth up to £200 and entitles you and your partner a complimentary double/twin room (*subject to a daily minimum spend person on Breakfast & Dinner) for a maximum of 2 weekend nights, at any one 60 listed establishments throughout the UK and Eire; Offer subject to availabili

For your weekend break, we would like to offer you a choice of locations fr a wonderful collection of independently owned hotels and coaching inns, wh have been specially selected for our readers.

The participating establishments are listed in our special Directory. All guests h to do is purchase Breakfast & Dinner at the minimum prices per person at listed establishments' standard tourist rates. Your account for meals is payabl full on departure.

The Offer commences on 1st November 2000. Closing date to apply the Directory (which details the establishments) is 31st March 2001, and the date to take up the Offer is 31st August 2001. Date restrictions may apply, ch with the hotel.

The helpline for queries is 020 8832 7474 (this is not a booking line).

To apply for your Directory of participating establishments, simply send your v till receipt clearly showing the purchase of 'Redemption Blues' (rrp £5.99 Tim Griggs, together with a large SAE to 'Redemption Blues' Offer, PO Box 24 London W5 4GW. Proof of posting is not proof of delivery. Allow 28 days delivery of your Directory. Invalid applications will not be processed. The C excludes employees of Hodder Headline, their families and agents.

'WEEKEND BREAK OFFER'
Voucher Number **346721**